Also by Amanda Brown

Elle Woods

Elle Woods: Blonde at Heart

Family Trust

Legally Blonde

Also by Janice Weber

Hot Ticket

Devil's Food

Frost the Fiddler

Customs Violation

The Secret Life of Eva Hathaway

School of Fortune

Amanda Brown *and*

Janice Weber

St. Martin's Griffin

New York

This is a work of fiction. All of the characters, organizations, and events portrayed in this novel are either products of the author's imagination or are used fictitiously.

www.stmartins.com

Library of Congress Cataloging-in-Publication Data

Brown, Amanda.
   School of fortune / Amanda Brown and Janice Weber.—1st ed.
     p. cm.
   ISBN-13: 978-0-312-36673-5
   ISBN-10: 0-312-36673-6
   1. Weddings—Fiction. 2. Mothers—Fiction. 3. Children of the rich—Fiction.
  4. Rich people—Fiction. 5. Texas—Fiction. I. Weber, Janice. II. Title.
   PS3602.R65S36 2006
   813'.6—dc22

2007013157

First Edition: July 2007

10 9 8 7 6 5 4 3 2 1

School of Fortune

Amanda Brown *and*

Janice Weber

St. Martin's Griffin

New York

SCHOOL OF FORTUNE. Copyright © 2007 by Amanda Brown and Janice Weber. All rights reserved. Printed in the United States of America. No part of this book may be used or reproduced in any manner whatsoever without written permission except in the case of brief quotations embodied in critical articles or reviews. For information, address St. Martin's Press, 175 Fifth Avenue, New York, N.Y. 10010.

www.stmartins.com

Library of Congress Cataloging-in-Publication Data

Brown, Amanda.
    School of fortune / Amanda Brown and Janice Weber.—1st ed.
        p. cm.
    ISBN-13: 978-0-312-36673-5
    ISBN-10: 0-312-36673-6
    1. Weddings—Fiction.   2. Mothers—Fiction.   3. Children of the rich—Fiction.
4. Rich people—Fiction.   5. Texas—Fiction.   I. Weber, Janice.   II. Title.
    PS3602.R65S36   2006
    813'.6—dc22

                                                                    2007013157

First Edition: July 2007

10   9   8   7   6   5   4   3   2   1

To my three girls
—A.B.

School of Fortune

One

The elastic on Wyeth McCoy's sleep mask snapped just as his nightmare reached a horrific climax. In his dream he had been best man at a squillion-dollar wedding. The bride had arrived late, drunk, then had fallen into a pew while barreling up the aisle. Her nosebleed left hideous splotches on a gown previously owned by Elizabeth Taylor; the sight of blood caused the groom to become sick all over his powder-blue tuxedo. When the organist wouldn't stop playing "Take Me Out to the Ball Game," people began pelting him with their cell phones until he fled, taking all four harpists with him. The preacher couldn't remember the names of the couple getting married and neither could Wyeth, a humiliating snafu since he had known the groom since childhood. Nonetheless the ceremony stumbled on until Wyeth, desperately searching for the wedding ring, discovered it dangling from his own pierced earlobe. The mother of the bride began pulling it with all her might, tearing it free just as his sleep mask gave up the ghost.

Wyeth awoke with a scream to find the sheets damp with his fear. His ear hurt where the ruptured elastic had stung it. His sleep mask lodged uselessly over his nose. However, grateful to be experiencing the light of dawn, he poured himself a glass of sweet vermouth from the bottle at his bedside. Sipping, he revisited his nightmare, the seventh in seven nights. Always a ruined wedding, always ending in a scream. Always the same mother of the bride. Even now that he was safe in the real world, the image of her perfect blond bouffant and glacial blue eyes made him shudder: that witch was Thayne Walker, the most intimidating woman he had ever met. Wyeth poured himself a second glass of courage. Only a fool ignored his nightmares. Today he would put an end to them.

As he showered away the night's terrors, Wyeth rehearsed his resignation speech. The shorter the better. In and out, like a dagger. He'd be gone before she found anything to throw at him. "Madam," he orated to the swirling steam. "I regret to inform you that, due to personal reasons which I am not at liberty to disclose, I can no longer oversee your daughter's nuptials. You must immediately engage another wedding coordinator. I wish you well. I am certain this will be the most riveting event in Dallas since the Kennedy assassination."

Perfect! He left the shower. Wyeth repeated his speech half a dozen times as he donned his best linen suit and a supersized red bow tie. Decades ago, when he believed he would be the greatest Hamlet since Sir Laurence Olivier, Wyeth had studied drama. It hadn't been a total loss because now, with each syllable, his classical enunciation was coming back to him. Soon he'd sound like Shakespeare himself. Again Wyeth shuddered, remembering that Hamlet hadn't exactly punched out in a cloud of glory.

When the last drop of vermouth was gone, Wyeth strode to his beloved Hummer, the only one in the country (if not the world) painted metallic lilac. He felt this was a brilliant artistic statement showing his creative side while shielding him from aggressive idiots in SUVs. He was worth protecting: Wyeth was not only the whirlwind behind Happily Ever After, Inc., crème de la crème of wedding coordinators, but he was a potent good-luck charm. After twenty years in the business, not a single one of the weddings he had put together had ended in divorce. Was that a world record or what? Naturally the word had spread. Now superstitious and superwealthy clients on every continent hired him to make their unions a permanent reality, and Wyeth always delivered. He ran a fond hand over the gold letters on his car door. Happily ever after, indeed!

He was not going to allow Thayne Walker to break his unblemished record, even if it meant abandoning Dallas's bash of the century. Thayne had been planning this wedding since the day her daughter was born; even now Pippa liked to joke that she felt like a stage prop rather than the bride. For the engagement party, a Venetian-themed fête, Thayne had had a gondola shipped from Italy and lowered by crane through a skylight into her swimming pool. That petite soirée had started a six-month crescendo toward the main event. At this very moment Thayne was midway through a five-day pentathlon of luncheons, cocktail parties, dinners, and nightclubbing that would culminate in a ceremony attended by five hundred nearest and dearest friends. There would be roses, trumpets, unfurled carpets, and choruses of angels. There would be Vera Wang, five hundred place settings of Flora Danica, a major spread in *Town & Country,* and respectful coverage in the *New York Times.*

Wyeth had organized it all; in addition to the karma, he was renowned for staging weddings of stratospheric visibility. For months his every waking thought had been focused on this merger of two quasi-royal Texas families, the Walkers and the Hendersons. He had drifted to sleep running the numbers through his head: seventy people to help with décor, six thousand hydrangeas flown in from Colombia, two thousand rolled beeswax candles, one hundred hand-embroidered tablecloths, hot air balloons, fireworks, two blimps . . . eat your heart out, Cecil B. DeMille! For the wedding feast itself he had ordered a four-foot-high Sylvia Weinstock cake. Sylvia would be there and so would Sirio Maccioni, owner of Le Cirque, along with one hundred staff members flown in from New York on a chartered jet. Also arriving by jet were seven hundred lobsters, four kilos of triple-zero caviar, and half a ton of filet mignon. The sheer volume of the event would have traumatized an ordinary wedding coordinator, but Wyeth was no mere mortal.

Until the nightmares began.

He couldn't put his finger on it, but something about this affair was definitely off. Maybe it was just too good to be true. Pippa Walker and her fiancé, Lance Henderson, were a publicist's dream. Cameras loved Pippa, who had a body made for couture, the sweetest heart-shaped face, and a bewitching smile. Although Wyeth had difficulty imagining how this adorable blonde could be the offspring of a termagant like

Thayne, he was very happy for her. Lance was the perfect groom: agile, energetic, natural as a colt, with looks that caused women (and Wyeth) to swoon. Recently drafted into the NFL after four years as a Big Ten quarterback, Lance had a quiet humor and eyes that shone like dark pools as he answered questions at press conferences or signed autographs for hordes of besotted females. He'd make a fine husband for Pippa.

Yet a tiny voice kept nagging Wyeth in the dark of the night, warning that this would be the marriage that spoiled his perfect record. This morning the reason had hit him like a bolt of lightning: it wasn't the couple at fault, it was the mother-in-law! No marriage could survive Thayne's meddling. Wyeth should know: six months of her demands, insults, and wheedling had left him exhausted, and he was used to dealing with the Chanel Pastel Mafia. He couldn't imagine a son-in-law putting up with Thayne for more than a month. Lance might even kill her! Wyeth shivered: that would be the kiss of death for Happily Ever After, Inc. The break in his karmic chain would end in bankruptcy.

He sighed, acknowledging the sad truth: this wedding, despite its pomp and circumstance, just wasn't worth it.

Wyeth pulled up to Fleur-de-Lis, the Walker mansion. Thayne's exquisite home was inspired by the palace of the Comte de Mirabeille, a nobleman beheaded in the French Revolution. The fleur-de-lis was also the official flower of Kappa Kappa Gamma, Thayne's beloved sorority.

Recognizing the Hummer, the guard opened the iron gates. "I won't be a moment, Charlie," Wyeth said, smiling pleasantly. "You might just leave those gates open."

"Against house rules, sir."

"Then keep your damn finger on that button. I may be leaving in a rush."

After parking behind the dozen vehicles lodged in the driveway, Wyeth stood a moment wistfully observing the hubbub he had orchestrated. Gardeners were trimming the shrubbery and edging Thayne's already perfect lawn one last time before tomorrow's wedding reception. As florists installed fifty marble pedestals for the hydrangeas, a crew of half-naked men scrubbed the massive front staircase. Foodies with crates of produce rushed in and out of refrigerated trucks. Wyeth and Thayne had argued for months whether to have an indoor or outdoor reception; after consulting three top meteorologists and an Oklahoma farmer famous for predicting rainfall, they had decided to go *en plein air.* Again Wyeth sighed. Saturday would be clear and temperate, perfect wedding weather. He hated to exit just as the curtain went up on the greatest show of his career.

Careful not to slip on the wet granite steps, he proceeded to Thayne's doorbell. Margarita, the maid, ushered him into a foyer the size of an urban train station. The house was so cool, empty, and startlingly quiet that Wyeth needed a moment to gather his wits. *Now or never, old boy!* He threw his shoulders back, his chest forward. "I must see Thayne," he pronounced. "Im*mee*jetly."

Margarita frowned. "But you know Mrs. Walker exercises this time of day, sir. She cannot be disturbed."

"Oh, stop! I've seen women in tights! It does nothing for me!" Wyeth stormed off toward the gym, quite a long walk in a fifty-thousand-square-foot edifice. He finally arrived, out of breath, at the glass doors of the indoor swimming pool. Marching past the water, a terrified Margarita at his heels, Wyeth entered Thayne's gym.

Thayne was deep into the Alpine-slope portion of her treadmill routine as she watched her favorite show, *Growing Up Gotti,* on TiVo. The volume of both the television and the treadmill was deafening. For a long moment Wyeth contemplated his client's ultrahoned body, her perfect ponytail, moisturized-for-workout face, her raspberry/blueberry striped unitard: Thayne didn't even sweat without controlling every aspect of the experience. For a moment he considered slinking away like a whipped cur.

Over the grunts of three Gotti sons at the dinner table, Margarita shrieked, "I could not stop him, Mrs. Walker!"

Thayne coolly glanced over. Without breaking stride, she pressed the mute button on her remote. "Thank you, Margarita." The maid receded forthwith. "What are you doing here, Wyeth? Surely you have plenty to do for the next forty-eight hours."

"Tonight's the rehearsal dinner," he replied lamely. "I don't work for Rosimund Henderson."

"What's the problem, then?" Thayne increased the speed on her treadmill until her silver Pumas looked like two flying bullets. "Spit it out. I have four minutes left."

"It's about my perfect record. And my nightmares," Wyeth sputtered.

"Can't hear you!" Thayne shouted over the whirring of the treadmill.

Wyeth cursed himself for taking on a High Black Tie wedding that would make Emilia Fanjul's Dominican Republic nuptials look like amateur hour. The financial rewards were great, but oh, the ethical sacrifices, the groveling! He felt terrible about abandoning Pippa, the loveliest bride he had ever known, but his no-divorce record was as sacred as virginity: once violated, it wouldn't come back. The sight of Victoria Gotti onscreen, having her roots touched up, suddenly gave him courage. Wyeth pulled Thayne's $250,000 check, ten percent of the cost of the wedding, from his pocket. "Madam," he began, "I regret to inform you that—" His mind went blank. Too late Wyeth realized he had even forgotten to employ his faux British accent. Damn! "I quit!"

Thayne ratcheted up the treadmill another notch. "You must be suffering from exhaustion," she panted. "I know how you feel. But quitting is unacceptable."

"No deal," Wyeth shouted.

"I'll send you to Hawaii when it's over."

"No! I won't continue another minute. It's not the exhaustion, it's the bad karma."

Thayne's eyes darted to her full-length mirror. Botox kept her expression serene but she was reddening with anger. Worse, her tomatoey complexion clashed violently with the raspberry stripes in her unitard. How dare Wyeth desert her on the biggest weekend of her life! "Karma? Since when did you become a Hindu, Wyeth?"

"Karma's Buddhist, not Hindu."

"I don't care if it's Rastafarian, you can't back out now. I'll give you a fifty thousand bonus. And a hundred cases of that appalling vermouth you seem to live on."

Severely tempted, Wyeth wavered. As he battled with himself, Thayne raised her hand and confidently pointed the remote at her television. At just that moment, the light caught her triple diamond ring.

Wyeth's eyes boggled: that was the ring she had tried to yank out of his ear in last night's nightmare! The gods had sent their final warning. "Sorry," he shouted, tearing the check in half. "My decision is final."

Thayne continued to walk vigorously as the paper bits fluttered to the floor. "Yes, you will be sorry," she pronounced finally. "You will never do another wedding in Dallas. Consider yourself dismissed." Thayne did not watch him leave. Instead she pressed the mute button, smiling as sound reavalanched throughout her gym. If this hapless twerp thought quitting was going to ruin *her* wedding, he was sadly mistaken. She had been through much worse and landed on her feet. Thayne concentrated on toning her calves for an extra two minutes. Presently her complexion lost its ruddy hue and calmed to a vernal pink. She shut off the treadmill, stripped naked, and dove into her swimming pool, where she did her best thinking.

As she was completing her tenth lap on the kickboard, her husband, Robert, entered, dressed for the golf course in apple-green slacks and an impeccable white polo shirt. He knew immediately that something was very wrong; Thayne never destroyed her hairdo unless Armageddon was at hand. "Good morning, dear. Can I do anything for you today?"

From the middle of the pool she said, "Wyeth McCoy just quit. He thinks this wedding has bad karma."

"What rot! Do you really need him?"

"Are you joking? That's like Eisenhower quitting on D-day minus one."

"But you've rehearsed everyone to the bone." Thayne had probably ground away most of the bone, too, but Robert let that slide. After twenty-five years of marriage he and his wife had come to an understanding: she ran the show and he played golf.

Thayne reverted to scissor kick. "Fortunately I know a dozen wedding planners who would cut off their right leg to be part of this event."

More likely they'd cut off both legs *not* to be involved, but Robert called, "You are absolutely right, darling. I'm sure you'll have a replacement within the hour." He turned to leave.

"Robert! Make sure you're at the hotel at four. The rehearsal begins promptly at five."

"Certainly, dear. Call if you need me." That had been Robert's exit line for the last quarter century. Thayne had not once taken him up on it.

She left the pool after eight more laps and wrapped herself in a thick terry robe. Without showering, Thayne went to an upstairs bedroom that had been converted into Command Central. Striding to her desk through a jungle of dry erase boards, mannequins, printers, slide projectors, spreadsheets, invoices, faxes, swatches, and mountains of brochures, Thayne opened her laptop and located a phone number. Seconds later she was calling Steve Kemble, the hyperfabulous event planner whose show, *Whose Wedding Is It Anyhow,* held a national audience spellbound week after week. "This is Thayne Walker," she said in an unusually melodious, carefree voice. "Connect me to Steve, please."

"I'm sorry, ma'am. Mr. Kemble is in Madagascar for two weeks."

A tinge of irritation crept into Thayne's voice. "He doesn't have a cell phone?"

"Excuse me, who is calling?"

"Thayne Walker from Dallas. I'm sure you're aware I have a wedding this weekend."

All too aware: Wyeth had been wailing to Steve almost daily about his tribulations. "How may we help you, Mrs. Walker?"

"You may connect me to Steve, as I have already asked."

"I'm sorry, ma'am. Mr. Kemble is in Madagascar for two weeks."

"Are you a robot? I understood you the first time." Thayne needed a moment to resettle her voice to a more honeyed level. "Would you be so kind as to tell me exactly what he is doing there?"

"Filming the nuptials of a supermodel and an Iranian prince. I'm sorry I can't be more specific, but this is all very secret."

"Would he be able to fly to Dallas this evening?"

"I believe I just explained he was in Madagascar."

"Thank you for telling me a third time," Thayne snapped. "I could have my jet there in seven hours. He could disappear for a day. No one would be any the wiser, certainly not a supermodel and an Iranian."

A frosty silence elapsed. "If you leave me a number, I'll have Steve return your call as soon as possible."

"If you were Pinocchio, your nose would be longer than the Texas panhandle." Thayne slammed down the phone, resolving to have a word with Steve about the rudeness of his staff. She proceeded to the next name on her list.

"Gizelle? This is Thayne Walker." Hearing no reply, she continued, "Something has come up. We need a little extra help with the wedding this weekend."

Last January Gizelle and her six employees had spent two solid weeks preparing a proposal for Pippa's wedding. Thayne had chosen Happily Ever After, Inc., instead; she didn't like the looks of that sleazy z in Gizelle's name. "Surely Wyeth can find some extra help for you," Gizelle replied, hanging up.

Thayne proceeded to the third name on her list. "Bartholomew? This is Thayne Walker."

"Don't bother me." Click.

What was the matter with these people? Business was business. Were Pippa not an only child, were another Walker wedding a future possibility, Thayne was sure that Steve, Gizelle, and Bartholomew would be falling over themselves to assist her now. Clearly they were still hurt that she had chosen Wyeth to do Pippa's wedding. Thayne related to that. She had felt the same crushing disappointment when she didn't get into Kappa Kappa Gamma on the first try.

Thayne called two more wedding planners, both "busy," neither able to recommend anyone else who could help. Her lower digestive tract began to feel her pain. Thayne rushed into her pink marble bathroom, there to swallow her first pint of Kaopectate as she considered her options. Maybe she should take over. No, bad idea: if she had learned anything over the last six months, it was that underlings didn't respond to her laser-sharp management style. Besides, this was her time to reap the harvest of all her hard work. The mother of the bride should now be basking in the reflected glory of her daughter's white gown. She should not be down in the sweatshop with the peons.

Margarita, the maid, tapped on the bathroom door. "Are you all right, madam?"

"What is the problem, Margarita?"

"The pastry chef is fighting with the fish chef over the lemons. They want to speak with Mr. Wyeth right away."

"He just left on an errand that will take all day. Buy another crate of lemons and tell them to grow up."

"They are fighting with knives, Mrs. Walker. I am afraid."

"Margarita, I can't deal with this right now. Go downstairs and remove their knives."

"But—"

"Do as I say! That's an order!" Thayne flushed the toilet, drowning out her maid's protests. She took half a step toward the shower before the need to return to the toilet became overwhelming. Her arms were beginning to itch from the chlorine in the pool. Thayne thought she saw a few blotches forming on her face as well. To think that an hour ago, she had been jogging on her treadmill, happy as a victor of *Survivor!*

The phone next to the toilet rang. Surely that was one of the wedding planners coming to his/her senses, about to grovel for mercy. "Yes?" Thayne snapped.

"Mama? Are you all right? You never miss my wake-up call."

"I'm sorry, Pippa. It's been a busy morning. Are you and the girls done in the gym?"

"Yes. We're getting ready to go for our manicures."

"Good. I'll see you at the bridesmaids' luncheon."

"Weren't you going to get your nails done with us?"

"Don't push me!" Thayne shrieked. "If I can, I can, if I can't, I can't!"

Like her father, Pippa knew when to back a few miles off. "Sounds good. I'll take care of everything here. Don't you worry."

"Thanks, sweetheart," Thayne replied weakly. "See you at the luncheon."

She managed to take a shower before her intestines recurdled. Thayne considered calling Wyeth McCoy and promising to lock herself in her bathroom for the weekend, if only he'd come back. Then her phone rang. "Yes?"

"Twinkie? How are you bearing up?"

Dusi Damon, Thayne's old college roommate, was calling from Rangoon, where she and her husband, Caleb, had gone for a month-long, four-star vacation involving a bit of plastic surgery. Thayne was the only person in the world who knew that Dusi and Caleb hadn't gone to Asia to photograph sampans in the Bay of Bengal. "I am not bearing up at all," Thayne answered, breaking down into sobs. "Wyeth just quit on me. He thinks the wedding is jinxed."

"He quit the day before the wedding? That is unconscionable. I would sue, if not hire a hit man."

"I would do both if I could leave the bathroom." Thayne told Dusi about her digestive troubles. "How am I ever going to manage the rehearsal tonight? Wyeth is the only one who could keep all the marching and music straight."

"Hire a band leader. Like John Philip Sousa."

"This is my daughter's wedding, not intermission at the Cotton Bowl!" Thayne screeched. "God is punishing me, Dusi. I should never have created the wedding of the century. I should have settled for wedding of the half century."

"That's nonsense, Twinkie. You can do it. No one's irreplaceable, including Wyeth." Dusi thought a moment. "You must call the Mountbatten-Savoy School of Household Management in Aspen. Their people are used to handling events with a guest list of thousands."

"Mountbatten-Savoy, you said?" Thayne weakly scribbled the words in lipstick on the pink marble tile nearest the toilet. "Thanks so much. How was your surgery, by the way?"

"Fantastic. Caleb looks so much better. I'm devastated we can't be there with you."

"You're an angel." Thayne sniffled.

"You go out and show Rosimund Henderson who's in charge! She's just a Theta."

Reinvigorated, Thayne got the number of the Mountbatten-Savoy School of Household Management in Aspen. "I'm Thayne Walker of Dallas," she announced grandly.

"Hello! You're having a wedding this weekend."

"Who is this? How did you know?"

"I'm Olivia Villarubia-Thistleberry, director of the school. We're following events in Texas with great interest. It's not every day that the American equivalent of two royal families are united in marriage."

Thayne immediately liked this woman. "My wedding planner has come down with a case of adult measles. I'm in need of someone who can handle a rehearsal involving a symphony orchestra, a two-hundred-voice choir, two brass quintets, a bell choir, an organist, and thirty-one attendants, not to mention an obstreperous mother of the groom. I'll pay you fifty thousand dollars to get someone here this afternoon. On top of your usual fee, of course."

"I don't think that would be a problem for Cedric," Olivia said after a gut-wrenching hiatus. "He has personally dressed the Duke of Mecklenburg-Strelitz for twenty years. He has organized three royal weddings. And he happens to be here this week presenting master classes on Large Scale Events Requiring Hats."

"Hire a jet and fly him to Dallas at once."

"This is very exciting, Mrs. Walker. I'm so glad you called."

"I'll e-mail you all my files. Cedric can study them en route."

Thayne consumed another half pint of Kaopectate before feeling confident enough to venture into her fifteen-hundred-square-foot closet. She conducted a phone interview with Zarina, a Hollywood society reporter, while Margarita fixed her hair. She phoned Rosimund, Lance's mother, to say she'd be late for the bridesmaids' luncheon. She phoned Pippa and told her to proceed with the food service; she would get there as soon as possible. After choosing eight items of pearl jewelry to wear, Thayne finally allowed herself a smile. They didn't call her Superwoman for nothing.

Two

Six months ago, within minutes of learning that her daughter planned to marry Lance Henderson, Thayne had phoned the Mansion on Turtle Creek to reserve the presidential suite as well as the upper four floors of the hotel. By acting with lightning speed she was able to get a group rate and, better yet, prevent Rosimund Henderson, Lance's mother, from booking the best rooms for the groom's family and friends. Thayne thus ensured that her lifelong relationship with Rosimund, a formidable social rival, began on the correct footing.

That done, Thayne had focused on the daunting task of selecting ten perfect bridesmaids. At SMU Pippa had been a very popular member of Kappa Kappa Gamma. As word of her engagement torched through the sorority, Pippa was besieged with requests to be included in her wedding party. She would have loved to accommodate all her friends, but that was impossible. Thayne solved the crisis by holding a competition for the ten precious places. Each candidate had to submit family credentials, four photographs (front and rear shots in bathing suit and debutante gown), and write an essay entitled "Why I Should Be Pippa's Bridesmaid." The winnowing process was fraught with peril because the most socially desirable heiresses, including some of Pippa's absolute best friends, were not necessarily inheritors of the most graceful faces and forms. Thayne also had to deal with the girls' mothers, many of them powerful social matriarchs, all masters of flattery, bribery, and blackmail. After great deliberation she chose ten bridesmaids and three alternates and had them sign two-page contracts outlining their obligations. The zaftig bridesmaids were told exactly how many pounds Thayne expected them to lose if they wished to remain in the wedding party; each Monday all thirteen young ladies were required to phone in their vital statistics to Thayne's personal trainer.

When the bridal entourage arrived in Dallas a week before the wedding, the Walker limousine delivered them directly to the scale in her gym. One bridesmaid, having filed false reports about the thirteen pounds she had gained, was sent home in tears. Pippa tried to intercede on her behalf but Thayne held firm and installed an overjoyed alternate. Her final team was rewarded with a week of horseback riding, film screenings, shopping, fittings, and spa treatments.

At eight A.M. the day before the wedding, as Wyeth was confronting Thayne at her treadmill, Pippa and her bridesmaids were feverishly working out in the hotel gym. Thayne had engaged Richard Simmons for the week to keep the girls in tip-top shape. It was a gruesomely early hour to be sweating, but workouts were part of the contract each bridesmaid had signed. Afterward they regrouped in the presidential suite for a date with eleven Korean manicurists.

"Where's Kimberly?" Pippa wondered aloud, checking her Patek Philippe, a gift from Lance. No occasion; he just thought it would look nice on her wrist. "She knows we're getting our nails done at ten."

"She's probably still in the sauna," replied Charlotte, a willowy brunette. "One extra ounce shows when you're only four foot eight."

"And addicted to chocolate," added Hazel.

"Where's Ginny?" Pippa continued. "She's never late."

"She's probably doing an extra five miles on the treadmill," sniffed Chardonnay. "Just for fun." Chardonnay wasted no time grabbing an unattached Korean for a pedicure.

"I think she's taking her shoes back to Neiman's to be stretched," Francesca said. "She's got incredibly wide feet, you know."

"Do you think any guy on earth notices her feet?" Steffani snorted. "Pul—eeese." Ginny was endowed with full, nonman-made breasts, a great derriere, and a swanlike neck, in short, the best body of all the bridesmaids. She looked absolutely smashing in the slinky aqua silk gown Vera Wang had designed for them. Her mere existence annoyed the other females in the bridal party, six of whom had blown thousands on breast implants. The other two had had nose jobs. Nobody could do anything about their necks, however.

"No more cat talk!" Pippa interrupted. Ginny was her oldest, dearest friend. "I want everyone to say only nice things today. And tomorrow. Then you can go back to normal."

Everyone laughed: they could more easily fly to Mars than go forty-eight hours without trashing a rival. As the bridesmaids settled down with their manicurists, conversation turned to the groomsmen. None of them were married, either, so chances of Pippa's wedding resulting in half a dozen more weddings were quite high. "Tell us everything you know about Lance's friends," Cora demanded.

Actually Pippa didn't know much. Lance and his retinue had spent a great deal of the last six months in football camp. "I shouldn't prejudice you one way or another. You'll meet them all at the rehearsal tonight. Just turn on that Southern charm."

"Can you at least tell us who's richest?"

"I haven't noticed. Money isn't everything."

"Easy for you to say, Pippa. You're going to be swimming in it."

The door burst open. In teetered Kimberly wearing a body-hugging slip of a little black dress with slits up either side, Asprey sunglasses, four-inch-high Christian Louboutin pumps, and an enormous black bonnet with pink ribbons.

"Kim! You look fantastic! And that hat!" Pippa's manicure-in-progress prevented her from hugging the shortest bridesmaid. "Find a seat and get your nails done."

Instead Kimberly flopped onto the presidential bed. "I'm breaking up with Rusty," she cried. "He told me it was safe to have thermal reconditioning and highlights and now look!" Removing her hat, she exposed a swatch of overprocessed blond hair. "Split ends! My hair's broken. My spirit's broken. My Vedic astrologer thinks I might never heal." Kimberly burst into tears. "I hate him!"

Fortunately Thayne had arranged for Brent, the famous jetrosexual hairdresser (he would only do clients who had their own planes), to be in Dallas for the weekend. In fact he and three assistant trichologists would be waiting for the bridesmaids when they returned from their luncheon. "That's nothing a few deep conditioning treatments won't cure," soothed Leah, the ecstatic alternate.

"Absolutely," Pippa confirmed. "Brent can perform miracles."

Kimberly smiled through her tears. "I knew I could count on you, Pippa."

"Don't thank me, thank my mother. This is her wedding."

Kimberly laughed although this must have been the hundredth time Pippa had repeated her good-natured jest. Any normal daughter would have spat out those words, Kimberly thought. Or eloped. She could not imagine having a mother like Thayne, but Pippa seemed to adore the woman. She claimed Thayne was not only brilliant but *sweet*! Alas, Pippa thought well of everybody, Kimberly noted with disgust. Such an attitude was not conducive to survival in the real world. "This is not Thayne's wedding, Pippa. *You're* the lucky bitch marrying Lance Henderson."

Kimberly presented her hands to a manicurist. Thayne had decreed that all one hundred fingers in the bridal party be painted Flamme Rose Naturel Pink, a Chanel shade that perfectly matched their Blahnik sling-backs. As her nails were buffed, Kimberly shut her eyes and concentrated on another mortal enemy: Wyeth McCoy, the wedding planner. First he had convinced Thayne that no one deserved to be maid of honor. Then he had ordered the bridesmaids to process down the aisle by height, tallest first. Obviously Kimberly would be last onstage. She would enjoy only a few seconds in the limelight, admired by Lance's friends, before Pippa appeared and usurped all the glory. Kimberly had no intention of lowering her chances of matrimony simply because she was the size of a Munchkin. Whatever it took, her high heels were going to be first to click across that marble floor tomorrow at five o'clock.

"Kim!" shouted Leah. "You asleep there, honey?"

Kimberly snapped out of her trance. "You were saying?"

"Where did you get that superb *chapeau*?"

"London. Daddy flew me over in his plane last weekend."

"Well, you definitely win the prize for best hat." Pippa smiled, hoping to cheer her up. Kimberly had been in a sour mood all week.

"And you were so clever to come up with the Mad Hatter theme for the bridesmaids' luncheon."

"It wasn't *that* clever, Pippa. This wedding is already a lot like *Alice in Wonderland,* isn't it?"

Kimberly never imagined that Pippa would marry before she did. Instead of finishing school, Pippa had flitted off to Prague with an actor who looked like Jude Law. Meanwhile Kimberly had graduated with honors then enrolled in the Christie's training program in New York. It was a job but not a jobby job, fortunately, because Kimberly couldn't care less about art. Her sole aim in moving to Manhattan was to acquire a last name like von Furstenburg or at least Kravis. One year later Kimberly still hadn't managed to become serious with any "sons of riches." The best bachelor she could land was Rusty, who owned a chain of upscale florist shops and therefore got invited to lots of charity balls. When she heard that Pippa had become engaged not one tiny month after a humiliating return from Prague, Kimberly almost threw herself in front of the A train. She had intended to marry Lance Henderson herself.

"*Alice in Wonderland?*" Pippa laughed. "At least it beats *A Series of Unfortunate Events.*"

Half an hour later, their fingernails, hats, plaids, and polka dots in place, all bridesmaids absent Ginny packed into the elevator. Their aggregation of loopy millinery caused quite a stir in the hotel lobby. Paparazzi, camped out in the piazza, swung into attack mode as the ladies walked to their private dining room. Since Thayne had leaked the Mad Hatter theme to two of her favorite society reporters, two media types knew what the costumes were all about. Everyone else thought the luncheon was themed on either Abraham Lincoln (who had worn a top hat like Kimberly's) or Jiminy Cricket.

Lorenzo, the maître d', led the entourage to a room containing a round table set for sixteen. "Please be seated," he announced. "Mrs. Walker will be a few minutes late."

Thayne was never late for anything. "Maybe her treadmill ate her," Francesca said.

Pippa and the bridesmaids snuggled into their deep brocade seats. Their wineglasses were emptied within minutes. Two hovering waiters offered only water for refills: *I'm sorry, mademoiselle, Mrs. Walker's orders.*

Pippa's cell phone rang. "Start lunch," Thayne commanded.

"Is something wrong?" Pippa asked. Her mother sounded unusually stressed.

"Damn traffic!" Thayne hung up.

Pippa instructed the waiters to bring on the meal. The first course consisted of tiny mounds of buffalo tartare on transparent wafers. Each bridesmaid received two. The second course was a pair of rather small lobster tacos.

"Will Lance's mother be coming?" Cora asked, still hoping to gather critical information on the groomsmen.

"Of course," Pippa said. "Mama's probably picking her up this minute."

"Who else isn't here?" Cora persisted, staring at the six empty seats. "Besides Ginny."

"Two reporters. And Wyeth McCoy."

Across the table, Kimberly shuddered: Wyeth, her archenemy. She should have brought some arsenic for his wine. "Maybe his Hummer fell into a sinkhole."

Now that they didn't have to behave like proper ingénues for Mrs. Henderson and Mrs. Walker, nine bridesmaids miraculously located flasks of vodka in their purses. The table was acquiring a nice buzz when the doors swung open and Ginny, the missing bridesmaid, entered. Despite her black and white striped top hat, red polka dot bow tie, and wild orange plaid jacket, she looked as elegant as Greta Garbo. "Sorry I'm late." She found her seat next to Pippa. "Getting nervous?"

Pippa laughed. "I'm too busy to even think about it."

"That's the whole point." Ginny snickered at the costumes the nine other bridesmaids were wearing. They looked like a coven of demented Freemasons. "Whose Mad Hatter idea was this anyway?" She turned to Kimberly. "Yours, I bet."

Kimberly kicked herself for not bringing two doses of poison. "Thank you."

Ginny stared at the two buffalo crackers on her plate. "This is lunch?"

"That's your starter." Steffani couldn't take her eyes off Ginny. Something was *wrong,* even in the flattering light of the dining room. "May I ask what you did to your hair?"

"I got it cut." Ginny beckoned a waiter. "Whatever you just served for the main course, could you bring me two plates of it? I'm starving."

"So are we," nine voices chimed in.

"In that case bring nine more plates. My treat. And bring it fast, before Thayne gets here."

"Ginny! Take off your hat!" Steffani called.

Ginny obliged, revealing a pixie that showed off her neck to perfection. "Something wrong?" she asked, amused at the surrounding looks of horror.

"Omigosh, Thayne's going to kill you. Six inches minimum was in the contract! You signed it!"

"Oops. Guess I forgot."

Even Pippa looked worried. Ginny had always been a free spirit, but this was pushing the limits of independence. Hopefully Brent would think of a fix before Thayne saw the damage.

"Are you making some sort of statement, dear?" Hazel drawled.

"No, I'm leaving for an expedition right after the wedding." Ginny loved taking trips to jungles and deserts and other horrible places with giant bugs and no electricity. Although a triple legacy to Kappa Kappa Gamma, she hadn't even rushed, an aberration that made her little above a leper in the bridesmaids' eyes. After her first debutante ball, she had never been seen in a gown again—until now. No one could understand what Pippa saw in Ginny.

"You mean you won't make it to the reception?" Cora asked.

"Correct. My plane leaves at eight and flies directly to Costa Rica. I have to be at camp by midnight to see the kinkajous feeding in the trees."

The bridesmaids sat stonily processing Ginny's information. The bad news was that her haircut made her look sexier than ever. The good news was that she was disappearing immediately after the wedding. "Maybe you should leave a little early," Kimberly said hopefully. "Security and all."

Ginny patted Pippa's hand. "I'll stay as long as I can."

Their second helpings arrived. Ginny easily convinced the waiter to supplement lunch with buttermilk biscuits and two bottles of Belvedere vodka. When all of that was gone, the waiter brought dessert, an artful arrangement of five strawberries and another waferlike object.

Pippa glanced at her watch. Thayne was now an hour late. "Something awful must have happened," she whispered to Ginny.

"Relax. A Sith Lord couldn't stop Thayne from getting here."

Kimberly unsteadily rose to her feet and cultivated a warm smile. "I'd like to propose a toast to Pippa. Congratulations on snagging the most eligible bachelor in Texas. Without even trying." *Sneaky bitch,* she added under her breath, softly enough so that only her side of the table heard her.

"Thanks, everyone, for being my bridesmaids," Pippa replied, raising her glass. "I appreciate the huge effort you made to be here."

Obviously she was referring to her mother's mini Miss America competition. "No problem," Tara said. "We all had the pictures lying around anyway."

Thayne burst in, resplendent in a pink linen pantsuit, matching pink top hat, green leather gloves, and a Milky Way of pearls. She looked less like a Mad Hatter than a transvestite version of Mr. Peanut. Thayne's two favorite society reporters entered with her. "Sorry I'm late, girls," she called, sweeping past the maître d'. Thayne placed two Coach totes and her laptop on an empty chair. "How was lunch?"

"Delicious, Mrs. Walker! Thank you so much!" chorused ten suddenly modest, sober young ladies.

"Did you get enough to eat?"

"More than enough! Thank you so much!"

Pleased, Thayne looked around the table. She spotted Ginny's hair, or lack thereof, at once. "What have you done with your hair, Virginia?"

"Tucked it into my hat, ma'am. It got seriously knotted up in the gym this morning."

"Thank God we've got Brent upstairs." Thayne placed a small fuchsia box with a purple bow in front of each bridesmaid. As she did so, her perfume saturated the room. Its floral overtones were heavier than a state funeral. Only Leah was stupid enough to sneeze.

Kimberly astutely rushed into the void. "What is that fragrance you're wearing, Mrs. Walker? It's delightful."

"I'm so glad you like it." Thayne beamed. "Do open your gifts."

The girls had a bit of trouble with the tight purple bows but eventually everyone managed to unwrap a bottle of perfume with THAYNE etched in the glass. "Maison Ricci has created a special fragrance for

the wedding," the honoree disclosed. "Perhaps you'd be kind enough
to wear it tomorrow."

"Of course, Mrs. Walker! We love it!"

As she circled the table distributing another small box to her bridesmaids, Thayne told the two reporters about the thousands of scents she
and Madame Ricci had tested before creating Thayne, a fragrance
unique in the universe. She gave each reporter a precious bottle as a
keepsake before rounding back to her seat. "Pippa and I are thrilled to
present these small tokens of appreciation to you, our bridesmaids."

Each young lady screamed with delight upon unwrapping a pair of
diamond and Tahitian pearl pendant earrings from Mikimoto. "These
will look lovely with your gowns." Thayne described her search for the
perfect ten-millimeter pearls as the reporters scribbled in their note-
books and took even more pictures. After presenting each reporter
with a lavish gift box and an invitation to lunch elsewhere in the hotel,
Thayne dismissed them: she and the bridesmaids needed to review tomorrow's top-secret plans.

Once the door shut behind the reporters, Thayne ordered the waiters to clear the table of everything but the centerpiece. As she opened
her Vaio, the maître d' set up a picture screen. He attached Thayne's
PC to a projector. "Pay close attention, girls," Thayne announced, in-
serting a CD into her laptop.

Emboldened by the four ounces of vodka in her veins, Cora reiter-
ated her burning question. "Wasn't Mrs. Henderson coming with you,
Mrs. Walker?"

"I'm afraid she has a touch of upset stomach. She's nervous about
the rehearsal dinner tonight, poor thing."

"Will Mr. McCoy be coming?" asked Kimberly. She was going to
try one last time to get him to switch the order of the bridesmaids'
walk down the aisle.

"He is indisposed as well. Turn down the lights, Lorenzo." Thayne
pressed a key on her laptop. Onscreen flashed a head shot of a model
with a perfect French twist. "As you know, Brent has arrived from
New York to do your hair. For the wedding rehearsal, everyone will
wear this style." Consumed by the image onscreen, Thayne did not see
the grimaces passing between Ginny and the other bridesmaids. "Tomorrow we'll go with a more romantic look. I just love this, half swept

up, off the face, secured with a gorgeous barrette, and down in the back. You all have such lovely long hair and this style will show it to perfection." She paused. "Were Mrs. Henderson here, you would have your barrettes. They are her gift to you. I hope she doesn't forget to bring them to the rehearsal dinner tonight."

"Is that style our only choice?"

"Yes." Thayne didn't have to look to know who had asked: Ginny, of course. Pippa had threatened to elope if her SMU suitemate wasn't in the bridal party. Thayne had acquiesced but considered Ginny her second serious mistake, after Wyeth McCoy. "Moving on to undergarments."

Onscreen flashed another model wearing a knee-length body suit attached to a bawdy push-up bra. "They don't call this Lipo in a Box for nothing. Has everyone purchased a set?"

"Yes, Mrs. Walker," chorused the angels.

Onscreen flashed a pair of pink slingback shoes. "Everyone has virgin Manolos ready to go?"

"Yes, Mrs. Walker," responded the chorus, even louder.

Thayne thought she heard a giggle in the dark. She decided to ignore it. Onscreen appeared a pink Gucci clutch. "And your purses?"

"Yes, Mrs. Walker," the chorus nearly shrieked. This time Thayne definitely heard three people laugh. Pausing in her presentation, she glanced imperiously at the faces beneath the Mad Hatter hats. "May I remind you that looking perfect at a wedding is a very serious business?"

No kidding. Each bridesmaid had shelled out over eight thousand dollars for gown, handbag, shoes, fur, and girdle, and that was just one outfit in a week of special events. Add Mad Hatter costume, gifts, dermabrasions, hair coloring, luggage, cocktail dresses, jewelry, airfare and whatnot, and the bottom line edged close to fifteen thousand dollars per bridesmaid. Fortunately each girl's parents recognized that this wedding was a critical investment in the family pedigree. No one was about to complain when Thayne was spending four times that much on each bridesmaid.

"Quiet, girls!" Kimberly hissed. "I don't know what's gotten into them, Mrs. Walker."

"Thank you, Kimberly. You're such a grown-up. Had Wyeth allowed a maid of honor, you would have been it." Thayne returned to the last slide, showing a model in a white fox stole. "Everyone has purchased her Maximilian?"

"Yes, Mrs. Walker!"

Was that a hiccup? "Hopefully this is what you will all look like tomorrow evening. Fabulous doesn't even begin to describe what I see."

A Russian supermodel sashayed down a runway in the gown, shoes, purse, stole, earrings, hairdo, and presumably undergarments that Thayne's ten bridesmaids would be wearing tomorrow. "I'll let you dream about that overnight," Thayne said, swiftly packing up her laptop.

"Where are you going, Mama?" Pippa whispered in the dark.

"Last-minute details." Thayne kissed her daughter's cheek. "The perfume was a huge hit, no?"

"Definitely."

Thayne paused at the door. "Your limo will be at the hotel at five sharp to take you to the rehearsal. Wear your prettiest dresses, please." With that, she rushed off to her next appointment.

"Something's wrong," Pippa whispered to Ginny. "She didn't stay to yell at the waiters about poor service."

The flasks of vodka resurfaced immediately. Kimberly nodded to Lorenzo, who went behind a screen and emerged with a cart piled with gifts. "Pippa, we all wanted to give you a little something for your wedding night. Of course we're all terribly jealous and wish we were screwing Lance ourselves."

Pippa blushed, thinking Kimberly was joking. "Is this a staglet party now?"

"Whatever." Kimberly read the first card. "From Charlotte." That was an edible teddy. From Francesca: crotchless silk panties. Tara: illustrated book of top one hundred sex positions. Hazel: cream formulated to heat up on contact with sex organs. Steffani: black lace garter belt and fishnet stockings. Cora: white peignoir. Kimberly: a pound of See's chocolates. Leah: silver handcuffs. Chardonnay: large vibrator for when Lance got tired. Ginny: season ski pass to Aspen.

Kimberly frowned. "What does a ski pass have to do with Pippa's wedding night?"

"Nothing. That's where I'll be after Costa Rica, in case the newlyweds want to visit."

A knock: Harry, Rosimund's majordomo, stood in the doorway. He held a silver tray mounded with small boxes. "Mrs. Henderson sends her apologies for missing the luncheon." Harry pretended not to see the pile of feathers, garters, and other unmentionables in front of Pippa. "She hopes you will accept these small tokens of appreciation for participating in her son's nuptials."

Harry distributed ten little boxes. Inside were platinum barrettes containing subtly larger diamonds and two Tahitian pearls slightly larger than those on the earrings Thayne had just given everyone. Harry receded while the bridesmaids were still gasping in shock and awe.

Pippa tapped her water glass with the silver handcuffs. "Sorry to break up the fun, but in ten minutes we're expected in the presidential suite for a final fitting. Thanks for all these incredible gifts! Each of you can expect a personal thank-you note from Lance." That didn't get as big a laugh as she would have thought. Pippa loaded her presents into the Coach totes as all the bridesmaids save Ginny left the room. "That was strange," she said.

Ginny shrugged. "They can't decide whether they love you or hate you."

"Hate me? I thought I was doing them a big favor."

"You snagged the top dog." Ginny picked up the heavier of the totes. "Where is he anyway?"

"Drinking tea with his mother. Playing rugby." Pippa was not amused. "I haven't seen him in days. I hope he's not getting cold feet."

"Let's find him. Make sure he knows where to go tomorrow."

Pippa hesitated. "What about our fitting?"

"We've had five this week. Come on. You need fresh air."

They tossed the totes and their hats into Ginny's Lexus SUV and drove around Dallas. She was right: it felt great to get away from The Event and pretend this was just another lazy Friday in June. "Bet they're here," she said, pulling into the SMU campus.

Sunbathers stared as they crossed the lawn. One even called out, "You guys clowns?"

"Maybe we should have ditched the costumes," Pippa said, her eyes raking the field for Lance.

"Nah. Good cover." Ginny had no interest in Lance's groomsmen: between expeditions she was seeing a rookie on the Miami Heat. Fortunately, since both Rosimund and Thayne frowned on interracial couples, the NBA finals precluded him from offending either of them this weekend.

"There they are." Pippa headed for a softball game near the athletic center. "Hi, guys. Where's Lance?"

"He and Woody went shopping for cummerbunds."

Pippa immediately hit the speed dial on her cell phone. *Hi. Leave a message and I'll call back.* "Do you know where?"

"No idea."

"Does anyone have Woody's number?" Ginny asked. The guys just stared at her like parched sheep so she steered Pippa back to the SUV. "You okay?"

"The groomsmen had their cummerbunds months ago. I bet Woody took Lance to a whorehouse to enjoy his last hours of freedom."

"Come on! They would have done that last night at the stag party." That went over like toads in a bra. "They're probably at NorthPark."

As Ginny was driving to the mall, Pippa's cell phone rang: Thayne. "How's the fitting, baby?"

"Perfect. Now we're all going to see Brent for our hair." Pippa thought she heard a voice in the background announce a flight to Vancouver. "Where are you, Mama?"

"At the florist." Click.

Pippa stared glumly out the windshield. "Why is everybody lying to me today? Do I look really stupid or something?"

"Excuse me, but didn't you just lie to your mother?"

"I'm protecting her. She sounds overwhelmed." Pippa frowned at her friend. "Couldn't you have waited one day before getting that damn haircut?"

"No. Look at the schedule. Anyway, in twenty-four hours you'll be Mrs. Henderson and I'll be on a plane to Costa Rica."

Pippa's stomach catapulted with terror. "Pull over," she whispered. "I think I feel sick."

Three

Rosimund Henderson was not accustomed to taking second place to anyone, anywhere, ever. On her home turf, the superior city of Houston, she was considered royalty. Her family fortune originated in the earliest days of Texas oil, when her great-great-grandfather Enoch Hicks had uncapped a ninety-thousand-barrel-a-day gusher in the Spindletop field. Rosimund was the product of four generations of magnificent breeding and she had preserved the line by marrying Lyman Henderson, scion of an equally illustrious Houston clan. Rosimund and Lyman produced Lance and, eighteen years later, a surprise they named Arabella.

Lance was the apple of his mother's eye. For twelve years, until he went to boarding school, they were inseparable. Rosimund instilled in her son a sense of chivalry toward women, respect for his elders, social grace, and civic obligation. Her heart burst with pride as he grew into a young man who regularly made the dean's list and the varsity team. Although he could have gone on to grad school, Lance chose to play football after becoming a first-round draft pick for the Dallas Cowboys. Rosimund wasn't happy about the Dallas part, but she recognized that once Lance led his team to Super Bowl victory, he could easily become governor of Texas and from there president of the United States. She had a game plan and Lance subconsciously knew it.

In most respects, Rosimund thought, Lance could not have chosen a better wife than Pippa Walker. She was his social equal, not some gold-digging tart. Pippa would produce gorgeous children. She was loyal to a fault: look at her devotion to Thayne. Rosimund only wished that Pippa had finished college and had some sort of career that she could give up for Lance. He was not terribly forthcoming about why she had not graduated from SMU. The rumor mill hinted that Pippa had followed some sort of Marxist auteur to Prague; Lance assured his mother that this sordid episode in his fiancée's life was over and not as bad as she had been led to believe. He had even gone on to suggest that he, too, had had a few episodes in his life that Rosimund would not be thrilled to hear about. She had dropped the subject there and then.

Upon reflection Rosimund had to admit that she had no problem with Pippa. It was Pippa's mother who seriously threatened her peace of mind. Furthermore, no amount of money in the bank could erase the blot Dallas from the Walker pedigree. It was always, and would forever remain, downscale to Houston. Although the Walkers had struck oil a mere twenty years after the Hendersons, Rosimund considered Thayne nouveau riche. In fact, Rosimund had detected symptoms of lowerclassitis as soon as Lance had announced his engagement last Christmas. She had phoned a discreet inquiry to Dallas's finest hotel, the Mansion on Turtle Creek, only to be informed that Thayne had booked the upper four floors of the hotel just an hour before! Rosimund had immediately summoned Lance to her chambers and asked if he *absolutely* wanted to go through with this marriage. Truth be told, he had proposed to Pippa not one month after the girl had returned in disgrace from Prague. For a moment Rosimund thought she saw a flash of terror in her son's eyes. Then he had said, "Mother, it's what I want more than anything in the world."

For the next six months Rosimund could only watch helplessly as Thayne created an extravaganza meant to delude people from Houston into thinking that people from Dallas were their equals. For Lance's sake Rosimund maintained icily cordial relations with her co-grandmother-to-be. However, she missed no opportunity to discreetly obstruct or trump Thayne whenever possible.

Like her idol Nancy Reagan, Rosimund wore nothing but red. She was also fond of astrology. After realizing with a shock that once Lance married Pippa he would be lost to her forever, Rosimund had sought the consolation of numerology. As luck would have it, not one week after her seer instructed her to avoid anything to do with the number ten, Thayne announced that there would be ten bridesmaids at the wedding. She hoped Rosimund would be able to produce ten groomsmen. Still smarting from the theft of all those hotel rooms, Rosimund had flatly refused. Her son would be attended by nine groomsmen and two pageboys. Little Arabella would be a flower girl. Thus war was declared.

Six months later Rosimund still had no intention of attending a luncheon for *ten* bridesmaids. That would be like asking lightning to strike her in the head. She planned to call in sick at the last minute and was even practicing a demure cough when Thayne called to say that she'd be late.

"Exactly how late?"

Thayne could not answer with any degree of certainty: diarrhea was an affliction with its own timetable. "Hopefully not more than fifteen minutes. It depends on traffic."

Rosimund had let a damning silence elapse. "Please arrive as close to the scheduled hour as possible. As you may recall, I have a ball to oversee this evening."

"You never hired a planner?" Thayne crowed. "Good Lord! You're doing all that grunt work yourself, Rosimund?"

"My dear woman, an event as vital to me as my son's rehearsal dinner is not something I would ever entrust to outside help. By the way, did you read the newspaper this morning?" There had been a lengthy article purporting that Rosimund's rehearsal dinner cost as much as Thayne's entire wedding.

"No. Robert told me there was nothing of interest." Thayne hung up.

Annoyed that she had not been able to edge in the last word, Rosimund returned to the bed in her parlor suite, the largest room available to her after Thayne's usurpation of the presidential, terrace, master, and executive suites. Across the bedspread Rosimund had arranged forty disks the size of dinner plates, each representing a table for tonight's rehearsal dinner. She was attempting to distribute four hundred one-inch Velcro tabs, each inscribed with a guest's name, ten to a table. Red tabs represented her friends, blue were Thayne's, green were Pippa's and Lance's. Rosimund had been working on the seating plan for months and had yet to feel secure that the red tabs were arranged in slightly superior position to the blue tabs. Engrossed in place setting, she barely noticed an hour slip by. Her phone rang again.

"I'm on my way." Thayne felt no need to apologize.

"Take your time. I've made other arrangements for lunch." Rosimund hung up. *Touché!*

After two hours of hell, she settled on the final seating configuration for the Henderson Ball, as she liked to call tonight's rehearsal dinner. She phoned her majordomo, whom she had brought from Houston along with her entire household staff. "Harry? Is everything all right over there?"

"Totally under control, madam."

In keeping with her numerologist's reading of four as her lucky number, Rosimund's ball would take place in four sumptuous climate-controlled tents that had been erected in Texas Stadium, home of the Dallas Cowboys. The Hendersons considered Texas Stadium "family" since Lance would be working there come September. "Send someone to my room for the seating chart. I've finally finished it."

"Right away, madam."

After carefully stacking the disks and their Velcro tabs on her desk, Rosimund ordered jumbo shrimp with dandelion greens from room service. She was famished and a bit exhausted. Her personal attendant would arrive at four to help her bathe and dress. Until then, she needed to rest. As she was wrapping herself in a red silk robe, Rosimund heard a soft knock on her door. "Pippa!" She had been expecting room service or, even better, her peerless son. "Please come in."

"Are you feeling better, ma'am? I brought some hot and sour soup." While at the mall, Ginny had forced Pippa to consume a second lunch to replace the one she had just barfed.

"How kind of you." Robe fluttering about her long, slim legs, Rosimund took the tray into the living room. She moved with the grace of a purebred stallion; from certain angles her face even looked equine. No question Lance had inherited his athletic prowess from his mother. "I'm sorry to have missed the luncheon, Pippa. Perhaps in Dallas it is customary to make a respectable woman wait over an hour. In Houston it would be scandalous for me to keep the appointment after such an indelicacy."

"I see." Pippa tucked yet another rule of Houston etiquette into her memory bank. "I'm afraid my mother was suffering a touch of jitters herself."

"Thayne may have bitten off more than she can chew, poor dear." Rosimund opened the white carton. "This smells divine. Tell me about the luncheon."

Pippa related a few innocent highlights as Rosimund tucked into her soup. "The girls are so excited at meeting all those eligible bachelors."

Dallas hussies! "I do hope they will concentrate tonight. I fear this rehearsal will be extremely difficult to coordinate."

Pippa's wedding was to take place in Meyerson Symphony Center. Workmen had constructed a marble-covered extension to the stage in order to accommodate the Dallas Symphony Orchestra and chorus, a bell choir, two brass quintets, the bridal parties, and last but not least, Pippa's bridal train, a confection embossed with what Thayne claimed to be her family crest. When fully extended, the train occupied its own zip code. In an attempt to work out the complex logistics before the wedding rehearsal, Thayne and Wyeth had twice rented Meyerson, musicians, thirty-one actors, and tried a few dry runs. Wyeth had reached a peak of frustration when, even on the fifth go, the small army of attendants was still receding from the hall when the Hallelujah Chorus ran out of notes. He finally calculated that everyone had to walk at a pace of twenty-two inches per second in order to evacuate the auditorium by the time the brass quintets opened fire.

"The bridesmaids have been practicing their paces for months," Pippa said. "They should be able to march up and down that aisle in their sleep."

Rosimund smiled thinly. She had been young once herself. She knew that the moment the bridesmaids set their eyes on Lance's retinue, all training would go out the window. "We shall see."

Room service appeared bearing Rosimund's shrimp and dandelions. She ate that, too, with gusto: it would be eons before dinner and she had played two sets of tennis with Lance this morning. "Did the bridesmaids like my gift?" she asked, refilling her glass with Evian.

"They loved the barrettes. Thank you so much."

"And Thayne's gift? I hope they didn't notice her pearls were smaller than mine."

"I didn't see any calipers at the table." Pippa waited until Rosimund finished her shrimp before asking, "How's Lance holding up?" She and Ginny had never located him.

"We had breakfast followed by tennis. I believe he's off playing rugby now. I hope you will forgive me for taking him away from you today, Pippa. It was my last chance to have him all to myself."

"That's perfectly all right." Actually it was perfectly infuriating, but Pippa tried to put herself in Rosimund's satin mules with the little red pompoms. "I'm sure I would only bore him with my tempests in a teapot." She stood to leave. "I'll be so glad when this wedding is all over."

Pippa burst into tears, surprising herself as much as her mother-in-law-to-be. Rosimund gathered her in her arms. "There there, dear. Courage!" Rosimund cursed Thayne for making Pippa's nuptials a nightmare instead of a fairy tale. "Would you like me to call my numerologist? She's excellent at jing luo massage."

"That's okay," Pippa sniffled. She needed Lance, not a massage. "I'm sorry to be bawling like this."

"I was exactly the same the day before my wedding." Rosimund's husband and his groomsmen had spent the day at the racetrack. "But I did what I had to do. And tomorrow so will you."

"I haven't heard from Lance in days."

"My dear, that is completely normal. Between you and me, all men view marriage as half prison, half death sentence. You must not be simpering now. You must wait for Lance to come to you. Do not appear weak or he will despise you forever."

That sounded pretty asinine. "Who's this groomsman Woody?"

"My son's physical therapist. He has a large clientele on Fifth Avenue. Why do you ask?"

"He and Lance were shopping for cummerbunds this afternoon. That's rather bizarre, seeing as the groomsmen already have them."

Rosimund's eyes flared then went quickly still. "I asked them to purchase one for Harry, my majordomo," she lied.

"That's such a relief. I was thinking much darker thoughts."

"Shame on you, dear." Rosimund rose to her full six-foot-two height. "Now go make yourself beautiful for my boy. Thank you for the soup."

Pippa took the elevator upstairs. Stress was making her paranoid. *Of course* Rosimund would want her majordomo's cummerbund to match the groomsmen's. *Of course* Lance would want someone to go shopping with him. *Of course* Woody, a New Yorker, would have the most fashion sense.

Her calm was momentary. As she opened the door of the presidential suite, Pippa heard Brent shriek, "You slut! How am I supposed to make that gopher fur into a French twist? How how HOW?"

Pippa rushed inside. There stood Ginny, arms folded, calm as a Cheshire cat while Brent ranted at her pixie. The hairdresser had had a trying afternoon. Repairing Kimberly's split ends had put him an hour behind schedule. He had never imagined that she would be followed by six bridesmaids with long blond hair the texture of last winter's hay. What was it with Texas girls and big blond hair? Farrah Fawcett and Linda Evans had been on the trash heap of hairdo history for almost two decades. And what was the attraction of having breasts as large as their heads? Physically and mentally these women were just one step away from mooing. He had been out of his mind to come to Dallas. To think that tomorrow he'd have to comb out the French twists and start over again!

"Is this some sort of joke?" he shouted at Pippa. "Your mother's going to pulverize me if I don't get ten twists on that runway tonight."

The door swung open. In strode Thayne, dressed in a light blue cashmere suit with midnight-blue mink cuffs. Her sapphires sparkled. Her hair and makeup were perfect. Despite the maniacal glint in her eyes, she looked very attractive. "Are you ready for my comb-out, Brent?" Then she saw Ginny. "What in God's name is *that?*"

"I didn't do it!" the frazzled hairdresser shrieked.

Thayne sighed; the gods were lobbing nonstop catastrophe at her today. "You would have had plenty of attention as you were, Ginny. That hair will look ridiculous with a large barrette." No one even tried to refute that. "You're fired."

"No!" Pippa cried, grabbing the cell phone out of Thayne's hands before she could call a replacement. "You can't do that!"

"I certainly can. We will not have a neo-Nazi in our entourage."

"Ginny goes, I go!" Pippa screamed. "This is my wedding, not yours!"

Thayne stared at her daughter, mystified by the outburst. "Honey, are you having a bad day?"

"Yes, I am having a Very. Bad. Day." Pippa collapsed onto a presidential couch. "I should have stayed in Prague and become a *ménage à quatre*."

Brent rushed over with a box of chocolate kirsch bonbons. "Take three, sweetheart." Last thing he needed was the bride going up in smoke: Thayne had only paid him fifty percent of his fee. "I have wigs," he announced, pulling one from a trunk. "We'll fix her in no time."

Ginny was not enthusiastic. "Sounds like I'm getting spayed."

"Humor us," Thayne hissed.

Did she have a choice? Ginny slid into the salon chair. "I'm doing this for you, Pippa."

"Thank you," her friend whimpered into the cushions.

After Ginny left, bemused and bewigged, Thayne went to the couch. "What exactly is the problem, honey?"

That was a complicated issue. "I think Lance visited a whorehouse today."

"That is ridiculous! He could have any woman he wanted simply by snapping his fingers." Belatedly realizing that this was anything but reassuring, Thayne added, "And if he did, that's nothing to get upset about. Believe me, in a year you'll be begging him to go back whenever he has the urge."

Someone knocked. Arming himself with a can of mousse, Brent went to the door.

"Mrs. Henderson sends an ornament for Pippa's coiffure," Harry the butler announced. "If she would wear it tonight we would be so pleased."

Brent returned with a little box. Inside was an heirloom hairclip encrusted with four carats of old mine-cut diamonds. "Pretty," Pippa said, knowing full well the barrette was less a gift for her than ammo against her mother.

"You're not *thrilled*?" Brent cried.

"Rectangles are so passé," Thayne informed him. "I would have had the diamonds reset in a platinum oval. I suppose you'll have to wear it or Rosimund will be crushed." To her surprise Pippa barely moved. "Enough tantrums, baby. Please. People are depending on you."

That did the trick, as always. Pippa slid off the couch. As Brent swept her hair into a twist, she watched Thayne chain-smoking at the window. "Nervous about tonight, Mama?"

"Not a bit."

Actually, Thayne was surprised she wasn't lying on her back in the cardiac unit of Baylor University Medical Center. Wyeth had gotten her day off to a poor start by quitting. The bridesmaids were on the verge of caloric mutiny: chances of them gorging themselves at the Henderson Ball were great, and there would be no more gown fittings. Wyeth's replacement Cedric was a terribly eccentric man. Thayne was anything but confident he could handle the situation. Worst of all, Pippa was about to snap. Lance at a brothel? Rosimund had probably bought him an all-day pass out of pure spite. "Have you been crying, dear? Your eyes look red."

"I ate some hot and sour soup. It always makes my eyes water."

"I hope there wasn't any MSG in it! It will keep you awake all night." Thayne glanced at her gold Cartier Tank Française watch. "Go to your room and put a cucumber pack on your eyes. I want you looking perfect."

So did Rosimund. So did everyone. Pippa kissed Thayne's cheek. "I'll do my best, Mama."

Thayne was already dialing out on her cell phone. "Cedric? Call the bell choir. The large bells must be polished again. I saw fingerprints." She hung up.

Pippa paused at the door. "Who's Cedric?"

"Did I not mention I dismissed Wyeth this morning?"

"No, you didn't." So that's why Thayne had been an hour late for the luncheon. Why she had called Pippa from the airport. "Where'd you find his replacement?"

"He was referred to me. Cedric is a veteran of three royal weddings. I should have hired him in the first place."

"What happened to Wyeth?"

Thayne wasn't about to tell her daughter that bad karma had caused Wyeth to tear up a check for two hundred and fifty thousand dollars. "He couldn't take the heat, honey. Run along now."

Pippa immediately called Wyeth, who didn't answer. She phoned Lance, who didn't answer, either. Room service delivered one perfectly chilled cucumber as she was fighting back tears of frustration and a growing fury. Pippa put a few slices on her eyes but got no beauty rest: every two minutes a bridesmaid flew in with some crisis regarding her dress or complexion. To make matters worse, word had just leaked to the press that Thayne's wedding had an A list and a B list. Everyone on the A list had received a lacquer box filled with gilt-edged engraved invitations and response cards for a multitude of barbecues, receptions, and the wedding itself at Meyerson Symphony Center followed by dinner and dancing to six different bands at the Walker mansion. Those on the B list received only a plain invitation to the wedding followed by a buffet in a downstairs function room at Meyerson, where the wedding party would appear later in the evening. Needless to say, quite a few Dallas socialites went berserk when they realized they weren't on the A list. After a dozen verbal confrontations, Pippa told the front desk to hold all incoming calls. She worked on a difficult sudoku puzzle and ate half the chocolates Kimberly had given her. When her migraine only intensified, Pippa ate the rest of the sliced cucumber as well.

At the stroke of five the bridal entourage convened in front of the hotel. Since Thayne had forbidden pantsuits for the rehearsal, each young lady now sported a skimpy cocktail dress and very high heels. Their attire delighted the crowd gawking from the veranda. As onlookers cheered and flashbulbs exploded, the girls ducked into the first of three stretch limos waiting at the curb.

"Debbie Buntz offered me four thousand dollars for an A-list invitation," bragged Chardonnay, passing around her flask of vodka. "I said there was nothing I could do. That old bag didn't invite me to her Sadie Hawkins dance last fall."

"Roxie Hooper offered me ten grand and a week at Canyon Ranch." Francesca rapped on the window separating her from the driver. "Do you have a pair of scissors up there? This is an emergency."

A hirsute hand passed a pair of nail clippers through the aperture. Francesca snipped the spaghetti straps off her lime green cocktail dress. She disposed of the straps and the clipper whence it had come. "Where's Pippa? And Kimberly? Traffic is horrible on Friday night."

Hazel could not take her eyes off Ginny, who looked scrumptious in a teal taffeta frock that hugged her every curve. "Is that a wig?" she finally asked.

"No, I've been drinking Rogaine," Ginny replied pleasantly.

Pippa finally arrived wearing a vintage yellow chiffon princess gown. She looked pale but totally exquisite. "Thanks for waiting."

"Where'd you find that fantastic dress?"

"It was my mother's." That went over like a pie in the face.

"Where'd you get the necklace?" Steffani asked with a slight note of accusation. She had always wanted a choker of graduated diamonds. "Lance again?"

"It was my grandmother's." Pippa looked around the white leather seats. "Where's Kimberly? She was in my room five minutes ago, all set to go."

"Omigosh, here come the Hendersons," Cora squealed.

The limo almost tipped over as nine bridesmaids surged to one side to get a better glance at Lance, his parents, and little sister Arabella boarding the vehicle behind them. "Pinch me. I must be dreaming," Leah murmured as her nose left a smudge on the glass.

Outside, several scantily clad women broke through the restraining barriers as Lance walked by. "You're going to put up with that the rest of your life?" Ginny asked as he stopped to sign autographs.

Seeing the disdain in Lance's smile as he scribbled in their football schedules, Pippa felt infinitely better. "If he can, I guess I can."

The Henderson entourage had all boarded the second limousine when Thayne emerged from the hotel, cell phone at her ear. She was accompanied by husband, Robert, back from a few last holes at the golf course. Robert held his wife's Judith Leiber handbag, a second cell phone, and a Ferragamo tote stuffed with emergency supplies. Kimberly walked at Thayne's right side.

"Is she trying to sneak someone onto the A list?" Charlotte frowned.

In fact, moving some third-rater onto the A list was far down Kimberly's list of priorities. Five minutes ago Pippa had told her Wyeth

McCoy had been replaced; Kimberly had immediately seized her chance to rearrange the bridal procession. She had contrived to bump into Thayne in the lobby and was now waiting for her to get off the phone. Finally Thayne did so. "What a pretty dress, Kimberly," she said. "Outrageously short, however."

"The cleaners must have shrunk it." The dress was brand-new. "Could I have a word with you about the procession, Mrs. Walker?"

"Is there a problem?"

"I just wanted you to know that I can move twenty-two inches a second like clockwork. I guess that's because I have a lower center of gravity than the other girls."

"Yes, we're quite aware of that." Kimberly's lack of height had almost eliminated her from the bridal party. Thayne ripped the other cell phone out of her husband's hand. She had four missed calls on that line. "Please get to the point."

"I think it's crucial that I lead the procession. Ginny's sense of co-ordination may not be as sharp as it was at lunchtime."

"What makes you think that?"

"Well, maybe *she* can walk a straight line after drinking a bottle of cherry vodka. I know *I* couldn't."

Thayne's cell phone rang. It was Cedric reporting that the organist had just fallen off the stage extension and sprained his wrist. They were calling replacements but so far had gotten nothing but answering machines. "Get into your limo, Kimberly," Thayne snapped. "I'll sort this out later."

"A few of the other bridesmaids have been drinking, too," Kimberly added for insurance. Thayne would have thirty minutes en route to Meyerson Center to chew this distressing cud. "Only Pippa and I are totally sober, and Pippa certainly can't go in first."

Mission accomplished, Kimberly dove into the bridesmaids' limo. "Sorry, guys! I forgot to spray myself with Eau de Thayne." Unscrewing her flask, she swallowed several ounces of vodka.

As their limousine transported them through Dallas, the brides-maids fixed their makeup, drank, and grilled Pippa about her honey-moon to a secret location: first one to snitch to the newspapers would earn several thousand dollars. Pippa revealed nothing, but *she* didn't even know where she'd be spending her honeymoon. She and Lance would be boarding the Henderson jet and taking off for destinations unknown. A gift from Rosimund.

Engrossed in discussion, no one noticed Thayne's limo shooting ahead of them in traffic. By the time the bridesmaids arrived at Meyerson Center, Thayne had already been there ten minutes. The young ladies were met in the lobby by a tall, humorless chap in tails who introduced himself as Cedric, the new wedding coordinator. A forty-year veteran of drunken orgies, Cedric could immediately see that the bridesmaids had arrived even more inebriated than had the groomsmen.

"Where are the boys, Cedric?" Leah asked, tottering ever so slightly (or so she thought) on her high heels.

"In the rear lounge, madam. Drinking coffee as fast as they can swallow it." Cedric eyed the shortest woman in the entourage. "Kimberly?"

"Yes, sir!"

"Please walk from here to there at twenty-two inches per second." Cedric assessed her progress. "Attention! Mrs. Walker has requested a change in the order of procession. Bridesmaids will now enter the auditorium beginning with the shortest and ending with the tallest. Kindly rearrange yourselves as I fetch the gentlemen. We will pair up and proceed with the rehearsal."

Cedric disappeared for ten long minutes. He had not foreseen that one third of Lance's friends would be seriously passed out.

Meanwhile, affairs were not proceeding well in the auditorium. The replacement organist was there but had forgotten reading glasses in his rush to leave home. Thayne had ordered the back lights turned down so low that the orchestra couldn't read their music, either. The officiating Reverend Mark Alcott, who owned four evangelical television stations and was considered the Protestant equivalent of a cardinal, had a bad cold and would have to confine his mellifluous baritone to a whisper. Only one brass quintet had arrived, dressed in jeans and scruffy T-shirts instead of the dark business suits Thayne had requested. As the two boy pages played a rough game of tag, the ring bearer was frantically crawling under the auditorium seats trying to find the ring that had just rolled off his satin pillow. The bell choir was rehearsing, badly, a twenty-second intermezzo Thayne had commissioned John Williams to write for that magical moment when Lance would kiss his new bride.

Thayne was ricocheting between mishaps, shouting into a bullhorn, as Rosimund and Lyman Henderson made their way up the aisle to the front row of the auditorium. After a few seconds in her seat, Rosimund raised her hand. "Thayne! Oh, Thayne, dear!"

Thayne walked swiftly over. She was dismayed to find Rosimund wearing a tiara with her red pantsuit. "Yes, Rosimund? What can I do for you?"

"I'm afraid this seat is unacceptable. I'm so close to the extension that I'll have a terrible crick in my neck by the end of the ceremony."

"Would you rather sit halfway back in the auditorium?"

Rosimund pointed to the first tier of boxes, where visiting Windsors or Ross Perot would be placed. "I think that would be a suitable location for the mother of the groom."

"I'm so sorry. I've put a brass quintet there."

"Is that so? Who are those five ruffians with tubas on the edge of the stage?"

"One of the quintets. There are two."

A tremendous crash nearly caused Thayne to drop her bullhorn. A chorus riser had just collapsed, flooding the percussion section with sopranos. The orchestra manager hurtled onstage to tell Thayne that, due to union rules, the rear of the stage had to be evacuated while the risers were repaired. Everything should be back in position in fifteen minutes. "You don't understand," Thayne screamed into her bullhorn although the man was not an arm's length away. "We're already thirteen minutes late. The entire bridal party must be at Texas Stadium in one hour for a nationally televised broadcast on *E!*"

The manager merely shrugged: no one argued with the union.

Outside in the lobby, Cedric had finally rousted the groomsmen from the lavatory and herded them upstairs. He was pairing them off with the bridesmaids according to a list Wyeth had bequeathed to him. Kimberly's euphoria at being first was deflated by the discovery that she would walk up the aisle with the homeliest guy in sight, a middle-aged turkey with a mangy mustache and potbelly. His name was Woody and he appeared to be completely, disgustingly, sober.

"And what might be your relation to the groom?" she asked.

Woody gazed with pity at Kimberly's cleavage. She had freakishly large breasts for a woman of her height. "I'm Lance's physical therapist," he replied.

"So you've seen him naked, you lucky shit."

He pretended not to have heard. "I haven't seen so many French twists since *Gigi*."

Kimberly looked desperately around the lobby. Ginny, now tenth instead of first in line, would process down the aisle alone since Rosimund had provided only nine groomsmen. Too late Kimberly realized that entering last, in solitary splendor, would have been infinitely better than walking down the aisle with Woody. Worse, the eight other couples were chatting comfortably arm in arm. Half of them looked like they were already going steady. Kimberly felt like killing someone. "Excuse me, Woody."

She went to the ladies' room and finished every last drop of vodka in her flask.

Four

The worse the rehearsal, the better the performance: if that axiom were true, Pippa's wedding would be flawless. Despite her bullhorn, Thayne was nearly hoarse by the time the chorus, symphony, bell choir, and brass quintets had regrouped following the collapse of the risers. When the musicians were finally tuned and ready to go, she repaired to the vestibule with Rosimund. Sight of the two matriarchs marching down the aisle toward them struck terror in the bridesmaids. Within seconds drunken strumpets became demure damsels standing in a line. The groomsmen apishly followed suit.

Thayne paused to sniff the air in the lobby: was that beer or her perfume? Madame Ricci had advised her it would smell different on other people, and she was absolutely right. Thayne's frown deepened as she observed the indecently exposed flesh on parade.

Rosimund didn't help by commenting, "I feel as if we're in a bordello."

"At least they're not wearing crowns with pants. Are we ready to process, everyone?"

"Yes, Mrs. Walker!"

Thayne sensed something odd about the young couples. They

seemed to be propping each other up. Aha: the high heels. The girls hadn't eaten since lunch and were probably feeling dizzy. "We'll be at dinner in no time," she announced. "Where is Pippa?"

"She's getting her train reattached," Kimberly replied. "One of the harness straps broke."

"Are we ready to begin back there?" Cedric's voice boomed from the front of the auditorium.

"Yes," Thayne shouted back through her bullhorn. The music began. "Tommy! Come here."

Tommy, the ring bearer, was a professional child actor. After scouring every possible cousin in the Walker family and failing to find a boy four feet tall with curly blond hair and excellent deportment, Wyeth McCoy had called a talent agency in Hollywood. Although he looked six years old, Tommy was actually thirteen. He had been smoking heavily for the last few years in order to stunt his growth. Thayne told everyone he was a third cousin once removed.

"Where is the groom's ring?" Thayne cried in horror, spying only one band on the pillow.

"It got lost." Bored with all the waiting, Tommy had tried it on. That's when it had slipped through his fingers and rolled away.

Rosimund clucked in disappointment. A Henderson would have chopped off his right arm before letting go of that ring. "Wherever did you find this boy, Thayne?"

Thayne knelt beside the lad. Was she hallucinating or had he been smoking? "Where did this accident happen, Tommy?"

"Somewhere around there." He pointed.

"Where is the f-ing mother of the groom?" Cedric fulminated from the other end of the hall. "You're fifteen seconds behind the music."

Rosimund clamped her hands over little Arabella's ears. "Such language! Please tell that man to control himself!"

"Cedric, we've lost a ring," Thayne called.

"I don't care if you've lost your f-ing cat, send the mother of the groom out NOW." Cedric instructed the orchestra to start over again.

Rosimund rehearsed walking from the rear of the auditorium to her front row seat on the groom's side while gazing beatifically at her son, Lance, who was waiting onstage with the Reverend Alcott. It was a very heady experience. Then Cedric shouted, "Thayne! Get your ass on the carpet! What's taking so g-damn long?"

"Is that man insane?" Rosimund fumed to her husband. "This is a holy occasion."

Lyman put aside his *Robb Report* devoted to motorcycles. "He's working with raw recruits, darlin'. Cut him a little slack." Lyman returned to the magazine.

Thayne now paraded up the aisle and seated herself in the front row, bride's side. She was breathless with excitement and had to restrain herself not to ask Cedric if she could try that once again, just to be sure she got it right.

"Ring bearer! Where's the little prick?" Cedric barked into his bullhorn.

"I just fired him," Thayne called upstage.

A voice across the aisle intoned, "You fired your own third cousin once removed?"

"Yes, Rosimund, I did." Thayne returned her attention to Cedric. "Let's keep moving."

"Pages! Flower girl! Where's the flower girl?"

Back in the lobby, Kimberly roughly pushed little Arabella into the auditorium. Besides being saddled with the homeliest groomsman, Kimberly had just discovered that the cutest girl on earth, Lance's wee sister, would be preceding her up the aisle. Rosimund had been rehearsing Arabella for months because this wedding was, in a sense, her daughter's debut in society. Arabella instinctively rose to the occasion; when she dug her little gloved hand into her basket of rose petals and strewed them in the air, she could have stolen the show from Judy Garland, Shirley Temple, and the Olsen twins combined.

"Bridesmaid one! Come out!"

Kimberly could only smile, pretend her escort was George Clooney, and concentrate on walking toward the stage at a steady twenty-two inches per second.

"Are you intoxicated?" Woody whispered as they were halfway into the hall. "You seem to be having difficulty keeping to the middle of the aisle."

"Shut up, you disgusting troll."

"I detect hostility in your voice, Kimberly. Are you unhappy with some element of your life?"

"Silence," shouted Cedric from a distance. "You're not at the f-ing movies."

"Where did you find that chimney sweep?" Rosimund asked Thayne in a stage whisper heard above the entire Dallas Symphony. "If he continues using such foul language, I will have no choice but to take Arabella home."

"Cedric, please!" Thayne rasped. "Do dukes and duchesses talk like this?"

"Where do you think I learned it, madam? Attention! Rear of the hall! Where is the next pair of attendants?"

That would be Cora, currently sharing her first kiss with partner Denny. They finally separated when Cedric threatened to perform an instant clitorectomy with the Leatherman in his pocket.

"Thayne, really," Rosimund reprimanded. "You must dismiss that beast at once."

"And replace him with?"

"We know several generals at Fort Hood. Any or all could be here within the hour."

"This is Dallas, not Baghdad. Continue, Cedric. Please temper your language."

Cedric continued to issue marching orders amid avalanches of shocking profanity. Unable to stand it anymore, the Reverend Alcott finally tore the bullhorn from Cedric's mouth and stomped it to an electronic pancake, to show Cedric what would happen to him in the afterlife if he continued using F, G, and C words. He then held Cedric in a viselike grip and commenced quite a long private prayer that was broadcast throughout the auditorium thanks to the microphone on his lapel.

Cedric finally broke loose. He was pleased to see that the entire bridal party had arrived during the Reverend Alcott's tête-à-tête with the Almighty. "Pippa! Up the aisle!" he shouted.

As the orchestra surged into Mendelssohn's "Wedding March," all eyes turned toward the rear of the auditorium. Pippa and her father, Robert, walked slowly up the aisle, trailed by Pippa's just-repaired wedding train. It was heavy enough when she was pulling it on a marble floor; pulling it along a carpet was nearly impossible. Both Pippa and her father were leaning forward, straining like two beasts of burden, as the train clung to the carpet every inch of the way. Every few steps they could hear a little rip as the threads binding the train to Pippa's custom-designed titanium harness broke. Sensing that his daughter was on the verge of panic, Robert regaled her with a long-winded joke about a priest, a rabbi, and an ayatollah on the golf course.

Pippa didn't hear a word her father was saying. Her eyes were glued to Lance, who was watching in adoration as she neared. Robert was just about at the punch line of the golf joke when he and Pippa arrived at their destination. The music stopped so he reluctantly stopped as well.

Reading from a script, the Reverend Alcott cleared his sore throat and quietly began. "Dearly beloved, we are gathered together to witness the union of two young hearts and two great families, the Walkers and the Hendersons. It is a historic, joyful occasion."

"Excuse me," Thayne interrupted. "You forgot 'unforgettable.' "

The Reverend Alcott squinted at his script. "That's been crossed out."

"What? Who?"

"I did," Cedric replied. "The word is inappropriate."

"Put the word back in," Thayne ordered. "Cedric, have you been tampering with my ceremony?"

Rosimund leaned over the aisle. The Walker family crest, so crassly embroidered in gold on Pippa's train, was giving her a violent headache. "Could we move on? Four hundred guests are waiting for us in Texas Stadium. I'm sure that you and your hired man can sort out this 'script' later."

The Reverend Alcott continued, "Who gives this woman to be married?"

Flustered, his mind still on the golf joke, Robert replied, "I do."

Thayne leaped to her feet. "No no no, Robert! Please concentrate! One more time!"

The Reverend Alcott repeated the question. Robert gathered his wits for five full seconds before replying, "Thayne Ardelle Beatrice Brattlewood Priscilla Inge Walker and I do."

Thayne went nearly purple. "No no no, Robert! You forgot 'Tuttle'! One more time! Inge Tuttle Walker!"

The Reverend Alcott repeated the question. There was an even longer silence before Robert replied, "Thayne Ardelle Beatrice Brattlewood Priscilla Ingle Tuttle Walker and I do."

"Inge, not Ingle!"

"Inge Tuttle Walker and I do," Robert said. "That's the last time I'm saying it."

"That's more like it," Thayne beamed.

The Reverend Alcott was only a few sentences into a reading from the Song of Solomon when Chardonnay swooned. On the way down, she grabbed the elbow of the violinist sitting behind her. Chardonnay's head and the violinist's Guarneri del Gesù hit the floor at about the same time. The violinist went ballistic. "Will you calm down," Thayne shouted. "It isn't the end of the world. I'll buy you another one."

"You sure as hell will," the violinist screamed back as four people tried to restrain him. "Hope you've got a spare three f-ing million!"

Again Rosimund leaned over the aisle. "Thayne, this is the last time I'm going to ask you to control the language in this pigsty."

Arabella began to whimper, but not from the four-letter words she heard every day in kindergarten. "What happened to that lady, Mother? Is she dead?"

"She's had a little too much excitement, that's all. Come here, darling. Sit with me."

Arabella had no intention of leaving the stage. Some corner of her brain knew that she was one step away from being the star of the show. "I'll be okay."

Rosimund settled back into her seat. "If only that ring bearer had one ounce of Arabella's gumption," she commented loudly to her husband.

After Chardonnay and the violinist were removed from the auditorium, the Reverend Alcott wisely decided to stop reading from the script. It was an indecipherable mess of overstrikes and insertions. "After the Scriptures, there will be a choral interlude." The choir sang "How Lovely Are Thy Dwellings" from the Brahms *Requiem*. "Then I will read a love poem by Tennyson." Fortunately Cedric had not edited any of that. "After which the orchestra will play the overture to *Romeo and Juliet* by Tchaikovsky."

"Isn't that a bit heavy?" Rosimund asked across the aisle.

"Your son requested it," Thayne shot back.

"I will then read a brief history of the Walker family, followed by a brief history of the Henderson family. I assure you that each reading will be exactly the same word length," the Reverend took care to add. "Then the brass quintets will play the *Royal Fireworks Music* by Handel."

Thayne noticed that three bridesmaids looked fairly chartreuse. "We'll skip that for now."

"Next the bride and groom will exchange vows. Lance, please join me here." Every distaff heart in the auditorium broke as Lance stepped forward and mumbled his wedding vows with Pippa. Cedric stepped in for Tommy, the banished ring bearer. "Then I'll say, 'Mr. Henderson, you may kiss your wife, Ms. Walker.' "

Rosimund sprang to her feet. "Excuse me, Reverend Alcott! You do mean *Mrs. Henderson,* don't you?"

He studied the script. "It says *Ms. Walker.*" In boldface italics, 20-point type.

Rosimund trained her sweetest, deadliest smile across the aisle. "I'm afraid this won't do, Thayne. It is inconceivable that a woman fortunate enough to be marrying a Henderson would not take the family name."

"I've told Pippa it's all right, Mother," Lance said quietly.

Deeply shocked, Rosimund sank into her seat. A moment later, everyone could see her dabbing her eyes with a handkerchief. "What about the grandchildren?" she moaned to her husband.

Once again the Reverend Alcott leaped into the breach. "When I say 'kiss the bride, Lance,' the bell choir will play 'O Happy, Happy Day' by John Williams. Let's rehearse that, shall we?"

Upset at his mother's tears, Lance could only muster a perfunctory kiss for Pippa as the bell choir chimed out a triumphant theme that sounded a little like *Raiders of the Lost Ark.* When the piece finally ended, Thayne stood up. "Lance, you're going to have to do much better than that. Mr. Williams has composed twenty seconds of music for this climactic moment, at five thousand dollars per second I might add, and you're expected to be kissing Pippa for the full count."

"Mama, this is really embarrassing," Pippa said. "Could we leave it until tomorrow?"

Stung, Thayne looked across the aisle. She felt Rosimund's pain. "What's gotten into everyone today?"

"I don't know, dear," came the hurt, muffled reply.

His voice on its last legs, the Reverend Alcott whispered, "The musicians will then join forces for the Hallelujah Chorus. The bridal party will follow Lance and Pippa out." He looked at the pale couple. "I'd scram if I were you."

Lance and Pippa nearly ran out of the auditorium, followed by their attendants. Pippa ditched her train in the lobby, then piled into the first limousine with Lance, who was already dialing Rosimund's cell phone. Pippa waited until he had smoothed his mother's ruffled feathers. "I'm so happy to see you," she cried, plastering his face with kisses. "Where have you been?"

"Keeping the guys out of jail." Lance buried his nose in Pippa's neck. "Diorissimo?"

Lance had always been exceptional at identifying perfume. "It's a custom Ricci blend. Ginny and I were looking for you today."

"So I hear."

"You haven't introduced me to Woody."

"He's in the next car."

"Did you two find a cummerbund?"

Lance put two fingers under her chin and raised her face. "Is this an interrogation?"

"Absolutely. I'm insanely jealous."

"Yes, we found a cummerbund."

"I would have loved to help you shop."

"And I would have loved to have you there. But I wasn't about to risk the wrath of Thayne by removing you from scheduled events." Lance kissed her. "Forgive me?"

Pippa's smile lit up the back seat. "Always."

Five

An hour before the Henderson Ball was to begin, seven hundred people had gathered outside Texas Stadium to watch guests arrive in their Bentleys, Aston Martins, and Hummer limousines. When it started to sprinkle, valets held umbrellas aloft, protecting the hair of Dallas from contact with ordinary rainwater. Crews from the local stations and *E!* recorded every step as women in glittery gowns and men in tuxedos traversed a red carpet into the stadium. The onlookers applauded almost nonstop. This was way more fun than rubbernecking at Oscar night because Dallas society women, unlike Hollywood actresses, did not believe that less was more, especially when it came to hair, jewels, makeup, sequins, ermine, and teeth.

Commandos in headsets kept the parade flowing evenly from vehicle to arena. Inside the stadium, guests wandered between four climate-controlled tents, one for each season, as they awaited the wedding party. Rosimund had borrowed the season idea after reading about a gala that the Emir of Kuwait had thrown for the Sultan of Brunei. In keeping with her Chinese numerologist's reading that four was her lucky number, she planned to serve a four-course meal that included black and white truffles, delicate game meats, rare grains, four wines, and Veuve Clicquot instead of the gassier Cristal that Thayne preferred. The first tent, stark white, was a winter garden containing a veritable forest of bamboo trees as well as two gigantic Plexiglas enclosures, one housing a pair of pandas, the other a pair of Siberian snow leopards. While sipping cocktails, guests could marvel at the animals, eat Kumamoto oysters, and watch a laser light show. A gamelan orchestra from Java serenaded A-listers who had come to Dallas for the wedding of the century. Souvenir booklets informed all that the laser exhibition was visible from the moon; the big hit of the evening was a gigantic hologram of Lance and Rosimund hovering like benevolent deities one hundred feet above the stadium.

When she was finally en route from Meyerson Center, Rosimund phoned her majordomo. "Begin moving guests into the second tent."

"Thank you, madam," Harry replied. The chefs were going ballistic because dinner was one hour behind schedule. "Did rehearsal go well?"

"As well as could be expected of a three-ring circus."

Within moments the word "dinner" began flashing over and over in the sky. Guests headed for the next tent. During their long wait to be fed something more substantial than oysters and finger sculptures, they had had ample time to study the seating charts situated throughout the bamboo forest. Everyone now poured toward their tables with a great sense of anticipation.

The décor of the second tent evoked springtime. Forty tables were set in soft blues and pinks; a brass cage ensconcing two mechanical lovebirds topped the floral centerpiece on each table. The birds chirped nonstop as Andre Rieu led the Johann Strauss Orchestra through a flurry of waltzes. Acres of sky-blue silk formed the canopy of the tent. Large fluffy clouds attached to invisible pulleys wafted overhead, occasionally showering those below with golden stardust (edible, in case it hit the food). The air was fragrant with just enough lily of the valley, Rosimund's favorite fragrance, to overwhelm Thayne's signature perfume.

Harry managed to seat everyone moments before the bridal party arrived. The spotlight found Rosimund, hard to miss since she was not only first in, but also wearing fiery red and a two-pound tiara. A shaft of light followed her to the microphone at the head table. As she welcomed her guests, waiters in pale yellow tuxedos commenced pouring Champagne.

While the cooks in the service tent went even more ballistic at the delay, Rosimund read a five-page, single-spaced essay entitled "My Son Lance." Her memoir shared significant moments such as his first solid food, his graduation at the top of his kindergarten class, his discovery of a football, his first barbecue, his eight trips to Europe with her, his fifteen full scholarships that they didn't need, his first-round draft pick by the Cowboys. Rosimund closed with names she would prefer for her grandchildren: Henrianna and Hart. She raised her glass of now warm Veuve Clicquot. "Lance, I wish you as much joy with Pippa as you've had with me."

"Hear, hear!" cried the guests.

"Thank you, Mother," Lance dutifully replied. Under the table he squeezed Pippa's hand. "She's not too bad once you get to know her. You can leave that bottle right here," he told the waiter refilling their glasses.

Pippa didn't want to say anything, but her fiancé had had plenty to drink already. Worse, just before the rehearsal, Lance had presented all his groomsmen with Tiffany flasks containing 150-proof bourbon. "Are you all right, sweetheart?" she asked.

"Couldn't be better. Why?"

"You don't normally drink Champagne." In such quantity.

"And I probably won't for another twenty years. Ah. You're worried it will impair my performance." He smiled as Pippa blushed. "I'll let you in on a secret. I have yet to discover *anything* that impairs my performance."

From the other end of the table, sensing that her son was already telling Pippa things he would never tell her, Rosimund felt a stab of pain. She remedied the situation by asking Lance to dance with her.

Watching her future husband and mother-in-law waltz around the parquet floor as artificial clouds dusted them with gold, Pippa felt suddenly weary. She was no psychoanalyst, but Lance did seem overly attached to his mother. She wondered if she would ever be able to turn that tide around. *Henrianna Henderson?* Out of the question.

"May I have this dance?"

Anson Walker, Pippa's beloved grandfather, took her hand. A legendary oilman and cattleman, Anson had decades of experience with petroleum, cows, and that other ruinous natural resource, Texan women. "You're looking mighty serious tonight."

"It's all beginning to hit me, Grampy."

"Perfectly normal. Don't worry about Rosimund. About now she's feeling like General Custer at the Battle of Little Bighorn."

Pippa smiled. "Are you calling me an Indian?"

"No, a little big horn." Anson steered Pippa onto the dance floor. "Did your mother tell you she wore that same dress at her rehearsal dinner?"

Pippa was surprised. "No."

"I wouldn't think so. She was somewhat under the weather, too. Apparently the prospect of marrying my boy Robert was impossible to face without the help of two bottles of Champagne. You should have seen her on the dance floor. That poor girl was more liquid than solid. Grandma Walker almost called off the wedding. She was sure Robert was throwing himself away on a spineless wastrel. And look how that little lassie turned out. We're all so proud of Thayne."

"So am I," Pippa said. "But I want to be an equal partner with my husband."

"Lance is a good boy. With your help I'm sure he'll outgrow his mother and become the man of the house." Anson smiled at Pippa's diamond choker. "I'm so glad you're wearing that necklace, pumpkin. It was my wedding gift to your grandmother."

"I'm honored to have it." They danced a while in silence. Then Pippa asked, "Were you in love with Grandma at first sight?"

"We were special friends whose friendship caught fire."

"Did it catch fire before or after you got married?"

"I'll tell you a secret. It was ten years afterward." Anson's eyes grew misty as he remembered. "Your grandma was napping on the porch swing. It was late afternoon on a perfect summer day. She opened her eyes and saw me. A little smile overtook her face. In that moment I fell head over heels in love with her and stayed that way for the next forty-three years."

"But how did you survive the first ten?"

"We got to know and respect each other better. I always knew she was a fine woman. I always knew we were rowing the same boat." Anson kissed Pippa's forehead. "It will be the same for you."

Pippa certainly hoped so. "Do you think I'm rushing into this, Grampa?"

"Of course not. You've known Lance for years. You have a good idea where he's coming from. Lord knows you two talk enough together."

Yes, Lance could chat all night long. That was one of his most endearing qualities. "Do you think I'm marrying on the rebound?"

Anson went quiet for a few turns around the floor. "I think it's good that you had a romantic disappointment before marrying. Makes you appreciate the good apples more. Mistakes are our best teachers."

"André was a mistake, all right." Pippa just wasn't sure what she had learned.

"I'm only sorry you gave him a year of your life, when you could have been in school."

The year wasn't entirely wasted. Pippa could speak a few words of Czech and she distinctly remembered the happy times. Both of them. "I'm not sure I want to stay in stage design," she said.

"Then find something else you love. I do wish you'd go back to school and finish a degree. Education was the key to my success. If I hadn't learned about agriculture and geology, I would have been useless with cows and oil."

"Once this wedding's over, I'm going to do something with my life, Grampa. Promise."

"I know you've got it in you. Lance will be consumed with football so you'll have plenty of time to study. All the money in the world won't make you an adult. You've got to get there yourself. Just like your mama."

Lance tapped Anson's shoulder. He looked flushed. There was a gleam in his eye that Pippa had not seen before. "May I?" he asked.

"Well, well! Had enough of dancing with Rosimund?" Anson handed Pippa to her fiancé. "Take care of my girl now."

Lance's fingers closed around Pippa's. They began circling the floor while the guests started in on the first course, truffled shad with roe. "Were you two discussing social Darwinism or something?"

"Survival of the fittest did come up."

As their offspring danced, Thayne and Rosimund looked dotingly on from the head table. "That boy of yours is the luckiest man on earth," Thayne commented, pressing her fork into a mound of shad roe. What a waste of a good truffle! "There aren't many women with Pippa's looks, personality, and pedigree. And accomplishments! Lord! Gold Girl Scout, cheerleading captain, debutante, Kappa Kappa Gamma, and she speaks fluent Czech."

"Her degree is in?" Rosimund inquired.

"Pippa is still deciding. Nowadays it's considered much wiser to take a few years off rather than major in something silly." Thayne meticulously removed a bone from the shad. "Lance is the only boy I know with a degree in ceramics."

"He has a fine eye for art. Since he has the means to become a major collector, it was a perfect choice of major. He can always study political science when he becomes bored with winning Super Bowls."

Thayne peered across the dining room. One of the bridesmaids seemed to be straddling one of the groomsmen. It was difficult to see clearly with all this gold dust Rosimund was blowing in everyone's eyes. "Those friends of his are mauling my bridesmaids."

"Perhaps you need glasses, dear. Your bridesmaids are doing all the mauling." Rosimund sighed. "I wish you could have had one Houston woman among them."

"For your information I did find one bridesmaid from Houston. She gained thirteen pounds in six months, lied to me about it, and had to be dismissed."

Rosimund quietly masticated her black and white truffles as she tried to think of a way to run Thayne over with her Volvo and get away with it. "Where did you find that suit? I seem to remember seeing something like it on the Paris runway eight or nine years ago."

"Alfred Fiandaca made it for me last month. Light and dark blue are the Kappa Kappa Gamma colors." Thayne squinted at Rosimund's ensemble. "Isn't red completely out this year?"

"Do you follow fashion fads? I suppose that's the difference between old money and nouveau riche." Rosimund lovingly straightened her tiara. "When did your ancestors come into wealth, dear? I've forgotten."

"Twenty years after yours did."

"Twenty years can be an eon. Ask Prince Charles. Well! Wasn't that delicious. I'm so looking forward to the smoked baby quail and purple rice."

Two groomsmen, both football players, wobbled over. The 150-proof bourbon previously in Tiffany flasks now raged through their veins. "May we have this dance, ladies?"

Pippa smiled as the couples joined her and Lance on the parquet. "How sweet! Your friends asked our mothers to dance."

"They have a little pool going. First guy to seduce either of them wins five grand." Lance laughed curtly. "Personally I'd rather service my horse."

Pippa couldn't believe what she was hearing. "I suppose I should be glad you find screwing your mother unattractive."

"That was a lovely comment, chickadee."

"So was yours. And don't call me chickadee. I'm not a bird."

Fortunately Pippa's father tapped Lance on the shoulder. "May I cut in?"

"Not a moment too soon, sir." Lance walked off.

Robert saw his daughter's eyes fill with tears. "What was that all about?"

"I think we just had our first fight." Pippa could barely eke out the words as she watched her fiancé stalk out of the tent. "I feel like I'm sliding down a well, Daddy."

"Preperformance jitters, darlin'. Perfectly normal." Robert guided his daughter between raucously whirling Rosimund and Thayne. "Lance isn't sure he can live up to expectations. In this case there are plenty. Believe me, I've been there."

"What is this, true confessions night?" Pippa snapped. "Was anyone in this family actually happy to get married?"

"Happiness comes later," Robert attempted to explain.

"How much later?"

"When you learn to balance what you've got with what you thought you had." Robert kissed her forehead. "Meanwhile, a well-bitten tongue comes in handy."

To please her parents Pippa danced with mayors and senators for what seemed like eons. Lance skulked back into the tent as the toasts began. As he slid into his seat beside her at the head table, neither offered a word of apology. In silence they watched Kimberly stagger to the microphone.

"Good evening!" she called. "Have y'all been enjoying those weird little mushrooms?"

"French truffles," Rosimund corrected from the end of the table.

"Truffles, wuffles." That got a nice titter. Encouraged, Kimberly continued, "The bridesmaids have come up with three reasons Lance and Pippa are getting married. One, it's no fun chasing your lover through Prague in the dead of winter. Two, Lance doesn't want to get confused with Oedipus."

Kimberly and her friends were laughing so hard that they barely noticed no one over the age of twenty-two was laughing with them. "Three, Pippa wants good seats for Cowboys games." To what she thought was universal cheering, Kimberly stumbled back to her seat.

"That was pretty vicious," Woody whispered. "I'm surprised at you, Kimberly."

"Go back to your own table!" she snapped.

"You're so drunk, you forgot the toast."

Woody went to the microphone. "Very nice job, Kimberly. I'm sure you won't remember anything in the morning, and neither will the rest of us, hopefully. I'd like to propose a toast to the best guy on earth, Lance Henderson. I wish you a lifetime of tribulation. Sorry! I meant jubilation. All this Champagne is going to my head. I'd like to congratulate Thayne and Robert, Rosimund and Lyman, for raising such wonderful children. Lance and Pippa, you're breaking every heart in Texas tonight."

Parents and children stood up for bows. "Who is that fellow?" Thayne whispered to Rosimund. "He's quite eloquent."

"That is Lance's physical therapist. He flies in every two weeks from New York to check the cartilage in Lance's knees. They're insured for seventy million dollars."

As waiters served the next course, a mélange of exotic greens and nuts atop a wedge of hard-boiled ostrich egg, Lance began dancing rather pelvically with the bridesmaids. Pippa sat and fumed: in three years they had only danced waltzes together.

"Just look at my boy." Rosimund beamed from the other side of the table. "So light on his fee—"

She dropped her fork as yet another groomsman yanked her chair back and planted his lips on her neck. "You've got my blood boilin', Mrs. Henderson. Say you'll dance with me or I'll kill myself."

"Why, Lawrence! You do flatter me."

Seconds later, as Thayne was grimly salting her ostrich egg, she received a similar invitation from another groomsman. The mayor of Dallas asked Pippa to dance. Off she went, leaving her father alone with Rosimund's husband, Lyman. "Weddings," he said, shaking his head. "You'd think this was the oil rush of '01."

"I'm looking forward to some semblance of sanity next week," Lyman said.

"I wouldn't count on it. If Rosimund is anything like Thayne, she's going to start planning little Arabella's nuptials the minute this one's over." Robert raised his glass. "Here's to many years of fine golfing, Lyman."

"And fine fishing, Robert."

At the stroke of midnight, just as the Johann Strauss Orchestra packed it in, the Lester Lanin Orchestra swung into high gear in the next tent. Those interested in dessert, coffee, and open bar simply followed the music to the Summer Pavilion. Here the canopy was made up of hundreds of yards of deep green silk embroidered with gold stars. The orchestra sat on a revolving stage in the center of a small lake teeming with goldfish and water lilies. Two gondolas—each longer than the single gondola Thayne had imported from Venice for Pippa's engagement party—were available for rides. Oarsmen expertly steered them through a Tunnel of Love made up of a hundred thousand red roses. Elsewhere in the tent, fountains modeled on those at the Villa d'Este overflowed with crème de menthe, Amaretto, Grand Marnier, Chambord, and other strong colors. In lieu of tables, hundreds of deck chairs were placed about the artificial turf for the comfort of spectators at croquet, bocce, and horseshoe courts: Rosimund was a devotee of English lawn parties. Unlike Thayne, she didn't expect her guests to cavort till dawn on fruit cups. She offered a sixty-foot-long chocolate buffet. Every conceivable manifestation of chocolate was there in profusion: cakes, puddings, bombes, gelatos, pies, truffles, brownies, candies, pots de crème . . . Thayne could only watch in impotent rage as her bridesmaids piled their plates with two and three of everything.

Dancing continued. The drinking never abated. Soon wading, swimming, and falling overboard ensued. No one knew exactly what happened between Kimberly and Woody while their gondola was in the Tunnel of Love, but it emerged upside down. Thayne had planned to make a dignified exit at the stroke of one o'clock but that was impossible when a handsome young swain was begging her to tango every two minutes. She even allowed herself a second helping of chocolate chiffon pie to keep her energy up.

At two o'clock Lance waded across the water to the Lester Lanin Orchestra and took the microphone. His pants were soaking wet. He was barefoot. "I'd like to make a toast," he said. "But first everyone has got to understand that I'm totally, hopelessly sm—smi—"

He paused, trying to form the words. The audience thought Lance was going to say, "Smitten."

Instead he said, "Smashed!"

Rosimund didn't cheer as raucously as everyone else. Sensing that her son was about to say things he might regret, she began working her way over to the man in charge of the PA system.

"I'd like to thank everyone for coming tonight," Lance began. "I don't know about you, but I really love this tent. It's like *Brideshead Revisited* stuffed with Texas heifers and longhorns. Hard to believe I'll be playing football right here in two months. Anyway, thank you all for coming tonight. I've already said that? So what, I really mean it. What a tent! There's nothing my mother enjoys more than dropping a couple million bucks on a party instead of donating to the homeless. You're my girl, Rosimund! Where are you, darlin'?" Lance blew a kiss into the crowd. "I know it's going to be a strain, me bringing another lady into the house, but remember, nothing in this world is permanent except death, taxes, and your mother."

Lance doused his face with water from the goldfish pond. "Some people think of marriage as a prison sentence. Just ask my father. But I hope that's not going to be the case for me. I hope it will be my refuge. That ring on my finger, that's going to be my little Pippa smiling up at me all day long." Lance staggered backward into the arms of the conductor. "Nice biceps there, sir. Anyway, everyone, I want to thank you for coming tonight. It's the eve of my execution."

Rosimund finally reached the PA engineer. "Pull the plug on that microphone."

"If I do, the whole tent goes out," he replied, which was a lie. Fifteen seconds ago Thayne had stuffed three hundred-dollar bills in his pocket, promising seven more if he turned the volume up.

Rosimund paled. She stepped to the edge of the pond. "Play the loudest piece in your repertoire," she commanded the conductor. "Lance, you're exhausted. Come down."

"You play one note and I'll break your arm," Lance growled. The conductor decided not to play one note. "Mother, stop ordering people around. You're a worse control freak than Tom Landry." Lance suddenly began to whimper. "You deserve better than me, Pippa. I'm just a jock."

"Lance, that's enough," Rosimund called. "You've had too much to drink."

"Tomorrow I'm going to inherit the mother of all mother-in-laws. Can you imagine what my life will be like with Rosimund AND Thayne coming to dinner? That's like playing the Raiders without a helmet!"

With that, Lance plummeted into the goldfish pond. His friends splashed in after him. As they carried him out of the tent, Rosimund waded over to a microphone. "Boys will be boys," she announced with a *wasn't-that-adorable* smile.

Pippa had been watching Lance's monologue from the croquet court. Drunk or no, he seemed at wit's end. "I've got to see if he's all right," she told her grandfather, pushing through the crowd.

Thayne intercepted her halfway across the tent. "We're returning to the hotel."

"Let me go! I have to see Lance."

Were that to occur, this wedding had a fifty-fifty chance of incinerating. "Honey, you've got to back off. He's under the influence. Mark my words, Lance will be throwing himself at your feet tomorrow." Thayne patted her daughter's hand. "I was in the same condition my own wedding eve. Your father has never mentioned it and I have never forgotten his gallantry." Thayne strong-armed Pippa into the cool night. "Before we go, let's peep inside that last tent."

Rosimund's fourth tent was a paean to autumn. The canopy was orange silk embroidered with apples. A twenty-foot-high *H,* constructed entirely of spray-painted foliage and sheaves of wheat, stood in the center. A fifteen-foot high *W,* constructed of gourds and black plastic bats, stood behind it. Guests could take hayrides on a path winding around the two towering letters. One thousand pumpkins, flown in from somewhere they were actually in season, had been carved into jack-o'-lanterns. They were arranged fifty across and twenty rows high on a gigantic scaffolding. Six men on ladders hastened to light their candles before guests migrated in. Caterers were already arranging a breakfast buffet. A rock band, effortlessly resembling scarecrows and ghouls, warmed up in half a barn that had been dismantled in Vermont and reconstructed here.

"Way over the top," Thayne snorted, leading Pippa away. "Rosimund should be ashamed of herself."

Six

Pippa didn't sleep all night. Something was terribly wrong with Lance. He had been unreachable for the past few days. He had muffed nearly every line at the rehearsal. En route to the Henderson Ball he had seemed oddly glib. He never did introduce her to Woody. As for that drunken, rambling speech, what was he trying to say? Did he really feel he was going to his execution? Pippa had never heard him castigate his mother, even in private; nor, judging by the dismay on her face, had Rosimund. Lance hoped his marriage would be a refuge rather than a prison. What did he need refuge from? Behind all the wild remarks, Pippa had sensed howling desperation. Was Lance marrying her simply to make his mother happy? Was she doing the same for Thayne?

Unable to come up with a definitive "no," Pippa stared at the moon. No question she and Lance had allowed this fest to get out of hand. Neither of them had made any attempt to slow down their mothers, although once those two runaway trains got rolling, nothing short of an atomic bomb could have derailed them. But that didn't mean Pippa and Lance were forced into the marriage, or that they didn't love each other.

She thought back to the first time they met, freshman year at SMU, History of Texas 101. Thayne had insisted Pippa take the course and note how many times the Walker family was mentioned. Lance sat next to her. For a football player, he was remarkably literate. And so nice! For the first six months, they only knew each other by first name. Neither wanted to intimidate the other by divulging negative baggage like "Henderson" or "Walker." Pippa always looked forward to seeing Lance and she increasingly felt the feeling was mutual. A true Southern gentleman, Lance proceeded slowly and chivalrously with her. He didn't ask her out until Thanksgiving. He planted his first good-night kiss on her hand, not her mouth. Three dozen roses arrived the next day with a note thanking her for her delightful company. Intrigued by his heavy cream stationery embossed with an *H,* Pippa thanked Lance for the roses on her own heavy cream stationery embossed with a *W.*

Next day the truth came out. "You mean you're one of *those* Hendersons?"

"You're one of *those* Walkers? We're almost kissin' cousins!"

Lance was too well bred to rush into a turbulent romance. Besides, he was obsessed with football. On his free nights they would study together and, over a few glasses of neat bourbon, discuss Princess Diana conspiracy theories and their mothers. Mothers were a favorite topic.

Then, in Pippa's junior year, along came André, a slovenly, profane, pack-a-day smoker from the backwaters of Louisiana. His blue eyes could burn holes in reinforced steel. He was brilliant, opinionated, and incandescently sexual. He wanted to make art films. André stopped Pippa as she was crossing the campus one morning en route to Psych 101.

"Stay right there." He whipped out a throwaway camera. "You're beautiful. Don't move! Turn your head. Look over the hill and smile as if your lover just ravished you and you're still in flames."

Pippa had no idea what that smile might look like. "How's this?"

"Way too virginal, but I'll take it."

André soon ushered Pippa into the garden of earthly delights, something she had been waiting for Lance to do for three long years. Although he tried not to show it, Lance was crushed by Pippa's desertion. He remained civil but their late-night talks ceased. Convinced that André was the next Truffaut, Pippa followed him to Europe, where he was shooting his first film, *Prague-Nosis.* It was about a student from Louisiana who, discovering he had terminal cancer, self-medicated with sex and drugs. Pippa got her grandfather to put up fifty thousand dollars for the project. She rented a luxurious apartment in the heart of the historic district and acted as André's secretary, paymaster, cook, and lover.

The year went from bad to worse. One day, after a fight with André, she called Lance. They began to have long chats, just like the old days. When Pippa inevitably caught André in bed with two Czech actresses, she flew back to Dallas. Lance was waiting at the airport with an armload of roses. Although he had a big game that weekend, he listened to Pippa's long, tearful tirade and never once said "I told you so" before taking her home.

After Thayne got over her shock at seeing Pippa on the doorstep, first thing she said was, "I told you so." She glared at Lance. "And who is this? The key grip?"

"Lance Henderson, ma'am." He held out his hand. "Very pleased to meet you."

"Rosimund's son?"

He smiled. "You know my mother?"

"I know *of* her." The gears were already clicking in Thayne's head. "Please come in."

"I'd love to, but the team has curfew." Lance hugged Pippa. "Good night."

"Do you know who that boy is?" Thayne cried the moment the door shut.

"I don't want to talk about it, Mama."

Next day a courier delivered one ticket to Lance's football game at SMU. Pippa finally met Rosimund, who said little but observed much: she had been pressing Lance to find a suitable fiancée for years. Lance played brilliantly, snapping a three-game slump. He didn't blow a game, nor did Pippa miss one, for the remainder of the season. He proposed to her at Thayne's annual Christmas Eve party.

Come to think of it, that was the only other time she had seen Lance drunk. Pippa watched an airplane slice through the night sky: lucky passengers, going somewhere else! Lance had swept her behind the Christmas tree and pretended to lose a cuff link. They were crawling around on the floor when he said, "Found it."

In his hand was a platinum ring with a fancy yellow diamond, over two carats, radiant cut, about seven millimeters square, held in place by two half-moon white diamonds. The ring was so big that at first Pippa thought it was a button that had popped off someone's Santa outfit. "I know just one of us is supposed to be on our knees for this," Lance said, suddenly serious. "But will you marry me, Pi—?"

Before he could finish the last syllable, a seismic hiccup shook him head to foot. Her name emerged as "Piccup." "That's quite a ring," she said.

"It belonged to my great-grandmother. Rosimund wants you to have it." Lance crawled over and slipped it on Pippa's finger. It fit perfectly. "May I take that as a yes?"

Pippa hesitated a moment. She knew she would never find another André, which was probably a blessing. But Lance hadn't exactly filled the month since their reunion with physical ardor. Maybe he was taking libido-suppressing steroids. Maybe he considered her tainted goods and was working that out with his inner self. "Do you love me?" she had asked.

"With all my heart." For the first time, he kissed her passionately.

Pippa closed her eyes, recalling that blissful moment. Lance *did* have it in him. "Then I accept. With all my heart."

Lance had spent most of their engagement either in football camp or hiking in the Andes. Just as well: prenuptial chastity was a sacred oath of Henderson men. After he swore he was not involved with another woman, Pippa let the subject drop. Where on earth would she find a man who understood her, or her mother, so completely? Lance and she were like brother and sister. Every marriage manual in the world recommended choosing a mate from a similar socioeconomic background: so much less explaining to do.

As night became dawn, Lance's strange speech kept turning over and over in her mind. What had happened to his shoes? Was he a closet alcoholic? What if he got smashed again and couldn't function on their wedding night? So great was Pippa's desperation that she nearly called André in Prague. Fortunately reason prevailed. Any sane woman would feel terrified the night before her wedding. "Lance is a good man," she told herself over and over. He would grow. They would grow together. She would return to school: Quarterback's Wife was not a serious career choice. For a Walker, anyway.

A fiddling at Pippa's door roused her from a dark trance. Kimberly, her dress barely on, stood in the hallway with a similarly *déshabillé* groomsman. "Oh! I thought this was my room! Sorry!" They stumbled away.

Pippa was almost asleep when someone knocked softly but insistently on her door. A woman stood in the hallway. She wore a navy tweed suit, matching navy hat, and enough scarab jewelry to sink a pharaoh. In her hands was a large lacquer box. "Forgive me for the early hour," she said, marching in. Her box hit the coffee table like a cinderblock. "Please. Open it." Inside was a stash of gold coins. "One hundred Krugerrands. Each contains one troy ounce of pure gold. A wedding gift from my husband, Bingo Buntz the fourth, and myself."

"Thank you so much, Mrs. Buntz."

"It is absolutely imperative that we be invited to the reception at Fleur-de-Lis this evening."

Pippa recalled seeing the name Buntz on one of Thayne's many lists. "Have you not received your invitation?"

"Young lady, are you aware that your mother has an A list and a B list for the reception? And that the B list is not the place for a woman of my social standing? Bingo and I have been pillars of the community for twenty-five years. We are scandalized by this slap in the face."

"Have you spoken to Thayne about it?"

"Hardly, as she placed us there in the first place. Surely you know of someone who wouldn't mind a quieter celebration with fewer people. We're happy to trade places."

"I'll do my best, Mrs. Buntz."

"Thank you, dear. Bingo and I will see you at the wedding. You may send a groomsman to our seats with a proper invitation. I'll be wearing a pale blue hat with tropical feathers. And please get some sleep. You look exhausted."

Pippa was disturbed no further until her nine o'clock wake-up call. It was Thayne, beside herself with anticipation. "Did you sleep well, honey?"

"Like a rock."

"Will Kimberly be rounding up the girls to meet Mr. Simmons in the gym?"

"I doubt it. She had a late night."

"Damn that Rosimund! Her chocolate buffet was a deliberate attempt at havoc."

"I'm pretty sure the girls ate of their own free will, Mama. By the way, Mrs. Buntz just dropped by. She would like an A-list invitation."

"Over my dead body. Bingo is a roué." He had made his millions in waste recycling rather than fossil fuels, as if there were a difference.

"She gave me a hundred Krugerrands."

Thayne did the math: forty-seven thousand bucks. "I'll think about it."

"I wonder if Lance is awake."

"I just saw him playing tennis with his mother. He looks fresh as a daisy. I told you he wouldn't remember a thing about last night. Do you think *all* the girls were up till dawn in that Halloween tent? I'll knock on their doors myself. They signed a contract and they are going to stick to it."

Pippa went to the gym. Only Ginny was there, minus the wig, working out with Richard Simmons. Since she lived down the road from the hotel, Ginny was not sleeping there with everyone else. She had left the Henderson Ball shortly before Lance's speech to catch the third game of the NBA finals. "Good morning, sunshine! Ready to walk down the gangplank?"

Pippa switched on her treadmill. "I believe 'aisle' is the word."

"Where is everyone? They have some nerve criticizing me for ignoring my contract."

Over the next thirty minutes the rest of the bridesmaids trudged in. Rosimund's chocolate buffet had done its damage, as everyone noticed when stepping on the scale. No one but Ginny felt better after an hour of aerobics. Moaning, the girls were marched into the steam room then weighed again. "What did you eat last night?" the distraught trainer cried. "Tell the truth."

"Three slices of chocolate cake, one brownie, a hot fudge sundae, three chocolate macaroons, and some fudge pie," Leah replied.

"What did you drink?"

"Anything I could pour into my glass."

"*Mon Dieu!* What about your diet?"

"I had a relapse, okay? Give me a break."

Pippa found Rosimund's majordomo, Harry, waiting in the hallway outside her room. He wore the turquoise plaid cummerbund that Lance and Woody had purchased yesterday. In his hand was a small package. "From Lance," Harry announced, weaving slightly on his feet. The poor man had now gone thirty-two hours without sleep. "With profound apologies for his behavior at the ball."

Pippa took the box. "He couldn't deliver this himself?"

"It is considered bad luck for the groom to see his bride on the wedding day. Before the event, that is."

"Oh. Right." Pippa opened the box. Inside was a pair of yellow diamond earrings that matched her engagement ring. "Good grief!"

"May I tell him he is forgiven, madam?"

"Of course. Get some sleep, Harry. You did a fantastic job last night."

Thayne smiled when Pippa showed her the earrings. "That is one hell of an apology. You should hope Lance gets plastered at least twice a year."

"That's not even funny, Mama."

They entered the elevator. "You must start remolding him as of tonight. Look what I've done with Robert. He was a hopeless mess when I married him."

"What is he now?"

Thayne thought a moment. "A six-handicap golfer."

The bridesmaids were waiting for them in a spacious terrace suite crammed with ornately wrapped boxes: Thayne thought a gift-opening party would provide a pleasant pastime for Pippa and her attendants on her wedding day. After setting up a video camera to record events for those who couldn't attend, like Rosimund, Thayne sat on a couch with her laptop, ready to record incoming gifts on a spreadsheet program that would also format the thank-you notes.

"Please monitor the hallway," she told the armed guard who had been protecting the boxes all week. Once he left, she turned off the video camera. "Today is the moment of truth, girls. I hope you're up to the task you've been training for these past six months. If I may be frank, last night's rehearsal was ghastly. Your behavior at the Henderson Ball was an embarrassment."

"The boys made us do it!"

"Surely you've been in contact with the male species prior to last night. By now you should be familiar with the proper countermeasures." Thayne sniffed the air. If anything, it smelled of alcoholic halitosis. "Have you forgotten to wear my perfume?" Many sheepish faces affirmed her suspicions. "That won't do. Kimberly, a small question. Early this morning I received a phone call from the *Dallas Morning News*. Their society reporter claimed you had relayed some information about Lance's unfortunate toast. Is that true?"

Despite her fierce hangover, Kimberly turned three shades greener. "I don't know what you're talking about, Mrs. Walker."

Thayne gave her a small envelope. "Open that, please." Inside were two tickets to a performance that evening at the Dallas Ballet Theater. "Enjoy the show. You are expelled from the wedding party."

"Mama!" Pippa cried. "You can't do that!"

"Don't cross me again, Pippa. The alternate is already en route. Leave the room, Kimberly. You are a traitor." Thayne watched as Kimberly stumbled out. Following a door slam that must have set the chandeliers quivering five floors below, she calmly continued. "I want *nothing* to stand in the way of a perfect day. Remember that I still have one more alternate just praying for the phone to ring." As Thayne switched on the video camera, her demeanor brightened for posterity's sake. "Our first gift is from Miss Louella Hackers of Houston." She handed a box to Pippa. "Read the card, darling."

In a daze, Pippa opened a box of napkins that looked as if they had just been ordered from Horchow. " 'Dear Pippa and Lance, These napkins belonged to my great-great-aunt, the Duchess of Saxony-Coburg-Gotha. They were used to entertain royalty, politicians, and legendary artists. The napkin with the corner missing was used by Charlie Chaplin as he demonstrated a new trick during a dinner party attended by the Duke of Bedford. I hope these napkins' history will enliven your dinner parties for years to come.' "

Six of the twelve napkins had corners missing. "They will certainly enliven dinner parties at the Salvation Army." Thayne tossed the box aside. "Continue, Pippa."

"From Mr. and Mrs. Trevor Hingham of Houston. 'We hope you will love this new hobby as much as we do.' " Pippa unwrapped His and Hers square-dancing outfits in a bright purple check. " 'They were designed by Bill Blass.' "

"Square dancing must be popular in Houston." Thayne sniffed, tossing that box atop Louella's. "What is in those pink boxes?"

A huge soup tureen and forty soup bowls, all embossed with a gold seal. "From the estate of Sam Houston," wrote the Digbys of Houston. "Our idol."

Thayne shook her head. "Couldn't they have found anything from the estate of John Neely Bryan?" He had founded Dallas. The soup set joined the reject pile. "Open a few of those envelopes, Pippa. Maybe we'll see some nicer things in small packages."

The first envelope contained a certificate of ownership for ten thousand barrels of crude oil, a gift from the Trumbulls of Corpus Christi. "That's more like it." Thayne nodded.

The next envelope contained a picture of a white pony. "We hope you and Lance will enjoy owning a genuine Lipizzaner stallion. Her name is Trudy," wrote Mrs. Anthony Ludling of Houston.

"Why didn't they just send a Ducati?" Thayne sighed. "Trudy can stay in the Henderson stables until you and Lance find a house."

Next Pippa opened a few gifts from Lance's friends: a gold-plated football, a case of bourbon, and a two-person sleeping bag. She got ten bread machines. Another small envelope contained a photograph of a white Yamaha baby grand piano. "We know Lance is musical," wrote the Pembertons of Houston.

"Yamaha?" Thayne frowned. "That sounds Japanese."

"It looks like a nice piano, Mama. Maybe I'll take lessons."

"They didn't include a year or two of lessons?" Thayne's eyeballs rolled toward the ceiling.

Mr. and Mrs. Harvé Pruett V of Fort Worth sent six Fujiwara chef's knives. Thayne's annoyance at receiving another Japanese import abated when Chardonnay informed her that they retailed for four hundred dollars each.

Noticing that the bridesmaids were having difficulty staying awake, Thayne asked everyone to read a line from the bridal registry that she had been compiling for months.

"Eight settings of Flora Danica," yawned Leah.

"From?"

"The Burtons of Amarillo."

"Very nice. Pass the book along, Leah."

"Eight settings of Flora Danica," read Cora, passing the book to the next lap. "From the Huddlestons of Dallas."

"Eight settings of Flora Danica," read Francesca. "From the Crawfords of Plano."

"Eight settings of Flora Danica," read Tara. "From the Jeffersons of El Paso. How many place settings do you need, Pippa?"

"Fifty," Thayne replied. "Pass the book along, dear."

"Thirty settings of Waterford crystal, Lismore pattern," read Ginny. Rather than a wig, she wore a monumental polka dot turban and gigantic reflective sunglasses. Neither Pippa nor Thayne had the energy to inquire what kind of statement Ginny was making today. "From my mother."

"How nice of her," Pippa said.

"My father sent the other twenty settings." Ginny's parents were divorced. "You're going to have to buy a castle to store all this crap."

"Are you calling Waterford and Flora Danica *crap*?" Thayne inquired icily.

"I'm just wondering where one might find a cupboard for fifty place settings. Not to mention a dining room table."

"They will be custom built," Thayne informed her. "Pass the registry along, Ginny. We've barely made a dent in that mountain of gifts."

"Fifty place settings of silver from James Robinson in New York," read Hazel. "Who's that? Is he married?"

"*That* is a company, one of the last in the world making handmade silver. It is very difficult to scratch. What a fantastic gift. Who sent it, Hazel?"

"Dusi and Caleb Damon of Las Vegas."

"My college roommate." Thayne smiled at Pippa. "She and Caleb are in Rangoon for double surgeries. They send their regrets."

Pippa smiled vaguely. Rangoon sounded pretty good about now.

The opening of boxes dragged on for three hours, by which time six of the girls were snoring robustly. Thayne did not dismiss them until every last gift had been catalogued and critiqued. Pippa received more ewers, decanters, candy bowls, salt and pepper shakers, butter dishes, and platters than she could use in ten lifetimes. She received enough food processors to open a kitchen supply store. She got Italian mirrors, Aubusson rugs, Tiffany lamps, rare maple trees, a Nakashima table, and a pair of historic Smith & Wesson revolvers with pearl grips. Her arms ached from tearing open the wrapping paper. Her face ached from smiling.

Finally Thayne looked at her watch. "My goodness, time to get our hair done again! Hurry upstairs, girls."

The room emptied. "Thank you for keeping track of all that, Mama."

"We didn't do too badly." As she switched off the video camera, Thayne was already calculating changes in a dozen of A- and B-list invitations. "A Lipizzaner! Now that takes the cake."

"I wish Lance could have been here."

"Truly you don't. Men find this sort of event boring to the hilt. Honey! What is it?"

A sharp pain in Pippa's stomach had doubled her over. "I'm getting nervous."

"Why, baby? Cedric has been at Meyerson Center all night reinforcing the chorus bleachers and your train. The girls will pull themselves together. They always do. All you have to do is walk a decently straight line on your father's arm. If you can't remember to say 'I do,' simply nod your head. Just don't faint on me! That would be the mark of a rank amateur."

"I've never fainted in my life. I'm not going to start today."

Sliding an arm around Pippa's shoulder, Thayne walked her to the elevator. "I am so proud of you. This is a historic day for the Walkers."

"Or else?"

"Don't even make a joke like that." They boarded the elevator. "Rest a bit, Pippa. Wipe that look off your face. You're too young for worry lines. I'll send Brent down as soon as he's done with the girls."

"I hope tonight will be a total triumph for you."

"Thank you for humoring me, darling. I've had a lot of fun putting this all together."

Pippa's stomach twisted into another painful knot as she left the elevator. A split of Cristal and a dozen chocolate truffles, consumed in the bath, helped somewhat. Pippa semidozed as Brent did her hair and a cosmetician applied her makeup. Margarita arrived with the wedding gown, a stunning confection of seed pearls and silk organza. Its strapless, beaded bodice limned Pippa's torso like fondant on a wedding cake then, a few inches below her waist, blossomed into a gossamer waterfall of silk organza. Girls dreamed of such dresses when they gazed into the mirror and imagined themselves walking down the aisle; Pippa's dream was now coming true.

"Why you do not smile, Pippina?" Margarita asked, drenching her with Thayne perfume. "You are not happy?"

"Just nervous. I think I strained my back pulling the train yesterday."

"*Santa Maria!* Tomorrow you relax the back. With Lance," Margarita winked.

Anson knocked and entered. His eyes teared up at the sight of his granddaughter in her gown. "You look stunning, Pippa."

"Thanks, Grampa. I'm so glad this is almost over."

He patted her hand. "So are we all, pumpkin."

Thayne, Robert, and two photographers awaited them in a white limousine. "I don't think I've ever seen two more beautiful women," Anson said.

Thayne blew him a kiss. "Thank you. I do feel special today." Besides the family diamonds, she wore a lilac chiffon gown with a belt of hammered gold. The brim of her lilac hat created a three-foot no-fly zone around her head. "Pippa, I don't care if the roof comes tumbling down, just keep walking forward. When Lance takes your hand, everything will fall into place. The fate of the Walkers rests in your hands."

"That's a bit over the top, luvvie," her husband remonstrated.

"Shut up, Robert! I'm talking about your grandchildren, not the eighteenth hole."

The bridesmaids were already at Meyerson Center, excitedly applying their final ten layers of mascara. Everyone's half up, half down hair looked stupendous with the Henderson barrettes and the Walker earrings. Thanks to Lipo in a Box, their gowns flowed like rivers of aqua cream over their hips. The new bridesmaid, Carola, had absorbed three years' worth of gossip in the thirty minutes she had been with the bridal coterie. She was the only one not too hungover to drink now.

Ginny, regal in her second wig, swaggered over. "Where's something old?"

Pippa pointed to her diamond choker. "My grandmother's."

"Something new?"

"My bra."

"Something borrowed?"

Pippa displayed an ankle bracelet belonging to Thayne.

"Something blue?"

"The tattoo on my butt. Would you like to see it?"

"No thanks." Ginny wrapped Pippa in a ferocious hug. "You're ready to rock."

Arabella, the flower girl, arrived in an embroidered Victorian gown. The bridesmaids all screamed when Pippa wriggled into her train: fantastic! As the minutes ticked toward five, the excitement became almost unbearable. Florists distributed bouquets of gardenias and yellow roses. Seamstresses tacked emergency darts. Carola doused ten necks with Thayne perfume. Out in the hall, brass quintets began to play ceremonial introductions.

Cedric rapped on the door. "Everyone in the lobby in two minutes."

His words precipitated a final death cloud of hairspray. Then the door swung open. The girls—even little Arabella—shrieked in horror as Lance walked in. He looked to die for in a black and gray morning suit. "You can't be here! It's bad luck on your wedding day! Get out!"

His eyes found the bride-to-be. "I must speak with you, Pippa. Alone."

Seven

*B*ridesmaids, photographers, florists, and seamstresses fled the dressing room as if Lance were radioactive. When they had all gone, he quietly locked the door. He and Pippa looked across the room at each other for a long moment, each taking in the other's sheer beauty. "You look ravishing," Lance finally said. His voice sounded sad.

Pippa led him to the sofa. "Something's wrong, isn't it? I've known for days."

He sat without blinking for an eternity. When he finally spoke, Lance seemed his old self again. "Pippa, never doubt that I love you totally. To be your husband would make me the happiest man alive. I've hoped and prayed that we could have a normal life together. But mother nature has conspired against me."

"Are you ill?" she cried. Cancer? Brain tumor? "I'll take care of you. You'll get better."

Lance shook his head. "I'm gay. Always have been, always will be."

Pippa hardly breathed as the calamitous news sank in. Finally she whispered, "I think I need a drink."

He produced a flask from his coat. "Here."

They nearly emptied it. "Why didn't you tell me?" Pippa whimpered, near tears.

"I thought I could change. I feel more attracted to you than to any woman I've ever met."

Tears stung her eyes. How could she have been so stupid? "All this time I thought you were obeying the Henderson code of honor."

"I'm deeply sorry, Pippa. I've been in therapy. Confession. Taken hormone shots. I even rented a whore for a week in Peru." He laughed to himself. "She may as well have been a teddy bear."

That was fairly annoying. "How could you have let this charade go on so long?"

"I didn't have the courage to stop it once things got up to warp speed. I've been feeling so guilty and craven and worthless. After that speech last night I felt like killing myself."

All things considered, that wouldn't have been a bad resolution to the problem. "Does Rosimund know?"

"She suspects. That's why she's been pushing the wedding harder than Thayne." Lance covered his face with his hands. "Thank you, mommy dearest."

"I'll be the laughingstock of Dallas forever." Pippa swallowed the last of the bourbon then threw the flask at a mirror. Lance winced as it shattered. "You stupid ass!"

"We could go through with the wedding and divorce after a year. Woody and I will take care of you financially for life."

"*Woody?*" Pippa cackled. "You're dumping me for that fat slob?"

"Please, *please* don't take it personally. And he's not a fat slob." Lance swallowed with difficulty. "What do you think? One year, then we call it quits?"

After a moment's reflection Pippa shook her head. "I don't think so."

Cedric pounded on the door. "What's going on in there? Everybody's waiting!"

"Tell them to play Beethoven's Ninth," Lance shouted. "We're not ready."

After a stream of expletives, Cedric called, "Three minutes. Then I'm coming in with a shotgun."

Lance and Pippa listened to his footsteps recede down the hallway. "We could run away," she said. "Make a break for the limousine and disappear to Tahiti."

"Our mothers would never recover. I'd never play football again."

Lance began to sob. "God, what have I done? I've let everyone down so hideously."

No kidding. "We have to make the best of it. We'll just walk in there and tell them the wedding's off."

"What would be the reason?" Lance wailed.

"It will come to me." Pippa's mind locked into gear. "We can donate the flowers to the children's hospital. Thayne can still throw a Derailed Wedding party. People don't need a bride and groom to drink themselves under the table."

"Wouldn't it be easier to just go through with it?" Lance repeated tearfully. He began to tremble. "Rosimund will never forgive me if word gets out."

"If I can take it, she can," Pippa snapped. "Look, I'll say it's all my fault. She'll believe that."

"But it's not your fault."

"It's half my fault. I should have known."

Lance fell to his knees and put his head in Pippa's overflowing organza lap. "I don't deserve you. I never have. I love you so much."

As she forlornly patted his head, Cedric returned with a small army. "At the count of ten, we're breaking down the door," he shouted. "Ten! Nine! Eight!"

Pippa sprang into action. "Get up, Lance." She caught a glimpse of hot-pink underwear as he hastily tucked his shirt back into his pants. "We're coming, Cedric."

"Seven! Six! Five!"

As her fiancé stood before her in all his male glory, Pippa's heart broke. What a man never to have had! "I love you forever," he whispered.

"And I you. Could you unhook this damn train?" Pippa stifled a tear as he unsnapped the titanium harness: that was the closest Lance would ever come to undressing her.

"Four! Three! Two!"

She swung open the door. "Hold your fire."

"Do you realize what a mess you've made?" Cedric screeched, dragging them outside. "The organist has been improvising for the last ten minutes. The new bridesmaid started in without waiting and the rest of those f-ing cows followed. Now everyone's onstage staring at the chandeliers."

Pippa's father, pacing the foyer, was most relieved to see her. He held out his arm. "Ready to go, darling?"

"Daddy, go sit with Mama. Lance and I have decided to walk up the aisle together."

"That's a switch. When do I recite your mother's eight names?"

"You don't." Cedric shoved a potted geranium into Robert's hand. "Pretend you're a bridesmaid." He pushed Robert into the packed auditorium.

A murmur ran through the crowd as Robert slowly proceeded up the aisle. His wide smile allayed fears that anything could be wrong. "Where's Pippa?" Thayne hissed as he sat beside her. "My God, you're hopeless! Go back and fetch her."

"I'm staying right here."

"Where's Lance?" Today Rosimund was dressed in a deep red gown that clashed badly with her hair and fatally with Thayne's lilac outfit.

"Right behind me, ladies," Robert responded.

Receiving a signal from Cedric at the back of the auditorium, maestro launched the orchestra into Mendelssohn's *Wedding March*. Hand in hand, Lance and Pippa came down the aisle.

"Where's her train?" Thayne glared across the stage extension. "Have you stolen Pippa's train?"

"I wouldn't touch it with a ten-foot pole." Rosimund was glad to see Lance smiling for the first time in days. She reached for her lace handkerchief. "Aren't they beautiful?"

"Yes, darling. Perfect," her husband replied.

The bridal couple walked quickly up the ramp. The Reverend Alcott, majestic in a white cassock emblazoned with gold, smiled as if the gates of heaven had just opened. "Dearly beloved, we are gathered—"

Lance turned around. "Could you hold off for a second?"

Thayne's gasp could be heard in the last row. "Get up there, Robert," she said, pushing her husband out of their pew. "Tell them who gives the bride away. And don't forget to say Tuttle!"

Confused by the nonscripted material, the conductor motioned the chorus to rise. Two hundred voices began singing "How Lovely Are

Thy Dwellings" from the Brahms *Requiem* while Lance conferred with the Reverend Alcott. Thayne and Rosimund nearly had heart attacks when the minister closed his Bible, walked to the far end of the stage, and stared serenely at the chandelier along with all the bridesmaids.

Thayne craned her neck at the ceiling. "What are they looking at?"

"What next, Thayne?" Rosimund asked as the music swelled. "A monkey and an organ grinder?"

"It's all right, Mother," Lance said. "Could you come up here with Dad?"

"You come up, too," Pippa told her parents. She would never be able to make a speech with Thayne glaring at her from the first row.

Brahms finally ended. The audience of five hundred waited for something to happen. It was painful to view Rosimund's and Thayne's dresses side by side; each brought out the worst shades in the other. Finally Pippa took a deep breath and stepped forward.

"Thank you for coming here today. Lance and I are so happy to see you. Marriage is such an exciting adventure, like climbing Mount Everest. Before you begin that climb, you have to be sure you've got the proper equipment. Oxygen. Sherpas. You've got to avoid blizzards. But the view from the top is worth it all." She paused, wondering where to go from here. The room was beginning to tilt. When her grandfather blew an encouraging kiss from the front pew, Pippa got an idea.

"Life is full of surprises and we're all engaged in a long process of self-discovery. Sometimes people don't even fall in love until ten years after they're married, on a nice warm summer afternoon, when one of them has been napping in a hammock."

She noticed many sidelong glances in the auditorium, as if people were having difficulty following her train of thought. Strange, her speech made perfect sense to her. "I think love means acceptance of the good, the bad, and the ugly. There's not much of the latter with Lance, of course." Everyone laughed. "When he asked me to marry him, it was one of the happiest days of my life." Pippa frowned, remembering the other truly, outstandingly happy day of her life, that being the afternoon André first took her to bed and ravished her. That man knew a woman's body better than a woman did. His hands were like pools of warm light. His mouth—

Anson Walker gently cleared his throat. Pippa's thoughts snapped back to the task at hand. "Lance and I have had a wonderful six months watching our mothers plan for today. In a way, that was our gift to you." The auditorium filled with applause as Rosimund and Thayne bowed stiffly.

"Please wrap this up, Pippa," her mother muttered under her breath.

"Lance and I believe love must be a little blind if it is to survive. That doesn't mean it should be deaf and dumb. We will love each other until our dying day. What do we need a little piece of paper for? Who makes the laws anyway, our hearts or a bunch of politicians in Austin?"

Pippa's heart began racing as Rosimund slowly raised her wrist and studied the face of her diamond watch. "How much longer will you be expatiating, dear?"

The room began to spin. Pippa looked desperately at Lance and was flustered to see him standing with his eyes shut. He seemed to be mumbling to himself. "To make a long story short, Lance and I will not be exchanging wedding vows today. It wouldn't be right. We're very fond of each other, of course. It's just that—there's someone else!"

After a second of deathly silence, pandemonium erupted. Pippa felt herself float to the ceiling as events roiled around her. She was dimly aware of Rosimund gathering up Arabella and Lyman and leading a platoon of outraged Hendersons from the auditorium as Lance stumbled after them, begging for mercy. Rosimund paused only once, to whap her son's face with her red beaded purse. "Don't you dare ask for mercy! You're the first cuckold in Henderson history!"

Things weren't going much better in the Walker camp. Thayne had collapsed to the floor in a furze of lilac. The only doctor present was Seth Shapiro, the society dermatologist who Botoxed most of Dallas. He was having difficulty making his way to the stage against the flood of exiting Hendersons. Cedric tried to revive Thayne with a stream of bourbon from his flask, but succeeded only in ruining her makeup. He instructed the orchestra to begin Tchaikovsky's *Romeo and Juliet.* When this had no calming effect on the riot, he shouted at the bell choir to begin "O Happy, Happy Day," the twenty-second kissing interlude by John Williams. That did nothing, either, so Cedric told both brass quintets to blow their brains out.

Realizing there would be no celebration at Fleur-de-Lis, no catching of the bridal bouquet, and little hope of parlaying Dallas's wedding of the century into nine more, every bridesmaid save Ginny crumpled to the floor in tears. Woody also dropped to his knees, sobbing more loudly than any of them. Pippa stood alone and forgotten in the eye of the hurricane. She looked up to see Anson gazing at her with a mixture of surprise and bemusement. "I'm sorry, Grampa," she heard herself call. She saw him smile as if he understood. A second later he clutched both hands to his chest and pitched forward.

"No!" Pippa screamed. Then everything went black.

Eight

When Pippa came to, she was lying on a backstage couch at Meyerson Symphony Center. Ginny was daubing her forehead with a cool, damp cloth. A cacophony of brass, bells, tympani, and organ muddled the air. Far-off people were shouting. Pippa looked down at the big white dress she was wearing. "What happened?"

"You blew the wedding."

It all came rushing back to her. "What a nightmare."

"Seriously." Ginny winged her wig into the shadows. "Would you like to come to Costa Rica with me?"

"Now?"

"I suggest leaving Dallas for a few days. You really stepped in it."

Pippa recalled Thayne sinking to the floor. "Is my mother okay?"

"She's indestructible. The paramedics took her away. Along with your grandfather." Ginny didn't elaborate on that.

Pippa's head swam. "Where's Lance?" she wailed.

"Last I saw, he was sniveling down the aisle after his mother. Count your blessings, girl. You did the right thing. There's only one woman in his life, and it ain't you. Sorry."

"Rosimund left?"

"The Hendersons all marched out. The Walkers rushed the stage.

The bridesmaids took off with the groomsmen. I carted you back here. Hey! Scram!" Ginny shouted at one of the photographers before slinging an enormous duffel bag over her shoulder. "Think you can stand up? I've got a cab waiting." She had booked it weeks ago to take her to the airport. "You've got to disappear."

"Dressed like this?"

Ginny took her firmly by the arm. "Now."

They retrieved Pippa's cell phone from the deserted dressing room. Before hustling Pippa into the cab, Ginny disposed of two paparazzi outside the artists' entrance by tossing their cameras into oncoming traffic. "Drive until I tell you to stop," she told the cabbie. He didn't understand much English so she twirled a finger in the air. "Drive! Circles!"

While he was putting a few miles between them and the carnage, Ginny located two sets of tank tops and cargo shorts in her duffel. She had only one pair of hiking boots; for the moment Pippa would have to navigate in her white Blahniks. "It's not the presidential suite," she said, unzipping Pippa's wedding dress. "But our options are limited."

As the cab circled Dallas, they changed into camping gear. "As I see it, you have two choices," Ginny said as she compacted the soft, white mountain that used to be Pippa's gown into a tight roll. "You can stay at my place while I'm in Costa Rica or you can come with me to Costa Rica."

"Can't I just go home?" Pippa wanted nothing more than to crawl into her nice warm bed and hibernate for six months. "I feel really sick."

"I'd rather face a mauled tiger than your mother. You presume she'll even let you in the house." Ginny looked at her watch. "My plane leaves in two hours."

"You know I can't just run off," Pippa moaned. "It wouldn't be right."

Ginny gave the driver an address in Wellington on the Creek. With a wry smile, she leaned back in her seat. "You've got to admit, it was fun while it lasted."

"It wasn't fun at all. I'm never going through that again."

Ginny appraised Pippa through half-open eyes. "So who's the third wheel?"

Pippa's first inclination was to admit the story was a farce. Then she realized that further clarification could ruin Lance. "I can't say."

"Is it André?"

"What? No!" Why did Ginny automatically presume *she* was the one with the third wheel?

Ginny patted her hand. "You were brave to come clean. The most eligible bachelor in Texas will never live it down, though."

"Yes, I'm sure he won't be dating any more cheerleaders for a long, long time."

"Wow, that was bitchy." Ginny rolled down her window at the security gate of Wellington on the Creek. "This is my friend, Stanley. She gets carte blanche."

"No problem, Miss Ortlip."

The cab driver braked in front of Ginny's palatial home. "Wait for me," Ginny told him.

She unlocked the door to her villa, which Pippa had visited many times before. "You'll be safe here." Ginny tossed their wedding gear into a chair. "I'll be back in two weeks. On the fridge is a list of restaurants that deliver."

"I can never thank you enough."

Ginny handed over her car and house keys. "SUV's in the garage. Sorry I can't stay."

Pippa was sorry, too. From the balcony she watched Ginny's cab speed off. After the roar and confusion at Meyerson Center, the calm here was surreal. Where'd everyone go? Shouldn't she be slicing wedding cake with Lance about now? Her insides felt like rope. Settling numbly into a couch in the home theater, Pippa turned on the sixty-inch LCD television. What should appear but *Fantasy Weddings*. The bride looked obscenely happy.

"Go away!" Pippa screamed, hitting the remote. Now she got *Weddings of a Lifetime*. Wyeth McCoy was giving an interview. In horror Pippa heard him explain that he never took on weddings he didn't think would last, even if it meant resigning in midstream. "You knew!" she cried, jabbing the remote. On came *My Big Fat Greek Wedding*. "No!" Pippa shrieked, flying off the couch. She attacked Ginny's stack of DVDs, searching for anything not involving a man, a woman, a wedding, or romance of any kind.

She watched *The Hunt for Red October* as she robotically consumed a few boxes of crackers and a half gallon of milk. Why didn't

Lance call to see if she was okay? Why didn't a bridesmaid call? Her grandfather? She checked her cell phone: full batteries, in ring mode. Surely people must wonder where she had gone. Someone must be worrying. Someone must want to hug her and whisper, "There there, it's not your fault. You've been more than noble about this."

Dream on. At wit's end, Pippa speed-dialed her ex-fiancé. "Lance? Are you all right?"

"Pippa?" he managed to squeak. "Where—"

"If you dare come near my son again," Rosimund thundered, "I will have you prosecuted to the full extent of the law. You are evil!" The line went dead.

"You sniveling *turd*!" Pippa screeched so loudly that her tonsils nearly blew out. Somehow she was not surprised that Lance hadn't told his mother the truth. Alas, his cowardice was exceeded by her own stupidity. She should have gone through with the wedding, as he suggested. They could have chastely cohabited for an interval, then split. There would have been gossip, but nothing like the firestorm she had now generated all by herself. Pippa stared morosely at the huge diamond ring on her left hand. Rosimund would demand it back, of course.

Thank God the Walkers took care of their own! Once Thayne heard the real story, Pippa would be forgiven and protected. Venerated as the saint she was. She called star one on her speed dial: Thayne.

The number was no longer in service.

Pippa called Fleur-de-Lis: ditto.

Traumatized, she hit mute and went into a semivegetative state, her jaws slowly grinding caramel popcorn as talking heads occupied the television screen. Weather. Sports. Pippa saw but didn't immediately comprehend when her grandfather's picture appeared on the screen. When two four-digit numbers appeared under his name, she snapped back to life. With trembling fingers she grabbed the remote and toggled mute.

"Anson Walker, the legendary oil billionaire, collapsed this evening at a family gathering. He was rushed to Baylor Medical Center and pronounced dead upon arrival. The cause was cardiac arrest. According to unconfirmed reports, Walker was attending his granddaughter's wedding, although a family spokesperson has denied that a wedding took place. Our investigative reporters are on the scene. Stay tuned."

Spoons and popcorn went flying as Pippa leaped off the couch. A minute later, barefoot, she was in Ginny's SUV, driving home as fast as she dared. Her tears nearly blinded her. Grampa dead? How was that possible? He had the heart of a bull. Just last night he was dancing with her. He was the only one who understood!

Traffic began knotting up a half mile from the Walker mansion. Pippa plowed over lawns and curbs, between limousines and news crews, barely missing gawking pedestrians and bicyclists who loved a good show despite the late hour. Cutting off a Bentley, she screeched to a halt at the front gate and rolled down her tinted window. "Charlie! It's me!"

The guard peered at her. "Hello, Miss Walker." He didn't make a move to open the gate.

"What's the problem? Open up."

"I'm sorry. Your mother has given orders not to let you in." Charlie tried not to stare at her Day-Glo camouflage T-shirt. "Never to let you in, as a matter of fact."

"She's not feeling well! You know that!"

Charlie removed an envelope from his jacket. "Your father asked me to give you this."

With shaking fingers, Pippa read the terse note.

My dear girl,
    This has been a very sad night for the Walkers. Your mother is prostrate with shock and grief. I suggest you allow her sufficient time to regain her spirits before making further contact. Someday I hope she will come to you.
                                                            Love, Daddy
P.S. I wish you had let us know.

Inside the envelope was an inch of crisp C-notes. Pippa stared at the wad of bills for a moment before dangling half of them in front of Charlie. "Please let me in."

"Can't do it, Miss Walker. I suggest you turn around."

Pippa stared through the heavy iron gates. Fleur-de-Lis looked as if it were being looted. Workmen were dismantling tents, long barbecue grills, floral arrangements, Porta Potties, tables, chairs, and loading them onto trucks as fast as possible. Caterers were streaming down the front steps with trays of food and shoving them into vans. All the housemaids were standing on the porch helplessly wringing their aprons and crying. Every light in the house was on except those in Pippa's bedroom.

The Bentley behind her honked its horn. "We have an invitation to the party," the driver called.

"The party has been canceled," Charlie called back. "Please go home."

"I beg your pardon! We have come all the way from Kilgore."

"That's where you should return."

"How very rude, sir! Thayne will hear about this!" The Bentley slowly reversed and joined the traffic stuttering in the opposite direction.

Charlie listened to his headset. "The trucks are coming out," he told Pippa. "You've got to move."

"What if I don't?"

"You'll be towed. I'm sorry, Miss Walker. Those are my orders. After all your mother has been through, I think it would be better to go quietly."

Defeated, Pippa put the Lexus into reverse. "I'm at Ginny's, if anyone cares."

If he heard her, Charlie did not reply.

Cringing as she passed dozens of people she knew, Pippa crawled Ginny's SUV back to Wellington on the Creek. She returned to the couch in the home theater. For hours the only moving parts of her body were her occasionally blinking eyelids and her right hand tirelessly working the remote as she surfed for news. As the next morning progressed, her grandfather's life and death received increasing air time, as did the circumstances surrounding his collapse. Adding to the excitement, each person interviewed by crack local telejournalists seemed to have a different version of events at Meyerson Center.

In horror Pippa watched her bridesmaid Leah say, "We were all so worried about Pippa. She was unnaturally quiet all week. Her mother was obviously forcing her to get married. Thayne Walker is like the godfather. You do what she says or you wake up with a dead horse in your bed. Don't be surprised if I'm found floating in the Rio Grande for saying this."

Cedric the substitute wedding planner was interviewed next. Impeccable in a dark blue blazer and ascot, laying on the upper-crust British accent with a cement trowel, he presented quite a different picture than had Leah. "Mrs. Walker is a brilliant and sympathetic woman. Family means everything to her. While she deeply mourns the passing of her father-in-law, her daughter's happiness is paramount. If Pippa loves someone else, even though she may have chosen a less than optimum moment to make the announcement, Mrs. Walker fully supports that."

The interviewer looked skeptical. "So who's the lucky guy?"

"Mind your own *bleep*ing business, you lowlife *bleep*!"

Lance, of course, was declining any interviews. About an hour later scandalmongers unearthed Pippa's old flame André in Prague. "Pippa and I lived together for a year," he announced nonchalantly. With each syllable, the cigarette in his mouth bobbed up and down like a needle in a polygraph machine. His eyes were as blue and languid as ever, Pippa noticed.

"Have you been seeing her?"

"No comment."

Pippa threw a pillow at the television. "You schmuck!"

Kimberly was interviewed next. "I think Pippa acted in a truly hideous way. Lance Henderson intended to marry her yesterday. She has caused him major humiliation and she has caused me major inconvenience. I personally spent about ten thousand dollars to participate in the wedding."

"Will you sue?"

"My only concern is that Lance will find a more suitable wife."

"He already has, you rat!" Pippa shouted.

Another news station had set up camp outside Fleur-de-Lis. Their cameras followed the parade of trucks leaving the grounds of the Walker mansion in the dead of night. "This feels like a funeral," a reporter intoned. "And in fact it is the first of two funerals this week for the Walkers. The family remains in seclusion." He walked to the guardhouse. "What can you tell us about last night, sir?"

Charlie shut the glass window in his face. Undeterred, the reporter walked to a white Mercedes idling nearby. "Excuse me." The window rolled down. "Are you a friend of the family?"

Mrs. Bingo Buntz IV, resplendent in a sapphire-blue suit with matching hat and feathers, glared at the reporter. "I am here to ask for my wedding gift back. Obviously a wedding did not take place."

Barely suppressing a grin, the reporter glanced at the forty or so vehicles waiting behind Mrs. Buntz. "Is this the returns line, then?"

"You could call it that."

"May I ask what your wedding gift was?"

"Approximately fifty thousand dollars in gold coin."

"Ha ha! Sure it wasn't a fondue pot?"

Her window rolled shut.

Pippa staggered to the bathroom and swallowed a handful of aspirin. If she thought Thayne's wedding was a media circus, this was ten times worse. She took every cereal box out of Ginny's kitchen cabinets and returned to the sofa. Her eyes burned.

"Where is Pippa Walker?" an anchorwoman asked. "No one's talking." She held up that morning's newspapers. Pippa gasped as she read the headlines. QUARTERBACK SACK. WORDS KILL BILLIONAIRE GRANDFATHER. "One can't blame her for disappearing." She shared a chuckle with her coanchor. "What do you think, Harvey? Mata Hari or Runaway Bride?"

"Mixed-up kid," was all he said. Anything else was a lawsuit.

The stations had a field day with Thayne, then made a show of balancing that with long obituaries of Anson. Psychologists gave interviews about wedding jitters and why wealthy people married at all. Wyeth McCoy, while not divulging financial details of Thayne's extravaganza or even letting on that he had been fired, gave a self-serving talk on the cost of society weddings and how Happily Ever After, Inc., made those dreams a reality. Legal experts wondered if a prenuptial agreement had been signed. Experts on etiquette explained how couples went about returning their gifts in the event of a meltdown. The blather was endless. In a trance, Pippa listened to every word.

Finally, late in the afternoon, the phone rang. It was Ginny. "Holding up?"

"No. My grandfather died."

"I'm so sorry about that. You didn't kill him, in case you were wondering."

"I tried to go home," Pippa sobbed. "Thayne doesn't want to see me, maybe forever."

"Amen! Sorry, bad joke."

"I want to go to the funeral."

"Pippa, you can't. Think about it."

"I could wear a disguise."

"Every paparazzo in the country is looking for you. Security will be tighter than at a presidential inauguration. The press will be there in droves. Can you imagine the fracas if they discover you there in a costume? You've got to put your own feelings aside and let your grandfather be buried with dignity."

"Maybe I should kill myself," Pippa whispered.

"Fine, just not in my house, okay?" When Pippa didn't laugh, Ginny said, "Don't forget to turn the GPS on your cell phone off. It can be traced."

When the press nicknamed her Balker Walker, Pippa collapsed in bed and remained there for two days, sobbing. How could such a bad thing happen to such a good person? Through her tears she watched news of the funeral and infomercials. She rummaged obsessively through Ginny's kitchen in search of trans fats. The phone rang day and night as reporters offered Ginny zillions for an exclusive interview. Pippa intermittently turned on her cell phone to check messages. The same reporters offered her the same zillions. Wyeth McCoy called once to say he knew all along that something was wrong and he'd be happy to give her a thirty percent discount on the second wedding. Kimberly had the gall to ask if Pippa had returned Lance's engagement ring. Not a word from Thayne. The silence was making Pippa ill.

On the third day, as she was finishing the last of Ginny's frozen pizzas, the doorbell rang. Pippa nearly gagged on her pepperoni but made no move to answer it. The caller remained, patiently ringing every thirty or so seconds, until she tiptoed to the door and put her eyeball to the peephole. On the stoop was Sheldon Adelstein, her grandfather's lawyer, holding a briefcase and a grocery bag. Sheldon had been considered a member of the family for at least fifty years. In fact, he was Pippa's godfather.

Never so glad to see anyone, she unlocked the door. "Sheldon!" She hugged him so hard his Stetson hat fell off. "How did you find me?"

"Charlie at the front gate mentioned you might be here." The rest was a matter of paying off the guard out front. Sheldon stepped back and observed Pippa with some concern. Last time he had seen her, she was a perfect vision in white. Now she looked uncombed, unwashed, and unhinged. The Day-Glo T-shirt didn't help. "I take it you haven't ventured outside."

Pippa's eyes welled with tears. "Where would I go?"

Antarctica was an option. "I brought cookies from Margarita. Let's have a cup of tea, shall we?"

They went to the kitchen, where Pippa put water on to boil. Sheldon placed a tin of lemon snaps on the table. "Are we alone?"

"Yes. Ginny's in Costa Rica."

"I was referring to the Other Man."

The other man was with Lance! "As I said, we're alone. How's my mother doing?"

"Not terribly well. This wedding meant a lot to her, as you may imagine. To have that go up in smoke and lose Anson the same day has been a severe blow. Fortunately Thayne responds well to medication." Juniper berries, in the form of gin.

"She'll recover. Embarrassment is different than guilt." Pippa shut off the screeching kettle. "I killed my grandfather, Sheldon."

"Nonsense. Anson was eighty-four years old. He had been partying hard for a whole week. He could have died during a normal wedding, for all we know." Sheldon cleared his throat and straightened his string tie. Had Pippa known him better, she would have realized he was about to utter a monumental lie. "As they put him in the ambulance, I was at his side. Do you know what his last words were? 'Tell Pippa she didn't do this to me. Tell her I love her and understand completely why she called off the wedding.'" No point in saddling the poor kid with a lifelong guilt complex.

Pippa's eyes brightened. "Did he really say all that?" It seemed a lot of words for someone who had just suffered a catastrophic heart attack.

"Yes. I swear on a stack of King James Bibles." Easy for Sheldon to say: he was Jewish.

"That is such a relief. I feel like a huge rock has been lifted off my heart."

"One reason I came here was to tell you that relatively good news." Sheldon opened his briefcase. "We also have a few legal matters to discuss."

His tone of voice did not bode well. Pippa brought the tea and sat opposite Sheldon at the kitchen table. "You must understand that your mother is not quite herself," he began. "That said, she is mentally alert enough to have had papers drawn up this morning."

Pippa tried to remember what all those lawyers on the talk shows had been jawing about. "Is she suing me for breach of contract?"

"No, dear. She intends to disown you."

Pippa trembled. What a cruel word! "What does that mean?"

"That means you will no longer be considered her daughter. Her fortune will not be passed on to you. You will no longer be able to consider Fleur-de-Lis your home. Legally, you should consider yourself an orphan, like David Copperfield."

"What about my father?" Pippa croaked. "Does he want to disown me, too?"

"As of yesterday, he was playing golf in Morocco. Your mother ran him out of the house with an antique candelabra. He feared for his life."

"I have to call him," Pippa said. "He'd never agree to this."

Sheldon's silence suggested that this could be a misassumption. "Pippa, some decisions are very difficult to understand. You are no longer a child. You must assume responsibility for your actions. Thanks to you, Thayne is in a precarious social position, perhaps for the rest of her life. You can hardly expect her not to be furious and a little vengeful."

"You call disowning me a *little* vengeful?" Pippa shrieked. She dropped her head into her hands. "I'm sorry, Sheldon. This is a bit of a shock." Out on the streets! No college degree. No roof over her head. No allowance. No professional skills. Pippa didn't even know if she was capable of operating the cash register at Taco Bell. "How will I survive?"

Sheldon somberly sipped his tea. "Destiny works in strange ways. Your grandfather always believed you had great potential. He encouraged you to follow your dreams, be it making movies in Prague or marrying a Henderson." Sheldon tactfully refrained from mentioning that neither of these endeavors had amounted to a hill of beans. "He always wanted the best for you, but he wanted you to earn it. To that end he put a trust fund in place, effective upon his death." Sheldon took a few papers from his briefcase and donned a pair of reading glasses. "You will receive an allowance of sixty thousand dollars each month."

"Thank God!"

"There's a catch. 'This trust shall provide for you so long as you are in school.'"

"What kind of school?"

"That is your choice." Sheldon continued reading. " 'If and when you earn your diploma, you will receive the remainder of the trust.' Since that's somewhere in the neighborhood of a billion dollars, I suggest you try to pass final exams."

"How can I go back to school? I'm infamous."

"The wording is ironclad. You've inherited most of Anson's estate, Pippa. He has left a mere pittance, fifty million or so, to your father. Which is why Thayne may have attempted to kill him with that candelabra."

"I don't understand! Why did Robert get barely anything?"

"We can't question the dead. I suspect Anson feared your mother would fritter away the Walker fortune. Her lavish tastes are well documented. Whereas he had complete faith that you would do something more meaningful with the money." Sheldon removed his glasses. "Any questions?"

"Sorry. I'm in shock."

"I'm afraid we all are. Would you mind if I made one suggestion that might make life easier for everyone? Change your name immediately. Go to school and begin a new life."

"That's three suggestions."

"Just change your name then. I can draw up the paperwork immediately." Sheldon uncapped his Montblanc pen. "Henceforth, you would like to be known as . . . ?"

"How am I supposed to know? It's not as if I've been thinking about this for the last few years."

"Yes, of course." He put a business card on the table. "That's my private line. Call anytime, day or night. There are more cookies in the bag."

Pippa stopped him at the door. "Do you think Thayne will ever speak to me again?"

"You've got to give it some time, child. You have inflicted a deep wound."

"But there's more to the story. I haven't told her everything."

Sheldon shuddered. "I'm not sure her constitution can withstand any more revelations. Goodbye, dear. Think about that new name. And where you might like to live, not necessarily Dallas."

After he left, Pippa poured herself a good shot of scotch, her first strong drink since the wedding. She would soon be rich beyond her wildest dreams, at the price of losing her family and reputation. That was not a good bargain. Pippa would gladly have traded every last cent for the chance to turn back the clock to Saturday afternoon, shortly before five. If money couldn't do that for her, what good was it?

Nevertheless, for Sheldon's benefit, she began paging through Ginny's *Town & Country* magazines in search of a suitable alias. How about Starlene? Bertha? Binky? Each was worse than the last. How about last names? Pippa rearranged the letters in Walker: Krelwa. Lawrek. Wrakel. Everything sounded like a Latvian terrorist. Forget names, how about a new place to live? New York. San Francisco. Paris. Shanghai. Maybe she should stick to Texas, hide out in Hico or Flatonia, someplace so dusty and lifeless that no one would ever think to look for her there. She could lie on a couch, tube out, and nosh all day like Gilbert Grape's mother.

That was beneath a Walker's dignity, so Pippa tried to figure out what she might like to study. Shopping 101 was not offered at any university. Media studies? She was great at watching television. Once upon a time Pippa had wanted to teach kindergarten. A month's internship, dealing with irrational parents, had changed her mind. After Prague she had no further interest in making movies. Law, science, business, medicine: way too cutthroat. Back to square one.

As she finished the tin of lemon snaps, Pippa listed her strong points: listens well, kind person, neat appearance. Sighing, she put down her pencil. To be completely honest she did have a career, and that was Daughter of Thayne. That's what she truly excelled at. Where she felt at home. She wistfully toyed with the gold chain around her ankle. Her mother had given it to her for the wedding so that she would be wearing something borrowed. It was all she had left of her now.

Once again Pippa collapsed in tears on the couch. She would never again walk in the garden at Fleur-de-Lis, never wake up in her canopied bed to the aroma of fresh coffee, all because she had tried to help a condemned man. Where the hell was he now? Where was his mother? *Anybody?* The walls were closing in on her. Pippa had to get out before she slit her wrists in Ginny's Hydro Spa.

Neiman's to the rescue!

Pippa shot to her feet. After a fairly violent scrubbing in the shower, she faced the problem of what to wear on her excursion. None of Ginny's clothing fit, nor did she have much of a mascara collection. Pippa couldn't possibly go out in that camouflage T-shirt and white Blahniks. Defeated before she had even begun, she slumped into the chaise longue by the cathedral window.

A hard cushion lodged against the small of her back. It turned out to be her rolled-up wedding gown. Sight of her lovely dress now wrinkled and abandoned almost precipitated a fresh fit of sobbing; then Pippa realized she was holding the only clothing here that was her size. She found a pair of scissors and snipped three feet of material off the hem, turning her Vera Wang gown into a strapless frock with a short but extremely full skirt. Pippa located her Lipo in a Box and her four-inch Blahnik heels under the bed. She had never taken her engagement ring off. Now she added the yellow diamond earrings Lance had sent her the morning of the wedding and the diamond choker her grandfather had given her as an engagement gift. She looked in the mirror. There stood a young woman wearing a fortune in gems, an abused dress, and six-hundred-dollar shoes: perfect Texan shopping attire!

Ginny was a fan of huge sunglasses and safari hats. Pippa borrowed the least offensive of these from the walk-in closet. Locating a small beaded purse with the price tag still on, she stuffed it with cash from her father. She doused herself with the Thayne perfume on Ginny's dresser then slipped the flacon into her purse. It would go everywhere with her from now on. On the way out she folded Sheldon's business card into the wad of bills in case she happened to come up with a new name, a place to live, a school to attend, or a path in life.

The automatic garage door opened. Pippa backed Ginny's Lexus SUV out the driveway. Fresh air! Sunshine! Movement! Drunk with freedom, Pippa couldn't resist taking the huge vehicle on the highway for a spin. She turned the CD player up full blast and, singing along with Josh Groban, motored around Dallas. Near the end of the CD, somewhere on Route 75, Pippa glanced into her rarely used rearview mirror and was surprised to see flashing blue lights directly behind her. She put the music in pause and opened her window a crack.

"YOU! PULL OFF THE HIGHWAY *NOW! * LAST WARNING!"

So that was the strange noise she had been hearing for twenty minutes. The man sounded incredibly angry. Pippa veered across three lanes of traffic and pulled onto the shoulder. She waited nervously as the patrol car phoned in Ginny's license plate. In her sideview mirror she watched a stony-faced Goliath of a policeman stride toward her window.

"Yes, Officer?" she asked meekly.

"I've been following you for twenty miles. You've been speeding for all twenty of them."

"I'm sorry. You just tap the gas on this thing and it goes forward."

"Do you know what a rearview mirror is for?"

Putting on lipstick, obviously. Pippa didn't think the officer would relate to that. "For seeing what's behind you?"

"Right! License and registration, please."

Pippa found Ginny's registration in the glove compartment. "This is my friend's car. She's in Costa Rica. I'm staying at her house. I'm afraid I've left my license at home. I only have a little bit of money in my purse. Well, Ginny's purse. My father gave me the money when I tried to go home the other day. My mother won't let me home because I'm an orphan now so I'm staying at Ginny's while she's in the jungle studying nesting habits of the—"

"Get out of the car. Pop the trunk." He found nothing inside but a gigantic striped top hat.

"That's Ginny's Mad Hatter hat! Isn't it sweet?"

His lips didn't move. "Name and address, please."

"Pippa Walker," she whispered. "I live at Fleur-de-Lis on Royal Lane. Used to live, anyway."

The officer's eyebrows rose half an inch. The butchered dress, the diamonds and white shoes, the bright yellow sunglasses were beginning to make a little more sense now. He recognized the face that had been dominating news broadcasts for the last few days. "You just had a wedding."

Her face fell. "Sort of."

Poor kid looked like a ghost. Last thing Balker Walker needed was more public trauma. Still, he had sworn to uphold the law. The officer began filling out a triplicate form. "You'll have to appear in traffic court and pay a fine for speeding. Bring your license, if you can find it."

"Court? With lawyers and police? Photographers?"

She looked about ready to lunge into oncoming traffic. He felt sorry for her. She was so outrageously cute, even in that nutty safari hat. "Or you can go to traffic school."

Pippa stood absolutely still for a long moment. Then she asked, "Could I make one eensie little phone call? Please, it's a matter of life or death."

She found a little card in her beaded purse. "Sheldon! Does traffic school count as school?" Hardly breathing, Pippa listened to the answer. Life and color returned to her face. "I'll go to traffic school, Officer," she said, nearly giddy with excitement. One would think he had just presented her with a flying carpet. "Thank you so much!"

Nine

Unaware of the road rage she was creating in her wake, Pippa drove at a rock-solid thirty miles per hour to Neiman Marcus as she talked with Sheldon on her cell phone. He promised to look into the driving school schedule and get some electronic funds transfers going once Pippa was officially enrolled. "You won't be using your given name, will you?" he asked. "One media circus is enough for the time being."

"I'm still thinking about an alias. It's harder than you think."

After parking in a remote corner of the lot, Pippa took the escalator to American Designers, a department she could navigate blindfolded. She was only halfway through the Zac Posen rack when a nearby voice drawled, "That is not your style, Katherine."

"Give me a break, Mum. What would you know about my style?"

Pippa cringed to see Mrs. Bingo Buntz IV not ten feet away. Her daughter was modeling a white gown that only accentuated her Rubenesque contours. "You are not wearing that to the cotillion. It is extremely tacky."

"But it's seven thousand dollars!"

Mrs. Buntz inspected the price tag. "I suppose it's a possibility.

There has to be something on this floor for at least ten. Miss! Could you help us?"

Pippa took the opportunity to slink to a far-off rack containing loud pinks and turquoises by Lilly Pulitzer. She was pawing through that when who should emerge from a nearby dressing room but Leah and Cora, her erstwhile bridesmaids. In a panic Pippa dropped to her knees and began crawling to the far corner of the American Designers department.

"May I help you, ma'am?" a voice asked as she was trying to break through a clot of floor-length gypsy skirts.

Pippa glanced up at a pair of shins. "I seem to have lost my contact lens."

The salesgirl was too polite to ask how that could occur if Pippa was wearing huge sunglasses. Instead she knelt beside her. "What color was it?"

"Listen," Pippa whispered. "Forget the contact lens. I'm sure it's crushed. I want you to bring me everything you've got in Zac Posen size six." When the girl merely stared at her, Pippa added, "I've got agoraphobia. It's a miracle I made it this far. And don't tell anyone I'm here!"

The diamonds convinced the salesgirl that Pippa, though insane, had disposable income. "Stay calm. I'll be right back."

The girl quickly returned with an armful of dresses. "Fine," Pippa said. "Can you bring me a couple of Laundry skirts and tops? Also a dozen panties and some 34C La Perla underwire bras? A little leather jacket by Andrew Marc would be good. I need a pair of sneakers, white sandals, and black flats. Size eight. Ferragamo if they're not too pointy."

"I don't think Ferragamo makes sneakers."

"Whatever." Pippa handed over an inch of hundred-dollar bills. "Here's some cash."

As soon as the girl left, Pippa wriggled out of her nonwedding half-gown. She chewed the price tag off a ruffly red dress and was sliding it over her head when she heard Mrs. Bingo Buntz IV say, "Look at those nice long skirts, Katherine."

Seeing two pairs of approaching shoes, Pippa rolled behind a rack of DKNY trousers just in the nick of time. "You can't be serious, Mum," the daughter said, removing a gypsy skirt for inspection.

"These are so Woodstock." Pippa watched in horror as Katherine lifted her wedding dress off the floor. "Hey, this is kind of cute."

"Never pick something off the floor! Look at that hem. This has been seriously vandalized."

"But I love the bodice. We can get a seamstress to fix the bottom, can't we?"

"Miss! Can you help us? We'd like to purchase this dress."

Pippa saw a third pair of shoes join the Buntzes' clodhoppers. After a moment the salesgirl asked, "Where did you find this?"

"Right here, mixed in with the gypsy skirts."

"It doesn't seem to be in salable condition. I'm not sure this is one of our gowns."

"Of course it is. Look at the label. You do have a Vera Wang boutique, don't you?"

"Let's take a look." Three pairs of shoes, and the wedding dress, went away.

Pippa bit her own hand so that she wouldn't scream. She counted to one hundred as she rocked back and forth. After another eon she heard a voice.

"Ma'am?" Her salesgirl was squatting beside her. "I think I've got everything."

"Not quite! Go to the La Prairie counter and get me foundation, sunscreen, blush, eyeliner, shadow, mascara, foam cleanser, exfoliator, antiwrinkle cream, and three lipsticks. My color is three point four. Then meet me with everything in sports memorabilia." No female Pippa knew would ever go there. She handed over the chewed-off price tag of the ruffly dress she was wearing. "Add this to the bill. Wait! Do you see two blondes with big hair anywhere?"

The salesgirl stood up. "There are about twenty of them duking it out at the Moschino sale. Don't worry, no one's looking over here."

Pippa scuttled downstairs as rapidly as dignity allowed. Every few steps, it seemed, one of her friends, or Thayne's friends, or someone who looked like a wedding guest, or a musician from the Dallas Symphony, stepped in her path. She put one foot ahead of the other until she stood in front of a glass case containing autographed baseballs, boxing gloves, and hockey sticks. A few weeks ago, at this very counter, she had bought Lance a signed photograph of Roger Staubach's "Hail Mary" pass to Drew Pearson.

"May I help you, ma'am?" the salesman asked.

"Did you sell that autographed picture of Lance Henderson?" Pippa asked, trying to kill time. "I saw it here a while back."

"We're totally sold out. Every girl in Texas wants a picture of him now that he's back in circulation." The salesman had no sooner spoken than two girls came to the counter asking for a Lance Henderson picture, preferably from the rear in football tights.

"He's got such a cute butt," one girl told the other.

Pippa severely bit her tongue. Luckily her salesgirl and three assistants laden with boxes were approaching. Pippa led them out to the SUV and rocketed out of the Neiman's lot. She did her grocery shopping at a Hispanic supermarket on the down side of Dallas. Everyone there presumed her jewelry was fake and/or she was a stray from a halfway house. She got back to Ginny's place just in time for reruns of *Another World*. After consuming half a pint of Häagen-Dazs Rum Raisin, she listened to her phone messages. Sheldon had called six times, so she called him back. "Good news. Driving school starts tomorrow. It goes for a week."

"Then I'll be a billionaire?"

"If you pass the course, yes, I'm afraid so. You will enroll under what name?" Silence. "It's almost five o'clock. If I don't get you in today, you'll have to wait another month."

Pippa watched the credits scroll by on television. Zoe, Patty, Vonda, Carly, Perdita . . .

"Perdita," she said. That had a nice ring to it. "Bacardi."

"Where did you find that name?"

"On the credits for *Another World*."

"You can't possibly do that. The real Perdita Bacardi will sue you for the entire billion. Give me another last name. Quickly."

Pippa looked around the room. Ginny had left a stack of Central America travel books on the dining table. Panama. Honduras. Nicaragua. Costa . . . "Rica."

"Perdita Rica? Are you serious?"

"Do it, Sheldon! It's just a name."

"I'll get back to you in a few minutes. Don't go anywhere."

Pippa unfolded the Dallas *Morning News,* which Ginny had forgotten to put on hold when she left town. Her calm vaporized as she saw an article on the front page. LOVERS' LAWSUITS LIKELY. Apparently Rosimund was seeking full restitution from Thayne for the cost of the Henderson Ball, a mere ten million dollars. That figure would double if Rosimund compensated her guests, as any respectable Houston woman would, for plane fare, meals, clothing, and mental suffering. Never one to pass up a good catfight, Thayne was countersuing Lance for twenty millions dollars for sexual harassment plus the cost of her guests' plane fares, meals, clothing, mental suffering, *and* liquor. Neither Lance nor Pippa was available for comment. In fact they had both disappeared, giving rise to rumors that the couple had eloped, playing a practical joke on two overbearing matriarchs.

Spinoff articles jammed the Living section of the paper. Gossip columnists had a ball with the several dozen men who had come forward claiming to be Pippa's secret paramour. After reading every last word, Pippa sleepwalked to the freezer. She opened the remaining half carton of Häagen-Dazs, filled it to the brim with rum, shook vigorously, and began to drink. Instead of abating, this story was spreading like an Ebola virus.

Sheldon called back. "You're to be in school tomorrow at nine sharp. If you pass, you'll be forgiven the moving violation and two points. You will inherit a fortune. Pippa, are you there?"

"Pippa is not here. Perdita is here. Pippa is dead."

"Are you speaking with food in your mouth?"

"I've been reading the newspapers."

"That is something I can't prevent, but would advise you to stop doing at once."

"Mama's being sued."

"If you pass driving school, you will be able to reimburse both Thayne and Rosimund all by yourself. I hope that gives you some sense of purpose, if not poetic justice."

Pippa cringed at the reminder that Thayne's current difficulty was all her fault. "I'll make it up to her, Sheldon. In one week this will be all over."

"I certainly hope so." He explained that Pippa must take care not to let anyone know her true identity. It hadn't been easy convincing the police that an alias was in everyone's best interest because, every so often, they liked to make an example of a rich and famous scofflaw. "Don't socialize with anyone in class. Try to obliterate any traces of Pippa Walker."

"But I just bought a new wardrobe at Neiman Marcus."

"I hope it's very unassuming."

"What do you mean?"

"I mean you're going to blend into the linoleum. Perdita Rica should be a waitress or someone of that ilk."

Pippa went to the bedroom. The pile of clothing on the bed included a red ruffly dress, a purple leather jacket, some hot-pink tops, a tight white skirt, and a black V-neck sheath, all very clingy and obviously designer. That wouldn't do, so Pippa changed back into camping gear. She grabbed the Lexus keys, then paused: last thing she needed was a DUI citation. She called a cab. When it appeared out front, she donned the safari hat and sunglasses. "Take me to Wal-Mart," she told the driver.

As they slogged to a less privileged section of town, Pippa studied young female pedestrians, hoping to gain a few wardrobe tips for her Perdita Rica persona. Apparently rule number one was Less Is More, particularly when covering the gluteus maximus. Rule number two was No Pastels, Earth Tones, or Small Prints. Rule number three was Tight. As she observed the flesh bursting from every available gap, Pippa realized that if she really wanted to blend into the linoleum, she should put on fifty pounds and wear short shorts, a rayon halter top, and five-inch platforms to driving school. Rule number four was Dark Hair.

"Wait for me here," Pippa said when the cab reached Wal-Mart.

She had never been inside such a store before. The place smelled like fake food. She didn't see one carpet on the floor. People pushed their carts around as if they were in a demolition derby.

"Hi," greeted a guy in a wheelchair. "Looking for something in particular?"

"Do you have a designer clothing section?"

"Like Fruit of the Loom? Sure. Over there."

Pippa grabbed a shopping cart and zigzagged forward until she found a sea of tank tops. She tossed a handful of those and two skirts into her cart. Taking a cue from teenage girls at the next rack, she acquired a pair of flip-flops with thick rubber soles. She was at the jewelry counter buying a watch when the woman next to her said, "Excuse me, but are you that bride? Pip something?"

Stay calm, Pippa commanded herself. "I'm afraid not. My name is Perdita." She raised her voice a few decibels. "Perdita Rica."

"Perdita! That means 'little lost girl' in Spanish. And *rica* means 'rich.' So I guess you're a poor little lost rich girl! Just like that old movie with Betty Hutton."

Pippa forced herself to smile. "Yes, people have been kidding me about that my whole life."

"You really look like that girl, you know. You could make money impersonating her at parties."

"Now that's a thought." In a panic, Pippa hit the drugstore for black hair color. What had given her away? Only her mouth and a few inches of cheekbone were showing. The saturation coverage must have made her instantly recognizable, like the Hulk. She picked up a tattoo kit and some truly offensive nail polish before joining the checkout line. Her shoulders ached from trying to make her neck disappear. Fortunately those next to her in line were either reading the magazines, attending to screaming infants, or filching malted milk balls from two-pound bags. As she inched forward, Pippa read the Clairol instruction booklet. Dyeing one's own hair seemed more complicated than open heart surgery; no wonder professionals like Brent charged six hundred dollars to do it in a salon.

Pippa was about to drop out of line and look for the wig department when the woman ahead of her stuffed the *National Enquirer* back in the rack. Pippa was stupefied to see a picture of herself, in her wedding gown, on the front page. In fact she was on the cover of *Us, People,* the *Examiner, Globe,* and *Sun.* MURDER PLOT UNCOVERED. TEXAS FIZZLE. WHAT WENT WRONG? QUARTERBACK SNEAK. I DON'T! Beneath the headlines were shots of her dancing with Lance at the Henderson Ball, high school yearbook pictures of them both, football shots, pictures of her grandfather, even a blurry photo purporting to be Thayne and Rosimund slugging it out in a mud pit. There was a fifty-thousand-dollar reward for finding her.

"That slut should be strung up," the woman commented, noticing Pippa staring at the rack.

"It was all arranged by the mother." The beanpole at the register spoke with the accumulated wisdom of fifty years in front of a television set. "So she could get Rosimund's money."

"That poor boy," the first woman clucked, departing with four floor fans. "Have a blessed day."

The beanpole began whipping Pippa's tank tops past the bar code reader. "You buying that box or just reading it, hon?"

Keeping her chin down, Pippa handed over the Clairol kit. "Sorry."

"That comes to seventy-eight fifty."

Something was seriously out of whack. Pippa's cheapest skirt at Neiman's had cost three times as much as the entire cartload here. She might be a fugitive, but she wasn't a thief. "Are you sure?"

The woman checked. "Dang! That code didn't read right." Now everything came to seventy-*one* fifty. "Out of one hundred cash."

Pippa hardly dared breathe as the woman studied the bill from many angles, making sure it wasn't counterfeit. She accepted her change and ran into the withering heat of the parking lot. Her cab was idling in a handicap space. "Get me home," she cried, diving into the back seat.

Each time the cab passed a newsstand, drugstore, or supermarket, half of her wanted to leap out and buy every tabloid in sight. The other half of her wanted to join a monastery in Tibet. When the driver finally stopped at Ginny's place, Pippa gave him a hundred dollars and rushed inside like a vampire singed by the light. She triple-locked the door and pulled every drape shut. She sat in the dark, numbly waiting for someone to turn the lights on and tell her this was all a bad dream.

Ten

Driving school met in the function room of Happy Hour Motel on Harry Hines Boulevard. Situated next to train tracks, it got poor online reviews for noise and fumigation. Local hookers were the motel's biggest clients; the Texas Department of Public Safety ran a close second. State officials thought of it as a de facto penal institution and hoped, correctly, that after a week in a classroom reeking of roach bomb and fried eggs, miscreant drivers would do anything never to go back.

Officer Vernon Pierce glanced up from the lectern as his final student rushed through the door at one minute before nine. "Perfect timing," he said as she slid into a front row chair and flipped down the writing table. Nice legs! The rest was pretty atrocious, though. He had never seen such a bad hair dye job. She may as well have stuck her head in a bucket of tar. Tattoos disfigured her arms and the bluish-gray nail polish looked straight out of the morgue. She was wearing two halter tops, each covering a couple of inches that the other one missed. The white skirt with little cherries on it, stiff as cardboard, was obviously brand-new. Wal-Mart special. The girl's footwear looked like a wedge of Dunlop tire. The heavy gold ankle bracelet didn't fit with anything at all. "And you are?"

"Perdita Rica."

Strange, she didn't look Hispanic. In fact her eyebrows were blond.

"Good morning, everyone. My name is Officer Pierce. We're going to be best friends for the next five days, so let's get started by telling each other why we're here." He pointed to a gangly teenager in overalls in the front row. "Billy. You first."

"I didn't commit no offense. I'm innocent."

"Then tell us what offense you were unjustly accused of."

"Driving my tractor."

Officer Pierce studied his printout. "Billy is correct. He was driving his tractor. What he neglects to mention is that he was driving it in downtown Dallas although his father's peanut farm is in Abilene. The laws of Texas forbid operating a tractor over one hundred and fifty miles from one's farm."

"My pickup broke and I had to get to a prom."

"Your date must have loved that." Pierce passed on to the next student. "How about you, Tom?"

A paunchy man who looked shortchanged by life said, "It's really unfair that I should lose my driver's license when I wasn't even driving and causing any danger."

"My heart bleeds for you." Pierce consulted his printout. "Unfortunately you dropped two empty Whopper cartons, two supersized Cokes, a bag of Reese's Pieces, a package of Pringles, and half an ice cream cone out the window of your car although you were in a rest area not thirty feet from a trash bin."

"That is disgusting, man." Billy twisted around in his seat. "You ate all that?"

"No sermons, please," Pierce interrupted. "If one chooses to litter in the beautiful state of Texas, one will lose one's driver's license and incur a fine. How about you, Gordon?"

A thirtysomething redneck muttered, "I was in my boat, minding my own business."

"Perhaps so, but you had a blood alcohol level of point one seven. According to the laws of Texas, those who choose to go boating while intoxicated will lose their driver's license."

"Everyone drinks a few beers while they're fishing," Gordon protested. "Otherwise it's not fair to the fish."

Pierce addressed an elderly black woman in the rear row. "Hattie! Tell us why you're here."

"I don't know, Officer. I've been driving for seventy-five years and never so much as hit a jackrabbit. Then the other day this officer came up out of the blue and pulled me over."

"Let me explain, then. You were going twenty-five miles per hour on an interstate highway where the maximum speed limit is seventy and the minimum speed limit is forty. You were therefore driving fifteen miles per hour under the minimum."

"You mean I'm being punished for going too slow?"

"Correct. Let's hear from you, Seymour."

A skinny black teenager wearing pants that would have been voluminous on Humpty Dumpty said, "I'm an urban artist, man. That's all I'm gonna say here."

"Artist? The police report states you were defacing private property. According to the laws of Texas, if you choose to cover other people's walls with graffiti, you will lose your driver's license."

"That's so white," Seymour fumed.

"And you, Carrie-Jo?"

Scrawny trailer trash answered, "I was just talking on my phone."

Pierce perused a few sentences in his printout. "If we gave a prize for understatement, you'd win. In the state of Texas it is illegal to follow a fire truck at a distance of less than five hundred feet. It is also illegal to cause a crash while talking on a cell phone. Carrie-Jo managed to crash into the rear of a fire truck while talking on her cell phone."

"It was an important call," she pouted.

"How about you, Lola?"

A bodacious young woman minimally dressed as Santa Claus replied, "I'm a professional valet."

"You were going thirty miles an hour in reverse and T-boned a Jaguar. According to the laws of Texas, reckless driving will cost your license."

"Give me a break! He should have had his lights on."

Shaking his head, Pierce focused on his last student. Cute little face, if you could get past the hair. "Perdita. What brings you here?"

"I was speeding."

The class erupted in cheers. "You go, girl! Glad to know we got one legit criminal here!"

"Quiet! You were also driving without your license and you ignored the flashing blue lights behind you for twenty miles."

"I'm sorry. I was singing along with Josh Groban."

Pierce passed a hand over his eyes. This class made skid row look like Princeton. "As I listen to your stories, I detect a common thread. NOT MY FAULT! I DIDN'T DO NUTTIN'! Let me set the record straight. You are not victims. You broke the law. That's why you're here. Rule number one: driving is a privilege, not a right. Any questions?"

He waited a full ten seconds for an answer. Finally Perdita finished scribbling in a spiral notebook. "No, sir."

"In order to pass this course you're going to show up on time every day. You're going to do your homework. You're going to score seventy percent or better on a rules test, a signs test, a vision test, and a driving test. That's four tests! Do you think you can handle that?"

Eight coconuts would have responded with more animation. Officer Pierce finally detected movement in the front row, in the form of a teardrop rolling down Perdita's cheek. "What's the problem, Perdita? Surely you've taken tests before."

"I'm sorry, Officer Pierce. It's just that you look like my ex-fiancé." She removed a lace handkerchief from her purse.

Carrie-Jo ceased chomping her bubble gum. "Sweetie! Did he dump you?" Women never cried if they did the dumping.

"Quiet! In this room you open your mouth if I ask you a question. Otherwise you keep it shut tighter than the trunk of a Cadillac." Pierce walked up and down the rows, dropping a little booklet on everyone's desk. "Here is your own personal Texas Drivers' Handbook. Consider it your Bible for the next five days."

"For shame, sir," Hattie gasped.

"I was speaking figuratively." As he dropped a manual on Perdita's desk, Officer Pierce noticed her perfume: heavy but intriguing. "Open to chapter one. 'Your License to Drive. Who May Operate a Motor Vehicle in Texas. One: residents who have a valid Texas driver license.'"

Gordon, the beery fisherman, raised his hand. "Are we going to sit here and read to each other all week? I can read the book at home and come back for the test."

Excellent suggestion, but this course wasn't about making life easy. "Since you claim to be literate, Gordon, why don't you read the manual for us right now. Start on page one."

Gordon began reading a soporific text describing the nine types of driver who could legally operate a motor vehicle in Texas. Officer Pierce observed the class as Gordon droned on. He already knew who would pass and who would fail. Old Hattie would pass, if she got through the vision test. So would Perdita, who was underlining nearly every sentence in the manual with her yellow highlighter. The guys would mostly fail because they all thought they knew this stuff and could wing it on test day. Carrie-Jo's passing depended on her ability to cheat. Lola wouldn't finish the course.

Pierce let Gordon read for thirty minutes then asked Tom the litterer to take over at the Anatomical Gifts paragraph. Having eaten a large breakfast, Tom didn't enjoy reciting about organ, tissue, and eye removal but did as he was told. As his monotone pushed the class further into narcosis, Pierce's gaze returned to Perdita. Her parts didn't add up to the whole. She looked smart but lost. She didn't seem the type to have a drug problem. Runaway was possible, but who in her right mind would run away to Dallas? Pierce studied her tattoos. The blobs on her left arm looked like Minnie Mouse; everything else was a blurry mess. He wondered if she sported a few rings on her nether body parts, as did many women with tar-black hair. She wore a huge ring on her left hand. Pierce presumed it was one of those cubic zirconia monstrosities because he knew that rich people never took this course. They hired lawyers instead.

When Tom's voice gave out, Pierce asked Lola to come to the front of the class and read about Court-Ordered Suspensions, Alcohol-Related Offenses, and the Point System for Moving Violations. After thirty minutes Pierce turned to the young man who had never removed his eyes from Lola's microscopic Santa costume. "Seymour, tell us the fine for a first DWI."

The graffiti artist replied, "I never heard of a dwee. Is that a bird or something?"

"D.W.I. That's shorthand for driving while intoxicated. Drunk driving."

"Oh, that," Seymour pooh-poohed. "What about it?"

"What is the fine?" Pierce repeated through clenched teeth.

"Fifty bucks?"

Pierce tapped his fingers on his desk. "Let's take a ten-minute break," he suggested. "Fresh air. Coffee. Bagels. Don't forget to use the litter basket, Tom."

The classroom emptied except for Perdita, who seemed eager to tell him something. "The fine for a first DWI is one thousand dollars a year for three years."

"Very good, Perdita. I notice you've been paying close attention to everything."

"That's because I really need to pass this course. My whole life depends on it."

When women confided such things to him, they usually shoved their décolletage in his face. Apparently Perdita's mind didn't function that way. Pierce was relieved because in her case, the temptation to barter would be great. "I'm sure you'll do very well," he replied. She had pretty green eyes, he noticed. Soft and trusting. "May I ask what is that perfume you're wearing?"

"It's called Thayne. There are only fourteen bottles in existence. It was custom blended in Paris." Pippa almost showed him the flacon in her purse before realizing that a waitress would barely possess hand lotion, let alone French perfume. "I got it at a garage sale for ten cents."

"I see." Not really. "Why does your life depend on passing the course?"

"My grandfather will—" Her face went cherry red. "Increase my allowance. I'm a waitress," she added for no reason whatsoever.

He watched her skitter out of the room. Perdita's rap sheet said she was driving a Lexus SUV when she was pulled over: that was a hell of a lot of tips.

When class resumed, Carrie-Jo the trailer trash got things off to a rocky start by hoisting her boobs in Officer Pierce's face and asking, "Is parallel parking going to be on the driving test? Like, it's not my particular favorite thing to do in the car, if you know what I mean."

"Just for you, Carrie-Jo, I'll make parallel parking fifty percent of your driving test."

"That's not fair! I won't do it!"

"You'll automatically fail if you refuse to follow instructions."

Pierce turned to the class. "FYI, you'll fail the course if you have a crash between now and your exam." He noticed Perdita scribbling furiously in her notebook. "It's all on page fifteen, Perdita. You don't have to recopy the entire manual."

She put down her pen. "Sorry, sir."

He made her read two chapters covering Vehicle Inspection and the Liability Insurance Law, written in English but incomprehensible to anyone but a judge or William Shakespeare. Finally his wristwatch beeped: noon. "Let's break for lunch. See you at one o'clock sharp for a review of road signs."

Pippa followed Pierce down the hallway. All was dead quiet except for the embarrassing squish of her flip-flops as she gained on him. Although she was sure he could hear her, Pippa saw Pierce walk faster and faster away. "Officer Pierce! Stop!"

He obeyed, of course. He'd have to be made of stone not to. "What can I do for you?"

"Do you tutor?"

Every molecule of testosterone screamed in protest as he answered, "Absolutely not."

Humiliated, Pippa fled to the parking lot. Her cell phone rang as her key turned in the ignition. She recognized Lance's number. If he was calling for sympathy, this was not a good time. "Let me guess," she snapped. "You want your SMU varsity pin back."

"Pippa?" a man asked.

"Yes!" Wrong answer, in case it was an enemy. "No!" Wrong again, in case it was a friend. "Maybe! Who is this?"

"Woody. Lance's physical therapist."

"Emphasis on physical."

He let that pass. "If it's any comfort to you, Lance is catatonic with grief and guilt."

"That's the best thing I've heard all day."

"What rage!"

"Just shut up, okay? You two weasels deserve it."

Woody sighed. "Yes, we do. Pippa, you're the most selfless woman we've ever met. Mother Teresa doesn't even come close."

"What is the purpose of this call?"

"How would you like to have Lance's Maserati?"

That sounded fantastic. However, on second thought, "That sounds like a bribe."

"A more gracious person would call it a gift."

"A more grateful person would have offered the gift himself." Pippa turned up the air-conditioning: Woody's voice made her blood boil. "As you may guess, I'm not looking for souvenirs of our relationship right now. Thanks to Lance, Thayne will disinherit me. My grandfather's dead. I'm hiding out like a criminal at Ginny's. Enriched plutonium has more friends than I do."

"I feel your pain. Lance has been banished to Brazil until Cowboys training camp."

"I couldn't care less about your pain." Pippa felt an invisible hand squeeze her heart. "I want my mother to know the truth. She'll forgive me when she knows the whole story."

"Are you sure?"

Not totally. Thayne would not be above strangling Pippa for terminal naïveté.

"Thayne must first get past her fury," he counseled. Besides ministering to Lance's knees, Woody considered himself a gifted amateur psychoanalyst. "She must want you back. Need you in her life again. Your mother must understand why your wedding meant so much to her in the first place. That's going to take a lot of self-analysis."

"And meanwhile I disappear and wait for the Second Coming?"

"That's a good way of putting it. Yes."

Pippa sighed: Jesus had already taken two thousand years. Thayne wouldn't settle for a minute less. "I can't believe I was so blind. Lance really had me fooled."

"He didn't do so deliberately."

"You mean he honestly thought he was AC-DC? Give me a break."

Woody sighed. "Can you move on, Pippa? Find someone else?"

"Just like that? It's going to be a long time before I trust a man again."

Women were so messed up, Woody thought; they actually had to know and trust a guy before they could bend over for him. "Lance wants you to keep the ring. Keep everything. He told his mother under no circumstances was she to ask for any jewelry back, even if she wins the lawsuit."

"That is so heartwarming, Woody."

"What about the Maserati?"

"Take the tailpipe and shove it." Pippa snapped her cell phone shut. Woody *help* her? That was like Henry VIII offering to sew Anne Boleyn's head back on.

Carrie-Jo rapped on her window. "Can you lend me three bucks for lunch?"

Pippa looked in her wallet. All she had was a pair of hundred-dollar bills. "I'll come in with you," she sighed.

They entered the motel's humid, moldy coffee shop. Pippa got a cup of coffee that tasted as if it had been simmering since St. Patrick's Day. While paying for that and Carrie-Jo's lunch, she happened to glance at the television above the cash register. She gasped to see Thayne, her father, and another woman emerging from a limousine. Thayne's black veils floated in the breeze as she and Robert followed a horse-drawn wagon into a cemetery. Pippa recognized the gravestones of the Walker family plot in Crockett, Texas. She saw Anson's favorite horse, Scamp. That big long box in the wagon must be his coffin. On top of the coffin stood his alligator boots with the six-inch spurs. Anson claimed they spun a bit whenever he was standing on top of oil.

Pippa's father, back from golfing in Morocco, looked as if he had just swallowed a divot. Thayne seemed emaciated and unsteady on her feet, perhaps because she was wearing a pair of Guccis with four-inch spikes, not the best choice for walking on grass.

A television reporter appeared and said, in case any of his viewers were totally blind, "This is a sad day for the Walker family."

Transfixed, Pippa watched live coverage of Anson's funeral. The Reverend Alcott, back for an encore, read from the family Bible. Cedric the substitute wedding planner was there, standing tall in a tartan kilt and reflective sunglasses. Pippa was surprised to see Kimberly, her erstwhile bridesmaid, standing at the graveside in a strapless black dress and her Mad Hatter hat, recycled for a second media blowout. For the benefit of the paparazzi's zoom lenses, Kimberly dabbed at her dry eyes with a handkerchief at regular intervals. At Thayne's elbow stood a vaguely familiar woman in a black hat with a swooping brim. Pippa finally identified the face behind the sunglasses as that of Dusi Damon, her mother's college roommate. Dusi hadn't been able to make the wedding because she was having plastic surgery in Rangoon. Now sufficiently mended to be seen in public, Dusi wore a low-cut black sheath, three-quarter-length black gloves, and a neckful of rubies. Whenever Kimberly whipped out her handkerchief, Dusi gazed stonily at her. Pippa recognized some long-lost cousins from Corpus Christi, all fatter than ever. There were so many fluttering veils and hankies at the graveside that each time the wind picked up, the mourners looked as if they might sail away.

At the height of the ceremony Thayne wobbled over to the coffin and heaved Anson's boots into the open grave. Pippa bit her lip so hard that it bled: Anson had promised her those spurs! Now they, and his oilman's luck, would be buried with him? She watched in horror as her mother threw a handful of dirt on top of the boots. Her father tossed some more dirt on top of that. Dusi picked up a handful of dirt and, completely missing the large hole in the ground, sprayed Kimberly with soil just as Kimberly was pretending to wipe her eyes with her handkerchief. Fascinated, Pippa watched Dusi guide her parents back to their limousine.

"Anson Walker has joined the oilfields in the sky," the reporter said. His next attempt at poetic utterance was cut off by a commercial for dog food.

"From dust to dust," the little old lady at the register said.

Realizing that she had been staring at the television for almost half an hour, Pippa headed into the hallway.

"Hey! You in that driving school? You be goin' the wrong way." The cashier sped after her. Before Pippa could prevent it, she was marched back to class.

The shades were drawn. Officer Pierce sat behind a slide projector, whence he was flashing a series of geometric shapes against the wall and barking, "Octagon: stop signs. Triangle: yield signs. Circles: railroad warnings. Pentagon: schools." He paused. "Yes, Millicent?"

"This one tried to get away," the cashier reported. "She was watching a funeral."

"Don't just stand there, Perdita. Come join the party."

"Hey, doesn't she automatically flunk?" a voice whined from the dark as Pippa returned to her front-row seat. "You said we had to be here on time every time."

"I'm so sorry," Pierce answered. "Did I neglect to mention that each time you're late, you have to score five points higher on all four tests? That means seventy-five, Perdita. Across the board." Watching a funeral? That was pretty twisted. "Let's review colors for the late-comer. A red sign means stop. A yellow sign means warning. Orange means construction. Brown, recreation area."

"This is too hard, man," Seymour muttered. "There are like a hundred signs in the book."

"You're an urban artist, aren't you? You're supposed to have an eye for shapes and colors." Pierce turned off the slide projector and had his class recite another five chapters from the manual. "Home-work: duh! Traffic signs. We'll have a quiz tomorrow."

"Does it count?" Billy the farmer groaned.

"Absolutely." As Pierce yanked its cord, a window blind zipped upward, emitting a cloud of dead beetles as it slammed into the top of the frame. "Class dismissed. Perdita," he called as she was bolting for the door. "One moment."

She stood quietly in place as her classmates shuffled out. Pierce thought she looked pale, trembling almost. Maybe she thought he was going to smack her. His voice softened. "Were you really watching a funeral?"

"My grandfather," she blurted.

The poor kid was delusional. Nothing was on this time of day but the soaps. "The one who was going to increase your allowance if you passed the course?"

"Yes."

Pierce reached for his wallet. "How much allowance were we talk-ing about?"

"A billion dollars," she said with a straight face.

"Would you settle for ten bucks today and ten tomorrow?"

To his surprise she didn't snatch it out of his hand. She simply gasped and ran out.

Bawling, Pippa blasted the SUV out of the parking lot. Officer Pierce had no doubt meant well, but mistaking her for a charity case was humiliating beyond belief. Attending her grandfather's funeral via television had been equally crushing. And all the while she was endur-ing this unearned tribulation, Lance was in Brazil working on his tan!

Well, it was time to spread the misery. Houston was four hours south of Dallas. If she started now, she could be kicking down Rosimund's door by sunset. That seemed like an intelligent plan, so Pippa drove onto Route 45 and engaged the cruise control, careful to stay under the speed limit. Through her tears she studied the shape and color of every passing road sign: homework. She rehearsed exactly what she was going to say and imagined the look on Rosimund's face when she heard the truth about the perfect son who had ruined Pippa's life.

After an hour of vindictive nirvana Pippa was startled to drive past a large green sign for Crockett, where her grandfather had been buried just a few hours ago. She screeched over three lanes to the exit ramp: Rosimund could wait while she paid her last respects.

Thirty minutes later Pippa arrived at the cemetery where her great-great-grandfather Cougar Walker was interred along with his wife and four generations of progeny. Dinnertime was the high point of the day in Crockett, therefore the place was deserted. It was also one hundred ten degrees Fahrenheit on the open prairie, which tended to curtail lingering expressions of grief. Pippa parked the SUV beside the mound of fresh dirt in the family plot. She had almost convinced herself that the funeral had been an elaborate hoax when she saw a bunch of square holes in the grass where Thayne had been standing. Those punctures had been made by four-inch Gucci heels.

It really happened.

Pippa sank to the dry grass and sobbed anew. When she could see again, she read the names carved into the surrounding gravestones. She knew all their stories by heart: Uncle Landon had slipped into a vat of crude oil, lost his dentures, and gone toothless for the next fifty years. Despite getting struck twice by lightning, Aunt Eliza had outlived three husbands. Great-grandma Patsy, who never finished eighth grade, tripled the family business while her husband was fighting the Japanese. Cousin Jeb, aged seven, had shot and killed a thief making off with one of his mother's famous shoofly pies. The tales went on and on: the Walkers were proud, smart, strong people. Generation after generation had proven it wasn't the money, it was the attitude. Pippa could almost see her forebears shaking their heads, wondering how their superior genes had produced such a dud. She heard Anson's voice: *Get that diploma.* She heard her great-grandma Patsy: *Don't blow a billion, honey.* She even heard Officer Pierce: *You are not a victim.*

Chastened, Pippa drove slowly back to Dallas. Screw Rosimund. The Hendersons were losers.

Stanley, the guard at Ginny's gate, motioned for her to roll down her window. "A Maserati was dropped off for you today, ma'am." Pippa had told Woody to go shove the exhaust pipe. Apparently he had taken that as a yes. "We parked it in a corner of the garage. Under its cover."

"Keep the keys. It might be there for a while."

Pippa microwaved a few frozen dinners. She opened the Texas Drivers' Handbook and began cramming her brain with road signs. That beat thinking about her grandfather's spurs buried under six feet of prairie dust.

Eleven

The phone rang at seven o'clock sharp. "Good morning," Sheldon said. "How's driving school?"

"The teacher is really tough." Pippa yawned. Her legs felt like logs. "Officer Pierce."

"He's got an excellent reputation. Stern but fair. How's your alias working out?"

"I'm getting used to it." Pippa removed the manual lodged between her ear and the pillow. "I saw Grampa's funeral on television. I can't believe Thayne threw his spurs away."

"As I said, she's not herself."

"That's why I need to be with her."

"Most unwise, considering her reversal of fortune. Speaking of which, I've transferred sixty thousand dollars to your money market account. An envelope containing petty cash and a driver's license in the name of Perdita Rica has been delivered to the Happy Hour Motel. You are a student, after all."

His sarcasm was not lost on Pippa. "I know it's not exactly what my grandfather had in mind, Sheldon, but it's a means toward an end. I could do a lot of good with a billion dollars."

If Sheldon had a dime for every oil heir who had told him that, he could buy Conoco. "We'll revisit that concept once you graduate."

Pippa dressed in her second Wal-Mart outfit, a white piqué shift with large purple flowers. The color scheme looked putrid with her inky hair. Before leaving she studied herself in the full-length mirror. She was not a convincing Latino: the proportion of boob to butt was the inverse of the ethnic ideal. Another serious problem caught her eye: her tattoos had washed off in the shower.

Heart racing, Pippa looked at her watch. She'd never have time to restencil herself before class and she couldn't be late again, so she grabbed a couple of Magic Markers and the first sweater she found in Ginny's drawer. Rush-hour traffic was awful. The SUV tore into the Happy Hour Motel lot at two minutes before nine. Pippa sprinted past the exterminators fumigating the first floor. She slid into her front-row seat as Officer Pierce was opening the windows. "Sorry, class. AC's on the fritz today."

"You don't expect us to take a test in this heat," Gordon the fisherman protested as Pierce passed out the quiz.

"I not only expect you to take it, I expect you to pass it." Few people ever did; Pierce had made the quiz extra difficult in order to scare everyone into studying harder for the final. Perdita seemed to be much more with it today, except for the mohair sweater. It was heavy enough to suffocate a llama. "Those of you wearing ties or jackets may feel free to remove them." She didn't budge. "Perdita?"

"No thank you." She smiled as sweat teemed down her legs, forehead, and stomach.

He hoped she wasn't trying to hide needle marks on her arms. That sexy perfume of hers was billowing off her like heat from a radiator. Officer Pierce forced himself to keep moving. After ten minutes he collected the quizzes. "You may visit the water fountain while I mark these."

Pippa rushed into the hallway and peeled off her sweater. "Seymour," she called the moment he emerged from class. "Could I ask a huge favor?"

"You name it, cream puff."

Pippa gave him a Magic Marker. "Would you mind drawing a couple of tattoos on my arms? Whatever inspires you."

They went to the lobby. As a few hookers watched, Seymour expertly covered Pippa's arms with black lines and squiggles. "There you go. That ain't comin' off for a while."

Pierce did a double take as she returned to her seat, arms bared. They seemed to be covered with artistic renderings of male and female genitalia. Perdita seemed either totally unaware that everyone in class was snickering at her body art or she was taunting them with some twisted personal agenda.

"All but one of you failed," he said, dropping her quiz on her desk. She had scored a ninety-eight. Maybe she was an idiot savant. "That's phenomenal, negatively speaking. Explain yourselves."

"The NBA finals were on last night."

"There were too many signs."

"Morning is not my best time."

"Those are excuses, not explanations. Perdita, you may sit by the pool while we review road signs." Before she left Pierce handed her a thick envelope couriered to "Perdita Rica, Driving School, Happy Hour Motel." No return address.

From his desk Pierce observed Perdita at the swimming pool ripping open the envelope. It seemed to contain an enormous amount of cash. She tucked that into her purse then stared at the overchlorinated water for a spell. Then she made a call on her cell phone. Soon an Asian woman in a white lab coat arrived; Pierce watched in fascination as she gave Perdita a manicure, pedicure, and foot massage. He could barely take his eyes off Perdita's disturbingly long legs as the woman applied layer after layer of polish to her toenails. Perdita dozed for a while; the sight of her lying innocently on her back made Pierce very itchy to go outside and lie somewhere on his stomach.

Around eleven-thirty he saw a Lincoln roll into the lot. A uniformed chauffeur removed a picnic hamper from the trunk and snapped a tablecloth over the plastic table next to Perdita's lounge chair. The fellow's white-gloved hands removed china plates and a bouquet of roses from the hamper. As Perdita ate the first of three courses, the chauffeur retired to an imaginary sideboard, staring at the dilapidated train tracks beyond the chain-link fence as he waited to clear the table. The whole scene looked like a clone of *The Great Gatsby* but with major chromosomal damage.

Pierce gave his class a second signs test. This time four students managed to answer seventy percent of the questions correctly, so he dismissed them for lunch. Perdita was just paying the butler as Pierce sauntered to the pool. He read the insignia on the man's uniform. "Hotel Adolphus? That's a step up from McDonald's."

Perdita quickly said, "My grandfather works in the kitchen."

"I thought he just died."

She blushed a rich red. "That was my other grandfather."

Yeah, right. Pierce went to his official Texas state car. He had to pick up a video for this afternoon's class. He turned the keys in the ignition but nothing happened. "Son of a bitch!"

As he was bending over the hood, Perdita pulled up in her SUV. Its front grille looked like an automotive version of Hannibal Lecter's restraint mask. "Need a ride? I was just going to drop off some laundry."

"Heading anywhere near the motor vehicle agency?"

"It's right on my way."

Pierce sank into the passenger seat. The SUV had every bell and whistle imaginable, yet Perdita dressed like a pauper. He pondered this inconsistency as she waited for a break in oncoming traffic.

Ten breaks came and went. "Sorry," Pippa said. "You make me a little nervous."

"Take your time." He could stare at those legs all afternoon.

At last Pippa pulled onto the highway. She didn't dare talk lest Officer Pierce think she wasn't paying attention to driving safety. The SUV plodded forward, never getting within three car lengths of the vehicle ahead of it. "Relax," he said finally. "You're doing fine."

Her perfume was burning a hole in his nose. Last night he had searched for it online: no one on the planet made a scent called Thane or Thain. Google kept trying to wing him over to some society lunatic. "Left at the next light." He smiled as her blinker immediately went on; the next light was a half mile away. "You seem to be feeling better today, Perdita."

"Yes, thanks. I'm learning a lot. You're a good teacher. Stern but fair."

Stern? Where'd she get that idea? He said nothing until she made the turn. "New tattoos?"

"They're very big at my restaurant. I'm a waitress."

"Heard you the first time." Pierce didn't want to ask what sort of cave Perdita worked in. He had her drive in circles downtown as he etched the silhouette of her calves in his memory.

They passed the courthouse three times. Pippa didn't dare tell him he was lost. On the fourth pass he said, "There. Pull over to the curb. I'll just be a second."

"Officer Pierce, are you asking me to wait in a No Parking Anytime Tow Zone?"

"If anyone gives you grief, tell them you're with me." On second thought, with those tattoos, "Or maybe just circle the block."

Pippa watched him run up the crowded courthouse steps easily as a cat. Within seconds a meter maid rapped on the window. "See that sign? Move it."

She drove around the block. When she returned to her starting point, the meter maid was still waiting in ambush so Pippa cruised by the courthouse, searching for Officer Pierce. A space cleared on the busy steps and she glimpsed a flash of red. Pippa stared into the lunchtime crowd, not believing her eyes but yes, that was a tall, horsy woman wearing a crimson suit: Rosimund, flanked by two men with major briefcases. Photographers buzzed in their wake.

Lawyers! Paparazzi! Of course! Rosimund had just filed her lawsuit against Thayne!

The sudden blare of a horn snapped Pippa's attention back to the street. She stomped on the brakes as a Vespa zipped in front of her. The Mexican driving the overloaded pickup behind her did the same. With a great squeal of rubber, his vehicle stopped inches from Pippa's taillights; unfortunately the forty crates of chickens he was hauling to market kept going. Chatting on her cell phone, the woman in the Escort behind the pickup never even moved her foot from gas to brake. She was rear-ended in turn by a teenager who had been changing a CD in his mother's Volvo.

Videotape in hand, Officer Pierce emerged from the motor vehicle agency just as the Vespa cut in front of Perdita's Lexus. He heard the Mexican skid to a halt and he saw the chicken crates topple over the busy street. *Boff! Boff!* He witnessed the next two collisions. As he was hurrying down the steps, a tall woman in a red suit pointed at Perdita's car and shouted, "That's one of her nymphomaniac bridesmaids! I'm sure of it!" Pierce was almost trampled by a herd of photographers rushing past him toward the Lexus. He bolted after them.

Paparazzi were swarming the SUV by the time Pierce got to it. All telephoto lenses pointed at Perdita, who had had the presence of mind to cover her face with a lacy thong she was taking to the dry cleaners. Pierce collared the guy who was trying to yank open the driver's door and tossed him at a squawking chicken. "It's me, Perdita! Open up!"

By some miracle she heard his voice above the fray. She unlocked the door and slithered to the floor, keeping the thong over her face. Pierce hopped inside. "Can you get us out of here?" she whimpered. "I didn't do anything."

"I saw." Pierce rolled down his window. "You have three seconds to get lost," he told the photographer plastered to the windshield. "One. Two. Three."

Pierce floored the accelerator. The guy on the hood nearly broke his nose on his own Nikon before sliding over the fender. Pierce looked in the rearview mirror. The street behind him was a blizzard of angry chickens and drivers. "You can get up now," he told the thong.

Pippa crawled to her seat. "Are we leaving the scene of an accident?"

"You didn't cause an accident, the guy tailgating behind you did. Rear-end collisions are one hundred percent the fault of the driver in the rear."

She looked out the back window. "Oh no! They're still there!"

Pierce confirmed in the rearview mirror that a green VW Bug and a white Mini Cooper were bearing down on them. They probably weren't the meter maids. "Seat belt fastened?"

Yes. Pippa sat rigid as a mannequin as Pierce zigzagged through Dallas, never overtly breaking traffic laws but not exactly observing them, either. He blasted through a series of yellow lights; the VW and Mini shot through them red. "Persistent," he said, squealing onto McBride Boulevard. "Are you married to the mob?"

"No! Please leave marriage out of this!"

"The woman in the red suit said you were a nymphomaniac bridesmaid."

"She's a drunk."

"Your ex-fiancé is sending a posse to bring you back," Pierce guessed.

"You couldn't be more wrong."

Pierce gunned the Lexus past four cars in a row, narrowly missing an oncoming Airstream. As they approached Route 208, Perdita's voice became wild. "They're getting closer! I'll kill myself if they catch me!"

"They won't catch you." Maybe she was a streetwalker and her pimp was trying to kidnap her back into prostitution. Pierce sped down the highway while allowing the VW to pull up alongside on the right. He waved at the short, bald driver, then slammed on the brakes. When the VW shot a car length ahead, Pierce tapped its left rear end with his right bumper, throwing it into a spin. "One down," he said as it spiraled into the trees.

The Mini was still on his tail. When he saw a break in oncoming traffic, Pierce ripped on the hand brake. His locked rear wheels spun in a semicircle around the front wheels, pointing the Lexus in the opposite direction. In one smooth motion Pierce released the hand brake, hit the gas, and wrestled the SUV from the shoulder back onto the pavement. In seconds the Lexus blazed past the Mini going the other way. Whistling, Pierce exited the highway onto a residential street. "Not even close." He said, grinning.

"Where'd you learn that?"

"I was a stunt driver." Pierce hadn't had such fun since. "Why were those men chasing you?"

"They thought I was someone else. I do slightly resemble the person they're looking for."

Pierce drove a while before saying, "I learned a couple of things as a stunt man, Perdita. One is I can spot a phony a mile off."

"I am not a phony," she protested. "I'm just having a small identity crisis."

"You're a really bad liar."

Pippa brightened. "That's a relief."

Officer Pierce revised his theory for the tenth time: maybe she was a sadistic state auditor. Any minute now she'd whip out her badge and fire him for a multitude of infractions. "Whatever you are," he sighed, pulling into the motel lot, "I'm sure it's unique."

"Could you please teach me that reverse stunt? In case they find me again?"

"It's called a J-turn. I'll think about it." How could he say no to those big green eyes? Pierce parked behind the motel in case an all-points bulletin had gone out on a white Lexus SUV. He inspected the front of Ginny's car. Its fender had survived without a scratch. "Class starts in three minutes." He walked inside.

Pippa needed a moment to pull herself together. That was a *really* close call. When she returned to class, Pierce was calmly pulling down the blinds. One would think he had spent his lunch break practicing yoga instead of bashing cars off the road. "Since some of you have expressed boredom with reading the manual, we're going to watch a video on safe driving techniques," he announced.

Carrie-Jo raised her hand. "This roach bomb is giving me a headache. May I go home?"

"Yeah! My throat hurts," Seymour whined.

Class relocated to the patio for a recitation of chapters six through nine. After an hour even Officer Pierce was having difficulty staying awake in the heat. When landscapers began uprooting the chain-link fence around the swimming pool, he called it a day. "Quiz first thing tomorrow," were his parting words.

Everyone but Perdita fled. "Do you need a jump start, Officer Pierce?"

Yes. Several. After resuscitating his junker Pierce drove Pippa to a vacant strip mall west of Dallas. En route he told stories about his days as a stunt driver. Pierce's career had ended not on the set but in a farmer's market. He had been buying Black Jack figs when a geezer in a Miata plowed into him. He was in the hospital for nearly a year. Then his fiancée ran away with his doctor.

Pippa was horrified. "How did you recover from that?"

"I took up ballroom dancing. Very therapeutic. Okay, let's try a few J-turns."

The old parking lot was barely long enough to ramp up to speed, but after a few attempts Pippa got the hang of one-eighties. "You drive a stick?" Pierce asked.

"My ex-fiancé had a Maserati."

A police car, blue lights flashing, zoomed into the lot. The officer jumped out. "Show me your license and registration," he ordered.

Pierce showed him a badge instead. "I was just giving this woman a driving exam."

"We had reports of fishtailing behind the doughnut shop."

"Someone's pulling your leg, Officer. No one goes over twenty-five miles an hour on a driving exam in the state of Texas."

Peering inside, the policeman saw a pretty young woman disfigured by tattoos and hair dye. Instructor and student were strapped in tight as ticks. Something about the scenario didn't look kosher but it was a state vehicle and Pierce had a badge. "I didn't know the MVA gave exams here."

"We're testing the site. Thanks for stopping by. Dallas police are really on top of things."

"We have to be. The crazies were out today."

Easing onto the boulevard, Pierce realized he had broken enough traffic regulations in the last six hours to get jail time. Perdita must be emanating some kind of subliminal impulses that were jamming his law-abiding radar. He noticed that, at the sight of the policeman, she had plastered herself against the passenger door. "You're not a felon, are you?"

"No, sir. Never."

"Is this car stolen?"

"It belongs to my friend. She's in Costa Rica."

A few hundred witnesses had seen the license plate. "There could be some people asking questions at her place."

Perdita turned white. "You mean it's not safe to go there?"

"I wouldn't risk it." Heavy seconds passed. "You could stay with me."

"I wouldn't dream of imposing like that! Maybe there's a room at the Adolphus."

Sure, in the larder, where her other grandfather worked. "There's a Days Inn up the road. You could even walk to class in the morning."

Pippa hesitated; Thayne had always said she would rather sleep in an open sewer than a Days Inn. "I guess that would work."

She insisted on paying cash for the room. Pierce estimated she had five thousand bucks stuffed into her little purse. He then deduced that the jewels on her finger must be real and that, given the afternoon's wild chase, Perdita was attached to someone rich, annoyed, and violent. "Sure you're going to be all right here?"

"I'll be fine. Thanks for saving me today, Officer Pierce."

"Happy to help." He would have asked her to rhumba class tonight but the tattoos and flip-flops were highly inappropriate. "Study that manual now."

Pippa went to her room and obediently pored over the manual for an hour before realizing that she'd have to wear her purple-flowered shift to class again tomorrow. When coeds did that at SMU, it was a dead giveaway they had slept with the professor the night before. She called the desk. "Is there a boutique on the premises?"

"You should be happy there's an ice machine."

Pippa slumped against her headboard. Without Ginny's SUV she was stuck. And what was she supposed to do about dinner? The nearest food was three miles up the highway.

Aha! Maserati! She called the security gate at Wellington on the Creek. "Stanley? This is Ginny's friend. How are you doing?"

"People have been looking for Miss Ortlip. Looking for her car, I should say."

Pippa shuddered. "What did you tell them?"

"I said she was out of the country. I hope that was all right."

"Perfect. Could you do me a huge favor? Remember that blue car someone dropped off for me yesterday? You've got the keys, right? I'd like you to drive it to the Days Inn on Harry Hines Boulevard. If you could swing by a Chinese takeout on the way, that would be fantastic."

He thought about refusing but Ginny was his biggest holiday tipper. "My shift is over at ten."

"Thanks." Pippa resumed studying the manual. She wanted to delight Officer Pierce with a perfect score on tomorrow's quiz. Every few paragraphs, however, the facts and figures put her to sleep: this had been a long, perilous day. She wandered to the bathroom and splashed her face with water. There, under the fluorescent lights, Pippa noticed that her skin looked very uneven. She hadn't been paying much attention to it lately, but that was no reason to go around looking like a sea sponge.

Near the phone was a flyer for Nori Nuki, a spa in Las Colinas. It was open 24/7 and offered a full array of esthetic services. Patrons of the Days Inn would receive a ten percent discount. Even better, she didn't know a soul in Las Colinas, a neighborhood near the airport.

"I'd like a body scrub and a facial tomorrow morning," she told the woman who answered the phone. "And my makeup done. I have to leave at eight-thirty."

"Then you get here seven. What facial you like? Cucumber and rice vinegar? Sea salt? Clay and seaweed? How about chocolate facial? That very popular now."

"Yes! I'll have that one."

"For body scrub, facial, and makeup you pay two hundred bucks include tip. You be here seven sharp."

"Do you have a dress shop close by?"

"Forty bucks I get you good dress. What size?"

"Six. Thank you."

Pippa went downstairs to wait for Stanley. Her pulse faltered when a blue Maserati appeared without Lance Henderson behind the wheel. *Get over it,* she told herself as Stanley pulled up to the entrance. *This is your car now.* As soon as possible she'd change the license plate: HUDDLE had nothing to do with football. Another signpost she had missed along the speedway to matrimony.

The car's interior reeked of fried noodles. Stanley parked in a corner of the lot. Pippa gobbled four egg rolls as he told her about the men who had come looking for Ginny. To her immense relief they had been journalists, not policemen. "Were you in some kind of chase?" he asked.

"They were harassing me. Don't worry, Ginny's car survived. I left it somewhere else for a while."

Ginny's friends were scary. Stanley was embarrassed to look at the body art on this one. "Good idea. People at Wellington Creek aren't used to riots."

Pippa gave him three hundred bucks. She went back to her room and polished off the Chinese dinner. For the first time since the wedding she felt hopeful about her future. Tomorrow, sporting a new dress and a fresh face, she'd ace another test. The day after that she'd graduate from driving school. The vaults of Fort Knox would open. She'd kick off her new life by taking Officer Pierce out to dinner. Introduce him to Sheldon. Clear the air over a few bottles of Champagne. It would be a grand occasion except Thayne wouldn't be there.

Pippa shed a few tears onto her chopsticks. Not hearing her mother's voice was a deprivation that made each day fall short of complete. She missed her terribly; the feeling had to be mutual. *Don't count on it,* an inner voice said. Thayne was not known for her reverse gear. "Just give me a chance," Pippa prayed, spraying her neck with a tiny sneeze of Thayne perfume. "Two little minutes."

The front desk awoke her at six the next morning. Pippa wasted a good bit of time searching for the terry robe she assumed came with every hotel room. After giving up on that, she had to call downstairs for a razor. Maybe Thayne had a point: sometimes it was worth paying an extra thousand a night for the bare necessities. Pippa wriggled into her dress and the damp underwear hanging on the towel bar. She drove the Maserati out of the parking lot. At the first red light, noticing the guy in the next car motioning to her, she rolled down her window.

"Wanna drag?"

"No thanks." The slightest moving violation would kill her chances of a diploma.

Almost every time she stopped at a light, the guy in the next car would look over and rev his engine. Other guys drove in parallel with her for blocks at a time. Finally a woman with big blond hair pulled up alongside. "Excuse me, but is that Lance Henderson's car?"

Pippa nearly stalled the engine. "Who?"

"KYQX is giving a thousand bucks reward to the first guy to find him. He's supposed to drive a blue Maserati with the license HUDDLE."

"I don't know what you're talking about. My daddy gave me this car for not piercing my nose."

Pippa shut her window and stared straight ahead. She felt conspicuous as a boiled lobster on a white tablecloth. Damn! Why couldn't Lance drive a black Mercedes instead of this flaming homobile? She pulled over and, with a Magic Marker, changed the *H* on the license plate to a *P.*

Nori Nuki Day Spa occupied a humble storefront close to the airport. Pippa hid the car beneath an acacia and went inside. Despite the early hour, the place bustled with women. "You Padita for body scrub and chocolate facial," said the cheerful Korean behind the cash register. *Lifestyles of the Rich and Famous* blared from the television at her side. "I am Nori. Where your car?"

"Parked out back."

"You need sticker or they tow." Nori uncapped a felt-tip pen. "License number?"

"P-U-D-D-L-E."

Nori gave her the permit. "Put on dashboard please." When Pippa returned, Nori was holding a red silk sheath with mandarin collar, its side slit to the pelvis. "Much better than cheap dress you wear now. How about shoes? I get nice pair. Much better than what you wear now. Twenty bucks."

"Fine."

"How about hair? You need clip. Five bucks. How about wash off tattoo? Fifteen bucks. Lot of work but they not nice for young lady."

"I know that but you'll have to leave them on."

"Forget money. I do for free."

"NO! Thank you!"

Without skipping a beat Nori said, "Total two hundred eighty bucks now." She counted Pippa's cash. "Thank you very much, Padita. You go with Jung-Bo."

Nori spoke a few sentences to a white-smocked Korean with a face lively as a hassock. Jung-Bo gave Pippa a smock and key and pointed her at the locker room. "Remove jerly please. I keep for you."

Pippa changed into a towel. She gave Jung-Bo her Wal-Mart watch, her diamond rings, and ankle bracelet. "Don't lose this. It belongs to my mother."

Jung-Bo dropped everything into her pocket and led Pippa to a heavy door. "You stay twelve minute. I wait for you."

Pippa went inside. A sign said the temperature was 140 degrees. She sat on the floor with several Korean women who didn't seem to be sweating at all. Twelve minutes felt like twelve hundred. Next Jung-Bo pushed her into a dim inferno. The sand covering the floor burned Pippa's feet. *Timperture 160F.* Within seconds Pippa's heart began pounding fearfully. Sweat cataracted from every pore. Her head hurt; maybe her brain was swelling like a hot air balloon. She lasted two minutes.

"I'm sorry," she gasped, bursting into the hallway. "That room is very hot."

"Twelve minute." Jung-Bo tried to push her back in.

"No! I have an important test at nine o'clock! I need a brain, not scrambled eggs!"

Jung-Bo took Pippa to the next door. "Three minute in here."

Pippa stuck her head inside long enough to locate the sign on the wall. She managed to read "180F" before her eyeballs began pulling away from their sockets. One lone female lay motionless, perhaps mummified, in a dim corner. "Whew! That's enough of that!"

Displeased, Jung-Bo took Pippa to a whirlpool with steam rising from the surface. "Go in."

What the heck, the worst it could be was 212 degrees. Pippa dropped her towel and slid into the roiling waters. Jung-Bo stood guard at the ladder, making escape impossible. Finally she said, "We scrub now."

Pippa was taken to a white-tiled room containing six tables. Korean attendants wearing rough mitts scrubbed naked women lying atop four of the tables. As they worked, the attendants chatted and laughed, no doubt making fun of the bodies they were vigorously abrading. Every so often an old woman came along and sloshed a bucket of warm water over a reclining nude. After getting Pippa up on a table, Jung-Bo beckoned to a girl waiting by the sink. She began wringing Pippa's feet like damp washcloths. The pain was excruciating. "Could you go a little easy?" Pippa cried. "I'd like to walk out of here."

The girl began buffing Pippa's face with what felt like a petrified starfish. She applied an astringent to the raw flesh before coating Pippa's face with melted chocolate. "Close eye," she commanded, covering Pippa's eyes with rank, dripping cotton balls.

"What is that?"

"Tea from strong root. Good for you."

The chocolate quickly hardened to a bulletproof mask. Pippa surrendered to the scrubbing mitts as random paragraphs from the Texas Drivers Handbook floated through her mind. She dreamt she heard Thayne's voice, clear as a bell, say, *Don't come near me with those filthy mitts,* before a bucket of warm water sloshed the hallucination away. Pippa slid into a relaxing coma illustrated with hundreds of road signs. Soft Shoulder. Grooved Pavement Ahead.

"What do you mean you don't have a kimchee and volcanic mud facial? I didn't drive all the way over here to take a steam bath."

Pippa's eyes snapped open so quickly that both cotton balls fell to the floor. She turned her head very slowly. Thayne was lying on the next table. Unlike everyone else in the room, she wore an orange silk robe, pale orange mules, and her usual half pound of diamonds. Her hair was wrapped in a turban from Thibiant, her favorite Beverly Hills spa. She clutched a large Fendi handbag, obviously not impressed with security in the locker room.

"What are *you* looking at?" Thayne snapped, failing to identify the naked female with black hair, tattoos, and chocolate-shellacked face as her daughter. She turned to her attendant. "Don't tell me you don't have any volcanic mud on the premises. Every reputable spa in Dallas has volcanic mud."

"Why you not go to reputable spa then? Why you come here and make me trouble?"

"I thought I'd give you a try," Thayne said, albeit with a little less wind in her sails. "All right, forget the mud. Surely you have kimchee."

"Kimchee to eat. Not good for face. It burn face."

"That's why you mix it with the volcanic mud, you stupid twit." Thayne looked over at Pippa. "You there! What's that on your face?"

Pippa didn't dare respond in recognizable English. She raised her voice a few notches. "Sho. Clate."

"Chocolate? How disgusting. Miss! Did you say something about clay and seaweed?"

"That for body wrap," came the sullen reply.

"You don't consider the face part of the body?"

"It expensive."

"Just do it," Thayne said with a dismissive flick of the wrist. As her attendant went off to mix the clay and seaweed, Thayne looked around the room with a shudder. "Doesn't all that scrubbing hurt? I've never seen such rough handling. Or such a shocking lack of privacy."

"Is Korean style." What was Thayne doing here? Same thing she was, Pippa realized: avoiding recognition, poor thing.

The attendant returned with a ceramic pot. Thayne took one whiff and said, "I hope you don't intend to put that on my face."

"Excellent fo' you!" Pippa cried, terrified that her mother would get up and leave. "Must try!"

The desperation in her voice somehow got Thayne to relent. "Since I'm already here, you may as well go ahead," she told the girl. "Just try not to get any of that muck on my robe."

Pippa caught Thayne looking oddly at her as the clay was slathered on her face. She desperately wanted to reach across to her mother's table and hold her hand.

"Would you mind telling me what those tattoos are all about?"

"Ancient Korean symbols."

"They look like sexual organs to me. I'm surprised you haven't been taken for a prostitute. Forgive me if you are, of course."

All those stares Pippa had been getting for the last few days now made perfect sense. She blushed almost hot enough to melt her chocolate mask. "Fertility signs. For good luck."

"Fertility is luck? I have news for you. Children are a curse," Thayne whispered as the attendant mounded two wads of seaweed over her eyes.

While the girl scrubbed her breasts as if they were stains in the carpet, Pippa racked her brain for a way to proceed. She had pretty well painted herself into a corner by pretending to be a Korean. When Thayne discovered who was hiding beneath all that chocolate, her outrage would be heard in Kilgore. For the umpteenth time Pippa cursed herself for pretending to be someone she was not.

A young Korean woman in jeans entered the room with Nori Nuki. She had a camera. To Pippa's horror she pointed it at her. Pippa's first impulse was to play possum. Maybe it was a publicity shot; she happened to have the best-looking body in the room. Then it occurred to her that the woman could be pointing the camera at Thayne, who was lying on the next table.

"Be right back," Pippa said as the attendant began scrubbing her tattoos.

She marched over to the photographer. "Excuse me. What are you doing?"

"You be daughter of Thayne Wokker." Nori proudly exhibited Thayne's ankle bracelet as proof. She pointed to the mudpacked figure in the orange robe. "We believe that woman Thayne Wokker. You drive car own by Lance Handrison with license PUDDLE. We earn thousand bucks reward to find you."

"May I have my jewelry? Thank you." Pippa slipped her ring, watch, and ankle bracelet on then tossed the woman's Rolleiflex into the pot of melted chocolate. "Go fish."

"Bad lady! You destroy camera!"

Pippa ran to the locker room and zipped herself into her new red dress. She grabbed the little shoulder bag containing all her valuables. She was one step out the front door when a green VW skidded into the lot. Its driver was the jackal Officer Pierce had spun off the road yesterday. Pippa jerked back inside, locked the door, and ran to the body scrub room. Nori, the photographer, and Jung-Bo were yammering over the pot of chocolate, trying to fish the camera out with tongue depressors.

Pippa darted to Thayne's table. "Sorry to disturb you, Mama," she whispered, removing the seaweed from Thayne's eyes. "The paparazzi have found us."

Thayne stared at the chocolate-covered face bending over her. "Are you that Korean?"

"It's me. Pippa. Really. We have to go."

"Are you crazy? I can't go outside with my face under an inch of mud."

"Leave it on. For your own protection."

As Pippa dragged her mother past Nori and Co., Thayne regained sufficient presence of mind to shout, "You'll be hearing from my lawyer, you worthless lychee nuts!"

Pippa dragged Thayne out an emergency exit to the parking lot. "Is Lance here?" Thayne cried, seeing his car. Her hands flew to her face.

"Leave the mud on! And the turban. He gave me the car." Pippa shoved her mother inside and fired the Maserati into reverse. They shot out of the parking lot, but not before the little bald guy banging on the front door saw them. He rushed to his VW.

Pippa hit the gas. "How have you been, Mama?"

"Let me out of this car immediately!"

"You prefer to be picked up in Las Colinas in a bathrobe? They'll have a field day with that."

"How dare you stalk me."

"Wrong. I got there first." Pippa zipped around a corner. "Listen,

I know this isn't the ideal time or place, but I'd like to talk."

"If you're trying to get yourself undisinherited, don't waste your breath."

"There's a rational explanation. I was trying to protect Lance."

"How asinine! Rosimund can protect him far better than you ever will."

"Ah! Then you know?"

"Know what?"

What if she told her mother Lance was gay? Thayne would broadcast that throughout the solar system. Any mother would. Though sorely tempted to spill the beans, Pippa tried to open a back door to the truth. "I think Lance is sterile."

"So what?"

"I mean impotent." Pippa thought of Officer Pierce as she ran her second red light.

"Count your blessings. You would have had carte blanche with the chauffeur."

This conversation was not going the way Pippa intended. "Maybe he's neuter."

"Haven't you left out castrated and a transvestite? How about gay as a pink flamingo?"

"He might be that, too. Lance definitely might be that."

"Let's not forget serial killer and pedophile."

Pippa realized she may have overplayed her hand. "Do you think I'm making all this up, Mama?"

"Do not call me mother! Of course you're making it up. Let me scrape a little more mud off my face for you to fling at that poor boy."

"Leave it on!" Pippa shrieked. "I don't want anyone recognizing you."

"It's extremely uncomfortable."

"Believe me, chocolate feels worse."

Thayne sat in morbid disapproval as Pippa made an illegal left turn. "That awful Volkswagen is right behind us," she said, finally appreciating the gravity of the situation.

"Thanks. That's very helpful." The floor was beginning to burn Pippa's bare feet. Roughly shifting into fifth gear, she tried to think of a way to ditch her pursuer, drop Thayne off, and get herself to class in the next ten minutes. Just maybe, if she could whip into the Happy Hour parking lot before the VW made that last corner, she might get away with it. They were only a few miles away.

"Are you trying to kill me?" Thayne screeched as Pippa smoked around an island in the middle of the road. "You still won't get my money."

"Keep your stupid money. I would have liked Grampa's spurs, though."

"And I would have liked a son-in-law, so let's call it even. What you did was unforgivable."

"It was desperate and silly. Not unforgivable. I'm really, really sorry. How can I make it up to you?"

"Just like that? How dare you add insult to injury. You've desecrated the Walker name forever. Who is this Superman you spurned Lance Henderson for? It had better be Prince William or one of the Hunts."

"There is no one, Mama! I just made it up to call off the wedding!"

"To spite me," Thayne moaned, going limp. "You are truly evil." She gasped melodramatically as Pippa made a series of wild turns. Finally, exasperated, she said, "Didn't Lance carry a gun in the glove compartment? Can't we just shoot this fellow?"

Thayne didn't find a gun but she did locate a dozen condoms. "Aha!" she cried, waving a few in Pippa's face. "Does this look like the property of an impotent Dallas Cowboys quarterback?"

Unable to see, Pippa missed the turn into the Happy Hour lot. For the first time in her life she swore at her mother, shocking Thayne silent. It was six minutes before nine. Desperate, Pippa decided to cross the grass median and try again. If the Beetle was still behind her, she'd floor the Maserati into the lot of the Happy Hour Motel and make one of those J-turns Officer Pierce had taught her. Once she left the Volkswagen in the dust, she could drop Thayne off at the Days Inn to wash up while she jogged to class on time. Now that was thinking like a Walker!

Pippa cut across the grass median twice, with great success. Unfortunately, so did the Volkswagen. "Hold on," she told Thayne, zooming into the lot of the Happy Hour Motel at ninety miles an hour. "We're almost home."

Officer Pierce arrived early for class. He had taken a swing by the Days Inn up the road and called Perdita's room to see if she'd like a ride. The receptionist told him that she had left around sunup in a blue Maserati. Kicking himself, Pierce drove back to the Happy Hour Motel. He checked that the SUV was still safe and out of sight. He waved to the guys who were replacing the chain-link fence around the pool. Then he went to his car to await Perdita's arrival, obviously with her ex-boyfriend. Pierce was morbidly curious to see if they had made up.

At two minutes to nine he heard the whine of a highly taxed engine. Sounded Italian. Seconds later a blue Maserati blasted into the lot. Inside sat two bizarre-looking people with dark ski masks. The passenger wore an orange turban. Terrorists? Pierce watched in disbelief as the Maserati went into a dizzying 360-degree spin. Without once hitting the brakes, the driver floored the car through the gap in the chain-link fence and shot directly into the swimming pool.

Perdita! Pierce was running toward the splash when a green Volkswagen careened into the lot. In order to miss him the driver stomped on the brakes, swerved, and rammed Pierce's car with an earsplitting crash. Recognizing yesterday's paparazzo, Pierce left him to the airbags. He dove into the pool. The Maserati was about four feet underwater and sinking fast. Presuming the ex-fiancé was at the wheel, Pierce set about rescuing the passenger. He opened the door and unbuckled . . . it looked like a woman . . . feisty minx . . . *mud* all over her face? Fortunately the turban and most of the mud came off as he pulled her to the surface. She was wearing huge rings, like Perdita's. Good-looking blonde. Excellent body. Then she opened her mouth.

"What an awful little sinkhole."

"You're welcome." Pierce dove back underwater. Seeing the driver's tattoos, he had the worst adrenaline rush of his life. Nearly beside himself, he motioned Perdita to roll down her window. She wriggled out. They clung gasping to the ladder as the Maserati hit bottom.

Some of the stuff on her face had gotten into his mouth. "Is that chocolate?"

"Yes." Pippa peeled it off in waxy sheets. "Guess I need a little more practice with that J-turn."

"You over there! Recover my handbag at once. Chlorine is hell on leather."

"Who is that woman?"

"My ex-mother." Pippa had another calamity on her mind. "Did I just fail driving school?"

Correct. Pierce noticed that every student in class had gathered around the VW in the parking lot. No one had a clue there was a Maserati in the swimming pool. "Was he chasing you again?"

Pippa nodded miserably. "Can you arrest him?"

"Sure. If he's alive."

Thayne was now ranting at the grounds crew to fetch her purse. "She can't be here when the police come. Officer Pierce, you've got to help. She's just an innocent bystander."

That was hard to believe. Nevertheless Pierce said, "Your SUV is still out back. The keys are in the ignition." He had been hoping someone would steal it. "I'll write the accident report. You both went to seek medical attention. We can sign any papers later."

Pierce allowed her to precede him up the ladder. The gods rewarded him with a sight he would never forget: Perdita in all her glory, without underwear. She was a natural blonde, as he had suspected. Too bad she had such toxic baggage. Her mother, ex-mother, whatever, was the *coup de grâce.* "Good luck, honey," he told Pippa. "Wherever you're going, I hope you make it."

Thayne, her robe dripping wet, stood on the diving board watching one of the grounds crew recover her purse from the sunken car. "Now get my turban," she ordered, pointing to an orange towel floating underwater.

"Leave it, Mama," Pippa said, pulling her sleeve.

"Are you out of your mind? Look at my hair!"

"Hear that siren? The police will be here in ten seconds."

Thayne checked that her Chantecaille powder compact had not been water damaged. Then she flung a hundred-dollar bill into the water. *"Mi sombrero,"* she shouted, running after Pippa.

Three guys dove in after it. Thayne got her sopping turban back as Pippa packed her into the SUV. "What an awful car! Did you steal it?"

"It's Ginny's. I'm taking you to a hotel up the street. You can clean up there and go home." Pippa made one more attempt to mend fences. "I'm sorry I caused you so much trouble. Can you try to see things from my angle?"

"How dare you even ask! Thanks to you, your grandfather is pushing up daisies in Crockett. Cedric has been returning wedding gifts by the hundreds. We had to shoot the Lipizzaner. We had to pay Mrs. Bingo Buntz the fourth six percent interest on her Krugerrands. Rosimund insists on her day in court. I'm the laughingstock of Texas." Thayne turned her anguished face toward Pippa. "How could you have humiliated me so?"

"Can we get away from you you you? Real people call off weddings. Granted, we did so at the last moment, but did you see Lance crying up there when I made the announcement? He was the happiest guy on earth. Think about that." Pippa pulled in front of the hotel. "Well, here we are."

"Days Inn?" Thayne stared in dismay at five Japanese businessmen waiting outside for the shuttle bus. "You really know how to rub my face in it, don't you?"

Pippa got out of the SUV. "Take the car, then. Drive home."

Thayne slid into the driver's seat. She surveyed the dyed, crayoned, dripping mess that used to be her beloved daughter and felt like shooting herself. Then she noticed a triple gleam on Pippa's left hand. "My God! You're still wearing his ring!"

"Lance insisted I keep it." Pippa took it off. "Here. You earned it."

Try as she might, Thayne was constitutionally incapable of refusing three huge diamonds, especially when they were booty from Rosimund. "I suppose I could have them reset."

"And here's your ankle bracelet. I'll borrow it again next time." Her mother didn't even smile. "Really, Mama, are you still mad at me?"

Thayne's eyes went cold as an adder's. "Goodbye, Pippa. Never contact me again."

"But I love you!" Pippa wailed.

"If only the feeling were mutual." Thayne roared off.

Pippa stared after the SUV until it was just a speck on Harry Hines Boulevard. She felt someone tap her arm. One of the Japanese businessmen proffered a pair of green plastic flip-flops. "Please have. She is not nice lady."

As Pippa put them on, the shuttle bus pulled up. "Comin' with us, miss?" the driver shouted. "Twenty-two bucks to the airport."

Pippa stepped on.

Twelve

At the airport Pippa bought a humongous pair of sunglasses. She ducked into a ladies' room and washed the last chocolate smears from her face. After a hard look in the mirror she concluded that the bedraggled apparition with black hair, Mao sheath, and flashing green flip-flops didn't look a bit like Pippa Walker: she was safe. At a newsstand she collected ten magazines covering everything from weight lifting to gardening. Waiting in line, Pippa saw that people ahead of her were smiling at a windup doll on the counter. It was a plastic bride. Blonde. She squinted at it through her sunglasses: that damn thing was not only wearing the same wedding gown as hers, but its smile looked familiar. The cashier turned the key in the doll's back. Instead of going forward it went in reverse, squeaking, "I don't! I don't!"

BALKER WALKER DOLLS, the sign said. $12.99.

As a familiar nausea clawed her stomach, Pippa paid for the magazines and dove into the nearest bar. She sat facing the wall in the darkest corner, ordered a screwdriver, and started reading the advertisements in back of the magazines. It was imperative that she find another area of study, fast. Cooking school? She was terrible in the kitchen. Cheerleading school? Never again. How about horticulture? Murder on the manicure. Carpentry? Shoemaking? Travel agent?

Canine obedience school? "Get a grip," she muttered. That diploma was for dogs.

"Ready for a refill, hon?"

"Thanks." How did people find their paths in life? The lucky ones saw a fire truck or an airplane when they were three years old and knew right away that they wanted to be firefighters and astronauts. Way too busy with shopping, primping, and parties, Pippa had experienced no such bolt of lightning. In fact, the concept of working for a living hadn't occurred to her; she had thought her job in life was to redistribute the Walker wealth, preferably in retail establishments. *Thank you, Mama, for setting that fine example.* Pippa swallowed her drink and kept turning pages.

She saw nothing remotely interesting until the tail end of the last magazine in her pile, *Poker Today.* Three pages of ads for escort services: how hard was it to accompany men to dinner and the theater? Pippa already knew how to make an entrance in a five-star restaurant.

She phoned the ad with the prettiest girls. "I'd like to become a professional escort. Could you recommend a school?"

"School?" The guy laughed. "Oh, you're quick."

"I'm not trying to be quick. I'm trying to get the number of the school." He hung up on her. "Jerk!"

The waitress dropped off another screwdriver. "Somethin' wrong?"

Pippa pointed to the ad. "I'm trying to go to escort school."

"You can do better than that, honey."

Such as escort manager? Pippa had always enjoyed setting up coeds from Kappa Kappa Gamma with Lance's friends on the football team.

The ad almost leaped off the page. LEARN MATCHMAKING FROM A PRO! *My three-day certified bullet course will launch your career!* Maybe the force was with her after all. In great excitement Pippa dialed the number.

"Marvy Mates," sang a syrupy voice. "Leave nothing to fate, your soul mate awaits. Marla Marble speaking."

Pippa needed a moment to digest all the M&M's. "I'd like to take your course. Where are you located?"

"Warm, sunny Phoenix."

"I can start tomorrow. Can you fit me in?"

"We'll certainly try. Your name, please?"

"Perdita Rica" was scorched earth. Pippa noisily flipped to the middle of the poker magazine and skidded over an article. "Chip . . . Chippa . . . Flush . . . Chippa Flushowitz."

"That's very unusual."

"Yes. I'm Polish."

"You have no accent whatever."

"I grew up with my uncle in Oklahoma. Do you give every graduate a certificate?"

"Absolutely. Tuition is two thousand dollars."

"My goodness, that's steep."

"A small commitment to making others happy. Please pay in cash." Marla gave Pippa the address. "And bring your résumé."

Pippa frowned. "Shouldn't I be asking for *your* résumé?" After a frosty silence, she realized her mistake. "That's what they do in Poland."

"Phoenix is not Poland." Marla's voice regained its syrup. "We'll see you tomorrow, Chippa."

Praying it wasn't the towing company, insurance adjusters, police, or Thayne calling for the hundredth time, Sheldon Adelstein answered his phone. Pippa sounded cheerful as a lark. "How's it going, Sheldon?"

"It's not every day I'm asked to fish a Maserati out of a swimming pool. Or prove it wasn't stolen by an illegal immigrant. Or explain why you were enrolled in driving school under an alias."

"I'm sorry. I was just trying to get away from that awful man in the Volkswagen."

"Lance isn't going to be happy about his car. The insurers will replace it, but—"

"Lance gave me the car. Could you do me a favor? Give the new one to Officer Pierce."

"He did save you a peck of trouble."

"If it hadn't been for that paparazzo, I would have passed driving school. That is so unfair. Did my mother make it back from the Days Inn all right?"

Sheldon merely cleared his throat. "Should I courier the accident report over to Ginny's? You can sign it tonight and we can put this episode behind us."

"That's one reason I'm calling. I'm no longer at Ginny's. Obviously I failed driving school so I've enrolled in matchmaking school." Silence. "In Phoenix." All quiet. "Tomorrow. It will be over in three days."

"I hope so, for your grandfather's sake."

"Could you find me a hotel nearby? Someplace with good lights in the rooms so I can study. And a car. And a small allowance for lunch and a few suits. I had to leave Dallas with nothing but my purse. Oh, and don't forget two thousand bucks tuition. Could you send a new cell phone with the accident report? Mine got wrecked in the pool. So did my debit card."

"Didn't I just send you a significant amount of cash?"

"The plane ticket was expensive."

"You do have your Perdita Rica driver's license, I hope."

"Of course! That's how I got on the plane. One last thing. I need some Polish-looking ID for Chippa Flushowitz. My new alias." Pippa spelled it. "It doesn't have to be legal."

"That's a wonderful thing to tell your lawyer." Sheldon hung up.

In an Internet café Pippa concocted a résumé for her new persona. Making something up took longer than expected and she nearly missed the flight out of Dallas. As she dropped into her last-row seat, the little old lady next to her smiled. *Please don't be a talker,* Pippa prayed. Then she saw the windup doll on the woman's lap.

Granny was sharper than she looked. In a moment she made the connection between her seat mate and her windup doll. "You should be ashamed of yourself, young lady." When Pippa failed to respond, the woman huffed, "Floozy!"

"Gesundheit!" Pippa barked back right in the woman's face.

While the old woman was readjusting her hearing aids, Pippa smiled, pleased with her counterattack: maybe she was finally getting back on her feet. She was now two aliases removed from the woman formerly known as Pippa Walker. Perdita Rica and Chippa Flushowitz had never met that doomed bride, nor would they. In a way Pippa never wanted to run into her old self again, either. She pulled her hat down over her face as the plastic doll squeaked, *I don't! I don't!* After half an hour the cheap screw broke and the doll went quiet. The old woman spent the rest of the trip bashing its head against her snack tray while Pippa self-medicated with toy bottles of vodka.

She located a walk-in beauty parlor at the Phoenix airport. "I've got sixty bucks. Can you get rid of the black?"

The girl inspected a lock of Pippa's hair as if it were attached to a skunk. "Who did this to you?"

"I did it myself. Never again."

"Have a seat. Where'd you get the shiner?"

That must have blossomed on the plane. "I was in a minor collision this morning."

The girl yammered on about a big fat Hispanic wedding she was doing that weekend. She didn't know if she could manage coiffures for six bridesmaids, two mothers, a stepmother, bride, and groom for three days running. Pippa tuned her out by trying to compute how many zeroes there were in a billion. She even managed to doze under the dryer. Next thing she knew the girl was standing over her with a mirror. "What do you think?"

Pippa's hair was the color of a plastic banana. It felt as coarse as raffia. "Was that the best you could do?"

"Considering what I had to work with, yes."

"But I'm trying to look like a matchmaker!"

"What's that?"

"One step below a marriage therapist, you dope!"

"A little trim will fix everything. I'll do it no charge."

Four inches came off. Instead of calming down, Pippa's hair now stuck straight out in every direction. The girl had never seen anything like it. "Hmm. That's odd."

"Odd?" Pippa shouted, beside herself. "I look like a blowfish on acid!"

She stomped to a phone at the other end of the airport and called Sheldon. He had booked a suite at the Phoenix Ritz-Carlton, bless his heart, and had honored her other requests as well. "Are you all right, Pippa? You sound stressed."

"I just had my hair done. It's the color of egg yolks." In combination with her red sheath and green flip-flops, she looked like a seriously disturbed van Gogh canvas.

"Very Polish." Sheldon hung up.

Pippa caught a shuttle to the hotel. Ignoring the stares of other guests, she walked to reception. "My name is Chippa Flushowitz. Mr. Sheldon Adelstein has booked a room for me."

The old fool had sent a cornucopia of gifts up there already. "Any luggage, ma'am?"

"No."

The manager handed over a key. "Will you be needing anything else?"

Pippa thought a moment. "Would you have anything that takes Magic Marker off?"

"Off what?"

"Skin."

"I'll take care of it. Have a pleasant stay." *Try not to snuff the old geezer on my shift.*

Pippa's mood improved somewhat when she saw that Prada had delivered three suits, one for each day of school, plus accessories and makeup. Extra halogen lights had been installed in her suite, even in the bathrooms. A new PC and several books about Poland were on her desk, as was an envelope containing six thousand dollars. Rather than take a chance on Pippa destroying any more cars, Sheldon had arranged for 24/7 livery service with a chauffeur named Mike, who was Polish. There was an ATM card for Chippa Flushowitz on the coffee table. *If you don't get through this one,* everything practically screamed, *you're hopeless.*

Mike Strebyzwynkiwicz tossed his kielbasa sandwich away as a very attractive woman approached his limousine at eight-thirty the next morning. Her suit looked like blueberry ice cream. Her dazzling blond tresses reminded him of his three sisters, all executive secretaries at prestigious trucking firms. That shadow peeping out beneath her sunglasses looked like a black eye, which meant she had been in a brawl. She looked a little hungover. What a woman! "Miss Flushowitz? I'm Mike. At your service."

"Hi." Pippa saw that the back seat of Mike's Lincoln contained a writing desk with DSL hookup. "I've got a nine o'clock class at Marvy Mates."

"Right up the road." Mike wondered what was so damn hard about matchmaking that you had to go to school for it. Come on! You took a piece of wood, diced it up, put red stuff on the tip. Maybe it took a lot of practice to cut each one the same size. He looked in his rearview mirror. Chippa was holding an ice cube to her black eye. "A bag of frozen peas works best," he called. "There's plenty of time to stop at Albertson's."

"Could you pick up a bagel and frosted coffee while you're at it?"

Mike reached for the other half of his kielbasa sandwich. "This is what you need. My own mother made it." She fervently believed in the curative powers of garlic.

Starving, Pippa ate the whole thing as she waited for Mike to fetch the frozen peas. She caked more concealer over her discolored eye before chugging the coffee. "That was delicious. Thanks."

"This school have any lunch breaks or will you be making matches all day?"

"I have no idea. Can you wait for me?"

"Sure. You got me 24/7." Mike pulled into the lot of a derelict strip mall. Everything was Space Available except for Marvy Mates and a gun store. "Here we are."

Pippa stepped into the blistering heat of the parking lot. "Wish me luck."

Little bells tinkled as the door of Marvy Mates shut behind her. She looked around the room, wondering whether purple velour couches, pink walls, and red heart-shaped rugs were good indications of what was to come. Cupids adorned every lampshade, pillow, statuette, mobile, poster, and clock. "Can't Buy Me Love" blasted from the sound system. Empty carbohydrates in all forms were piled on a table beneath the sign *MARVY MATES ALL YOU CAN EAT BREAKFAST BUFFET.* A fortysomething woman in a white business suit sat typing at her computer. Pippa saw at a glance that she spent every available penny trying to look twenty-five years younger than nature had wrought, with uneven success. "You must be Chippa!" she cried, bouncing off her chair. "I'm Marla!"

All those exclamation points knocked Pippa two steps backward. "Hello."

"Hot out there today, isn't it! At least it's dry heat!"

An oven made dry heat, too; that didn't mean Pippa wanted to spend time inside of one. She removed her hand from Marla's grasp. "I'm very excited to be here. Earning a degree in matchmaking means everything to me."

Probably had to do with her green card. "Please! Sit! Did you remember to bring your résumé?"

Pippa concentrated on a sappy Valentine poster as Marla read her résumé three times over. "So you have a degree in cheerleading from the University of Krakow?"

"Their course is world-famous." That didn't make a great impression so Pippa added, "I always like to see couples at sports events, cheering together."

"Then why aren't you a professional cheerleader?"

"I broke my hip doing a triple flip on the final exam."

"And you have a degree in pickling from the University of Warsaw?" Marla continued.

"Correct." Pippa had no recollection of having written this résumé. However, she'd have to live with it now. "Many cultures equate food with love. And Poles love pickles. So I thought I'd help people meet through food."

"What happened?"

"All of eastern Europe suffered a cucumber blight."

"Where'd you get the black eye?"

"I was in a car accident."

"Were you driving drunk?"

"It was nine o'clock in the morning." Marla still looked skeptical. "No, I was not drunk."

"Aha. Got a lover?"

Pippa's quicksilver repartee screeched to a halt. "Excuse me, but what does that have to do with a matchmaking degree?"

Marla removed her heart-shaped reading glasses and focused on Pippa. "People looking for life partners are in dire need of your help. They're sad. They don't need any more competition."

Pippa needed a few moments to even comprehend what that meant. "I'm not here fishing for a boyfriend, if that's what you're worried about."

"Many women come to do exactly that."

Through the pink gauze curtain Pippa happened to notice her

chauffeur unzip his pants and furtively relieve himself on a nearby tire. "If you must know, I'm involved with my driver." What the heck did he say his name was? "Mike."

Mollified, Marla let Pippa's résumé slide to her lap. "How did you find us?"

"In a poker magazine. Quite a unique place for an ad."

"Do you play?"

Disconcerted by Marla's hawkish stare, Pippa blurted, "Mike does. He's the Polish champion. In fact he's playing six games simultaneously as we speak. On the Net."

"I see." Something didn't add up here. Chippa reeked of garlic yet had a chauffeur. Why go to Krakow to study cheerleading? Pickles? The hair? If Marla didn't desperately need two thousand bucks for LASIK eye surgery, she'd reject this nutjob at once. "Have you brought your tuition?"

Pippa forked over two thousand dollars, for which she received a name tag and a one-page syllabus on purple paper. The course looked wonderfully flimsy. "I can hardly wait to get started."

The bells above the door jangled as Marla was stowing the cash in her safe. A buxom woman in a snakeskin miniskirt crashed in. She wore an almost vaudevillian layer of makeup and a Dolly Parton wig. Her white shaggy top would probably have looked better on a bathroom floor. "Morning," she called, going directly to the breakfast buffet. After piling her paper plate high, she nestled next to Pippa.

"Chippa?" she read between mouthfuls. "That's a doozy. I'm Patty."

The bells tinkled as a man evidently blowing through the final stretch of male-pattern baldness bounced in. He wore plaid pants, a polka dot shirt, and green socks with his sandals. "Hi, girls. I'm Sal. Single and available."

A Jewish grandmother marched in on Sal's heels. Her red polyester pantsuit fit perfectly with the cupid décor. "What? No more bagels?" she cried, observing the table. "I want a rebate."

"Pipe down," Patty bellowed. On her plate were all three. "Get here on time tomorrow."

A small, swarthy man in a dark wool suit entered last. He poured himself three cups of coffee before settling onto the cushions. "Hi."

"Everyone's here," Marla chirped, distributing name tags. "Helen.

Aram. Meet Chippa, Patty, and Sal. I'd like everyone to introduce himself or herself and explain what brought you to matchmaking school. Aram, please start."

The diminutive fellow in the dark suit said, "I'm from Armenia. I'm also a doorman at a very prestigious Fifth Avenue apartment building in New York. There are lots of investment bankers in my building, including women. Since I know everyone, and they've already passed background checks, I had the idea to set them up on dates with each other. It's easy to walk home afterward, no drunk driving. People are spending more time in, what with gyms and gardens in the same building, so what better person than myself to get paid for a high-quality dating service?"

"You've come to the right place." Marla smiled, although she would never in a million years heed advice from a doorman of such questionable origin. "How about you, Helen?"

The Jewish grandmother said, "I decided to take matters into my own hands when my daughter Sadie turned thirty and still had no boyfriend. I went online and pretended I was Sadie. Right away I found her a nice Jewish lawyer down the block from us in Los Angeles."

"Wonderful!" Marla clapped.

"Would you believe my own daughter turned around and sued me for false representation? Then she married the lawyer! So I have talent. I know who fits who."

Patty disentangled a raisin from her shag loops. "Did she win the case?"

"Yes, of course. I didn't set her up with a half-wit! Forty thousand dollars they cost me."

"How about you, Sal?"

Sal stood up, a riot of clashing plaids and dots. "I'm a used-car salesman from Little Rock. I have never been married. I guess I don't know how to look for a woman. When I started losing my hair, my customers stopped buying cars."

"Sure it wasn't your outfits?" Helen asked.

"No, it was my negative attitude. Now I embrace my baldness. I'm going to set up a national baldies dating service." He looked significantly at Helen. "That includes bald women, by the way."

"I'm seventy-two years old! What do you expect, Rapunzel?"

"Patty!" Marla intervened. "Tell us about yourself."

"I'm from Jacksonville. My rat bastard ex doesn't pay enough alimony to keep me styled as accustomed. So I need money. My idea is I read the obituaries and send the surviving partner a note that I know how to find a replacement quickly and efficiently."

"You do that before the funeral?" Helen gasped. "Not very high class."

"Oh! Pretending you're your daughter is?"

"Be nice now! Chippa, what about you?" Marla asked pleasantly.

Figuring her cheerleading and pickle fibs would never get past Helen, Pippa said, "I come from Poland, where many people are Catholic, meaning they can only get married once. So it has to be right the first time."

Class waited. "You call that a colorful story?" Helen finally asked.

"Let's move on." Marla strode to a whiteboard easel near a heart-shaped beanbag chair. "What sort of person becomes a matchmaker?"

A meddling control freak, Pippa thought, but dared not say.

"A happiness enabler!" Marla wrote the words in tight, cramped block letters. "What sort of person needs a matchmaker?"

A stupid loser, Pippa thought, but dared not say.

"A happiness seeker!" Marla scratched on the board. She drew four arrows going back and forth between the words and stepped back to admire her work. "There you have it in a nutshell!"

Everyone stared at the words, mentally calculating that, at two thousand bucks for twenty-four hours of instruction, they had just passed the one-hundred-dollar mark. It didn't seem like much of a bargain, even with breakfast. Thinking all the frowns represented profound appreciation, Marla plunged ahead. "How many people does it take to make a perfect match?"

"One," Helen volunteered. "The matchmaker."

"Two," Patty countered. "The matchmaker and the matchee."

"Three," Aram said. "The matchmaker, the matchee, and the other matchee."

Sal went with, "Four. The matchmaker, the matchee, the other matchee, and the mother-in-law."

"Five," Pippa said. "The matchmaker, the matchee, the other matchee, the mother-in-law, and the other mother-in-law."

"We're getting warm," Marla said. "Do you see how complicated it is? The match is only the tip of the iceberg of everlasting happiness."

"What's the right answer?" Helen was still sure it was "one."

"Ten," Marla crowed, writing each word as she went down the list. "Matchmaker, matchee one, matchee two, mother-in-law one, mother-in-law two, domesticated animals, motor vehicles, matchee one's job, matchee two's job, and religion. Ten!"

"You said people, not things," Helen complained. "Otherwise I could have told you that whole list. I was married for sixty years. I should know."

Sal was aghast. "You got married when you were twelve? Rapunzel?"

"My parents and his parents fixed it in the old country. We were very happy together."

"The laws of probability dictate that even forced pedophile marriages can work," Marla assured her class. "Remember, if seventy percent of couples end up in divorce court, thirty percent do not! Chippa, may I ask what you're doing?"

"Writing down the ten tips of the happiness iceberg." Pippa was sure this would be a major exam question. "What did you say after 'sex'?"

"I did not say 'sex'," Marla said icily.

Patty was dumbstruck. "People have to be compatible in bed, don't they? I mean, most husbands want sex seven times a week. Most wives will tolerate it seven times a year. Shouldn't the matchmaker try to hook up the nymphos with the sex fiends and the frigid women with the numb nuts?"

Marla jammed the cap back on her dry-ink pen. "That would be futile. Women hunting for spouses always overstate their sex drives. Men always minimize it."

"I thought the whole point of going to a matchmaker was to present an honest picture of yourself."

"That concept is so off the wall I'm not even going there." Marla laughed. "Here's the real situation: there are over *one hundred million* single adults in the United States, all searching for an ideal partner who doesn't exist."

"Doesn't exist?" Pippa was aghast. "I had an ideal partner."

"Is that so! What happened to him?"

"He died," Pippa faltered.

"Consider yourself lucky. He punched out before the lights came on."

"Such attitude!" Helen gasped. "I had a 'marvy mate' for sixty years, miss. It's not a fantasy."

"Fine. I'll revise my statement: there are over one hundred million people out there searching for a needle in a haystack. I'm going to teach you how to line your pockets assisting them." Marla passed out a sheaf of papers. "Sign this first, please."

Aram couldn't get past the first line of legalese. "Could you translate this into English?"

"It's a noncompetition clause. I will be sharing my trade secrets. Therefore you will promise not to teach matchmaking within five hundred miles of Phoenix." Marla dry-erased every word on her whiteboard as her students signed the contracts. "Let's get right down to interviewing techniques. Your road to riches begins with the interview." *Bait the hook*, she wrote. "Patty, would you mind going next door and asking for a volunteer?"

"From the gun store?"

"Yes. The place should be crawling with bachelors."

Marla sang along with "You Are My Sunshine" until Patty returned with a fellow in a plaid flannel shirt. "This is Brad."

"Good morning, Brad! Help yourself to breakfast then come a little closer." Marla studied her volunteer as he consumed a banana muffin. "Chippa! What do you notice about this person?"

"Ah—he's a male," she said cautiously.

"Age?"

"In the prime of life."

"How is he dressed?"

"For hunting."

"His physical condition?"

Oh boy. "He seems hearty."

"Very good, Chippa. You're trying to put a positive spin on a client who is sloppy, obese, and probably illiterate."

"That's pretty malicious," Sal muttered.

"A good matchmaker is objective." Marla scratched the word on the whiteboard. "Able to assess raw material quickly and accurately. Sit down, Brad."

He sprawled on a heart-shaped beanbag chair, smiling at Patty. She was a hot mama in his book. "What does his body language tell you?" Marla asked. No one wanted to touch that one so she continued. "Observe the knees apart, the genitals in your face. That means he's sexually insecure. Probably not well endowed. The poor posture means low self-esteem. Arms outstretched over the chair? Not at home in the corporate world. Probably destitute. Looking for a woman with money. What does the matchmaker do at this point?"

"I'd tell him to go home, lose forty pounds, get a haircut, and come back when he's more presentable," old Helen said. "Otherwise there's nothing I can do for him."

"I'm sorry, that's the wrong response. A loser like this is your best customer. He's going to come back ten times to get set up with a date. At one hundred dollars a shot, that's a thousand bucks in your pocket. Observe closely." Marla warmly shook her specimen's hand. "Thanks for coming in, Brad. I'm so happy we'll be working together. Tell me about yourself." She pulled up a chair and leaned forward, electric with curiosity. "Notice my posture, class. I want to telegraph that I *care,* but in a professional way. I want to telegraph that I find this tub of lard attractive, fascinating, and unique."

To no one's surprise but Marla's, Brad ended the interview. "I'd rather date a muskrat than a bitch like you." He left, slamming the door so hard that the bells fell off their hook.

"He'll be back," Marla shrugged. "And I'm going to charge him a hundred-dollar reenlistment fee. Chippa, would you mind taking Brad's place on the hot seat?"

Pippa unenthusiastically sat on the warm cushion.

"Miss Flushowitz," Marla continued pleasantly. "Before I find your perfect mate, we need to get a few things straight. Number one, do you have a police record of any kind? That means arrests, convictions, current or pending DUIs, spousal abuse, pedophilia, restraining orders, kidnapping, or just plain spitting in public."

"No, ma'am."

"I think you're lying to me, Chippa."

"I was just trying to absorb that list of criminal offenses." Pippa saw that wasn't the correct answer. "I did get a speeding ticket a few weeks ago."

"Ah! I knew it!" Marla turned to the class. "Speeding indicates aggressive behavior."

"I wasn't being aggressive, I was just listening to the stereo and lost track of the speedometer."

"So you were being careless! Daydreaming! Arrested juvenile development," Marla crowed. She smiled sweetly. "Chippa, do you have any sexually transmitted diseases?"

"Excuse me?"

"That's an outrageous question," Patty sputtered. "You can't be asking people that."

"Why not? It's a legitimate concern, isn't it? After 'are you rich?' it's the next topic on most people's minds, if we're honest about it."

"I don't think it's constitutional to ask medical questions," Sal said. "If people like each other, they'll find out soon enough."

"Chippa, what is your sexual orientation?"

"For someone who left sex off the happiness iceberg, you sure are nosy," Helen sniffed.

"A matchmaker has to know a client's sexual bent or there will be disaster. Look what happened to that jock in Texas. Jilted at the altar. Millions of dollars wasted because he never realized his fiancée was a serial fornicator."

"The guy is gay," Patty snorted. "You can tell just by looking at him."

"She led him on," Aram said. "Gold digger."

"She did not!" Pippa shouted. "She had just as much money as he did!"

"Enough! We're not here to talk about a couple of buffoons in Texas," Marla cut in, waving her hands. "Chippa, just answer the question. What is your sexual orientation?"

"I believe I've made that clear."

"Oh, yes. The chauffeur," Marla drawled. "Well, I won't be setting you up with any college professors. What is your annual income?"

The room became very still as Pippa did a few calculations based on passing the matchmaking course. "Eighty million dollars."

Everyone burst out laughing. "This just goes to show how outrageously people exaggerate," Marla said.

"Take it or leave it." Pippa shrugged.

Marla left it. "What do you require in a mate, Chippa?"

"Character, integrity, ambition, intelligence, wit, discipline, talent, patience—"

"Whoa! Whoa! We're looking for a mate, not Superman!" Marla shook her head. "Do you notice what Chippa left out, class? Loads of money and great sex. The first two requirements on everyone's list. This client is a problem. Do you consider yourself good in bed, Chippa?"

"Are you serious?"

"Absolutely. How can I match you with someone if I don't know you like it?"

Pippa sighed. Two more days and she'd be out of here. "I suppose I am good in bed."

Aram raised his hand. "Do you really expect me, a doorman, to ask people in my building, female investment bankers and the like, if they are good at blow jobs before I set them up with their neighbors, also investment bankers?"

Marla covered her face with perfectly manicured hands. Maybe she was just showing off her eight turquoise Navajo rings. "I am trying to teach you how to conduct a meaningful interview. Online dating services ask much more invasive questions and people answer them without batting an eyelash."

The door burst open: Brad had indeed returned, with a gun. He proceeded to shoot every heart-shaped balloon and cuckoo clock in the room to smithereens. As the class dove for cover he obliterated every dish on the buffet table. "How's that for inadequate!" he shouted before flipping the table over and leaving.

Marla watched his truck fishtail out of the parking lot. "I had no idea hunters were that neurotic. Get off the floor, everyone. He's gone."

"What if he comes back with reinforcements?" Aram cried.

"He wouldn't dare. I know the type. I married five of them."

Sal cleared his throat. "If you don't mind, Marla, I'd like my money back."

"Sorry," she murmured, inspecting a muffin for bullets. "Tuition is nonrefundable."

"Since when?"

"I suppose you didn't read the small print at the bottom of the non-competition clause. Is anyone going to help me clean up this mess?"

Day one of matchmaking school didn't adjourn until six because of the precious time lost cleaning up the buffet table. In addition to covering Legal Risks of Matchmaking, Handwriting Analysis, Pros and Cons of Sleeping with Clients, Raising Fees Without Raising Eyebrows, Developing Client Dependency, Decorating Your Office, and That Winning Smile, Marla had passed out homework that would count for thirty percent of the final grade. The assignment dealt with client development, an area Marla harped on throughout the afternoon because, obviously, a successful matchmaker lost cash cows at a terrifying rate. Each student was to go to a bar of his or her choice and strike up a conversation with the first individual seen sitting alone. With the help of Marla's "conversation compost," as she liked to call a list of leading questions, the student was expected to harvest new fodder for matchmaking school by the end of the evening.

To prepare for this assignment Pippa lay in her bubble bath sipping Champagne as she studied Marla's suggested lines. When she felt confident with them, she dressed in a pink Prada suit and doused herself with the Thayne perfume she had brought in her purse to Phoenix. Hoping to counteract the negative visuals of a black eye and yellow hair, she donned a pair of stacked heels, a pillbox hat, and long gloves matching her pink suit. She had no jewelry, which made her feel naked, so she applied extra-thick lip gloss and mascara. At the stroke of ten she walked into the bar of the Ritz-Carlton.

There was only one lone man sitting amid the couples at the bar. Pippa quickly acquired the vacant seat next to him, noticing too late that he was the quintessential tall, dark, and handsome male of the species and would need a matchmaking service about as much as he needed a third testicle. *Don't be fooled,* Marla's voice reassured her. *Any guy who frequents a bar at ten o'clock needs help.*

"Hello." Pippa smiled. "What's that you're drinking?"

"Plantation rum." He tried not to stare. She looked as if she had just wandered in from the Macy's Easter parade, circa 1960, except for the hair and shiner. Nice perfume. "Care to join me?"

"I'll have a rusty nail," Pippa told the bartender, slapping a fifty on the bar. Under no circumstances was she to allow a prospective client to buy her a drink.

"Love the hat."

"This old thing? Thank you." He was disconcertingly handsome. He wore a gorgeous shirt and a Breguet watch with many complications. To Pippa's dismay, her mind went blank. She couldn't remember the first line of Marla's spiel if a billion bucks depended on it. And it did. To pass the time she laboriously adjusted her long gloves.

"What brings you to Phoenix?" he asked after what seemed like eons.

What would a matchmaker say? What what what? "I've been mating people."

"Really! How many people have you been mating with?"

If they get personal, change the subject. As her rusty nail arrived, Pippa finally remembered Marla's opening line. "My name is Marla." Shit! "I mean Chippa."

"Sure about that?" She was too busy chugging her drink to reply. "I'm pretty sure my name's Cole."

Pippa remembered Marla's second line. "How's your love life?"

"That's what I call direct. It's fine. How's yours?"

A wildfire blush overtook her face. "You're supposed to say something like 'could be better.' "

"Okay, it could be better. How's yours?"

Like a drowning rat Pippa leaped to the third line of Marla's scenario. "Are you presently married?"

"No. How about you?"

"Will you stop asking personal questions?" she snapped. "I've had a long day."

Cole watched her order a second rusty nail. Guys at the bar were beginning to notice her little pillbox hat and long gloves. With the hair and black eye, the combo was a huge turn-on. He sat for a long while simply inhaling her perfume. Every ten seconds a torrid blush swept across her cheeks. He watched her heavily glossed lips close around the tiny straw when her cocktail arrived. "Nice weather we're having," he said.

Weather? By now she should be leading him through the ten points of the happiness iceberg! As she tried to salvage an interview worth thirty percent of her grade, Pippa's straw began uncouthly sucking air at the bottom of her drink. *Think like a Walker, you idiot!* What would her mother do, backed into such a corner? Ah!

Pippa regained a grain of composure. "I have a proposition for you," she said, scratching a phone number on a napkin. "Call this number at nine o'clock tomorrow morning and ask for ten sessions with Marla. I'll pay you a thousand dollars."

Was she into threesomes? Maybe she liked to watch. Nine in the morning was a bit kinky, though. "I'd prefer ten sessions with you," Cole said. "Tonight. At the going rate, of course."

"What? How dare you!" Pippa smacked the guy with her Prada purse and fled.

The next morning at 8:45 sharp, Mike the chauffeur was waiting outside the Ritz-Carlton with a homemade kielbasa sandwich, iced coffee, and frozen peas. The temperature was already ninety-five degrees. Where was Miss Flushowitz? He hated delivering people late to their destinations. Mike was about to ring her room when Pippa burst through the revolving door and dove into the back seat of the limousine. "Floor it!"

Mike did the best he could with his hands full. "Everything all right back there?"

Absolutely not. After a sleepless night, steeping in humiliation, the last thing she needed was to see Cole in the lobby. He even had the effrontery to blow her a kiss! "Couldn't be better."

"Did you finish your homework?"

"Let's just say my homework finished me."

"I brought a little breakfast for you."

"Thanks." Pippa chewed in silence until they arrived at Marvy Mates. "Here goes nothing."

"You make those matches, now!"

Pippa's classmates looked even less eager to start a second day of instruction than did she. Yesterday's buffet having met an untimely end, there was no food on offer; in its stead Marla had inflated several dozen heart-shaped balloons and filled a bowl with cherry lollipops. Dressed in a turquoise pantsuit with one-inch pink stripes running horizontally on the jacket, vertically on the pants, she looked remarkably fresh. "Well! How did everyone make out last night?"

For his efforts Sal sported five stitches on his jaw. Aram had spent several hours in jail. Old Helen had gone to a McDonald's and had forty eager clients lined up, all aged twelve. Patty had slept with both of her prospects, not on purpose. One thing just led to another. Marla was beside herself with disgust. "What about the Polish Wonder?"

Before Pippa could respond, the phone rang. Marla ran to her desk. "Marvy Mates! Leave nothing to fate, your soul mate awaits! Marla Marble speaking!" She listened a moment, put the caller on hold, and announced, "Listen carefully, class, we're going on speaker phone!" She cleared her throat. "Ten sessions, you said? I'd be delighted! That will be one thousand dollars! A small investment in your happiness!"

"So I guess it's a wash," the fellow's voice said.

"I beg your pardon?"

"I was referred by Chippa Flushowitz. Would you know how I might reach her? She's a very persuasive saleswoman."

Marla knew exactly where he was going. "For your information, Miss Flushowitz's lover is the Polish poker champion. She is in the pickle business. Unless you're a hairdresser, she has no use for you whatsoever."

"Let's talk about it over lunch," the man said.

"Two thousand dollars."

"You drive a hard bargain, Marla. Where would you like to meet?"

"Coup des Tartes. You're buying." Marla hung up. "Gotcha! Nice work, Chippa. Is he cute?"

Pippa had been up all night thinking about the man's eyes, voice, mouth, hair, and hands. "He might be gay."

Marla bounced to the whiteboard. "Where were we?"

"Dating Techniques," Aram read tonelessly from the syllabus.

"I just *love* this chapter! Class, after you've racked your brain setting up your clients with a match, you'll have to give them a few pointers on etiquette. I need volunteers." No one moved. "Sal and Helen! Let's pretend this is your first date. You're both a little nervous. What's the first thing you're going to do?"

"Order a stiff manhattan," Sal said.

"Are you out of your mind? Do you want to tell the world you're an insecure zero before you even open your mouth?"

"But I would have done the same thing," Helen protested.

"Whatever. Let's say you're both slurping a couple of manhattans to get over the nerves. What are you going to talk about?"

"My husband Jerome." Helen beamed. "He was a prince."

"No no no! Do *not* talk about spouses living or dead! Do *not* dwell on the past! Do not discuss children, family, religion, sex, income, politics, your hip replacement, or any other hot-button topics on a first date!"

"So what's left?" Helen wanted to know.

"Omigod! The weather. Sports. Vacations. Food. Small talk! And all the while you're discussing your favorite denture creams and toupee glue, what are you *really* doing?"

Sal looked mystified. "Getting hungry?"

"You're observing body language. Reading between the lines."

"That's pretty hard to do after a few manhattans," Sal said.

"Which is why you *Don't. Drink. Them.* Chippa, what was this fellow's name again?"

Cole. His eyes were kind of like coal, come to think of it. "I forget."

"Did he look rich?"

All four feet ten inches of Aram shot off the couch. "Are we students or pimps? This course is a waste of my good time and two thousand dollars! You are pathetic, miss."

"I agree," Patty said. "No offense, Marvy Marla, but that outfit would scare a zebra."

Marla's lower lip quivered. "Is that the way you all feel?" Every head but Pippa's nodded in vigorous agreement. "Fine!"

She opened her safe and withdrew a piece of parchment paper. Marla signed it, melted some red wax, stamped it with a heart, and tied it up with red ribbon. She flung it in Pippa's lap. "This course is officially over. Everyone has failed but Chippa."

Pippa unrolled her diploma. It certainly looked official except for one thing. "Where's my name?"

"Fill it in yourself." Marla headed for the door. "I'm going for a walk."

"I want my money back!" Aram shouted. "Either my money or my diploma!"

Marla calmly took a big red hat from its red hook. "I repeat: you

have all failed the course. You do not have the fundamental humanity
to become matchmakers."

"I'll sue!" Patty screamed.

"Be my guest. After five divorces, I know who the killer lawyers are."

Little old Helen suddenly plastered herself to the front door, impeding Marla's exit. "Make you a deal, miss. We'll play you for our
diplomas. One quick game settles it."

Pippa felt the hair rise along the back of her neck as Marla's face
softened into an addict's narcotic smile. "Play?" she echoed.

"You heard me. Poker."

It all suddenly fell into place. Pippa nearly laughed at her own stupidity. "I'm afraid I don't know a thing about poker," she said with a
winsome smile. "Maybe I'll just leave and let you all sort out the refunds."

Marla snatched Pippa's diploma away. "You want your diploma,
you play for it."

"But I've only played once in my life!" With André in Prague. Strip
poker at that.

"Then get your Polack boyfriend to play for you. I've always wanted
to see how I stacked up against a champion."

"Can I please have that back?" Pippa whimpered, on the verge of
tears.

"No!" Marla pushed her out the door.

Pippa stood paralyzed in the blinding sunshine, staring at her
empty hands. Just a few moments ago they had held a signed diploma,
the passport to her new life. Now she was stripped clean. Looted!
How could she have stood there, flat-footed as an oaf, as events spiraled downward?

The limousine door swung open. "Taking a lunch break, Miss
Flushowitz?" Mike unstrapped the water bottle lashed to his shin.
"You okay? Here, have a drink."

"Tell me something, Mike. Do you play poker?"

"Now and then, at family holidays. I'm not a habitual gambler or
anything."

"Are you any good?"

He hadn't won a game in his life. All those combinations to remember plus smoke, whiskey, indigestion, football. "It depends on the
cards. Why?"

"I'm going to ask a big favor. Five people are starting up a game. I have to play or I lose my diploma. I'd like you to play for me."

He scratched a little sand out of his ear. "I thought you were all inside making matches."

"That didn't work out. I told a little white lie, Mike. I said you were the poker champion of Poland. Now everyone wants to play with you. Against you, actually. If you won my diploma back, I would certainly make it worth your while."

He thought a moment. "Happy to do it! You got me 24/7, remember?"

Pippa took two thousand dollars from her purse. "Here's something for the pot. That's all I know about poker. It takes money."

"Yikes! This is *really* money!"

She watched him fold the thick wad into his pocket. "The lady in the stripes is a little unstable. She thinks you're out here writing a book and playing six games on the Internet at the same time."

"I'll have to undestabilize her right away."

"Please don't." Pippa clutched Mike's sleeve. "Just go along with anything she says. It's good poker strategy. And I wouldn't talk much. Silence is intimidating."

Mike wasn't sure what she was telling him to do, but he didn't want to let her down. She looked pretty anxious about the diploma. "Let me get this straight. We're not in it for the money."

"That's right. But you can keep any money you happen to win."

"Sounds good to me."

They went inside Marvy Mates. The shades were drawn. Everyone was seated around a heart-shaped coffee table. In front of each player was a small pile of cash and a plastic cup full of whiskey. Aram expertly shuffled the cards. "Have a seat," he called. "So you're the Polish cham-peen?"

Rather than lie, Mike said nothing. "He doesn't like to talk," Pippa explained, sitting behind him.

In an effort to sap her opponents' concentration and get out of there by lunch, Marla had seriously unbuttoned the jacket of her turquoise suit. "Hello," she said. He was kind of cute in a bumpkin-lumpkin way. "Love the uniform. Is that a thinking cap?"

"Enough *small talk*." Aram smoothly dealt five cards to each player.

"Twenty bucks gets you in. No limits." As everyone tossed a twenty into the pot, he saw Helen reverently place a small plastic Virgin Mary on the table and rub the statuette's head. "What's that?"

"My good-luck charm."

Patty frowned. "I thought you were Jewish."

"So? You want me to put a Torah on the table?"

Marla went to her desk and opened a drawer. She donned a pair of velvet reindeer antlers and returned to the table. "If she can have a good-luck charm, so can I."

Aram shook his head in disgust. "Kiddies got all their toys? Let's get started then."

Helen picked up her five cards and uttered a foul oath at her Virgin Mary. "I fold."

Sal silently placed twenty bucks in the pot. Patty slid twenty in and added twenty.

Mike stared at the cards in his hand. Anything with a picture was good, he remembered. He had one of them, so he put a thousand bucks on the table. For some reason everyone gasped.

"You trying to kill us, Mack?" Marla cried.

"He's not the Polish champion for nothing," Pippa snapped back. "Where's that diploma?"

"In my bra." Marla put a thousand bucks on the table then added another hundred.

Aram folded. Sal and Patty asked for two more cards so Mike held up two fingers, too. He saw that they discarded two cards, so he did the same. Sal folded. So did Patty. Mike added another thousand bucks to the pot. Once again, everyone gasped.

"You rob banks or something?" Marla inquired, her velvet antlers bobbing. "I think you're bluffing."

Mike remained silent as he tried to remember what bluffing meant. Marla put another thousand bucks on the table, plus one dollar. After a few minutes of silence, Aram said, "You raising her, Mack? We don't have all day."

Erase her? Mike shook his head no. Aram said, "Okay, let's see what you got."

The table stared at his hand. Patty finally said, "You bet two grand on a stinkin' pair of jacks?"

That was apparently enough to beat Marla's pair of tens. "Take the money," Pippa whispered in Mike's ear. "You won."

Mike slowly acquired the drift of the game, although to Pippa's dismay he lost almost a thousand dollars in the process. Helen noticed that every time she swore at the Virgin Mary, Mike turned beet red then lost the round. Marla noticed that every time she coyly fingered her moose antlers, Mike turned beet red then lost the round. Patty noticed the same effect when she pulled at the loops on her shag top.

"Let's take ten," Aram said after an hour. "I need a smoke."

Pippa had a massive tension headache. Her diploma was still firmly ensconced in Marla's bra. She herded Mike into the limousine for a pep talk.

"I'm sorry, Miss Flushowitz," he said. "I started out with a bang then got lost."

"It's okay. I know you're trying." Pippa was already online in the back seat reading up on poker strategy. "We have to make Marla lose all her money so she antes up the diploma. Then we have to win that. Do you know what a royal flush is?" She read from a list onscreen. "Ace, king, queen, jack, and ten all in the same suit. It's the best hand in poker. Do you know what a straight flush is?" No. "Five cards in order, all one suit. That's next best after a royal flush." Pippa reviewed every possible combination as well as the rules of the game. Mike seemed to get everything but the concept of bluffing.

"That's like lying, isn't it? I'm not sure my priest would like that. Or my gambling."

"Bluffing is like a quarterback feint in football. And it's not really gambling when you're playing with someone else's money. If you get a good hand, go for the jugular."

"That's just below a full house, right?"

Pippa felt lightning behind her eyes. She should never have dragged the poor chauffeur into this shark tank. What would Thayne do in such a situation? Cheat, obviously. "I have an idea. If you hear me clear my throat, raise your bet." Mike looked uncertain about the ethics of that. "If everybody else has a little mascot, you can have me." Pippa gave him two thousand bucks. She only had twenty left in her purse. "I think Marla's a bluffer. So's Helen. Don't let them scare you when they raise the ante. Whenever Sal gets a good hand, he pulls his ear. When Aram gets a good hand, he bites his lip. When Patty gets a good hand, she plays with her shag loops."

"You noticed all that?" Mike had enough on his mind just remembering if flushes were better than jugulars. They went inside. No one spoke. As he took his seat Mike glanced at Marla, who had just put on a pair of heart-shaped reading glasses. They looked quite menacing with the stuffed antlers.

Marla smiled. "I'm going to kill you now, Polack."

Shivering, Mike watched Aram cut the deck. Oh, to be back in his limousine! He should have confessed right off the bat that he knew nothing about poker. *Polack!*

Pippa gently squeezed his shoulder. "You can do it. Stay cool."

Everyone put twenty in the pot. Mike was dealt a pair of nines. That seemed pretty good so when his turn came he bet a thousand dollars.

Marla peeled twelve hundred off a wad secreted in her bra next to the diploma. For an international poker champion, the chauffeur played quite inconsistently. Sometimes he bet big on low cards. Other times he bet small on high cards. He folded with medium cards. Was there a method to his madness or was he just an idiot? "Raise you two hundred, Polack."

Sal, Aram, and Helen folded. Patty pushed twelve hundred and ten bucks into the pot. She and Marla each wanted two cards. Mike took three cards and got a third eight. The table waited in tense silence for him to make his move. "You in, Polack?" Aram finally asked.

That was three "Polacks" in the last two minutes! Exercising superhuman restraint, Mike put a thousand and twenty dollars in the pot. Marla didn't meet that, nor did Patty. Mike won with his triple eights.

Helen unleashed a torrent of obscenities at her Virgin Mary. "I've never seen someone win so much money with such bastard cards."

"Polack," Sal muttered. "Makes a soufflé out of a friggin' pierogi."

"They're trying to get you angry, Mike," Pippa whispered as she noticed his ears redden. She couldn't lose him now: by some miracle he had won the last round. Marla was out of cash. Pippa could almost taste her diploma. "You're winning. Hang in there."

"Looks like you're going to have to play that diploma, Bullwinkle," Sal said.

Marla downed another plastic cup filled with scotch. She had tem-
porarily lost possession of the two thousand bucks earmarked for her
LASIK eye surgery. The Polack was cagier than she first thought, so
she would need a major good-luck charm. Marla went to the coat
closet, unearthed an old Navajo cape, and returned to the table.

"What is that rag?" Patty asked as Aram dealt. "I can smell the
horse piss all the way over here."

"Do you mind? I'm cold." Marla extracted the squished diploma
from her bra and tore off a corner. "That's twenty bucks."

Pippa shot to her feet. "No fair!"

Everyone agreed. "Fine," Marla sulked. "You lend me twenty to
get into the game then."

Pippa put her last twenty on the table. Helen, Sal, and Aram threw
their last twenties into the pot as well. After looking at their cards, they
uttered fireballs of profanity and folded.

Marla dropped the diploma on the table. "That's two thousand
bucks." She watched, mouth open, as Patty divested herself of fifteen
hundred in cash, her Seiko watch, her aquamarine navel ring, and two
earrings. "What do you call that trash pile?"

"Two thousand and fifty bucks. If you can bet a diploma, I can bet
jewelry. Those diamond studs alone are worth three grand."

"Those are cubic zirconia," Pippa shouted.

"Shut up! You're not even in the game!"

After a black silence Marla cooed, "Sweeten the pot, honey."

Patty flung a pair of tickets on top of the Seiko. "Skybox seats to
the next Diamondbacks game. Your turn, Polack."

Every cell in Pippa's body screamed at her to snatch the diploma
off the table and run. This was the round Mike absolutely had to win.
Summoning her last iota of courage, she peeped over Mike's shoulder
and nearly collapsed: he had just gotten the worst deal of the day.
Nothing! She cursed herself for having told him a signal to bet the
farm, not a signal to fold. *Fold! Fold, you idiot!* Pippa could feel
the tension rise around the table as everyone waited for the Polish
champion to reveal himself. She was acutely aware of warm scotch
fumes, Patty's struggling deodorant, and an increasingly vile odor emanating from the Navajo cape. Pippa's nose began to itch. Was that
thing made out of wool? She was allergic to wool.

As if she could read Pippa's mind, Marla refluffed the filthy material, sending a cloud of dander and dust into the air. Two seconds later Pippa sneezed. Then she coughed. Her sinuses were closing up faster than summer camp on Labor Day.

Mike pricked up his ears. Had Chippa just cleared her throat? Had she coughed or sneezed? She was definitely making odd nasal noises. Just in the nick of time, too. He had been ready to fold.

Everyone's heart skipped a beat as Mike pushed all his cash into the pile at the center of the table. Busy blowing her nose, Pippa didn't realize what had happened until Helen said to Marla, "You'll raise *that?*"

Marla caressed her velvet reindeer antlers. Through her alcoholic haze she realized that no one had any more money to bet with. She smiled: nothing was more exciting than driving six fellow humans to the brink of ruin. "No, I won't raise."

"Patty?"

Patty thought briefly about signing away her IRA and her two kids. "No."

"That's it, then," Aram said. "Winner take all."

Marla had a pair of fives. Mike had zilch. Patty had a pair of sixes. "Yeehaw!" she crowed, gathering cash, jewelry, and diploma to her shaggy bosom. "I WON!"

Pippa watched from another galaxy as Patty grabbed the diploma and ran into the bathroom. The toilet flushed. Patty emerged.

"Where's my diploma?" Pippa croaked.

"I used it for toilet paper. That's more than it's worth. Great game, guys! Happy matchmaking!" The little bells above the door tinkled merrily as Patty bounded out.

Sneezing, Pippa wavered to her feet. Her eyes were nearly swollen shut. The last thing she saw before stumbling out of Marvy Mates was Marla Marbles, ghoulishly regal in her Navajo cape, heart-shaped eyeglasses, and velvet reindeer antlers. "Some champ you turned out to be, Polack," Marla sneered.

Thirteen

Rather than knock Marla unconscious, which was very tempting, Mike raced out to the parking lot. Pippa was doubled over, sneezing. Her face had turned dark red. Her black eye looked like the dog's on the Bud Lite commercials. "Miss Flushowitz! Are you all right?"

"No. I am not all right," she wheezed, her eyes overflowing with tears. "Why on earth did you make that last bet? You lost everything!"

"I thought you cleared your throat."

"You can't tell the difference between a sneeze and clearing your throat? Thanks to you my diploma's literally down the toilet!"

She was crying as if her mother had just died. Mike felt terrible. "I was disrupted. Those women were calling me Polack and swearing at the Virgin."

"Just unlock the door, will you? Let's get out of here."

"I can go inside and get another diploma if you want."

She hesitated. "How would you propose to do that?"

How else? "Beat up Marla."

Guffawing, Pippa got into the back seat. Last thing she needed was an assault and battery suit from a professional victim. She opened the refrigerator, drank a pint of water, and plopped the mushy bag of peas over her black eye. Another school, another failure: what a nightmare.

Mike turned the AC on full blast. The temperature inside the limo could melt glass. "Can I take you out for a beer?"

"Just take me back to the hotel."

He drove dejectedly out of the lot. "Those guys were pros."

"No, just addicts." She sighed. "Guess my matchmaking career went up in smoke."

"So who needs matches?" He slid open the partition. "Use this."

Pippa inspected the small stainless steel case in her lap. It appeared to be a cigarette lighter.

"My brother made it custom," Mike said proudly. "He's a welder. Press the little white button and you get a flame. Press the black button, you get Mace."

"Are you joking? Isn't that dangerous?"

"Why? Sometimes I drive in bad neighborhoods. Sometimes there are vicious dogs. Sometimes people need to light their cigarettes. Why not combine everything in one handy gizmo? We already sent an application to the patent office."

Good luck with that one. "Have you ever sprayed Mace in a person's face? Or torched their dog by mistake?"

"I can tell the difference between a black and a white button. All we need now is a name. What do you think about 'Fire Bomb'?"

"It's a little strong." Pippa noticed a brochure for Marvy Mates on the seat. A squished pea covered the top of the *t* so that it looked like a *c*. "How about Marvy Mace?"

"I don't know about that Marvy. We need something about a lighter. Or a match."

"MatchMace."

"That's perfect!" How did she think of that so fast? Mike and his brother had been cracking their heads together for months. "We'll give you a penny for each one we sell."

"That's okay. I'm glad to help."

Looking in the rearview mirror, Mike saw a tear rolling down his passenger's cheek. Desperate to make her smile, he slid his hand into a puppet that he kept in the front seat. He was pretty good at driving with his left hand and putting on a puppet show with his right. Kids liked it. "How's the weather back there?" he bleated in a Tiny Tim soprano.

Pippa stared at the puppet. "What now?"

"I'm Clownie," the puppet squeaked. "Can you smile for me? A tiny one? A really tiny one?"

"Mike, put that stupid thing away."

"I am not a stupid thing," Clownie protested. "And I'm not going away until you smile. That's better! You're so cute when you smile. If I looked like you, I'd be smiling all the time."

"You're already smiling all the time. It's painted on."

Mike had to retire Clownie in order to make a few turns for the hotel. He opened Pippa's door and was glad to see the shadow of a smile still on her face. "I'll wait in the lot. You got me 24/7, remember."

Pippa tried to give his lighter back. "Keep this in case Marla shows up."

"No way! That's yours."

Pippa sneezed one last time as she slipped the thing in her purse. "Please go to the restaurant if you're hungry. Or the bar. Charge it to my room. I don't know how long I'll be." Forever, if she drowned herself in the bathtub.

In the hotel elevator Pippa tried to ignore a Rosimund-ish woman glaring at the bag of frozen peas pressed to her eye. Uneasy with the way another gold-plated harridan was studying her face, Pippa left the elevator on the third floor and took the stairs to her room. Matchmaking school was history before she had even unwrapped her second lipstick: Sheldon would go ballistic.

Her room was dim and as cold as an igloo at midnight. As she walked to the drapes, wondering how she'd present her latest failure to him, Pippa tripped over the cord attached to an extra reading lamp. She remained on the floor for quite a while before crawling to the phone. "Is there a guest named Cole at the hotel?" She should warn him off Marla. "I don't know his last name. He was in the bar last night."

The front desk searched. "He checked out this morning, ma'am." No last name offered.

Pippa couldn't remember the name of the restaurant where they were meeting for lunch. Didn't matter: Cole could handle Marla. He could probably handle any woman on the planet. Pippa asked for room service. Chocolate chip cookies, unlike the male of the species, had never let her down. As she devoured the life-affirming morsels, Pippa wondered what to do with herself next. If mistakes were the best teachers, as her grandfather had said, she should be president of Mensa by now.

Unfortunately she could think of nothing to do but leave Phoenix. After brushing the cookie crumbs off her Prada suit, Pippa rolled her belongings into a laundry bag and checked out of the Ritz-Carlton. "Mike," she called, tapping on the limousine window. "Wake up. I'd like to go to the airport."

His face fell. "But you only just got here."

"Don't worry. You'll be paid for the full week."

That's not what he meant at all. "Where's your luggage?"

"This is it." Pippa slid into the back seat. "Let's get this show on the road."

She was staring bleakly out the window when a high voice inquired, "Where's that smile?"

"Gone. Go away."

Clownie slid below the seat but popped up again, holding a two-inch square of paper. "I have something for you, Miss Flushowitz." It was a lilliputian Matchmaking Diploma. "Congratulations!"

"That's not remotely funny," Pippa yelled, tearing the paper in shreds. She burst into tears. "You have no idea what losing that diploma cost me! I may as well join the circus!"

Clownie clapped his hands. "Yes, be a clown! Then you'd smile like me."

The puppet's words slowly sank in. Pippa slid over to the laptop in the back seat and Googled "clown school." Why not? She excelled at disguise and slapstick. If she couldn't pass *that,* she might as well go on welfare. She called a place in Milford, Pennsylvania, because it was farthest away from Phoenix.

"Da?" a man snapped after eight rings.

"Is this the Russian Circus Arts Academy?"

"Da. I am Slava Slootski. You are who?" demanded his thickly accented *basso.*

Pippa looked in desperation around the back seat. Clownie? *Nyet.* "Cluny . . . Google."

"Gogol? You are Russian?"

"No."

"Then you not understand Russian clowns."

"Please, Mr. Slootski! I'm desperate to study with you! Your Web page says you're the best teacher in the world."

"I am best *clown* in world."

"That, too. I can be there tomorrow."

"What is your best trick?"

Pippa thought back to her cheerleading days. "I can do six back somersaults in a row."

"You dance?"

"Perfectly." Lance had thought so, anyway. "Cha-cha is my specialty."

"You are how tall?"

"Five feet nine inches."

"You like bears?"

Pippa thought he said "pears." "Love them."

"Okay," Slava agreed fatefully. "But you audition first. You must have talent or I don't take you."

"Thank you so much! I'll see you tomorrow."

Pippa found an overnight flight to New York on Travelocity. Mike watched his rearview mirror in fascination as his passenger rebounded from dead to very alive. She pulled out her cell phone. "Hi, Sheldon! I have good news and bad news. The good news is I actually did earn a diploma at matchmaking school."

"Did?"

"Unfortunately, I lost it in a poker game. Plus a bit of cash."

"You should have had four thousand dollars left after paying tuition."

"It was a close game. We almost won twice that amount."

We? Almost? Sheldon didn't want to know. "Any reputable institution will replace your diploma for twenty dollars."

"It's not that simple. The director of the matchmaking school was also in the game. She lost the diploma."

"How could *she* lose *your* diploma?"

"Look, she just did! It's literally down the toilet now. I can't get it back." What was his problem? "The point is I'm flying to New York tonight. I'll be back in school tomorrow. In a week I'll have a diploma for you."

"In which field this time?"

"I'm going to the Russian Circus Arts Academy." Pippa took a deep breath. "Clown school."

"You want to be a *clown?* And I thought matchmaking was bad."

"This is the Harvard of clown schools. Slava Slootski is a world-famous authority. It's like studying political science with Hillary Clinton."

Sheldon audibly shuddered. "And where might this 'clown Harvard' be located?"

"Milford, Pennsylvania."

Sheldon closed his eyes and thought of Anson Walker, his beloved friend. "I'll try to find a reputable hotel in the area," he said with deep resignation.

"How's my mother doing?" Silence. "My ex-mother? Sheldon?"

"Since you ask, she was arrested yesterday for assaulting a woman named Nori Nuki and allegedly defacing a spa with mud and melted chocolate. Would you care to comment?"

"Nori called the newspapers while we were having facials. She's the one who should be in jail. She nearly got us killed."

"Thayne certainly settled the score. Nori has a triple concussion. Ginny's SUV also sustained some damage." Actually, Thayne had totaled it when she drove it through the front of the spa. "The hearing is tomorrow afternoon."

Pippa was crushed. "I'll be right there."

"Absolutely not! Thayne is under sedation. Her doctors agree that seeing you put her over the edge."

"I had no idea she would be at that spa. You've got to believe me."

"She will go to a sanatorium in Kalamazoo until she recovers some degree of sanity. Your *ex*-father will return to Morocco. You are not to see or communicate with your *former* parents in any way. Even by coincidence. Is that clear, Pippa?"

"Thanks a lot, Sheldon."

As Mike watched his passenger revert to a zombie, he suspected that not even Clownie could bring her back to the land of the living. They rode in silence to Sky Harbor Airport. "American Airlines," Pippa said tonelessly.

The words felt like daggers in his heart. Mike opened her door. "When MatchMace hits it big I'll pay back all the money I lost."

"Don't even think about it." She kissed his cheek. "You were a good sport."

Inside the terminal Pippa hit bedlam in the form of fifty or so people toting large placards. At first glance it looked as if the baggage handlers were on strike. Then she read a few of the signs: MARRIED COUPLES EARN MORE MONEY. MARRIED PEOPLE LIVE LONGER. MARRIAGE WORKS! BE FRUITFUL AND LEGALLY MULTIPLY. "Who are those crackpots?" she asked the ticket agent.

"They're from WedLock. A coalition of dating services and marriage counselors."

She had to squeeze past the demonstrators to get to security. "Hello there," greeted a woman whose tight smile bore a frightening resemblance to Marla's. She had pamphlets. "Are you married?"

"Three times. I love it," Pippa called over her shoulder, ducking into line. Rub my face in it, schmucks! How kind of them to remind her she was destined for a B-minus job, an early death, and zero offspring. Pippa was nearly at the X-ray machine when she realized that her little souvenir, MatchMace, would be about as welcome aboard her flight as a shoe bomb. She didn't want to throw it away: it had meant the world to Mike. She had just enough time to find a FedEx outpost and send it to Sheldon, who was a heavy smoker.

The overnight flight was totally booked. Many seats were occupied by a marching band from Poughkeepsie returning home from a national competition. Sleep was the last thing on seventy teenagers' minds, as the other passengers swiftly discovered. Each time Pippa closed her eyes, shrieks would rend the air. Nonstop traffic in the aisle kept the odor of dirty sneakers, peanut butter, and French fries recirculating throughout the cabin. Worse, Pippa was wedged between two very large people. The one on the aisle had breathing problems. The other ate from a bottomless carry-on and had to visit the bathroom every fifteen hundred calories.

Between all that and worrying about Thayne's day in court, Pippa felt spry as a fossil when the plane landed in New York. She hit an ATM, then found a cab. "Take me to Milford, Pennsylvania."

"Miffa?" He turned down the steel drum music. "Whe' dat be, mon?"

The next cabbie found a filthy Esso map of Pennsylvania in his glove compartment. He and Pippa finally spotted Milford in the Poconos about seventy miles west of New York. "That's gonna cost," he said.

"Five hundred bucks door to door. Including gas and tip."

"You're on."

Pippa paid. "Wake me when we get there."

She dreamed of surreal characters and events. One vision involved Thayne in a vat of chocolate, playing poker. In another dream Pippa was in the woods fleeing a moose with heart-shaped sunglasses driving a blue Maserati. An insistent dinging finally evaporated her nightmares. Pippa opened her eyes to find herself sprawled across the back seat of the cab, soaked with more sweat than her Prada suit could handle. Her neck felt broken, having propped her head at a forty-five-degree angle for the last hour. She sat up. The cab was parked at a ramshackle one-pump gas station, receiving air in a rear tire.

Humidity engulfed her the second she got out. Huge mosquitoes attacked her ears and ankles. "Are we in Milford?" she asked, swatting them away.

"Yep." The little dings stopped when the driver hung up the air hose. "Now where?"

Pippa called Slava Slootski. After a distressing number of rings, someone picked up but didn't say anything. "Mr. Slootski? This is Cluny Google."

"Slava is gone," a woman with a Russian accent told her.

"Gone where?" Pippa tried to keep her voice calm. "He's expecting me."

"Yes, I know, you are where now?"

Pippa couldn't even read the paint above the rotting porch. "At a gas station with a blue sign."

"Go right, take fifth left, stop when you see elephant. Leave now. I meet you."

"Go right, take fifth left," Pippa repeated, diving back into the cab before the mosquitoes sucked her last drop of blood. "Someone will meet us at the elephant sign."

The fifth left was miles down the seedy, deserted highway. Pippa had never seen so many big dead animals in the road. "Think this is it?" the cab driver asked, stopping at a dirt path disappearing into the underbrush.

"Let's give it a try."

Before doing so, he reached under the front seat and handed Pippa a crowbar. The other he kept for himself. "Like the Boy Scouts say, be prepared."

Too bad her MatchMace was with FedEx. They bumped along the rocky way for what seemed like miles. There was no place to turn; Evel Knievel would think twice about backing out of here in reverse. "This don't look too promising," the cabbie observed nervously.

Pippa tried not to dwell on the fact that, were she raped and murdered in this godforsaken thicket, her remains would never be found. "Give it another minute."

They gingerly proceeded around a sharp curve. "Holy shit!" the driver cried, stomping on the brakes. "There's a friggin' elephant!"

Seeing them, the beast emitted a roar that threatened to shatter the windshield. It lumbered in their direction. As Pippa and the driver watched in horror, it raised its massive right foot. Two tons of that were about to come smashing through the hood when a voice called, "Mitzi! Behave or no dinner!"

Mitzi whapped the roof of the cab with her trunk a few times before shuffling off. A roly-poly woman with white hair and the features of an old potato appeared in the road. "Where is Cluny?"

Pippa got out, with the crowbar. The woman smelled like a swamp. "Pleased to meet you."

"I am Masha." She studied Pippa's suit. Shaking her head, she instructed the cab driver, "You turn here."

He was delighted to take advantage of a small roundabout and rocket out of there. "Hey!" Masha looked anxiously at Pippa. "He forgets your trunk."

Pippa batted away the instant swarm of mosquitoes. They weren't going near Masha, she noticed. "I'm afraid this bag is all I have."

"But your dancing shoes? Wigs and makeup? Where are they?"

"The airline lost them. Really lost them," Pippa added. "They got sent to Haiti by mistake."

"Slava will be furious."

A short, rotund man with a long white beard burst through the foliage. Briars clung to his patched clothing. His boots and face were monuments of mud. He carried a machete and a basket full of dark

mushrooms. Demonic forces radiated from his blue eyes. Pippa
screamed in fright. Sure that her end was at hand, she cowered behind
the older woman and, eyes closed, waited for the inevitable.

"Morels," she heard Masha say. "Very good, Slava."

Pippa peeped around the apron strings. "Mr. Slootski?"

He brandished his machete. "Off my property or I kill you!"

"Slava, stop! She is new clown, not tax assessor." Masha took
Pippa's hand. "Cluny."

Slava inspected Pippa head to foot, as one would a horse at auction. Despite the mosquitoes, she didn't dare move, sensing that this
examination was a critical part of her entrance audition. "Funny costume," he pronounced finally. "Grace Kelly suit, black eye, straw
hair."

"Thank you."

A large bear scampered out of the bushes. Seeing Pippa, it reared
on its hind legs and came at her, waving its paws in the air. Pippa
screamed a second time. Lunging backward, she tripped over her
crowbar and fell flat on her butt. The bear kept coming at her so she
covered her head with her laundry bag and kicked her shoes in the air,
hoping to ward it off.

"Ha ha!" Slava laughed. "Like overturned beetle! Very good."

Pippa slowly removed the bag from her face to find Slava feeding
red berries to the bear. "Meet Pushkin." Slava began humming "Tea
for Two." "Dance with him."

Swallowing her fright, Pippa did as she was told. She had to admit
that, claws aside, Pushkin had better moves than most guys at frater-
nity dances. "He likes you." Slava clapped his hands. "You like him?"

"He's adorable," Pippa replied, quivering with terror.

"Good. You come to school then." Slava plunged into the bushes
on the other side of the road. Pushkin disappeared after him.

Pippa nearly fainted with relief. "Are there more bears?" she asked
Masha.

"Only Pushkin. He dance boogie-woogie. He is star of our circus."
Masha frowned as the elephant unleashed another bloodcurdling bel-
low. "Maybe Mitzi is jealous. You do not be afraid of her. This way,
Cluny. I get you better clothes."

Masha headed briskly down the overgrown drive. After struggling for twenty minutes in her sling-back heels, Pippa debated whether it would be better to take them off and slash her feet on the rocks, or keep them on and break an ankle. She nearly stepped on a toad: keep the shoes on. Every once in a while Pippa swore she heard a menacing snort in the woods behind her. After an eternity the driveway ended and she found herself in a clearing.

Two young men and a woman were yanking at ropes and poles, apparently unfazed by another elephant just a few feet away. "Cluny! Come quick!" Masha yelled. Pippa ditched her shoes and ran over. "When I say three, pull rope. One! Two! Three!"

A gigantic swath of canvas rose from the ground. The other elephant curled its trunk around a telephone pole and poised it under a peak in the cloth. As the three workers hammered spikes into the ground, securing the tent, Masha pointed at another rope. "Pull!"

The elephant put a second pole in place, propping up the other half of the tent. "Good Bobo," Masha said, giving him an apple.

Pippa looked down at her scarlet hands. She had the makings of a major blister between her thumb and first finger. Her suit was a ruin of grass stains. There was no school building in sight. The three circus hands headed in her direction. An aroma of skunk cabbage enveloped them, same as with Masha. "Hi. I'm Cluny."

An elfin young woman squeezed Pippa's blister with excruciating force. "Lulu. I was with Cirque du Soleil."

Pippa had been around enough SMU cheerleaders to know that Lulu already considered her a mortal enemy. "That's wonderful."

A guy with a mangy ponytail stepped forward. Everything about his loose-jointed body said "airhead." His squidlike handshake confirmed the impression. "Benedict."

"Pleased to meet you," she said, slapping away a fresh cloud of mosquitoes.

Her third classmate, a fine specimen of manhood, undressed her with his eyes. "Cluny." His tongue luxuriated over the two syllables. "I'm Vik. Where'd you get the black eye?"

"I drove a car into a swimming pool." At least it sounded like a circus stunt.

"You come with me, Cluny," Masha said.

At the edge of the field stood three dilapidated trailers. Two were half buried in the dirt, like unexploded bombs from World War II. Masha opened the door to the most decrepit one. "You sleep here."

Pippa picked a path through piles of clothing to a tiny bunk. "Is this the dorm?"

"What is dorm? This is trailer, like circus."

"Where's the bathroom?"

Masha pointed out the window to the outhouse. "Very handy."

Pippa's nose wrinkled: a little too handy. "And the shower?"

"We have river."

"May I see it?"

Masha led Pippa down a briary path to the banks of a slow-moving body of water. "Delaware. Very warm this time of year."

A nearby *plupp* made Pippa jump. "What was that?"

"Bullfrog. If you catch, I cook for you. Excellent with mushrooms from Slava."

Pippa took out her cell phone: she needed Sheldon immediately. "If you don't mind, I'll be staying in a hotel."

"No! Everyone lives together, like circus." A moot point, in any case: no cell phone service. Masha led Pippa back to the second trailer. She emerged with rugged pants and shirt, socks, a pair of old boots, and a jar of oily brown liquid. "For bugs. Slava makes himself."

Pippa changed into the uniform. She sniffed Slava's insect repellent and almost passed out; however, since it appeared to work for everyone else, she slathered it on. When she emerged from the trailer, her classmates were setting plates on a nearby picnic table. Masha appeared with a steaming pot of oatmeal, a platter of smoked fish, and coffee. Everyone, especially Lulu, packed away an enormous amount of breakfast in very little time. "Eat up," she told Pippa. "You'll work it off."

The smoked fish made Pippa thirsty. She guzzled a mouthful from the glass at her plate before a fit of choking overtook her. "That was not water," she croaked, tears gushing down her cheeks.

"It's vodka." Lulu picked a bone out of her teeth. "Slava makes it himself."

Pippa's voice eventually returned. "You drink that for breakfast?"

"Breakfast, lunch, dinner," Vik said. "Russian circus tradition."

That was as much alcohol as Thayne slugged down when she lost important tennis matches. Impressed, Pippa took a second look at her tablemates. No one seemed in the least tipsy. How would she ever be able to polish off a glass of vodka at breakfast? She was already feeling the effects of the first swallow.

"What did you perform for Slava?" Benedict asked. "For your entrance skit?"

"I fell down backward over a crowbar and waved my feet in the air. Then I danced with a bear named Pushkin." As three forks paused in midair, Pippa realized she had touched a nerve. "He's quite good."

Vik managed to comment, "Pushkin is very particular about dancing partners."

"Masha says he's the star of the circus."

"Masha's a dumb cook. I'm the star of the circus," Lulu said.

"Excuse me. I'm the star," Vik corrected. "Just because you're small doesn't mean you're good."

"Back up," Pippa interrupted. "Is this a circus? I thought it was clown school. Balloons and honking noses. Big feet. Diplomas."

After a moment Benedict asked, "Does the name Slava Slootski mean anything to you?"

"He's the guy that hands out diplomas."

"He's one of the greatest Russian clowns that ever lived."

"Does that prevent him from handing out diplomas?"

"What's this diploma crap?" Lulu inquired. "You don't exactly need one to work in a circus."

Pippa took a deep breath. This school was off to a shaky start. "How did one of the greatest clowns who ever lived end up here?"

"He had an accident getting shot out of a cannon. Someone packed in a double dose of gunpowder and blasted him clean out of the tent. He broke both arms and legs and the explosion made him almost deaf. He came here and lived in the woods. In the middle of winter Masha found him fishing in the river with his bare hands. She took him in."

"Did they find the perpetrator?"

"It was probably Mitzi."

"That horrible elephant? Why didn't Slava make Dumbo burgers out of her?"

"Mitzi's a very talented animal. You don't just grind her up for a little temper tantrum."

Oy. "Tell me about Pushkin."

"Slava found him when he was a few days old. Orphaned." Benedict washed down a mouthful of smoked fish with Slava's vodka. "So Pushkin likes to dance with you?"

Lulu exhaled a stream of cigarette smoke in Pippa's face. "You strike me as rather clumsy."

For a pipsqueak, Lulu was a major pain, like a splinter under the fingernail. "From your vantage point, everything must look clumsy," Pippa replied.

Breakfast continued in silence until Vik leaped to his feet. "They're back."

Pippa saw Slava and his pet bear at the edge of the woods. By the time they crossed the field, all three students had cleared the table and were standing at attention, awaiting their master's orders. Pippa planted herself next to Benedict and made like GI Jane.

As if they were invisible, Slava proceeded into the kitchen with his basket of mushrooms. Pushkin paused to lick Pippa's ankles. "Bitch," Lulu whispered. "You put sugar on your feet."

"I did not," Pippa fired back. "I just have nice feet." Lance had often commented on their pulchritude.

Slava emerged from the kitchen. For a while he watched Pushkin's tongue explore the crevasses between Pippa's toes. Then, waving a fish in the air, he called, "Pushkin! Breakfast!"

Pushkin preferred to lick Pippa's toes. "In love," Slava announced blissfully. He yanked Pushkin by the scruff of the neck away from Pippa's feet. "Enough, greedy boy."

Slava led Pippa and Pushkin into the circus tent, where Vik was already circling on a unicycle, juggling. Pippa was amazed at his dexterity, particularly after the vodka. Slava was not. "Faster!" He tautened a low tightrope. "Walk!"

For a terrible moment Pippa thought he was addressing her. Then she saw Pushkin scramble onto the tightrope. Slowly and delicately, the bear sidled from end to end. "He shows off for you," Slava said. "Give kiss."

Pippa did so. She was beginning to warm to Pushkin, whose furry ears and pointed snout reminded her of a favorite gym teacher. Slava threw a small ball at Pippa. "Play catch."

Pushkin was a major leaguer. Once, instead of tossing the ball at Pippa, he gracefully kicked it to her. Once he caught the ball on his nose and balanced it while he twirled around in a circle. Slava was beside himself with excitement. "Look at him!" he cried over and over. Slava unearthed two pairs of roller skates from a trunk. Pippa was not surprised to find that Pushkin skated better than she did. He could certainly juggle better. Pushkin could also ride a unicycle.

"Enough!" Slava finally barked. "Time for nap." Pushkin didn't move. "Lie down with him for few minutes," he told Pippa.

"Here?"

"In bed, where else? Get bottle from Masha."

Although busy mashing turnips for lunch, Masha had Pushkin's milk bottle ready. "Is it good or bad that Pushkin likes me?" Pippa asked.

"Very good, Cluny. You travel all over world. Wear wonderful costumes."

"All over the world?" Pippa echoed unenthusiastically. Thayne would just love her ex-daughter joining the circus. "To tell the truth, I'd be happy with just a diploma."

"What is that, diploma?" Masha returned to her turnips.

Pushkin snatched his bottle from Pippa's hands and scampered into the last trailer, which was decorated like a seven-year-old's room. He nestled into a large basket lined with flannel sheets. Curling into a brown ball, he placed one paw around his bottle, the other around Pippa's foot.

"I hope you don't expect a bedtime story," she said.

In reply Pushkin removed a large-print edition of *Goldilocks* from a bookshelf. He dropped it in her lap, curled back into a ball, and looked imploringly at her. "Guess that answers my question," she muttered, and began to read.

The bear soon fell asleep. Pippa worked her foot free and tiptoed out of the trailer. At the far end of the field she saw Vik, Benedict, and Lulu doing chin-ups on a set of parallel bars as Slava paced before them, brandishing a whip. "Cluny! Show me strong arms!"

Pippa was hoisted up to the pole. She lasted about four chin-ups before falling off. Benedict let go after a couple dozen, then Lulu. Slava waited until Vik reached one hundred. "Enough." He turned to the three weaklings on the grass. "Good clown strong clown. Now do push-ups."

Once again Pippa conked out first. Lulu was up to two hundred when Slava threw ropes at them. "Stop. Jump rope now."

Pippa did so until her thighs gave way. Slava then had them race around the perimeter of the field. Despite having the shortest legs, Lulu won. "Boys, you let little lady beat you again?" Slava cried. "Go jump in Delaware."

Pippa followed her classmates to the river, where they stripped to their underwear. She reluctantly followed suit, exposing lace bra and panties.

"Very nice," Vik leered.

Scowling, Pippa dove into the water. Everyone swam to New Jersey and back. They dressed and did forty minutes of joint-popping stretches in the midday sun followed by a barrage of cartwheels and somersaults.

"You say back somersault your specialty," Slava said as she lay retching on the grass.

"I can do six in a row, Mr. Slootski. Not thirty."

"Lunch!" Masha called.

Pippa staggered to the picnic table. The midday meal consisted of mashed turnips, buckwheat groats, and collard greens accompanied by buttermilk and more vodka. "Very good food for clowns," Masha told Pippa, piling her plate high.

Pippa smiled wanly. "Is that what you do every morning?" she asked Benedict.

"Slava went easy on us today. We usually have to run up and down the mountain after the cartwheels."

Vik swallowed his vodka. "You've got to be in great shape to ride elephants and get shot out of cannons. Not to mention set up tents, fly on a trapeze, and dance with bears."

"When I got here, I could hardly do a push-up," Benedict said. "Now I'm up to ninety."

"In one week?" Pippa was astonished.

"Two years."

She did the math. "You mean you flunked Slava's course a hundred times?"

"The course lasts until Slava thinks you're ready to work. Don't worry, he doesn't charge you more than six hundred bucks no matter how long it takes."

Feeling ill, Pippa turned to Vik. "How long have you been here?"

"Four years."

Lulu? "One year. Don't try to escape, either. Mitzi can smell you a mile away. She's got razor-sharp tusks and can run as fast as a car. Swims like a fish, too."

"What about contact with the outside world? Going home for Thanksgiving?"

"You don't get it." Lulu finished her turnips. "This isn't Beer and Barf U. You're at the Russian Circus Arts Academy."

The damn Harvard of clown schools. "What if people flunk out? Then they can leave?"

"Clowns don't flunk out, Cluny. They either cut it or they commit suicide."

Banter ceased as Masha placed a fresh bottle of insect repellent on the table. The outhouse door slammed behind the trailer. Moments later Slava appeared, raring to go. "Lunch finish! Back to work!"

Slava's troupe paraded back to the tent. "Cluny, ride Bobo."

As she stared at the saddle behind the elephant's ears, Pippa wondered if she still had health insurance. It probably didn't matter: if she fell from that height, she wouldn't be worth saving. Slava snapped his whip an inch from her face. "Ride!"

Bobo stood placidly until Pippa mounted the knotted rope. Then he did his utmost to shake her loose. Fortunately, having received her first pony at the age of four, Pippa knew how to stay in the saddle. Finally even Slava grew tired of Bobo's rearing and stomping. "Quiet!" The elephant became still. "Cluny, dismount into net."

Pippa looked down. The net looked barely strong enough to catch a kitten. *Think diploma.* She amazed herself—and everyone else—by doing a perfect swan dive, bouncing a few times, and rolling off the edge of the net to terra firma.

"Bitch," Lulu hissed. "You took tumbling."

"Twelve long years, Tiny."

The class practiced juggling for several hours. Pippa thought her neck would snap when she brought her chin back down. "Break tent," Slava said.

Students and elephants flattened the tent in five minutes forty seconds. That was not a better time than yesterday, so Slava made them erect the tent and tear it down again. Still no improvement, so they had to do it a third time. "Five minutes," he finally announced. "Why you not do this first time?"

"Inexperienced help," Vik panted.

"You're welcome." Pippa's hands looked like 3-D blisters with fingernails. "Why must clowns pitch tents, Mr. Slootski?"

"You complain to help? You think you tsarina?"

"Eat!" Masha called.

Everyone trudged to the picnic table, there to be served glasses of cloudy liquid. Pippa sniffed. "What's this?"

"Beer from tree bark. Drink! Very good for clowns."

Slava downed his glass in one go and poured another. When that was gone, he felt refreshed enough to roar, "Now practice swallow the sword!"

Pippa couldn't help but think that, were she home in Dallas, she'd be sitting on the veranda at Fleur-de-Lis, sipping a mojito. Here she was poised on the rim of a slashed esophagus.

"Something the matter, Cluny?" Vik asked.

"I had no idea that being a clown was so life-threatening."

"Being good at anything is life-threatening."

"I see. Excuse me." Maybe her cell phone would work in the middle of the field.

Within ten steps Mitzi galloped out of nowhere to breathe down her neck. "She thinks you're trying to run away," Vik called.

Pippa held her cell phone up to Mitzi's tusks. "Phone! Dingaling!" She dialed Sheldon. *No service available.* Damn!

When she returned to the table, Slava made her open her mouth. "Wide! More wide!" He shook his head. "Not big enough for best sword. Vik, teach banana peel." Slava went with Pushkin into the last trailer.

Vik tossed a napkin onto the grass. "Say that's a banana peel, Cluny. Here's your basic fall." He splatted onto the ground. "Did you see how I broke the impact with my hands?"

"Ah . . . not really." Pippa watched Vik do it again. "I think I get it."

"Try."

Despite twelve years of tumbling, which Thayne had financed in hopes of becoming the mother of an Olympic gold medalist, Pippa swiftly discovered that fake falling required a strength and agility beyond her. Vik made her try again and again. "I'd appreciate a mat," she fumed. "Or at least a helmet."

Slava, dragging a large trunk, and Pushkin, holding a tambourine, exited the trailer. Spying Pippa flat on her back, the bear shot over to lick her face. Slava yanked Pippa's amour away by the ears. "Show me fall, Cluny."

Pippa hit the dirt. Pushkin expertly struck his tambourine at the moment of impact. "Very good," Slava commended. "We do more tomorrow."

"She only falls once? You made me do fifty my first day." Lulu whirled on Pippa. "You slept with him, you bitch."

"Never question Slava Slootski!" The master punished Lulu by having her walk on her hands across the field while he taught Pippa how to do Russian cartwheels. It was hard to say who was more disoriented by the time Masha called them for dinner.

The troupe ate mushroom stew with mashed potatoes. This time Pippa thought Slava's fiery vodka tasted exquisite. "You like stew with fresh mushrooms?" he asked.

"Delicious, Mr. Slootski." Pippa could barely keep her eyes open.

"Tonight you dance boogie-woogie with Pushkin."

"Okay." She tried to sound enthusiastic. "I didn't get much sleep on the plane last night."

Not Slava's concern. "Clown's life of illusion long, hard work."

Mitzi bellowed from the other side of the meadow, where she had been uprooting shrubs with her trunk. Pippa turned around. She could swear Mitzi was glaring at her. "Does she have indigestion?"

"She heard you're going to dance with Pushkin," Lulu whispered. "She hates other women touching him."

"Oh! Now I'm trying to screw the bear, too?"

"Shhh." Masha served another multiton *pièce de résistance*, cheesecake topped with huckleberries. Pushkin licked all but three off the top then scampered to the clothes trunk. He began pulling out all sorts of costumes and tossing them in the air.

"Look! Pushkin very excited to dance, Cluny."

"So am I, Mr. Slootski."

"Liar," Lulu hissed. "All you want is Slava."

"All I want is a diploma," Pippa hissed back.

"What you girls whisper?" Slava was getting annoyed. "Tiny, go wash tent. You too, Vik and Stupid." After they left, Slava dotingly watched Pushkin try on a few hats. "He is wonderful bear."

Pippa's courage made a fleeting appearance as she finished her vodka. "Mr. Slootski, may I discuss something with you?"

She removed six soggy hundred-dollar bills from her bra and secured them beneath the bottle of insect repellent. "First of all, I'd like to pay you for a week of clown lessons." She swallowed hard. "I will pay you ten thousand dollars when I get my diploma."

Slava's face clouded. "Why for?"

"Because I really want a diploma."

"Then you leave me?"

"Yes, that's a possibility." Oops, *very* bad move. "On the other hand, maybe not. This career seems to involve certain skills that I used to have, and could probably work up again, and you're the best clown in the history of circuses so this would be an honor and challenge, certainly an adventure . . ." Pippa's verbiage trailed off. "Let's just say I might stay a while."

His eyes narrowed. "You try to bribe Slava Slootski?"

"Never!"

"Then why you offer me ten thousand dollar? You think I care about money?"

"I didn't mean it that way. But you'll need at least that much to get those trailers moving. And feed Mitzi."

"I have plenty money in mattress. I need no more. I need dancer with Pushkin."

Never let them see you sweat, honey. A memory of Thayne driving a hard bargain with the Mansion on Turtle Creek flashed across Pippa's mind. What she needed was ruthless, overwhelming force. Pippa cleared her throat and leaned over the table. "Let's make a deal, Mr. Slootski.

You give me a diploma. I'll dance with Pushkin for six months and give you ten thousand dollars."

He thought that over. "One hundred thousand."

"Fine! One hundred thousand dollars."

Slava laughed from the belly. "Bravo, Cluny! You lie like Russian!"

Pippa realized she should have made at least a few faces before agreeing to the hundred grand. "It won't be easy, of course. My father will have to sell his farm."

"Farm?" Now Slava was the one leaning forward. "Animal or vegetable?"

Pippa racked her brain to think of a warm, fuzzy answer. Ah! "He grows mushrooms. Little white ones. They're very cute."

Slava's eyes burned with rage. "Your father works many years to make 'cute' mushrooms. Now you sell his farm like *that*?" He snapped his fingers. "Dirty your family name?"

"No! My family name means everything!"

"Never speak more about diploma, Cluny Google. I do not never steal man's mushroom farm."

"Wait!" Pippa shouted as he stalked off. "We'll sell my mother's shoe collection!" The outhouse door slammed in reply. Pippa put her face in her hands. Blithering idiot!

Now was the moment to run away. Mitzi and Bobo were nowhere in sight, nor was anyone else. Pushkin's nose was buried in the trunk of costumes. Pippa tiptoed away from the table, ducked beneath the kitchen window, and began picking up speed as she neared the Delaware River. She was nearly in the water when a rope flew over her shoulders and circled her waist. She was jerked into the air like a rodeo heifer and dragged over dirt and rocks back to the kitchen trailer.

Masha descended the steps, laughing as she set up an old record player on the picnic table. "You play cowboy with Pushkin? Is his favorite game."

Pippa smiled in resignation. "He's certainly good with a lasso."

Masha untied her. "He love you like Romeo and Juliet. Is very romantic bear."

Pippa tried to look happy about it. Slava returned with a fresh smile, having left his recent negotiations with Pippa back in the outhouse. He

squinted at an LP lying on the picnic table. "Find Cossack," he told
Pushkin.

Pushkin unearthed two Cossack costumes from the trunk as Slava
dropped the needle on a deeply scratched vinyl disc. "Dress! Dance!"

Over the next three hours Pushkin and Pippa hoofed their way
through every costume in the trunk: gypsies, Apaches, Viennese aris-
tocrats, astronauts, the Flintstones, pirates, cops, nurses. Pushkin's
energy never flagged. Pippa found herself strangely inspired: if she
closed her eyes, she could easily convince herself that the strongest,
gentlest man on the planet held her in his arms. It was a rare and ecstatic fantasy. When the moon appeared over the Poconos, she finally
sat down. "Sorry, fellas. That's the end of me for tonight. Thank you,
Pushkin." She kissed his nose. "May I go to bed now, Mr. Slootski?
Promise I'll have more energy tomorrow."

Had Pippa asked him for the Milky Way, Slava would have said,
"Of course."

Still in a nurse costume, Pippa drooped to the trailer. For the first
time since infancy she didn't bother washing her face, brushing her
teeth, or changing into pajamas. She fell into a deep sleep that lasted
until . . . what was that horrible rocking . . . an earthquake . . . Mitzi
upending the trailer . . . Pippa opened her eyes. Moonlight streamed
in the window. She smelled honeysuckle and the Delaware River. The
rocking was for real.

"Slower, you ape," Lulu whispered.

Aha: her petite classmate was having sex. Pippa didn't even want
to know with whom—or what; however, the mystery was solved when
Benedict's voice cut through the dark. "Shut up! I'm trying to sleep."

"Ditto," Pippa said.

The rocking instantly stopped. "You awake, Cluny?"

"Thank you for asking."

Vik's head swung over the bunk. "How was dancing, Nurse Ratch-
ett?"

Pippa went outside. Benedict joined her when Lulu's moans became Wagnerian. She rubbed her aching feet. "What I wouldn't give
for a hot tub."

"Let's go down to the river. It's almost as warm." He led the way, not in the least concerned that he was naked. They finally reached the riverbank. Benedict dove in. "Water's perfect."

Pippa unwrapped the Ritz-Carlton hotel soap that Masha had left in a community pail. It smelled fragrant but somewhat unreal, like her former existence. She hesitated a moment, then stripped off her nurse costume and waded in. The water was lusciously warm. Pippa was so entranced with making suds that she didn't notice a miasmal stench until it was, literally, breathing down her neck: Mitzi.

"Benedict?" she called softly, paralyzed. "Where are you?"

Downstream, smoking marijuana from a stash in the goldenrod. "What's up?"

"I need you here right now. We have company."

Thinking she meant the police, Benedict mashed his joint into mud and swam away.

"Benedict?" Useless! Pippa slowly turned around. There stood Mitzi, big as a barn. "Hi."

Mitzi emitted a deafening shriek. Pippa watched in horror as Mitzi's trunk slithered toward her like a giant cobra. The trunk stopped at the bar of soap. "All yours," Pippa said, placing it on a rock. She slowly backed away.

Fascinated, Mitzi ate the soap. Displeased at the aftertaste, she thundered after Pippa, who was already halfway up the hill, buck naked, running for her life. Pippa burst into the dorm as Lulu and Vik were winding down in gooey sighs.

"Make her go away," Pippa whimpered, diving into her bunk.

Vik peered over the upper edge. "Now *this* is a distinct improvement."

Mitzi rammed the trailer. Vik was knocked to the floor, where he remained, perhaps unconscious. "What's going on down there, Cluny?" Lulu asked, annoyed. "Surely you don't think Vik can get it up again tonight. Give me a little more credit than that."

"Shut up! Mitzi's trying to kill me."

A second ramming shook the trailer to its foundation. "Give yourself up, then. I need my sleep."

"Fine. If I don't dance with Pushkin, this circus goes nowhere."

"I knew you'd be trouble, bitch." Lulu hopped out of her bunk, squishing Vik. She removed a large plastic bag from a cabinet and flung open the door. "Come here, precious!" Lulu patted Mitzi's forehead as the pachyderm consumed enough marijuana for an army.

"That's not cruelty to animals, is it?" Pippa whispered as Mitzi shuffled into the forest.

"I save your neck and you worry about an elephant's drug habit?"

Benedict made a belated appearance around the side of the trailer. "You didn't," he said, eyes on the empty bag.

"Mitzi can return it tomorrow in nice neat loaves for recycling."

"That was the road kit, you sot!"

"Go ahead. Hit me."

He did, with force. Lulu grabbed a broom and started swinging back as Benedict fended her off with an old ladder. Half the time he missed, smashing a trailer instead. "Vik! Wake up!" Pippa cried. "Lulu and Ben are killing each other."

Vik came to and crawled to the doorway. "I put five bucks on Lulu."

Pippa got her cell phone after Lulu took a womb-crushing jab in the gut. "I'm calling 911."

"Won't do any good, Cluny."

Pippa noticed that, despite his amorous exertions, Vik was ten inches from calling it a night. "Get away from me."

"No way."

"Help! Mr. Slootski!"

"Save your lungs. Slava could sleep through the Battle of Stalingrad."

Vik was well on his way to forcible consummation when Pushkin, snarling ferociously, broke through the screen door and batted him away. Pippa fled to the outhouse where, to her amazement, her cell phone rang.

"I've been trying to reach you all day," Sheldon snapped. "Where are you?"

"Right this moment? In an outhouse. Apparently the only place in Milford, Pennsylvania, with cell phone reception."

"How's the 'Harvard of clown schools' treating you?"

Pippa forced back her hysteria. "Listen, Sheldon, I've made a mistake. I'm stuck in the woods with a bunch of lunatics, two wild elephants, and a dancing bear."

That was laying it on a bit thick, even for Pippa. Sheldon's voice became stern. "Don't tell me you won't be getting a diploma again."

He thought he heard a man and woman hurling coarse genital insults at each other. Then he heard an insistent pounding. A male voice, urgent with testosterone, shouted, "Listen up, baby! I'm naked, you're naked, what are we waiting for?"

"Are you naked?" Sheldon demanded. "The truth, young lady."

"Yes! So is everyone else! What does that matter?"

"You were going to buckle down and work. Not party all night long."

"I am *not* partying!" Pippa screamed. "My God! Bobo's trying to knock the outhouse down!"

"Bobo who? Is he French? I'll report him to student housing."

"Bobo's an elephant." Pippa screamed again. "Go away, Pushkin! Stop scratching on the door!"

"Is Pushkin the naked gentleman?"

"Pushkin is the bear."

Sheldon winced as she screamed a third time. "I'm going to call in the morning, Pippa. Thank heaven Anson isn't alive to see his only granddaughter drunk and carousing like a common tart."

"Don't hang up!" Too late. Pippa felt like dropping her phone down the two-holer.

"You alone in there, sweetheart?" Vik called.

"Mr. Slootski's with me."

That did the trick. "Have a nice night, guys! Let's go, Bobo."

Pippa counted to ten and cracked open the door. Only Pushkin remained, holding a Wilma Flintstone costume and *Goldilocks* in his teeth. Pippa slipped the toga over her head. "Thank you."

She followed Pushkin to his trailer and read aloud until his eyelids closed.

As dawn yellowed the Poconos, Pippa was awakened by sounds of gunfire. She found herself on the floor hugging a mound of brown fur. She shuffled outside to find Slava with a pistol, which he apparently used for reveille instead of a trumpet. "Good morning, Mr. Slootski."

Slava's mouth dropped open. "You sleep with Pushkin?"

"It got a little noisy in the dorm. You didn't hear anything?"

"Nothing. Where is Mitzi?" Slava trudged into the woods. "Wake other clowns, Cluny. We have big, big day."

Pippa popped her head inside the dorm. Vik was nowhere in sight. Lulu slumbered serenely beside Benedict: last night's brawl was mere foreplay. "Up and at 'em," she called, slamming the door.

She went to the river. Masha was there with a washboard and a basket of laundry. "Good morning, Cluny. Okay if I use nice soap?"

Masha had just scrubbed everyone's filthy underwear with Chanel Précision cleansing foam. The last quarter inch out of the tube barely produced enough suds to cover Pippa's nose. "Have you seen Vik?"

"He sleep with me last night," Masha said, eyes aglow. "Vik is verrrrry sexy boy."

Gross! "And you're a verrrrry sexy girl," Pippa replied, her ten years of etiquette school finally paying off. "Have you by chance seen my clothes?"

"I wash them." They were drying on the reeds.

Pippa checked the pockets of her soaking trousers. "Did you happen to see any little pieces of plastic?"

"Over there. You not need them. Slava take care of you now."

Pippa plunged into the razor-sharp cattails, where she located her Perdita Rica driver's license and a Chippa Flushowitz debit card. "When do you think that will dry?"

"Why you not wear cave outfit today? Very nice fit."

Very nice itch, too. However, Pippa had no choice. She returned to the trailer and tucked her last cash reserves into her bodice. Like a prisoner of war, she had to be ready to escape at a moment's notice. The flacon of Thayne perfume went in as well.

Her classmates were already doing chin-ups on the parallel bars as Slava paced before them chanting, "Good clown strong clown." His tone changed when he saw Pippa. "No chin-up for you today, Cluny." He kissed her hands. "Blister must heal."

"Whore," Lulu wheezed, her face a frieze of agony. "You screwed Slava in the outhouse."

"I read Pushkin to sleep last night. He didn't touch me and I didn't touch him."

"In that case you're the first couple in the history of dance to keep your pelvises apart."

"Pushkin is a bear. I don't believe I'm having this conversation."

"What you girls talk again?" Slava shouted.

"Nothing, Mr. Slootski."

Slava's hands formed a megaphone over his mouth. "Mitzi!"

Obviously no one had told him the animal was sleeping off ten pounds of weed. After an hour of calisthenics, Masha served Vik's favorite breakfast, turnip hash with dandelion greens. Pippa had to admit that the vodka tasted smoother with each passing meal, with each ripped muscle and weeping blister. "What you like to do today, Cluny?" Slava asked, anointing himself with insect repellent.

Pippa thought a moment. "Could we practice squirting flowers?"

"That's your idea of a clown?" Lulu choked. "Some nebbish with a squirting flower?"

"Yeah. And a big hat. Maybe a buzzing handshake. A happy guy."

"Enough!" Slava interrupted. "Is very difficult to do squirting flower."

To prove the point he got a box of artificial flowers, plastic tubing, squeeze balls, and glue from Masha's trailer. Everyone had to not only construct a corsage complete with hydraulic system but also hit a target in the eye from a distance of four feet. The only one who could perform this feat consistently was Pushkin. Pippa came in second.

"You practiced," Lulu seethed.

"I did not. I'm just good at wearing corsages." Pippa felt a tug on her toga. "What is it, Pushkin?"

"He wants to dance," Benedict said.

Pippa skipped around the table with Pushkin as Slava clapped and sang in delight. When they returned to their seats, Slava dipped Pushkin's paw in the insect repellent then pressed it on a sheet of paper. "You join Russian circus now, Cluny. Is great, great honor."

Pippa stared at the document. "Is this a diploma?" she asked, barely audible.

Slava smiled. "Da! Diploma."

It didn't look terribly official in the state of Texas but Pippa had three eyewitnesses, four counting Pushkin. "Thank you, Mr. Slootski, from the bottom of my heart. Do you think you could sign it for me?" After he scribbled across the lower corner, Pippa secured the paper in her fur belt. "Thank you so much!"

"*Thank you so much,*" Lulu mimicked.

Slava got up from the table. "Practice unicycle. I find Mitzi." He wandered into the woods.

"How are your unicycle chops?" Benedict asked Pippa.

"Nonexistent."

Benedict led her behind Masha's trailer, where six ancient unicycles stood in a rack. "Lean against the trailer and start pedaling." That worked fine until Pippa ran out of trailer. "Keep the pedals under your butt. If you start leaning forward, pedal faster. If you think you're going to fall backward, pedal slower."

"Does this thing have training wheels?" Pippa asked after her tenth crash landing. "I don't need another black eye."

"Keep trying. You'll get the hang of it."

Pippa shot around the side of the trailer and plowed into the picnic table. "Ever hear of brakes?" Lulu screeched, retrieving her squirting flower from the grass.

"Ever hear of a mouthful of knuckles?"

"Down, girls." Vik offered Pippa his arm. "I'll run alongside."

Pippa pedaled into the field. Each time she wobbled Vik caught her, invariably near a sex organ. She couldn't really complain since it was either that or a grass facial. If nothing else, Vik's groping motivated her to learn unicycling in record time.

"You've got the hang of forward." He sauntered off. "Now try ninety-degree turns."

Her classmates laughed each time Pippa fell. She thought she had broken every bone in her body when Pushkin swooped out of nowhere and suavely lifted her onto his back, all the while pedaling his own unicycle. "Thank you, darling," she whispered, clinging to his furry neck.

A force that she could not explain inspired Pippa to kneel on Pushkin's shoulders. It felt fantastic to be so high off the ground with the wind in her hair. *I have a diploma under my belt!* Sensing her elation, Pushkin went into an amazing series of pirouettes, hairpin turns, and seesaws, never once losing his center of gravity or his precious burden. Pippa laughed with delight. Pushkin was better than a flying carpet. Much better than Lance!

Through her euphoria she was dimly aware of rumbling. A thick, gray hose suddenly coiled around her waist, plucked her off Pushkin's shoulders, and vaulted her even higher into the air. *Hmmm! Mitzi has me in her trunk,* she thought calmly. *Those tusks look really sharp.* She relaxed as Mitzi shook her like a rag doll and unleashed a series of bellicose shrieks. Pippa saw her cell phone fly into the trees. Branches scratched her legs and ripped out her hair as Mitzi rampaged up a hill. The animal suddenly stopped short and unfurled her trunk. *I must be the first Walker flung off a cliff by an elephant,* Pippa observed, hurtling through space.

She had the presence of mind to hit the water feet first. Pippa torpedoed far down before her boots hit reedy muck. That shook her out of her reverie: she stroked wildly upward, breaking the surface as the last teaspoon of oxygen in her lungs expired. "Gaaaaaa!"

"Gaaaaaaa!" twelve Cub Scouts in canoes screamed back, terrified by the eruption in their midst. A few of the bigger ones began swinging their oars at Pippa as their counselors barked, *"SIT DOWN RIGHT NOW! I SAID RIGHT NOW!"*

"It's a mermaid! Don't let her in your canoe!"

"It's a pedophile!"

An oar whacked her in the head. Pippa saw meteors. *I'm going to drown,* she mused, sinking. *Thayne's going to sue the crap out of someone.* She sensed an overhead splash then felt a pair of arms cinching her waist. The touch was nowhere near as gentle as Pushkin's. *Thanks for that last ride,* Pippa thought, letting the Delaware swallow her.

Fourteen

Someone with wonderfully sweet breath was kissing her passionately. Trouble was he pinched her nose before each kiss. As her mind cleared, Pippa slowly realized that she was on the receiving end of mouth-to-mouth resuscitation and she was lying on a couple of sharp rocks. She let another kiss go by, then coughed and opened her eyes.

"Look, Mr. Flores!" a Cub Scout squealed. "She's alive!"

Pippa sat up. A dozen inner-city boys gazed at her in fear and fascination. The two adult leaders were also looking at her with mixed feelings: on one hand, she was gorgeous. On the other hand, anyone who jumped off a cliff into the Delaware River was probably on drugs. They had taken the Cub Scouts on a canoe trip precisely to get away from that sort of garbage.

"Are you a cavewoman?" one of the boys asked.

"No. This is just a costume." Pippa's eyes found her rescuer, a dashing Hispanic with great lips. "Sorry. I didn't mean to intrude on you like that."

He was almost disappointed that she had awakened: kissing this unconscious woman back to life was way more exciting than kissing his wife half to death. Aware that he was supposed to be a role model, Mr. Flores suppressed his lust beneath a fit of indignation. "Sorry?

You took one heck of a flying leap right in front of our canoes. That's not what I'd call showing a lot of concern for the safety of others. Not to mention yourself." He frowned at her sodden faux fur. "And where's your life vest?"

"I didn't think I'd be swimming," she replied feebly.

"A good Scout plans ahead," Mr. Flores preached to one and all.

"An elephant threw me off the cliff," Pippa snapped, relieving her boots of heavy water.

"Woooow! A real elephant? That is so cool!"

"That is anything but cool," Mr. Flores disagreed. Scouts were supposed to be truthful at all times. "In the first place, Pennsylvania is not a natural habitat for elephants. In the second place, elephants don't generally use their trunks as slingshots." He tore his eyes from Pippa's lovely throat. "What color was this animal, ma'am? Pink?"

"Gray. Her name is Mitzi." What was his problem? "Let's forget about her, okay? She's wanted to kill me from the moment we met." Pippa rubbed her aching scalp. She wouldn't be surprised if half her hair was still in the trees. As she touched the lump on the back of her head, it began to throb. "Would there be any aspirin in that first-aid kit? Four or five would hit the spot."

Mr. Flores made a show of reading the label. At last night's campfire he had been lecturing the boys on substance abuse. "Two is the recommended dose. Just this once I think we can make an exception. It's not every day you get thrown into a river by an elephant named Mitzi, is it?"

"Thanks." Pippa chewed five and drank from a proffered canteen. "You saved my life."

"Do a good turn daily. That's our slogan. Right, Scouts?"

"Right, chief!"

"My name is Geraldo Flores," he said, shaking her hand. "You are . . . ?"

Pippa needed a long, suspicious moment to respond. "Wilma."

Mr. Flores watched, perplexed, as she suddenly lunged for some paper in her belt and unfolded it as if it were the Magna Carta. "My diploma! Thank God it's okay!"

It looked more like used toilet paper. Wilma was definitely off her rocker. "Congratulations," Mr. Flores said. "That represents a lot of hard work, I'm sure." Now what was he supposed to do? Invite her to join them? The older boys were already agog at her endless legs and off-the-shoulder fur bathing suit. Even the six-year-olds were riveted by the red thong peeping beneath her hem. Once she got into a canoe, nobody would be paying the least attention to birds and clouds and trees, himself included. "Now that you're feeling better, Wilma, may we escort you home?"

To his chagrin she threw herself at his feet. "Please, Mr. Flores! Don't make me go back to the circus." She forced some cash from her bodice into his hands. "I'm happy to pay you."

None of the boys had ever seen one, let alone four, hundred-dollar bills before. "Wow! Can we have a look?"

"Sure," he sighed, handing them over. He helped Wilma to her feet. Much as he enjoyed a half-clad woman prostrate before him, this was not the right time or place for such mercies. "May I introduce you to Cub Scout Pack 35 from Philadelphia. We're canoeing to the Delaware Water Gap."

"That would be perfect. Thank you."

"Let me get you some warmer clothing." That was a joke, the temperature having shot well past eighty. "I mean longer clothing." Mr. Flores gave Pippa shorts, shirt, and cap from his own camp roll. As she went into the woods to change, the other scoutmaster pulled him aside.

"Is this a good idea, Geraldo? Chicks don't just fall out of the sky with four hundred bucks in their pocket. Maybe she robbed a gas station."

"In that outfit? Did you see the black eye? Scratched legs? I think she's escaping someplace bad. Maybe she was kidnapped."

"Could have been an act. She obviously made up her name."

"She's scared. Come on, this is a perfect lesson in helping a fellow citizen."

It helped when the fellow citizen was a hot blonde. "She doesn't think we believe that elephant crap, right?"

The words were no sooner out of his mouth than a feral shriek froze his blood. The boys clutched each other in fright: it sounded awfully close. Pippa burst out of the bushes with Mr. Flores's shirt half unbuttoned. "That's Mitzi! She's coming after me!"

"Into the canoes, boys," Mr. Flores commanded, unnerved by a second shriek. "No crying. Scouts do not cry. Scouts are brave."

Pippa didn't help the situation by whimpering, "Elephants can swim like fish. And they've got really sharp tusks."

"Zip it, Wilma!" Mr. Flores herded his charges back to the river. "Look sharp, everyone."

Pippa grabbed an oar from one of the taller boys. "Do you mind? I was on a rowing team." She planted herself in the rear seat and, energized by terror, paddled furiously out to the strong current. Pippa was dimly aware of Mr. Flores behind her screaming something about rapids. Canoe and Cub Scouts made horrible noises as they scraped over a patch of submerged rocks. "Hold on, guys," Pippa shouted. "We're doing fine."

They shot over a waterfall into a series of robust eddies. By some miracle Pippa's canoe remained upright. "Paddlepaddlepaddle!" she screeched to the kid in the front seat.

He didn't need to be told twice: every few seconds one of the smaller boys would look over his shoulder and scream, "I see the elephant!"

Pippa kept them going at maniacal speed for what seemed like miles. Only when they had rounded a bend in the river did she dare look backward. In her wake were three canoes but no Mitzi.

"Pull ashore, Wilma," Mr. Flores yelled, practically hoarse. "Over there."

Pippa steered the canoe onto the sand. "Nice rowing," she told the boy in front as they waited for the others to catch up. "You were awesome."

First thing Mr. Flores did upon alighting was march up to the lead boy and snap, "You call that safe rowing, Sancho? You nearly drowned half the pack."

"There was a man-eating elephant behind us! What was I supposed to do?"

"As for you, Wilma, if you weren't a woman, I'd beat the tar out of you."

Pippa hung her head. "I'm sorry, Mr. Flores. I must have panicked."

He gave her the four hundred dollars back. "There are some motels right down the road. I suggest you go there and contact—whoever people like you contact." He belatedly realized that this was not the greatest example of samaritanism on record. "Unless we can be of further assistance."

"You've done more than enough." Pippa pulled her sodden boots back on and began walking toward the highway. She turned to see twelve boys and two men staring at her in various stages of bewilderment. "Thanks for rescuing me. I'll never forget that."

"Will you be all right?" the littlest one called.

"I'll be fine." She gave a snappy salute and kept going: exit as gloriously as you enter, Thayne always said. Pippa's confidence waned as she got to the highway. What if Slava had a pickup truck and was already conducting a demented search-and-rescue mission? What if Mitzi was just a few yards away, ready to charge? If ever, this was the time to hitchhike. *Illegal in the state of Texas,* she heard Officer Pierce say.

Pippa stuck out her thumb. The third car pulled over. The driver, an obese woman about her age, was on her way to Bushkill. Pippa had no idea where that was but said, "Perfect!"

A self-help cassette was in progress. "Remember, only YOU can take charge of your life," a man's honeyed voice assured those of lesser mettle. "Only YOU can—"

The woman ejected the cassette and offered Pippa half a bag of Chips Ahoy. "I really shouldn't be eating these but I'm nervous."

"About what?" Pippa took six dry cookies. They were an exquisite change from Masha's fare.

"I'm going to a wedding. Seeing guys from my high school." The woman started to cry. "Why did I ever say yes? This will be so humiliating. There's my bridesmaid's gown. I can barely fit into it."

In the back seat was a pink monstrosity in a plastic bag. "Beautiful," Pippa chomped.

"We copied the design from that wedding in Texas. You know, the one that blew up?" Despite the absence of an affirmative, the woman continued, "If I was a bridesmaid at that horror show, I'd sue."

With difficulty Pippa swallowed half the cookie stuck in her throat. "I'm sure some of them already have."

"At least the mother went to jail."

The other half of the cookie sprayed all over the dashboard. "Jail? What for?"

"Disorderly conduct. She got into a fistfight with some guy named Wyeth."

Pippa forced herself to stay calm. "I thought she was resting in Kalamazoo."

"So was Wyeth. She broke his nose. The judge put her bail at a million bucks because it was her third incident in a week."

"Third?" Pippa barely eked out the syllables.

"The first was with a Korean masseuse. The second was with the mother of the groom. On the steps of the Dallas courthouse! Can you believe that?"

"Absolutely." *Way to go, Mama!*

"That was after she drove a Maserati into a pool. Covered with chocolate!"

"It was mud, not chocolate, and she wasn't driving." Pippa felt ill that some lardo in Pennsylvania knew more about her mother's tribulations than she did. "How far is Bushkill?"

"Ten miles. You all right?"

"Just anxious to get there."

The woman returned to her cassette. Pippa endured a self-help sermon so inane that even the narrator chuckled. Meanwhile the woman demolished the rest of the Chips Ahoys and cracked a bag of Pecan Sandies. Pippa inwardly groaned as they passed a huge billboard. WELCOME TO BUSHKILL, HONEYMOON CAPITAL OF THE POCONOS.

The car veered into the parking lot of a tacky motel. "Well, here goes nothing," the woman said.

"Thanks for the ride. Hope you catch the bouquet." Pippa walked down Route 209 and checked into the first dive that didn't advertise heart-shaped bathtubs. She handed the Junior Service Associate two hundred bucks. "I'd like a room for tonight."

A former Eagle Scout, he frowned at her blatant desecration of the uniform. "Would you have two forms of identification?"

Sure, except they didn't match. Pippa returned to the highway. She finally found lodging in a flophouse run by dour Indians. They took two hundred bucks and told her not to smoke in bed. Pippa's cabin was barely larger than the mattress it housed. Once inside, she lunged at the phone. By some miracle it produced a dial tone. "This is Pippa Walker. Connect me with Sheldon. It's an emergency. I've heard the most awful things about my mother."

Sheldon's personal assistant Gwendolyn-Sue replied, "I'm afraid Attorney Adelstein can't come to the phone. He's in the hospital."

"My God! Did Thayne break his nose, too?"

"He received a bomb in the mail. It was made to look like a cigarette lighter."

Pippa nearly collapsed. MatchMace! "Is he all right?"

"It's too soon to tell. His eyebrows and nose hairs got singed right off."

Pippa winced: Sheldon's intimidating eyebrows were his pride and joy. "Who could have done such a thing?" she asked innocently.

"He's not telling."

"Which hospital? I'd like to send flowers."

Gwendolyn-Sue took a deep breath. "Attorney Adelstein has specifically instructed me to tell you—and here I quote—'not to communicate with me in any way, shape, or form until my burning desire to strangle her ebbs into merely a desire to chop her legs off at the knee.'"

"What does that mean?" Pippa wailed.

"I'd say he's mad at you, honey."

"Wait! I have a diploma."

"Why don't you take a little vacation until he feels well enough to contact you?"

"I'll send my diploma for verification. And I won't budge from here until he calls." Pippa gave Gwendolyn-Sue her cabin number. "Is my mother really in jail?"

"Please, Pippa! Give everyone a rest!" The phone went dead.

Pippa spent two miserable weeks in her cabin waiting for Sheldon to call. Following its plunge into the Delaware, her Chippa Flushowitz debit card quit working. Afraid to venture outside lest Mitzi was still hunting her, Pippa lived on canned ravioli, Grape-Nuts, and old fruit from the convenience store across the street. She wore an increasingly grungy scoutmaster uniform or her Wilma Flintstone costume. She passed the time watching Bollywood films on in-house cable. She obsessed about Thayne, who seemed to be bouncing around the country from disaster to disaster in tandem with her. Following an erotic dream about Cole taking a naked moonlight swim with her in the Delaware, Pippa made a list of every boyfriend she ever had from the age of eight. The list was not only short but also discouragingly shallow . . . just like her. Lance was far better material than anyone who had preceded him. She should have married him. It would have been a tolerable nunnery; she would have spent the whole year unpacking wedding presents, and at the end of it, Pippa would be divorced but still a Walker. Ready to scream, she balled up her list and threw it at the television. She was far too depressed to even think about ways to spend a billion dollars.

Unable to stand the silence any longer, she called Sheldon's office. He still hadn't returned to work. "Did you get my diploma?"

"We did get an overnight letter billed to recipient," Gwendolyn-Sue replied. "Attorney Adelstein left instructions not to open anything from you."

"For Pete's sake, it's not a bomb, it's my diploma! It's critical that you open it. I'm down to my last fifty bucks. Please. I can't hold out much longer." That didn't cut much mustard. "If anything happens to me here, I'll have no choice but to sue you. Really major sue you."

Pippa was put on hold for a long while. "I've opened the envelope," Sheldon's assistant finally informed her. "Now I'm unfolding the paper inside."

Pippa waited an eon. "Well? What do you see?"

"A large brown stain." Accusing voice: "It smells like fecal matter."

"That's Pushkin's pawprint. It's the official seal of the school. What you smell is insect repellent used as ink. Very effective insect repellent, I might add." Pippa sensed she was not closing the deal. "Surely you see Slava Slootski's name on the bottom of the page. He's the most revered clown in the history of circuses. His signature alone is worth thousands of dollars."

"I see a centipede on the bottom of the page. Dead."

"Look, the diploma got soaked in the Delaware River by mistake. If you take it to an expert, I'm sure you'll see the signature."

"Expert or no expert, it'll take a miracle to convince a judge there's anything here but centipede guts."

"So you're telling me this isn't going to fly?" Pippa's voice began shaking. "I give you my word it's genuine. I have three witnesses."

Gwendolyn-Sue swore her fingers were beginning to itch from the damp, possibly bubonic paper. First explosives, now sewage. What next? "Pippa, you need professional help."

"No kidding. That's why I called Sheldon."

"I'm not talking about legal assistance."

"Are you calling me crazy?" Pippa screamed. "I'll tear your head off!"

"You're sounding like Thayne now."

That cooled Pippa's jets. "Is she out of jail?"

"It wasn't cheap, but she's out."

"Where is she now?" Nothing. "Please tell me. I'm not going to contact her. I just want to know where she is so I can worry about her better."

Gwendolyn-Sue sighed. The two of them were pathetic. If Anson Walker were alive today, he'd march Pippa and Thayne to the woodshed before you could say *Five percent executor's fee.* "She's traveling with an old friend from college. That's all I can tell you."

"Not that awful Dusi Damon!" The silence only confirmed her suspicion. "Give my regards to Sheldon. I'll call when I'm enrolled in another school. That will be soon because I'm really, truly, out of money."

Gwendolyn-Sue tried not to laugh. When people like Pippa said they were broke, that meant they were down to their last fifty grand. "Keep us in the loop." She hung up.

For a long while Pippa watched a fly crawl around the sole screened window in her cabin. A couple of days ago the fly had been full of energy and anger, bashing against the screen, sure it would find a way out. Now it was becoming lethargic. It no longer buzzed, it just wandered around the screen, an easy target for anyone with a swatter. Tomorrow its wings wouldn't be able to lift it off the sill. The next day it would be dead. Pippa understood completely.

You are not a victim. Jerk is pretty damn close, though.

Leave nothing to fate, your soul mate awaits. Yeah right. Hope you had a nice lunch with him.

You must suffer for your art. I've suffered enough and I miss Pushkin.

Pippa morosely sniffed her bottle of Thayne. There being only a half inch of perfume left, she didn't dare use any more of it. Around midnight she wandered across the street to the convenience store for a can of ravioli. As she was counting out a dollar and thirty-nine cents, the cashier asked, "Want a lottery ticket, hon? It's up to a hundred and thirty million."

Pippa laughed harshly. Her chances of winning the lottery were far better than her chances of acquiring a diploma. She picked a phone card off the floor. "Someone dropped this."

"Loser weepers, finders keepers. Call your mother." Seeing Pippa's face, the cashier said, "Call your boyfriend." The frown got worse. "Girlfriend."

Pippa handed over her last four pennies. "I don't have any friends."

"You found that card for a reason. There's a phone on the porch." Poor kid had eaten a whole shelf of Ravioli-O's and was looking more desperate each day. "Pick up that phone, you hear me? Someone's got to be worried about you."

Pippa inserted the phone card and dialed Ginny, whose number was one of the few she could remember. She got the answering machine. "Hi. Are you still in Costa Rica? I'm at—" She looked at the sputtering neon letters across the street. "Taj Mahal Cabins in Bushkill, Pennsylvania. Call if you feel like it." Pippa almost hung up. "Oh! Ask for Lotus Polo," she said before the card expired.

"There. Doesn't that feel better?" the cashier called.

"Tons." Pippa looked in all directions for an elephant. Then she dashed back to her cabin.

After the fly died, Pippa's only companions were the termites eating through the wall behind her headboard and the nearly empty bottle of Thayne perfume. Between recurring nightmares about Pushkin crying himself to sleep, Pippa became morbidly fixated on her black eye: like the fly and her ambitions, it had started out strong and was inexorably fading. It had almost disappeared when the phone rang.

"Lotus Polo." Ginny guffawed. "That's really scraping the bottom of the barrel."

When Pippa checked in at Taj Mahal Cabins, the proprietor's wife had been watching a polo match. Behind her was a statuette with ten arms in the lotus position. "It was the best I could do on the spur of the moment. Are you back in Dallas?"

"No, Aspen. There was nothing doing in Texas. Without the SUV, anyway."

"Sorry. I should never have let my mother drive."

"It's okay. I'll get the replacement soon. What have you been up to?"

Within three sentences Pippa's saga of the last few weeks degenerated into such weepy incoherence that Ginny feared for her friend's sanity. She couldn't believe that Pippa Walker, no matter how desperate, would sleep anywhere for eighteen bucks a night. "I've got an idea," she interrupted when Pippa started hallucinating about wild elephants and Cub Scouts. "Why don't you come out to Aspen? Get back into circulation?"

"I'm broke," Pippa wailed. "Thayne's cut me off. I have to go to school in order to get pocket money from my grandfather's estate. I won't be totally independent until I graduate."

"Hey! There's a school right down the street that would be perfect for you."

"What sort of place is it?" Pippa asked suspiciously.

"The Mountbatten-Savoy School of Household Management."

"Isn't that where Cedric came from? That stupid wedding planner who replaced Wyeth?"

"Think about it. You already know how to do a cream tea and ring a dinner bell. You'd breeze through."

"How long is the course?"

"I think it's two weeks. Like a vacation. I'll take care of your plane ticket and tuition. You can pay me back when you get your hot little hands around a diploma."

"Are you making fun of me?" Pippa shrieked.

"No! Get your butt out here. You need serious rehab."

The next day Lotus Polo received a FedEx box containing two thousand dollars, a pound of Schmidt chocolates, a Nike sweatsuit ensemble, and a book called *Rockies Unbuttoned*. She called a cab and checked out of Taj Mahal Cabins.

Fifteen

Ginny Ortlip prowled her brand-new BMW along the Arrivals curb, searching for a shapely blonde in a red Nike sweatsuit. She was sure Pippa's flight had arrived twenty minutes ago. Most of the passengers had already dispersed and Ginny was getting worried: her old friend had sounded none too coherent on their last phone call. Weeks of living like a fugitive had minced her reason. Thayne had accelerated the insanity by disinheriting her. Now Pippa was trying to validate her existence with some harebrained quest for a diploma.

On Ginny's third loop past the terminal, what appeared to be a Yeti flung open the passenger door and jumped in. "Whew, that was close! Let's get out of here."

A helmet of rough yak fur encased the intruder's head and most of her face. The four-inch sunglasses were postcataract-surgery specials. A floor-length Swiss cavalry coat smothered the Nike sweatsuit. What really threw Ginny, however, was the fake mustache. "Pippa?"

"It's Lotus."

"Where's your luggage?"

"I'm wearing it." Pippa tore the yak hat off. "I think my brains are stewed."

Ginny stared at Pippa's hair. Even soaking wet, its color was several shades brassier than a new trumpet. "Cute."

"It wasn't intentional."

"You wore that hat on the plane?"

"You better believe it." Aspen was one of Thayne's favorite playgrounds. Pippa peeled off the mustache and stuffed it in the ashtray. "I don't believe I spent the last two weeks in a honeymoon cabin in Bushkill."

"No wonder you're delirious." Ginny opened her window, trying to dispel the overpowering stench of yak. "Where'd you get the coat?"

"An army-navy store in Philadelphia. No one on the flight recognized me. In fact, the guy sitting next to me asked to switch seats."

Ginny patted Pippa's knee. "Still pretty wound up, aren't you."

"Wouldn't you be? I'm an orphan. There's a fifty-thousand-dollar price on my head. You're not going to turn me in, are you?"

"Honey, I'm going to turn you *out*. Shopping. Skiing. Parties."

Pippa had no appetite for any of that now. "How was Costa Rica? See any kinkajous?"

"A ton. And I've got videos." Ginny ramped onto Highway 82. "After the jungle I had a craving for snow so I went to the Italian Alps and took skiing lessons with Alberto Tomba."

"He's a serious hunk."

"No kidding. That inspired me to come here and hit the Nordic Track." Ginny's family's lodge in Starwood contained a huge gym. "I love Aspen in July. Much more room in the clubs."

"I really need to graduate from that school." How many damn times did she have to say it? "The thought of meeting ski bums and Arabian princes does nothing for me."

"Oh, right. There's someone else." Silence. "Isn't there?"

"If you insist. His name is Pushkin."

That bear: Ginny thought Pippa was joking. "Why don't you give an exclusive interview on prime time? Tell your version of events, then get on with your life."

"That would never work." Pippa remembered Officer Pierce's words. "I am a very bad liar."

"My God, didn't Thayne teach you anything? Sorry, bad joke." For a moment Ginny thought Pippa was going to punch her. "I think separation is going to be very good for you."

"Have you read one newspaper in the last month?" Pippa erupted. "Separating was the worst thing we could have done. My mother's been staggering from jail to sanatorium to fistfight ever since the wedding blew up. God knows what she's up to now with her friend Dusi."

"Calm down, Pippa! It's not your problem. Thayne's an adult. A very spoiled one. She's had everything go her way since the day she was born. She never developed a mechanism for dealing with adversity."

Pippa's mechanism for dealing with adversity hadn't fared much better. As the BMW pulled onto Main Street, Ginny called out on her cell phone.

"Olivia. Hi. Would four o'clock work? Great." She hung up. "You can't possibly go to school looking like counter help from Tulsa. You can't wear that yak rug, either."

"Would a scoutmaster uniform work?"

Ginny stopped in front of a hair salon. "Step one. You become a mousy brunette. Maid school, remember? Leave the coat in the car." She introduced Pippa to Kendra, a squat hairdresser with a fierce handshake. "This is my dear friend Lotus. The yellow has got to go."

Kendra sifted a bit of Pippa's hair between her fingers. The nicest thing she could say was, "There are whole clumps missing."

"I got caught in the trees. Hang gliding."

"I'll have to trim the ends."

"Again?" Pippa cased the salon. Short cuts seemed to be all the rage. "Whatever."

Ginny disappeared to shop while Kendra snipped away, chatting about ski conditions. Pippa's hair came out a lot browner and a lot shorter than she would have liked. "Quite a draft back there," she commented, rubbing the nape of her neck.

"Wear turtlenecks."

Ginny returned with a boxy pantsuit and shoes for Pippa. "You look adorable! Like Little Lord Fauntleroy."

Scowling, Pippa searched the bottom of the littlest bag for blush or eye shadow. "That's it?"

"Maids don't wear makeup. Go change in the back."

Even as a dull brunette in a unisex suit, Pippa turned heads. "No one's going to recognize me here, right?" she asked anxiously.

"No. Stop being paranoid." Ginny took her to Syzygy for lunch. She let Pippa vent at length about some Polish poker game. When dessert arrived, Ginny dropped a little velvet bag on the table. "You left these at my place."

Pippa stared at her diamond earrings, her grandmother's choker, Rosimund's barrette, and her Patek Philippe watch. They seemed less like jewelry than evidence from a crime scene.

"You can always pawn them." Ginny threw forty bucks on the table and moved Pippa outside. "Here's the scoop. Olivia claims to be an impoverished contessa. She married some Colombian drug runner and is in the middle of a nasty divorce. They both want the dogs." She took Cemetery Lane up a grand hill and pulled into a cul-de-sac, at the end of which stood a colossal edifice trying hard to pass for a log cabin. Heavy rattan chairs lined the front portico in case guests wanted to sit outside and watch the mountains move. Ginny confidently lifted the iron knocker. "Just follow my lead. You're supposed to be my butler taking a refresher course." The door swung open. "Hello, signora."

"Good afternoon, Miss Ortlip. Welcome, Lotus. I am Olivia Villarubia-Thistleberry, director of the Mountbatten-Savoy School of Household Management." Pippa was swept into the embrace of a five-foot-three, raven-haired bombshell struggling to take off those last ten pounds once and for all. As if to gird herself for the ongoing battle, which ended in defeat every day around sundown, Olivia wore black slacks and a black cashmere sweater that had fit perfectly on her honeymoon. She sported a towering bouffant and eyebrows penciled thick as macadam. "Quiet, Reed! Down, Barton!" she chided two white teacup poodles barking furiously at her feet.

Pippa and Ginny followed her into a room jammed with so much furniture that only the little poodles could navigate in a straight path. As they took their seats, Olivia's cell phone played cancan music. "Excuse me. That's my private investigator." Her smile faded. "Nothing in the safe-deposit box? Tap his phone, follow his car, and find those certificates. Or return every cent I've paid you with interest." She hung up. "My ex has fled back to Colombia with all our assets. Thank God

I have the school." As Olivia seated herself next to Pippa, two more teacup poodles bounded in. They were black. "Villeroy! Boch! Come, my darlings." Olivia gathered the four dogs to her lap. Approximately the size of Beanie Babies, they all fit. She rang a little bell and focused on her newest student. "I understand you've been managing Miss Ortlip's household for the last three years, Lotus."

Pippa tried not to laugh. Ginny was already diving for a handkerchief. "That's right, ma'am."

"Where did you receive your initial training?"

The four dogs in Olivia's lap gave Pippa an idea. "At the École des Chiens Domestiqués in Switzerland."

"I don't believe I'm familiar with that school."

No kidding. It was for Saint Bernards. Thayne had spent months on the phone with the breeder before deciding to go with a French bulldog. "It's very exclusive."

"I'm sure of that. Was Miss Ortlip your first placement after graduation?"

"No," Ginny interrupted. "I stole her from Gloria von Thurn und Taxis."

"Is that so! How did you like Gloria?"

Two of the poodles migrated to Pippa's lap and stood on their hind legs, attempting to breast-feed on her buttons. She patted their heads while keeping her eyes fastened on Olivia. "I'm not at liberty to discuss that."

"Bravo. Discretion is the soul of servitude. Look, my little dogs like you." Olivia's diamond rings clicked as she gathered four butterscotch chips from a silver dish. She was dropping them one by one into the poodles' mouths when a young woman entered with a silver tray. The ruffles on her apron, if laid flat, would reach from Aspen to Denver. The uniform and hat were hot pink. "This is Brenda," Olivia announced. "She works for the Pitts of Columbus. They own one of the largest sand and gravel concerns in the country. You may pour tea, Brenda." Olivia watched in silence as Brenda filled three cups. "What was wrong with that service, Lotus?"

Wrong? Pippa stared at the tray. "There appears to be a sixteenth-inch more tea in the first cup." Further commentary seemed expected so she said, "The steam is rising very haphazardly. If you pour slightly left of the handle and create a clockwise flow, you will get a perfect cloud of steam rising like a genie from the center of the cup."

"Excellent, Lotus! They certainly trained you well in Switzerland."

Pippa managed an apologetic smile at Brenda, who looked ready to kill her.

"Go to the kitchen and practice clockwise pouring, Brenda." As Olivia stirred heaps of sugar into her tea, two more micropoodles wandered in. They were brown. "Sub and Zero! Bad boys!" Olivia added them to the writhing commotion on her lap. "Why is Lotus here, Miss Ortlip?"

"She's generally good but she needs more finesse in dusting antiques and starching collars. Also more imagination in drawing baths. I would say an all-around refresher course would be appropriate, at the end of which I would like to see a sheepskin diploma suitable for framing. Two by three feet would be adequate."

"How long do you think this refresher course will last, Signora Villarubia-Thistleberry?" Pippa asked anxiously.

In Olivia's pocket was a check from Ginny for eight thousand dollars. She desperately needed two more checks just like that in order to finance her paramilitary divorce war. "That will depend on your progress. There may be a period of internship at the end of your course work." That way Olivia could charge both Ginny and the temporary employer for the extra week. "Lotus will be boarding here, I presume?"

"I would prefer she stayed with me. Now and then I require a toe massage in the middle of the night."

"Are you sure? Classes start at six in the morning." Olivia ignored little Boch, whose efforts to chew a hole in her cashmere sweater finally succeeded.

"Lotus stays with me," Ginny repeated.

"As you wish." Olivia's phone tinkled the toreador theme from *Carmen*. "Could you see yourselves out? Be here bright and early tomorrow, Lotus. No, he's not getting the dogs," she snarled into her phone. "Not one paw! Do not ask again."

"And you're sorry you didn't marry Lance?" Ginny asked when they were outside. "In six months you would have been haggling just like Olivia."

"Maybe," Pippa sighed. "Maybe not."

Ginny reversed the BMW out of the driveway. "You'll be happy to know your wedding is no longer front-page news. Without statements from you, Lance, or your mothers, the whole fiasco is dead in the water."

"What a nice way of putting things."

"You'll be fully rehabilitated in six months. Look at O.J. Simpson and Ted Kennedy."

"If only Thayne had as short a memory."

"She'll come around. You've immortalized her. Before the wedding she was just a generic Dallas social climber. Now she's a Texas legend." Ginny drove across the Roaring Fork River and headed up the mountain on the other side. "Let's not talk about her anymore. You came to forget."

Good luck with that one. Pippa rolled down her window to inhale the pure mountain air. "I'm beginning to feel a flicker of hope."

Ginny proceeded to a mammoth lodge and three outbuildings with a spectacular view of the Rockies. The Ortlips used it maybe two weekends a year; once Ginny's mother blew a couple million bucks decorating a place, she lost interest in it. "Want to watch my kinkajou videos? I have plenty of Cristal in the fridge."

"Perfect." Pippa showered and changed into camouflage pajamas, Ginny's favorite at-home attire. Outside the cathedral windows, late afternoon sun gilded the snowy peaks. Everything seemed unbelievably peaceful and permanent.

Downstairs, logs blazed in the fireplace. Ginny was setting out a platter of tapas. "Phew! What is that odor?"

"Thayne perfume. I've permanently borrowed your bottle."

"Keep it." Ginny raised her glass. "To Lotus. Aspen. Diplomas."

They settled on a couch to watch endless videos of Costa Rica and catch up on Dallas gossip. With each passing hour, each glass of Champagne, the fallout from Pippa's unwedding seemed increasingly comical. Apparently two of her bridesmaids had managed to snag engagement rings from two of the groomsmen; Wyeth McCoy was handling both weddings, which was probably why Thayne had decked him in Kalamazoo. Pippa was even beginning to laugh about Rosimund's lawsuit when the doorbell rang.

Ginny put down her glass. "Who the hell is that?"

Fearful intuition drew Pippa to the window. She half expected to see Mitzi outside pressing the doorbell with her trunk. What she saw was equally bad: a green Volkswagen. "It's the guy who nearly drove us off the road in traffic school," she whispered in panic, dropping to the floor. "He must have traced your Lexus plates."

Ginny handed Pippa the keys to her BMW. "I'll invite him in. While I'm roasting his ass, you go to Olivia's."

Outside, Pippa saw her breath: the temperature had dropped thirty degrees since sundown. Quiet as a thief, she crept around the lodge. Once she heard Ginny's front door slam, she tore over to the BMW and careened down the hill, by some miracle remembering the route back to Olivia's in the darkness. Pippa pounded the front knocker so hard that the porch vibrated.

"Coming!" Olivia had just polished off a box of animal crackers. The crumbs now clung to her turtleneck like bionic dandruff. "Lotus! This is a surprise."

Villeroy and Boch, the black teacup poodles, began joyfully shredding Pippa's camouflage cuffs. "If you don't mind, I'll be staying with you tonight. I don't want to be late for class in the morning."

"I'm so pleased." Three hundred bucks in her pocket! Olivia shut the door. "Are you ready for bed, dear? You're wearing pajamas." She didn't comment on Lotus's perfume, which could knock out an entire opera house.

"I'm sorry. This is Miss Ortlip's house uniform." Pippa noticed Olivia frowning at her purple-fleeced feet. "The slippers don't scuff her spalted Georgian maple floors."

"And that awful army hat?"

Pippa whipped it off. "My head was cold."

"Very well. Come downstairs. We're just finishing an evening class."

Olivia led Pippa to a capacious laundry where four students were ironing newspapers. Clapping her hands, Olivia announced, "May I introduce your new classmate, Lotus Polo, personal valet for Virginia Ortlip, heiress of a Dallas oil fortune and renowned wilderness explorer, with homes in Dallas, Aspen, and Manhattan."

Olivia led Pippa to the first ironer. "You met Brenda this afternoon. As you may recall, her employers, the Pitts, own a multinational sand and gravel empire." Too busy getting the creases out of *Doonesbury,* Brenda didn't look up. Olivia proceeded to the next ironing board. "This is Cornelius. He works for Ralph and Brando, the famous clothing designers with homes in Palm Springs, Palm Beach, and Provincetown."

"*And* Ibiza." A houseboy in head-to-toe white silk and waxed arched eyebrows extended his hand. "Camo is so *out,* Lo." He resumed ironing *W.*

"This is our dear Logan," Olivia continued, smiling at a petite Indonesian fellow in a pale orange tuxedo. "Personal valet to Biff Delaney, dot-com trillionaire from Seattle with vacation residences in Nantucket and Cancún. One of the most eligible bachelors on the planet, I might add."

"He's an animal," Logan muttered under his breath.

"Logan! No dissing employers during class time." Olivia winked at Pippa. "After class is a different matter." She proceeded to an elderly black woman struggling to iron the kinks out of *Reader's Digest.* "This is Maisie. She has worked fifty years for the Dudley Stringhammer family, which controls pork bellies futures on the Chicago Mercantile Exchange. They live in a chateau on Lake Michigan and summer in Newport."

A socially proud woman, Maisie took one look at Pippa's camouflage pajamas and sniffed, "Nouveau."

"What is Miss Ortlip's favorite reading material, Lotus? I'll purchase a copy and teach you to iron it properly."

"*Powder.*" Pippa had seen a copy on Ginny's coffee table. Alberto Tomba was on the cover.

"I had no idea she was interested in makeup." Olivia rapped two cans of spray starch together. "Attention! I'm showing Lotus to her room. When I return, I want everything ironed perfectly."

"That's pretty special, ironing newspapers," Pippa said, following Olivia up the back staircase. Even Thayne didn't expect her overworked staff to do that.

"Attention to detail sets my school apart." That and the astronomical tuition. Olivia led Pippa to a room on the top floor. Everything in it was yellow. "We spent all afternoon preparing this room for a visiting head of state. It was a wonderful exercise."

"Thank you. I love yellow."

"It was my private fitting room. Twice a year Saint Laurent flew in from Paris to hem my skirts here." If Olivia's lawyers performed up to spec, those days would return. She turned down the perfectly made bed. "May I be frank, Lotus? I wish you would reside with me for the entire course. It's difficult to concentrate on studies when you must return home every night and prepare blackened impala or whatever it is Miss Ortlip eats. The additional cost would mean nothing to her." Four thousand bucks: Olivia presumed that Ginny, like most people who sent their staff here, blew twice that every week on cocaine, Ritalin, and Lipitor.

"I'll discuss it with her at once."

Olivia helped herself to one of the chocolate truffles in a yellow dish. "It may not be easy. Miss Ortlip seems overly protective of you."

Pippa became worried. "Will staying with her affect my graduation?"

"It certainly can't help. Good night, Lotus. You'll get a wake-up call at sunrise."

Pippa pounced on the phone the moment Olivia left. She dialed Sheldon, who picked up because he thought Pippa's caller ID was that of an old client in Aspen. "Thankyou thankyou for answering, Sheldon. I've been so worried! How are your eyebrows?"

After a long pause he said, "I wouldn't know. At the moment I have none."

"I had no idea you'd try to use that lighter. Well, actually, I thought you might use it but I didn't think it would blow up in your face. There was a fifty percent chance that it wouldn't. It must have gotten shaken up in the mail. Half of it is Mace, invented by a welder brother of the limousine driver named Mike in—"

"How may I assist you, Pippa? As you may have guessed, that piece of damp paper you sent to me is not a qualified diploma. I don't care if Vladimir Putin himself signed it."

"Thank you for that vote of confidence. I'm now enrolled at the Mountbatten-Savoy School of Household Management in Aspen."

"You're going into real estate? Excellent. Aspen's a terrific area for it."

"Actually, it's more a school for managing homes from the inside out. Ironing newspapers, pouring tea, things like that."

Sheldon worked those images through to their abysmal conclusion. "You're learning how to become a *servant?*" That was even worse than a clown.

"I'm trying to get a damn diploma!" Pippa filled the frigid silence with details of Olivia's address, neatly printed on a card next to the truffles. "I owe Ginny Ortlip some money. I'll need about ten thousand bucks, a cell phone, and some more suits. Can you get my ATM card working again? It got soaked in the Delaware River."

"What happened to the Prada suits? Not to mention your cell phone?"

"I had to leave clown camp in a rush. Oh, I need a car."

"What for?"

"I just feel better with a car."

"And to whom might I direct these dire necessities? Jeevesina Butleroni?"

"Lotus Polo." It didn't sound like an improvement. "Thank you so much, Sheldon."

"I didn't say I'd do it," he fumed, hanging up.

Pippa immediately called Ginny. "Did you kill him?"

"Not yet. The swine is drinking all my beer and watching kinkajou videos. You may as well stay at Olivia's tonight. I'll come get my car in the morning."

"Could you bring a few more camo pajamas? I told Olivia it was my uniform."

Starving, Pippa finished all the chocolates. She had just gotten into bed when she heard tiny whimpers outside her door: Sub and Zero, the brown teacup poodles. They stationed themselves on either side of her pillow, like tiny clones of Pushkin. Pippa read aloud to them until they drifted asleep.

Next thing she knew her phone was ringing. "It's six o'clock, Lapis," Maisie said.

"The name's Lois. I mean Lotus." Too much Cristal. Dull headache. The dogs were gone. Where was she?

"We're waiting for you downstairs."

Crap! Pippa cycloned to the kitchen, where four immaculately uniformed classmates eyed her wrinkled pajamas with disdain. "Your boss allows you to be seen like that?" Brenda huffed.

"This is my tropics uniform. We just got back from Costa Rica."

Olivia and her six teacup poodles swept in. Today she wore a red dress that Saint Laurent had hemmed back in the halcyon days. A clip-on bow rested high on her bouffant, giving her the appearance of a standard-sized poodle. "Good morning! Today we will study the art of perfect toast." Olivia gestured to two dozen loaves of bread, six brands of butter, and a herd of jams and marmalades covering the granite island. "As you see, the variety is endless."

Maisie looked displeased. "I don't see any Wonder bread here, Signora Villarubia-Thistleberry."

"Correct. I wouldn't feed that to the squirrels."

"Mr. and Mrs. Stringhammer have been eating it every morning for the last fifty years."

"In which case I'm sure you already know how to toast it perfectly. You are excused from class. Go to your room and review the chapter on Orderly Medicine Cabinets. Be careful you don't step on my little dogs." They were spiraling between everyone's legs.

Maisie straightened her headdress and left. "She's such a snob," Cornelius the gay houseboy whispered. "Fifty years with pork bellies can really skew your outlook. What's she even doing here?"

"Maisie is taking the Ancillary Geriatrics course." It was a serious new source of revenue for Olivia. "And doing very well indeed. Find a serrated knife, everyone. Take a loaf. You have thirty seconds to cut it into half-inch slices." Olivia watched as her students sawed away. "Stop!" She gathered everyone around a stainless-steel box the size of a milk crate. "This is the most advanced toaster on the market. It works on color recognition, ejecting the toast the moment it turns amber brown. This model costs three thousand dollars and looks very handsome on the counter."

In a cultivated household, Olivia taught, melted butter must stop a half inch from the crust, otherwise it would soil the fingertips of those picking it up and shoving it into their mouths while they read the stock quotations. Olivia waited with a tape measure until each student had produced a slice of perfectly buttered toast. "Your next challenge is jam, which must go up to, but never over, one-sixteenth of an inch from the edge of the melted butter."

Again Olivia waited until each student had finished. "Bravo, all.

Lovely work. However, your toast is ice-cold. How are you ever going to manage breakfast for twelve?" No one answered. "Practice until you run out of bread." On the way out Olivia helped herself to a few slices.

"Is she making this up?" Pippa asked Logan. "No one butters toast to the sixteenth of an inch."

"Don't tell that to Olivia. She's serious about bringing back the Gilded Age."

Pippa practiced slicing as her classmates traded ribald stories about their employers. Cornelius's main purpose in life was to keep Ralph and Brando's daisy chain replenished. Brenda violently hated her employer Mr. Pitt now that he had married a woman two years younger than herself. Poor Logan was worn out keeping Biff Delaney's fifty mistresses from running into each other on the way into or out of his boudoir. "We looked up your boss on the Web," Cornelius called over. "Her only claim to fame was some outrageous wedding."

Pippa's stomach lurched. "Miss Ortlip keeps a low profile."

"Who's she sleeping with?"

"I have no idea." That got heavy guffaws: every servant on the planet kept a meticulous diary of the boss's fornications. Their retirement funds depended on it.

At nine o'clock, all convened under Olivia's Chihuly chandelier for a review of How to Announce Callers. Between phone conversations with her private investigator, Olivia passed along all she knew about intercoms and closed-circuit television deliveries as well. "Look, class! There's a real person outside."

"That's Miss Ortlip," Pippa cried.

"Show her to the parlor, Lotus. Everyone else practice security codes." Olivia settled in with Villeroy and Boch, Reed and Barton, Sub and Zero. "How are you today, Miss Ortlip?"

"Fine, thank you. I brought Lotus some fresh uniforms."

"Wonderful. I know you're anxious to go out and shoot a few reindeer, so I will come straight to the point. In my opinion Lotus should board at school for the entire course."

Ginny was not thrilled. "What do you think, Lo?" When Pippa remained frozen, she added, "I severely need you to wax my skis."

"I severely need that diploma," Pippa croaked, handing back the BMW keys.

"Have it your way." Shaking her head, Ginny left.

"Bravo, Lotus," Olivia said after the front door slammed. Four thousand bucks in her pocket! She looked more closely at the young woman in camouflage pajamas. Lotus did not comport herself like a domestic: quite the opposite. Nevertheless Ginny gave her anything she wanted. "May I ask—" Olivia's phone interrupted. "Mountbatten-Savoy School of Household Management. Olivia Villarubia-Thistleberry speaking."

"This is Leigh Bowes from Las Vegas," a woman's voice said. "Your name has been given to me by one of my dearest friends, Dusi Damon, who said you supplied Thayne Walker with a wedding planner on an hour's notice."

That would be Cedric, her former handyman, an ex-marine. For an enormous fee, Olivia had slapped on a phony résumé and shipped him off to that brouhaha in Dallas. To everyone's amazement he was still there. Cedric still sent Olivia two thousand bucks a month commission for landing him the gig. "How may I help?"

"I desperately need a new majordomo with impeccable credentials."

"We have a long waiting list," Olivia lied.

"This is an emergency. I'll pay you a fifty thousand finder's fee."

Leigh Bowes shot to the top of the nonexistent waiting list. Olivia forced herself to sound mildly bored. "Describe your requirements."

"All-around superior household management skills. Must make perfect martinis. Above all, I do *not* want an attractive woman. My husband is a disgusting lecher."

"I understand completely, Signora Bowes. My ex was the same."

"This weekend I'm hosting a celebration with three hundred friends. They are the cream of society. The event must go perfectly. If you get me someone by then, I'll pay an extra ten thousand."

Olivia nearly swallowed Villeroy. However, she managed to say, "Leave your number on my Web site. Please attach a personal recommendation from Dusi Damon." Olivia had never heard of her. She hung up. "Is something the matter, Lotus?"

"Did you say Dusi Damon?" Pippa gulped. "She's rather bad news."

Olivia didn't care if she was the Antichrist. Sixty thousand dollars!

She was so blown away she could barely deliver her next lecture, History of the Fork, in the library. "Logan," she said finally, giving up. "Prepare lunch while Maisie and I review Adult Incontinence. We'll all meet in the dining room at one. Lotus, what are you writing back there?"

"I'm taking notes for the exam."

Olivia's phone rang. As she plunged into a bitter altercation with a real estate lawyer, the doorbell rang. "Get that, someone."

Pippa went to the door. "Car for Ms. Polo," a man said.

A blue Maserati, the exact replica of Lance's drowned pride and joy, was parked at the curb. Damn it, that should have gone to Officer Pierce weeks ago! Sheldon had changed the license plate from HUDDLE to LOTOPO. Seething, Pippa signed for it and drove the man to the airport. She got back to school just in time for Advanced Place Setting in the dining room.

"Identify these dishes, class," Olivia announced, picking up various pieces of china from the table.

"Main course plate. Salad plate. Consommé cup. Butter dish. Salt well. Fish plate. Bread plate. Ramekin. Sauceboat. Caviar dish." Olivia was pleased to see that Lotus knew her away around a place setting. She pointed to an odd porcelain chalice. "And what is this?"

"Individual spoonbread dish?" Maisie guessed.

"Personal spittoon?" Logan tried.

Pippa raised her hand. "That is an eggcup, ma'am. For ostrich eggs." Rosimund had purchased four hundred of them for the Henderson Ball.

"My God, Lotus! You *must* give me the name of that school in Switzerland." If only Lotus were male, Leigh Bowes would have her majordomo by sundown! "When I say go, class, create an eighteen-piece place setting. All the dishes you need are on the sideboard. Careful! They're antique Sèvres."

When Pippa finished first, Olivia thought she'd break into hives. She led her students to the bar, there to learn that Pippa could identify every variety of her twenty Waterford glasses. Her voice barely above a whisper, she asked, "Can you make a martini, dear?"

"I've been making them for my mother since I was eight years old."

Weak-kneed, Olivia told everyone to study the Forbes 400 list until tea.

Olivia's evening class, Advanced Napkin Folding, was continuously interrupted by calls from lawyers and Leigh Bowes. Around midnight Dusi Damon sent an e-mail threatening to close down the school should Olivia fail to send a household manager to Las Vegas at once. Stressed, Olivia ate half a cheesecake. She awoke at dawn feeling like a rectangle of cream cheese. She had no sooner stepped off the scale when her bank called to say her mortgage payment was overdue.

She put a bow in her bouffant and entered the kitchen with a smile. Today Olivia wore a brown wool dress with six pockets down the front. A teacup poodle nestled in each pocket, giving her the appearance of a marsupial who had just birthed sextuplets. "Good morning, class. Today we will be dusting antiques, starching collars, and drawing baths." As she served herself a stack of crêpes suzette that Cornelius had made, the doorbell rang. "Get that please, Brenda."

Brenda ran out and returned with a large FedEx package. "For Lotus." She threw it with unnecessary force on the table.

Everyone watched with great interest as Pippa unwrapped, and nearly dropped, her souvenir MatchMace. "Miss Ortlip occasionally likes a good cigar," she explained, cursing Sheldon anew. He had sent ten thousand dollars cash in a plastic sandwich bag. Pippa also got a cell phone and five Chanel suits, which she didn't even try to explain.

Olivia watched in silence. First a Maserati, now this: Ginny Ortlip would rather lose an arm than lose Lotus. Domestics of her caliber came along once in a lifetime. Barely able to concentrate, Olivia gave every student a feather duster and told them to get the cobwebs out of the banisters while she and Maisie took a few turns around the wheelchair course in the basement.

Pippa adjourned to the driveway to call Sheldon. "The Maserati arrived yesterday. I thought we had agreed to give it to Officer Pierce."

"Couldn't find him. He disappeared after getting fired."

No! "For what?"

"Let's not even go there. You needed a car and it was taking up garage space. What do you think of LOTOPO? I tried to get TORPEDO but it was taken." Hearing no reply, he continued, "How's servant school going?"

"Fine. The diploma is a lock."

As Sheldon hung up, Pippa could hear him laughing.

Olivia was polishing off the last of the cheesecake when Leigh Bowes called for the tenth time that day. "I'm very close to making a decision," Olivia reported. "You will have to be patient."

"This is a desperate situation, Signora Villarubia-Thistleberry. I need a new majordomo by noon tomorrow. An extra five thousand for you if he arrives before midday."

"You will not be disappointed. Goodbye." Olivia could barely get the last forkful of cheesecake past her constricted throat. She had to think of something fast, *sixty-five thousand dollars* fast. Her phone rang again. It was Ginny.

"I must have Lotus back this afternoon. Alberto Tomba is visiting from Italy."

Olivia homed like a smart bomb onto the desperation in Ginny's voice. "I assess a fee for missed classes, Miss Ortlip."

"I'll pay you a thousand bucks to release Lotus at three o'clock."

"Two."

"Two o'clock is even better."

"I meant two thousand dollars, madam. At four o'clock."

"Damn, you're tough! All right."

Olivia hung up. Miss Ortlip . . . Cedric . . . Lotus . . . Las Vegas . . . plans were coagulating in her brain like amoebas in the primordial soup. She summoned Pippa to her parlor. Her little dogs wouldn't stop barking until Pippa picked them up. "Miss Ortlip has requested your assistance this afternoon. It seems she has planned a dinner party for Alberto Tomba."

"But I'll miss class."

"Never mind. We're covering Advanced Dogwalking Techniques and, to my knowledge, Miss Ortlip has no pets. Except you, of course."

Pippa sighed. Ginny wanted to party and this was payback time. "I'll finish as soon as possible."

"I need to ask a favor. Miss Ortlip was at that nasty Walker wedding, wasn't she?"

Pippa nearly dropped Sub and Zero. "Ah—yes. She was a bridesmaid."

"Could you get her feedback regarding Cedric and Mrs. Walker? I might transfer him to Las Vegas but that could be difficult if he's servicing the lady of the house."

"That's outrageous! Thayne Walker is happily married!" Realizing that she was shouting, Pippa forced herself to calm down. "At least that's what I hear."

"You've been misinformed, Lotus. Thayne Walker's husband has been golfing in Morocco ever since the wedding collapsed. It seems highly likely that Cedric has wormed his way into the master bedroom. Believe me, I know how he operates." Olivia couldn't figure out why Lotus looked so upset. She poured them both a glass of sherry. "Anyway, dear, could you please extract this information from Miss Ortlip for me?"

Pippa swallowed hard. "But doesn't Mrs. Walker need Cedric? You can't just rip him out from under her like a rug. Even if he is . . . you know . . . under her like a rug . . . which I doubt. Thayne Walker would never consort with the help."

Olivia looked oddly at her. "What's your interest in this, Lotus?"

"I know Margarita the maid. If Cedric left, she'd bear the brunt of everything. She's got a weak heart and bad bunions."

Olivia plopped onto the sofa and somberly stroked Reed and Barton. "Please extend some sympathy to me as well, Lotus. I am a single woman desperately trying to survive."

"Yes, ma'am." *It's the diploma, stupid!* "Forgive my insensitivity."

"I know you'll do your best. Do be back by eight. We're covering an important chapter on Etiquette at the Morgue."

"Thank you for excusing me, Signora Villarubia-Thistleberry."

Ginny no doubt meant well but it was time to let her know that a billion bucks were riding on graduation from school. Pippa looked carefully in all directions before dashing to the Maserati parked at the curb. She crawled fifty feet down the street then donned the yak hat, cataract sunglasses, mustache, and the Swiss Army coat she kept in the trunk in case that paparazzo was still snooping around Aspen. Pippa drove down Olivia's hill, through the village, and up Ginny's hill. She was drenched in sweat by the time she reached the Ortlip compound. Again Pippa looked in all directions before leaving the car. After ringing Ginny's bell she peeled her mustache off and stuck it to her cataract glasses.

Ginny, cocktail in hand, opened the door. She looked flushed: maybe Alberto Tomba really was here. "You're wearing *that* again?"

Pippa rushed inside. "Where's the VW guy?"

"On a wild-goose chase to Nebraska. Relax."

The house was set up for a party but Pippa sensed something off. The big WELCOME BACK sign over the fireplace was in English, not Italian. "When's Alberto getting here?"

"Screw Alberto!"

Twenty people, led by none other than Lance's lover Woody and the vile Kimberly, gushed out of the kitchen. "Surpriiiiiiiiiiiiise!"

Pippa bolted down the front steps and gunned the Maserati out of Ginny's driveway. She thought her head would explode. Blinded by the mustache stuck to her glasses, she nearly hit a trailer full of canoes on Main Street. She was dimly aware of pedestrians shouting obscenities at her as she blitzed through town. How could Ginny be so crass as to throw a surprise party for her? How could she invite Woody and Kimberly, of all traitors, or remotely think such a reunion would be *beneficial*?

Olivia was alone on her porch, having sent her students to Snowmass to return the four German shepherds she had borrowed for Advanced Dogwalking Techniques. One ear to the phone, Olivia tossed homemade biscuits to her poodles as she tried to stall Dusi Damon, an even worse shrew than Thayne Walker. "Harassment will get you nowhere," she said. "If you must know, I'm still checking the credentials of Leigh Bowes. Not to mention your own." Olivia hung up as Lotus's Maserati squealed into the driveway. A derelict staggered out of the driver's seat. "Excuse me! May I help you?"

Pippa whipped off her hat. She looked extremely distraught. "I've got to talk to you."

"Lotus! Come in. Take that foul coat off."

Pippa fell onto the couch in the parlor. "Something truly awful has happened."

"Did you scorch Miss Ortlip's newspaper?"

"It's a personal matter," Pippa croaked. "I just quit. I must leave Aspen immediately. I so wanted a diploma, signora! You have no idea how much I wanted one." Pippa began to wail so dejectedly that all six teacup poodles started howling along with her.

Olivia's brain went into overdrive. Ortlip was out of the picture. Lotus was out of a job. There must be some way to convert this tragedy into a sixty-five-thousand-dollar sitcom. "I can help. But you must have an open mind."

"Just make it quick."

"In lieu of class, you could do an internship at a wonderful home in Las Vegas. The woman of the house seems to be concerned about an upcoming fête. If that goes well, you shall have your diploma. I promise you."

"What's the catch?"

"She requests a male."

"Do you think I look even remotely like a guy?" Pippa shouted. The harshness in her voice set the dogs howling afresh. "Sorry, it's a touchy subject at the moment."

"You've already got short hair. You're tall and slender. In the proper uniform and underwear, I'm sure we could pass you off as a rather iffy male."

So Olivia proposed sending *her,* instead of Cedric, to Las Vegas. That would spare Thayne another rupture: an offer Pippa couldn't refuse. She unpeeled the mustache from her sunglasses and stuck it on her upper lip. "Does that help?"

"Very much." Frankly it was a stretch, but Olivia was willing to gamble. "Dry your eyes and come upstairs."

Olivia had a closet full of uniforms, remnants of the glory days when she and the ex had a staff of ten. "Saint Laurent designed these for me. Their inspiration is a Gainsborough portrait of the third Earl of Thistleberry, the cockroach's ancestor." Olivia removed the plastic bag from a gray military jacket with thirty brass buttons. Many loops of iridescent green-purple rope hung from the epaulets. The silk harem pants and porter's cap matched the ropes. "The colors of an English pigeon. Beautiful, no?"

"Do you have a summer uniform? Las Vegas is in the desert."

"Yes, of course." Rummaging in another closet, Olivia found the short-sleeved, short-pants version of the pigeon costume. She located several boob-flattening sports bras that had belonged to a maid who eloped with a ski bum. She found a pair of gray Rockport nubucks and gray socks. "Try these on, Lotus."

Despite its rigid lines, the uniform was surprisingly comfortable. The colors didn't look as awful together as Pippa had imagined. She wished Olivia hadn't told her about the pigeons, though.

Olivia studied the result: still too feminine. "Ah! One moment."

In a sewing table drawer she found a pair of oversized tortoiseshell glasses recognizable the world over. "Yves left them here on his last visit. They are among my most prized possessions." She poised them on Pippa's nose. "Perfect."

"But I can't see a thing."

"Take them to a one-hour store. Change the lenses to glass." Olivia got her cell phone. "Signora Bowes, this is Olivia Villarubia-Thistleberry. I have found a majordomo for you. His name is Cosmo du Piche. You will see him tomorrow morning. Please wire full payment to my account at once." Olivia knew all fourteen digits by heart. "He will not ring your doorbell until the funds have cleared." With a triumphant smile, she slipped the phone back into her pocket. "Well, that's settled."

"Cosmo du Piche?"

"My true love. He threw himself off a cliff when he learned I had married the cockroach. Go to your room and pack, Lotus. I'll book you a flight."

"I'd rather drive, if you don't mind. Immediately."

"But you must be in Las Vegas tomorrow morning."

"It's only six hundred miles. I've got a fast car."

"Very well." Olivia began gathering spare accoutrements for her protégé. "You come from a superior background. I'm sure you will be a success. And please remember that you are a man."

Think diploma. "I'll do my best."

In short order Pippa kissed the dogs goodbye and headed south.

Sixteen

Although she couldn't imagine why anyone would want to kidnap her, and she couldn't remotely imagine her husband, Moss, springing for a ransom should a kidnapping occur, Leigh Bowes had hired a bodyguard when it became apparent that she was the only socialite in Las Vegas without one. Samson was a disaster from day one. Sure, he looked impressive, but an armed man hulking six feet away at all times was, to say the least, intrusive. Plus he was a lummox. Each time Samson trailed her through the kitchen, he knocked something major off the counter, driving Rudi the chef bonkers. Samson insisted on locking Leigh into her bedroom every night, for her own protection. He ate nothing but aged prime rib. Nevertheless, since most female members of the Las Vegas Country Club had bodyguards and Leigh had been trying for eight gut-wrenching months to become a member of that superelite, she endured his company.

Unfortunately her majordomo had not been as flexible. He had recently marched into her bathroom, shut the door, and said, "Either Samson goes or I go."

Leigh was aghast: in one week she was throwing a birthday party for her bichon frise, Titian. Three hundred guests, their bodyguards, and their dogs had been invited. "What's gotten into you, Ferdinand?"

"He cleans his guns in the kitchen. Rudi hates that. He leaves his shavings in the sink and he's formed an intimate liaison with Kerry." The Irish maid. "I'm constantly walking in on them *in flagrante.*"

"How is that possible? Samson is with me eighteen hours a day."

Ferdinand peeped through the keyhole into the master bedroom. "They're defiling your mattress as we speak, madam."

Leigh passed a hand over her face. "You put me in a difficult position, Ferdinand."

He had said nothing further. He simply packed his bags and left. Out shopping, Leigh didn't even know Ferdinand was gone until that evening, when her martini failed to materialize at the stroke of five. Chaos had immediately overtaken Casa Bowes. Canceling Titian's birthday party was out of the question: such a faux pas would nuke her chances of membership in the Las Vegas Country Club. Leigh had called every employment agency in Nevada, to no avail. She had finally thrown herself at the mercy of her friend Dusi Damon, one of the last people she would even want to know about the catastrophe. Dusi had pointed her at Olivia Unpronounceable-dash-Supercilious in Aspen, who had coughed up a replacement after days of suspense. Leigh now owed Dusi so big time it bordered on moral bankruptcy.

Paranoid at losing yet another household employee, Leigh had said nothing to Samson or Kerry about their tawdry behavior. She didn't dare tell her husband about the fornication problem because Moss had never wanted a bodyguard in the first place. He already thought Casa Bowes had three servants too many, cheap bastard. Moss was even ticked that Leigh was replacing Ferdinand: in his opinion, she was perfectly capable of dusting the furniture herself. Then after all that ranting, he had blown a million dollars at auction for a tiny Poussin still life. Leigh was ready to kill him.

She was eating breakfast in her atrium, glancing through the Frederick's of Hollywood catalogue, when the doorbell rang. "Could you get that, Samson?" she asked after the third ring. "Kerry must still be tying bows on all the dog biscuits."

"Only if you come with me," he replied. His contract forbade him to wander more than six feet from his charge.

"Damn it!" Leigh threw down her antique silver grapefruit spoon. "Must I do everything myself?" She flung open the door. On her stoop stood a tall, slender—fellow?—in a gray jacket and iridescent green-purple silk shorts. He sported enormous eyeglasses and an Inspector Clouseau mustache.

"Signora Bowes." He bowed. "Cosmo du Piche at your service."

This was her sixty-five-thousand-dollar Superman? Leigh tried not to laugh. The boy looked seriously myopic. His voice was high as a girl's. "Come in. Did you have a nice flight?"

"I drove, thank you."

Cosmo didn't mention where he had driven from and Leigh didn't ask. Olivia had obviously filched him from another hapless society hostess; the less Leigh knew about that, the more innocent she could pretend to be when word got out. "Where might I park?" he asked.

Leigh was nonplussed to see a blue Maserati in her driveway. "Leave your car there for the moment. My chauffeur will put it in the garage."

As she spoke, a Brinks armored truck pulled up behind the Maserati. Four armed guards hopped out, unlocked the rear doors, and carried a large crate to the front door. "Moss Bowes residence?"

"Yes. I'm Mrs. Bowes."

"We have a painting."

That stupid Poussin! Leigh fought an overwhelming desire to refuse delivery. "Put it in the den."

"Not so fast." Samson barred their path. "Remove your weapons first."

The guards looked at him as if he had asked them to remove their gonads. "We can't do that while the painting is in our custody. Insurance regulations."

"And I can't let you in the house with weapons. Security regulations."

No one moved for a full minute. Leigh looked as if she had been shot. "Someone please do something!" she wailed.

Cosmo du Piche had met his first imbroglio. "I suggest you call your office," Pippa told the Brinks man. "And you call yours," she told Samson. "Let's get a dialogue going."

"Who's this bozo?" the security guy asked.

"My majordomo," Leigh replied. "Do as he says."

Chortling, the guard called his office. So did Samson. The situation was explained at least a dozen times to various managers. Brinks presidents phoned Goliath Protection Services presidents. Chubb agents were consulted. Lawyers were consulted. The Brinks men didn't budge from the doorstep, nor did Leigh, Samson, and Pippa budge from the foyer. After a passing patrol car got into the act, the dilemma was reexplained, with considerably less patience. By the time the police checked everyone's license to carry firearms, Leigh's front door had been wide open for thirty minutes. Her living room was at least eighty degrees and getting dustier by the minute. "Could we speed this up?" she asked, irritatedly tapping her foot.

Her cell phone rang. It was her art dealer in New York, advising Leigh that he had been rousted from bed at noon by Chubb, Brinks, and Sotheby's. She was mortified.

After the policemen left, no one spoke. Pippa took the opportunity to study the décor. Leigh's living room and foyer were stuffed with Louis Quatorze furniture that no human had dared sit upon for a century. A tremendous rococo harpsichord, the inside of its lid painted with a country scene, occupied a corner of the grand parlor. Dark paintings lined the apricot walls. Each canvas depicted a bird either dead with root vegetables, aloft in the wild, or cupped in a nobleman's hands. The place was pretentious, boring, and useless. Pippa noticed Leigh waiting anxiously for her pronouncement. "Beautiful," she smiled.

Leigh was an attractive thirtysomething blonde. She wore a large diamond in an aggressive setting. Her cerise sequined halter and four-inch heels seemed a bit much for this hour of the morning but she carried both well. She had dancer's legs. Although her exquisitely applied makeup had left no pore behind, she would have looked prettier with just moisturizer. Same with the jewelry: one knockout chain and bracelet would have looked better than the dozens garnishing her neck and wrists.

An apricot-colored Mercedes limousine squeezed into the driveway behind the Maserati and the Brinks car. Pippa saw a man leave the driver's seat. Tall, dark, handsome. He wore an apricot polo shirt, same as Samson's, with CASA BOWES embroidered in brown above the alligator. With a strange dread Pippa watched him approach the crowd on the stoop.

"Cole!" Leigh cried. "Can you believe this awful mess?"

Pippa nearly collapsed. *Cole from Phoenix!*

Cole presumed the babe in the iridescent pantaloons had just delivered a singing telegram to Titian, the dog. She was blushing in mortification: couldn't blame her. Then he stopped dead: despite the false mustache he recognized her mouth. It had been haunting him for weeks. *Chippa?* What was she doing here in that strange getup, pretending he was invisible? Either she didn't remember him or she didn't care to remember him: neither theory was complimentary. Cole decided to play dumb until he got his bearings. "I see the Poussin has arrived," he told Leigh.

"They can't bring it in or Samson will have to shoot them," she answered. "We've been standing here for half an hour."

The head guard snapped his phone shut. "Okay. We got a deal." He put his revolver on the doormat. "I leave my heat here and carry the picture inside. My three guys guard me. Your bodyguard guards the picture. If it looks as if I'm going to take off with it, everybody shoots me."

"That seems fair," Leigh agreed.

"Not so fast." Samson wouldn't let him in until he had run the scenario past his boss in Tucson. He frisked the guard. Then he cocked his gun and aimed it at the guard's chest. "Nice and easy. One false move and you're hamburger."

That got the other Brinks men so annoyed that two of them trained their guns at Samson's chest. "And you're chowchow," one of them replied.

"Let's try not to shoot a dozen holes in the painting, okay, fellas?" Cole said.

The guard with the crate tiptoed gingerly over the threshold. He had no doubt that should he somehow trip or hiccup, Samson would blast him. "Where would you like me to put this?"

"Right there against the umbrella stand. Thank you." Leigh signed a dozen receipts.

Snap out of it. He doesn't recognize you. Pippa was both relieved and a little hurt. She peeled four hundreds off a wad in her pocket. "Thanks for your patience, gentlemen. Excellent job."

"You're welcome." The guard glared at Samson. "You're not, asshole." They drove away.

"Nothing like a little shootout to get the day off to a good start. And you would be . . . ?" Cole asked Pippa when she made no sign of leaving.

"Cosmo du Piche," Leigh announced. "Our new majordomo."

"Cole Madisson. Nice touch, that tip." Picking up the crate, he walked down the hall.

Leigh's phone rang. It was her art dealer again. She had caused him to lose face with Sotheby's. If some cowboy was going to pull a gun every time he tried to deliver a French masterpiece to the Wild West, the Bowes family would be removed from his client list. "I told you I'm sorry," Leigh snapped, hanging up. She rubbed her flaming forehead. "Cosmo, can you do martial arts?"

"I can karate kick."

"That's good enough for me." Leigh turned to Samson. "You're fired. Wait here, Cosmo." Leigh accompanied Samson to his room. Five minutes later, his bags packed, they returned to the foyer.

"Good luck, fruitcake," he told Pippa on the way out.

When nothing remained of Samson but the dust cloud in her driveway, Leigh turned to Pippa. "I feel *so* much better already. Would you like a tour of the house?"

Having driven all night from Aspen, Pippa would have preferred a ten-hour siesta but, rather than get fired on the spot like Samson, said, "I would love that, Signora Bowes."

"We'll start right here with the front doors. I saw you admiring them. Aren't they fantastic?"

The Varathane had barely dried on two enormous rosewood doors. On the left door, beneath the inscription CASA, the figure of a woman in evening dress had been carved in bas relief. She bore an idealized resemblance to Leigh. On the right door, beneath the inscription BOWES, was the figure of a man in a tux, presumably the guy who had paid for everything. Twittering birds adorned the four corners of each door.

"I love the birds," Pippa said.

"My husband insisted on them. His company is the largest importer of feathers in the United States."

That explained the paintings. "Bravo."

"Fine Feather is also *the* purveyor of sequins, metallic fabric, whalebone, rhinestones, faux fur, and snakeskin in Las Vegas." Shutting the front doors, Leigh proceeded to a palatial room off the foyer. "I'm a bit of a Louis Quatorze nut. Casa Bowes is a thirty-thousand-square-foot replica of Versailles." Seeing Pippa's glazed smile, Leigh continued, "You're probably wondering why it isn't named *Maison Bowes*, aren't you?"

Actually Pippa was wondering if there were a death penalty in Nevada and, if so, when Leigh's interior decorator had been executed. "Yes, that did cross my mind."

"We didn't want to seem too pretentious."

"It's perfect." Pippa kept the smile glued on as Leigh showed her a Duesenberg, custom-painted apricot, parked in the garage: her toodling-around-town wheels. Pippa was led past six ballrooms, a coffin-sized silver chest, an indoor swimming pool, a bowling alley, and a cavernous library crammed with stuffed birds.

"My husband is an expert orthodontist, as you might imply."

Pippa didn't dare tell her new employer the correct words were "ornithologist" and "infer." "This is very impressive, Signora Bowes."

In the supermodern kitchen they ran into Rudi, a sixtyish chef in a white toque busy baking hundreds of tiny pie shells for tomorrow's birthday party. "Rudi's grandfather was pastry chef for Emperor Franz Jonah."

"Josef, *Dummkopf,*" Rudi shouted.

Leigh ignored him. "And this is our dear Kerry, in charge of laundry, linen, silver, and porcelain."

A blowsy, none too carefully washed young woman sat at the stainless-steel counter affixing white bows to a mountain of liver biscuits that Rudi had baked yesterday. "Who the hell are you?" she asked Pippa.

"Cosmo du Piche." There was no way to say that with a shred of dignity.

"I guess that means you're a guy. Where'd you get the threads? You look like a reject from *Cutthroat Island.*"

All of Leigh's staff wore an apricot polo shirt with CASA BOWES on the front and a floor plan of same on the back. No way was Pippa going to be seen in that: her gender would be immediately exposed. "These are the du Piche colors. My ancestors were ennobled by Pope Pius the Third in commemoration of their victory over the Saracens."

"No stuff." Kerry tied a few more bows on dog biscuits before figuring out what was wrong with this picture. "Where's Samson, Mrs. Bowes?"

"Standing in an unemployment line. He nearly massacred four Brinks guards this morning."

"That son of a bitch owed me a hundred bucks!" Kerry barreled out of the kitchen.

"Kerry has a temper," Leigh apologized. "She's also a lazy and disobedient slut." Her voice dropped to a whisper. "Rudi adores her. I won't risk losing the best pastry chef in Las Vegas. I'm sure you'll find a way to manage her."

As Pippa was trudging after Leigh up the grandiose main staircase, Cole called, "Excuse me, madam. Whose Maserati is blocking the driveway?"

"Cosmo's. Please park it in the garage and bring his luggage in." Leigh turned to Pippa. "Cole is my husband's valet and chauffeur."

Chauffeur? Wearing a Breguet watch? That was a lot of parallel parking. "Aha."

Leigh led Pippa through a tremendous shoe closet. She was inordinately fond of metallic sling-backs. Pippa soon saw why: the next closet was packed with sequined gowns in every loud color. "I'm a dramatic dresser," Leigh confessed.

"Good advertising for your husband's wares."

"Aren't you sweet. Actually, it's an old habit. I used to be a Rockette."

"Really! I took fifteen years of tap," Pippa blurted before realizing her mistake. There was nothing to do but plow ahead. "It changed my life."

Leigh deduced that Cosmo was gay or bisexual. At least with Samson gone, he wouldn't get beaten up for it. She led her majordomo through more palatial closets and the master bedroom, a nightmare of apricot pillows, shams, valances, and vanities. Leigh's master bath was even grander than Thayne's, no small feat, but the incessant orange was wearing on Pippa's nerves. They traipsed through a mirrored dance studio, where Leigh still took daily lessons. Pippa was shown the office, the safe room, and an adorable nursery for Titian, the bichon frise.

They proceeded to the servants' wing, where the appurtenances were lavish but still apricot. Leigh pointed to a door. "That's Cole's room. Here's yours. I hope you don't mind sharing a bath with him. It has a double sink and double showers. He's very tidy."

That was just great. "It's lovely, Signora Bowes."

Cole entered with two Hartmann wheelers covered with large red polka dots. Olivia had given them to Pippa as a going-away gift. "Here you go, Cosmo," he said, swinging them onto the bed. "Need any help unpacking? It's my specialty."

"No thank you. If you'll both excuse me, I'd like to get organized."

"Of course. Come to the kitchen when you've settled in. Kerry will bring you some Casa Bowes shirts in the proper size."

"If you don't mind, I'd like to remain in uniform," Pippa said. "My ensemble was designed by Yves Saint Laurent for a stately residence such as yours."

Leigh didn't dare protest. She had to admit that Cosmo's thirty brass buttons were fetchingly twee. "As you wish."

"Rule number one: establish your turf," Cole said after the door closed. "Well done."

Pippa felt her face burning. The room had suddenly gotten very hot. "I understand we'll be sharing a bath. If you would kindly avoid walking in on me, I'd appreciate it." Cole's only response was an exaggerated furrowing of the brow, as if he were trying to figure out the punch line of a moronic joke. "What's the problem?" she snapped. Looking directly into his eyes was making her dizzy. "Are you some sort of homophobe?"

"I don't think so. Are you?"

"Of course not!"

"Fine. Then let's share the bathroom. We both know what a penis looks like."

"You don't understand," Pippa whimpered. "I sometimes have dark urges."

"In that case I'll always knock, Cosmo." She was amazingly fun to tease. Cole looked at his watch. "Gotta pick up the dog. He's getting a comb-out."

"Wait!" Pippa didn't want Cole to leave. Something about his presence was powerfully reassuring. "Is this place all right?"

"Yes. You'll be fine."

Alone, Pippa tore off her glasses, which had already made major dents on the bridge of her nose. The guy at an all-night LensCrafters down the road had tried to get her to buy smaller frames, but she had held fast. That may have been a mistake. She unpacked her six du Piche uniforms. Pippa had brought one Chanel suit: that was probably another mistake; she shoved it way in back of her closet. She hid her jewelry roll beneath a skirted chair and went to the bathroom. Cole's toiletries were all Lanvin. He shaved with a fourteen-carat-gold razor and a Penhaglion boar-bristle brush. His sink was spotless. Under normal circumstances Pippa would have been delighted; now she realized that sharing space with such an intriguing man could be hazardous to her diploma. She would have to be incredibly cautious. After taking a shower, she adjusted her mustache and went to the kitchen.

Leigh and Kerry stood at the island testing a dozen microquiches that Rudi proposed serving for the birthday party. "What do you think, Cosmo?" Leigh proffered a tiny round tart. "This one's prosciutto and asparagus."

"Delicious."

"This is lamb and leek."

"Excellent. Rudi, you're a master."

"Smoked turkey and dill."

"Outstanding."

"All right. We'll go with those," Leigh said. "Three hundred of each, Rudi."

"Have you got anything for vegetarians?" Pippa asked. "There's one in every crowd."

"Vegetarians? These are for the dogs." The humans were getting tuna. Three fifty-pound bluefins, three thousand bucks apiece, were arriving tomorrow from the Tsukiji fish market in Tokyo. "How are you going to grill them, Rudi?"

"I do not never vork mit fish."

"Cosmo? Can you man the grill?"

Pippa swallowed hard. Nine thousand bucks was a lot of tuna to incinerate. "No problem, signora." Leigh would also be serving a ton of fussy salads. Titian's birthday cake was fifty pounds of sirloin tartare in the shape of a femur topped with mashed potato icing. The humans would get homemade sorbet and teeny-weeny chocolate cookies in the shape of Titian's head.

"What about drinks?" Leigh continued. No one knew a thing about that. "Cosmo, can I leave that to you?"

"Of course."

Leigh turned to Kerry. "And the entertainment?"

"Pin the tail on the donkey. Hide and seek," Kerry shrugged.

"I specifically told you games for dogs."

"And I specifically told you my job is linens, laundry, and silver."

"Cosmo, can I turn that over to you?"

"Certainly." Drinks, grill, and games for three hundred? Tomorrow? Pippa felt an incipient diarrhea gurgle in her intestines. "What is the budget, please?" Thayne *always* asked about money first.

"There is no budget. Spend whatever it takes."

Leigh left for a break dancing lesson, which her therapist had recommended to ease stress. Pippa poured herself a half cup of coffee. It took a tremendous effort of will not to pour a half cup of whiskey on top of that. *One thing at a time,* she told herself. If Cedric could bulldoze his way cold through Thayne's nonwedding-of-the-century, Pippa could muddle through a birthday party for a bichon frise. "Titian must be a very special dog."

"Who cares about that stupid mutt?" Kerry answered. "The whole point is to impress members of the country club. Getting in is harder than winning the World Series."

The game was familiar to Pippa. "In that case, someone has given the party serious thought. These events are planned like military campaigns."

"Ferdinand worked on it. The guy you replaced."

"Did he leave any sort of file?" Yeah, upstairs. "Could you get it for me?"

While Kerry was gone, a Tent Event truck arrived. Six guys asked Pippa where they were supposed to nail the stakes. *Proceed with confidence at all times.* "This way, please." Fortunately Leigh had a large backyard. "Over there. Don't wreck the cacti."

Kerry returned with a file named "Titian's First Birthday." Most of the plans were well in place, thank God. "May I rely on you to take charge of the tables?" Pippa asked Kerry. "Twenty rent-a-maids will arrive at ten."

"I know what I'm doing."

"And I don't have to worry about food, Rudi?"

"You don't vorry."

Games? Evidently Ferdinand hadn't gotten around to that. *Think big,* Thayne always said. *Make a statement.* Pippa recalled that dogs always seemed to enjoy themselves at shows, so she called the West-minster Kennel Club and arranged for three judges to fly in tomorrow for master classes and an informal competition. Pippa hired a stage designer from the Luxor to come over and build reviewing stands and a mini Hyde Park. Kids always enjoyed fingerpainting, so she booked an actor to come over in a Big Bird costume and supervise pawprint class. How about a few races in Leigh's pool? Pippa called the U.S. Olympic Committee and asked if they knew of a buff swimmer willing to officiate at a canine meet tomorrow. A fund-raiser, she added: after-ward he could sign a load of autographs for a thousand bucks a pop.

Drinks? Ninety gallons of zombies should keep everyone happy. Pippa ordered the booze while Kerry located a punch bowl the size of a baptismal font.

Grilling the tuna was a problem, though. Pippa didn't know what to do about that. She strolled past the kitchen window and nearly dropped her coffee as a gigantic tent rose from the flat earth. She found herself listening for the shriek of an enraged elephant.

Instead she heard Leigh. "Don't you dare interfere! This is my party!"

The mistress of the house stormed into the kitchen with a man at her heels. Blond, tan, toned: *Cool Hand Luke* in an Armani suit. With-out breaking stride Leigh grabbed an aluminum mixing bowl from the counter and hurled it at her pursuer. "Cheap bastard!" she cried be-fore running into the backyard.

The man stood in silence as two quarts of saffron mayonnaise drib-bled down his front. Rudi hit the ceiling. "*Dammi!*" he shouted, smash-ing a pot into the sink. "I yust make dat! By my hand, no mixer!" Chucking a second pot into the sink, he stomped out. "*Dammi!*"

Cole entered, assessed the damage, and rushed to the aid of the Ar-mani suit. "Sorry, sir. Titian took forever to poop."

As Cole was swabbing his lapels, the man noticed Pippa. "Cosmo du Piche," she bowed, unnerved by his steely blue eyes.

"The new majordomo," Cole explained under his breath. "Claims to be a male."

"*Columba livia,*" was all the man said.

"You know Olivia?" Pippa was floored. "She did spend some time in Colombia."

"*Columba livia,*" the man repeated. "That's Latin for 'domestic pigeon.'"

"Oh! You're absolutely right, sir. The du Piche colors are those of the noble pigeon. You're the first person who has ever made the connection. I'm so impressed."

That earned a sardonic smile. The man waited as Cole scraped most of the mayonnaise off his suit. He excused himself and strode into the yard. Within seconds the screaming match was back in overdrive.

"If you haven't guessed, that's Moss Bowes," Cole told Pippa. He threw her a pair of potholders. "Help me get these out of the oven before they burn to a crisp."

Pippa hurried over. "Do they always fight like that?"

"Nonstop. You'll get used to it." Cole rescued two sheets of asparagus tartlets. "How's the party coming?"

"Ferdinand paved the way." Pippa noticed that Cole was quite handy with a pair of oven mitts. "Are you busy tomorrow afternoon? I need someone to grill three tuna."

"Whole?"

"Of course! Presentation is *evvvverything.*" A quote straight out of Thayne's party book. "Could you rig them up like suckling pigs? There must be a spit somewhere in this house."

"I'll see what I can do. It depends on Moss's schedule. I'm his valet, not Leigh's." Cole removed his mitts. She really had the most adorable neck. He was dying to take a small bite out of it. "I'm also the referee," he said as the backyard shouts amplified. "See you later, Cosmo."

Pippa went upstairs to the study in search of the guest list. All she could find on Leigh's desk was a sheaf of handwritten pages, each containing four columns. The first column listed names like Harriet, Cornelia, Ardelle, Golda, Miri. The second list contained names like Tata, Checkers, Puzo, Oshkosh, and Nutkin. The third listed breeds like dachshund, pug, Portuguese water hound, bichon frise, and shar-pei. The fourth column listed numbers with long tails of zeros. Many entries were marked with asterisks, arrows, highlighter, and "very important."

"Cosmo?"

Pippa nearly shrieked in fright. "Hello, signora. I was just looking for the guest list."

Leigh had changed into a flimsy Karan wraparound. The jewelry and metallic high heels didn't add much gravitas. Neither did the fluffy white dog in her arms. "Have you met the star of the show? Say hello to my adorable Titian."

Leigh's bichon frise tried to bite Pippa's hand. He hated mustaches. "Bad boy! He's always so irritable when he gets back from the stylist."

Pippa rubbed the jagged scratch on her thumb. "As I was saying, signora, I'm looking for the guest list."

"You're holding it." Leigh passed a slender finger over the columns. "Name of guest, name of dog, breed of dog, guest net worth. I've been studying it for weeks."

"What do the asterisks mean?"

"Those women belong to the Las Vegas Country Club. I have to pay particular attention to them. It's very important I make a great impression or they'll blackball me. That would be a catastrophe."

"Are you sure? Very few people with shar-peis are even worth knowing. And how many people are actually coming? Where's your RSVP list?"

"It was regrets only and I haven't gotten a single one."

"You really have three hundred friends?"

"Let's just say three hundred women are curious to see my house. Do you think they'll like it, Cosmo? I've been decorating for months."

"Of course they'll like it. It's a knockout." Pippa handed Leigh the list for further study. "I presume you have a decent sponsor at the club."

"Yes, yes. You'll meet her tomorrow. She's wonderful. Knows everyone. She helped me make the guest list." Leigh was thrilled to hear what Pippa had planned in the way of entertainment. She didn't ask what anything had cost and, after that fight in the kitchen, Pippa didn't dare tell her. "I'm so glad you're here, Cosmo. You're a pro."

"I was recently involved in a large-scale event. By comparison this is a walk in the park." *Door prizes,* Pippa wrote to herself on a nearby notepad. *Personalized pooper scoopers studded with Swarovski crystals.*

Leigh had to rush off to a luncheon followed by a tea party, cocktail party, and dinner party, all with various members of the country club. At the door she abruptly stopped. "Is this dress okay?"

"You have excellent legs. No one will notice anything else."

Leigh got the message. "Would you help me pick an outfit tomorrow?"

"I'd be delighted. Go enjoy yourself now, signora."

Pippa was awakened at seven the next morning by shouts, a splintering crash, and a splash. She threw on her clothes and mustache and rushed to the kitchen. Rudi was cranking out hundreds of teeny-weeny chocolate cookies. Cole was calmly reading a newspaper. "What happened?" Pippa cried.

Cole looked up from the Money section. "Leigh threw a chair through a window into the Jacuzzi. With Moss in the Jacuzzi."

"And you're just sitting there?"

"I'm his valet, not his force field." Cole tried not to stare at her *very* nice calves. "Sleep well, Cosmo?"

"Yes, thank you." Pippa had conked out around eight. "Why did she throw a chair through the window?"

"She found an earring in Moss's shirt pocket."

"How'd it get there?" A shrug. "You're with him all day long. You should know."

"I drive his car, Cosmo. I don't follow him inside."

Pippa ran to the Jacuzzi. Moss was still in the water. So was a Biedermeier chair. There was glass all over the patio. "Are you all right, Signor Bowes?"

He ended a cell phone chat. "Heads up. She's not done yet."

Another chair flew out the bedroom window. This one landed on top of the tent in just the right spot to dislodge a critical support pole. Pippa watched in dismay as the whole thing collapsed to the ground. "Nice shot, darling," Moss called, stepping out of the pool.

"Sir! Please!" Pippa averted her eyes. "You're naked!"

"What's the problem?" Moss didn't understand. If Cosmo were a straight guy, sight of another naked guy would mean nothing. If Cosmo were a gay guy, he was getting a great peep show for nothing.

"We're expecting deliveries," was all Pippa could say.

"I presume the doorbell works." Moss shook the glass out of a pair of clogs and sauntered into the house.

Pippa fished the Biedermeier chair out of the roiling Jacuzzi, then returned to the kitchen. "Where's Kerry?" she asked Cole, annoyed. He had told her this place was totally fine.

"She never gets up before ten. It's in her contract."

"She knows damn well that twenty people are showing up at ten." Pippa went and pounded on her door. "Kerry!" No answer. She tried the doorknob. Kerry lay in bed, snoring robustly. Pippa shook her doughy shoulders. "Get up."

"Wha' you wan.'"

"I need your help." Snore. "Five hundred bucks if you're in the kitchen in five minutes."

A porcine eye opened. "You're a pain in the ass, Cosmo."

"Thanks. I knew I could count on you." On the threshold Pippa stepped on something round and hard: a pearl earring. She tossed it onto Kerry's dresser. "Four minutes."

She removed the second Biedermeier chair from the lake of canvas and briskly swept the patio. Thousands of last-minute details were streaming through her brain; she should have gotten up at four to tend to them all. The moment Kerry made an appearance Pippa herded her, Rudi, and Cole to the backyard and told them which ropes to pull: the tent juddered upward. Pippa replaced the main pole and bashed the stakes into the ground with an All-Clad skillet.

"Where'd you learn that?" Cole demanded.

"Girl Scouts." Damn! "Boy Scouts. Are you going to grill the tuna or not? The party starts at noon. We eat at one."

"I'll be here." Cole left to drive Moss to work.

Doorbell: HVAC for the tent. The sous chefs and place setters arrived. The florists and three judges from the Westminster Kennel Club arrived. Every few minutes someone delivered a case of wine, a massive bouquet, a basket of soaps, a tin of caviar, chocolates, a Smithfield ham, and so on: "For Titian" from Wooki, Pepper, Oodles, and so on. Pippa set up a gift exhibit in one of the ballrooms. The set designer from the Luxor arrived with a dozen fiberglass fire hydrants; Pippa put him to work making review stands and a replica of Hyde Park. For three hours she ran around in a frenzy, then suddenly realized she hadn't bought any game prizes. She tore upstairs. "Signora Bowes! How are you doing?"

Leigh had been in seclusion studying the guest list. Her cramming had not been assisted by the crew of six installing a new bedroom window. "Everything is mush," she moaned.

"Don't worry about it. We've got name tags for the dogs. I'll get the women so smashed on zombies they won't remember their bra size. Where did you get Titian combed out yesterday?"

"Canossal."

Pippa got them to deliver ten five-hundred-dollar gift certificates. "Okay. Let's take care of you." Pippa dragged Leigh into her suite of closets. "Show me what you're thinking of wearing."

A skintight white leather jumpsuit with fringe, red sequin sling-backs, red sequin cowboy hat. "That's a bit much," Pippa said. Leigh looked so hurt that she quickly added, "For midday." Pippa swished through hundreds of outfits. Nothing in the closet didn't involve se-quins, feathers, snakeskin, or rhinestones: Moss must have singlehand-edly skinned all the snakes, birds, and cows in the Third World.

"Have you got a pair of jeans? Plain jeans?" Yes, thank God. Pippa raided Moss's closet and found a white silk shirt handmade in Milan. "Here's your top." For the feet, a pair of pink Capezio T-straps.

"But those are dancing shoes," Leigh cried, horrified.

"You're a good dancer, aren't you? Flaunt it." Pippa looked at her watch. "I've got to change. Choose your own belt. Make sure it fits in the jeans loops."

"What about my hair?" Leigh cried.

"Ponytail and baseball cap *at most*. Not more than one necklace, one bracelet, and one ring. Not more than two-carat earrings. You want to show you have nothing to prove."

"But I have everything to prove," Leigh whimpered.

"Stop it! Trust me. The doorbell's going to start ringing in half an hour." Pippa charged downstairs. Cole was out with Moss, so the coast was clear in the bathroom. She hastily showered and changed into a fresh uniform. She noted with concern that her mustache was beginning to fray around the edges, not to mention that the glue was beginning to irritate her upper lip. Fortunately Olivia had packed her a wide sombrero made by Yves Saint Laurent, for summering in Bo-gotá. It would provide shadow cover.

Pippa tore through the ballrooms at Casa Bowes: tables set, balloons aloft, Poussin lit. Gifts ready for viewing. Zombies mixed. Dog show, Hyde Park, pawprint studio set up in tent. Canapés and caterers ready in kitchen. Bowling alley set. Nine thousand bucks of tuna on ice. Pippa called the Olympic Committee: buff swimmer en route. Kerry had managed to comb her hair and change into a fresh polo shirt. Leigh came downstairs looking like a million bucks despite the apricot sequined belt. Even Titian looked happy. Pippa smiled: this was almost as good as being back at Fleur-de-Lis.

"I'm nervous," Leigh said.

Pippa brought her a sip of zombie. "You drink nothing but water until the last labradoodle leaves, understand? Now come to the door and greet your guests. I'm right behind you."

At the stroke of one the doorbell rang. "Hi, darling!" Leigh said, embracing a woman in a Miu Miu suit and matching maize hat, gloves, shoes, and purse. She wore more jewelry than had Queen Elizabeth at her coronation. "You look beautiful."

The woman couldn't bring herself to return the compliment. She and her English bull terrier on a titanium chain leash stepped inside. "Those doors are too dark, Leigh. You should have done the birch stain, as I recommended."

Pippa felt the wind go right out of Leigh's sails. Who was this insufferable bag? "Birch stain is generally considered inappropriate for Bolivian rosewood, madam."

The woman gasped. "And who might this be?"

Leigh remained paralyzed so Pippa replied, "Cosmo du Piche, majordomo and personal bodyguard to Signora Bowes."

"Do you know who I am, young man?"

What a bore. And what a grotesque face-lift. "I believe you are one of three hundred guests who will be enjoying a wonderful afternoon at Casa Bowes." Pippa took the leash from the woman's gloved hand. "I see that both you and General Patton have similar taste in dogs."

"Well, I never! Is this the best that woman in Aspen could come up with, Leigh?"

Leigh shivered to life. "Cosmo, I'd like you to meet my sponsor and the woman who has made this afternoon possible. Dusi Damon."

Seventeen

*D*usi Damon! Thayne's college roommate! Pippa couldn't have been any more stunned had Leigh introduced her to Lucrezia Borgia. She hadn't seen the Damons in years. Dusi looked nothing like the broad-bummed, ball-nosed brunette Pippa remembered. Dusi was now a whippety blonde with gigantic breasts, high cheekbones, and the ghoulishly bisque complexion of the Heubach Koppelsdorf dolls that she flitted all over the world collecting. Pippa kicked herself for not recognizing Dusi's famous pink diamond ring sooner. *"Enchanté."* She bowed as condescendingly as possible: Thayne had always maintained that Dusi respected nothing but bullion and bullies. "So you are Signora Bowes's sponsor."

"Yes. I am chair of the membership committee at the Las Vegas Country Club." One would think she had just split the atom.

"Allow me to accompany you to the bar. You look parched."

"And my Giorgio?" Dusi's bodyguard.

"We've organized a luncheon for the bodyguards in the bowling alley. You'll be quite safe without him. I've placed five Delta Force snipers in the trees surrounding Casa Bowes." Pippa did not light the cigarette Dusi had just stuck in an Art Deco holder. "Or if you prefer,

Giorgio can go back to your car and wait in the hundred-degree heat for the next four hours."

"Oh, go to the bowling alley," Dusi grudgingly told the man. "Consider it vacation time."

"I'll be right back, Signora Bowes," Pippa told an aghast Leigh.

Dusi needed a few moments to compose herself as Cosmo chaperoned her down the hallway. Hermaphrodites had always fascinated her. This exotic creature looked like a cross between Truman Capote, Elle McPherson, and Ali Baba. Within twenty-four hours of arrival, he was obviously very much in charge of Casa Bowes, and he knew it. Cosmo had not remotely attempted to address her deferentially, or even as an equal, but as her *superior*! Not even Caleb, Dusi's husband, had the temerity to try that. "Where did that woman find you, Cosmo?"

"Are you referring to my great friend Olivia Villarubia-Thistleberry, whose name you've obviously forgotten?"

"Of course, who else?" Chagrined, Dusi repeated, "Where did she find you?"

"That is privileged information." Pippa collected a glass of punch from the bartender. "*Salut.*"

Hypnotized, Dusi not only failed to remind Cosmo that she drank absolutely nothing but martinis, but drained the zombie in one go. Pippa refilled her glass. "I suggest you see the new Poussin in the fourth ballroom before the crowds get too thick. What is the name of your English bull terrier?"

"Kappa."

"As in Kappa Kappa Gamma? By the way, smoking is only permitted outside on the patio." Pippa left Dusi openmouthed at the bar. She unhanded Kappa to one of the Westminster Kennel judges and returned to the front door. "How's everything holding up, signora?"

"Cosmo, I admire your bravado, but Dusi is not to be crossed. Without her, I'm toast."

"You might think this odd, but she loves getting slapped around. I have decades of experience with the personality."

"Do we really have Delta Force snipers in the trees?"

"There's nothing up there but locusts." Vehicles were beginning to congest the driveway. "Make sure you fuss more over the dogs than you do over the women. And don't neglect the bodyguards."

"Omigod," Leigh quivered. "Look. They're all wearing suits and pearls. I'm wearing jeans and a baseball cap."

"Perfect! This is a birthday party for a dog, not the Mayflower Ball. Don't introduce me to anyone. Don't even look at me. I'm wallpaper."

"That's a stretch, Cosmo."

"Shhh! Don't even pretend to know their names. Let them think their names weren't important enough to remember in the first place." Pippa hung around the front door for the first hundred or so arrivals. Leigh eventually got the hang of antipretension. Where was Cole? Moss? They should have been here at noon, schmoozing and grilling their butts off. *Someone will always let you down. Have a Plan B.*

Pippa strolled through the chattering crowd, happy to see that Leigh's guests appeared well on the way to zombosis. The bodyguards in the bowling alley were already cracking their second keg. There was a great fuss around the three Westminster Kennel judges and Big Bird in the pawprint atelier. Way more women had lined up to see the three gigantic tuna on ice than did to see Moss's Poussin in the ballroom. Rudi was playing to the crowd, opening oven doors to a chorus of oohs and aahs as he removed sheet after sheet of tartlets. "Not for you!" he kept shouting, slapping away gem-cluttered hands. Everyone thought he was kidding.

Pippa again returned to the front door. Most of the guests had arrived; Cole and Moss had not. "Where's your husband?" she asked Leigh.

"I couldn't care less where he is. Does that bastard really expect me to believe he has no idea how an earring got into his shirt pocket?"

"Maybe he picked it up off the sidewalk."

"And it was such a cheap pearl stud! So common!"

"You would prefer it was a sapphire? Cole promised to grill the tuna. My timetable is edging into Code Red." Pippa whipped out her phone. "Dial your husband, signora. Now."

Moss answered on the first ring. "Yeah?"

"Where are you, Signor Bowes?"

"Trying to earn your fee. Sixty-five grand, if I remember correctly."

"If you don't get here in ten minutes, we're going to steam three large bluefin tuna in your Jacuzzi. I mean it."

Pippa hung up as a taxi braked beneath the portico. A sleek young man in an Izod warm-up suit skipped up the steps. "I understand there's a meet here today."

Pippa blanched. She had not expected the winner of about twenty gold medals at the 2004 summer Olympics. "Thank you for coming, Mr. Phelps. I see you have a sense of humor."

"What happens here, stays here." Pippa didn't get the joke so he continued, "Actually I was in town, so the committee sent me over."

Pippa decided to start the swim meet. She brought Phelps to the pool, explained the situation as honestly as possible, and promised to finish in an hour. It didn't take long for word to get out that Michael Phelps happened to be paddling around Leigh's pool and would be available to sign autographs at a thousand bucks a pop after the swim meet. For two thousand a pop he would pose for pictures, all proceeds to benefit the Olympic Committee. He was a wonderful sport. The dogs were wonderful sports. After an hour, Phelps had raised a hundred grand and was still going strong. The ladies were beside themselves.

Moss and Cole finally made an appearance. Enraged to see one hundred dogs in his pool, Moss stomped to the library and slammed the door. Pippa hustled Cole to the grill. "Just where have you two been all day?"

"Meeting with Mafiosi, scumbags, and shysters."

"That's not funny."

"I wasn't joking."

Whatever. Pippa pointed to the three tuna lying in large vats of ice. "Get grilling."

He turned off the gas. "I've been thinking, Cosmo. There's a better way to do this."

"And that would be?"

"Sashimi."

Of *course* that was the way to go. "Good thought."

Cole knew his way around big fish. By the time Pippa had distributed prizes and presented Phelps with an oversized check for one hundred and sixty thousand dollars, the first tuna was arrayed in paper-thin slices over Leigh's Meissen platters.

"Beautiful," Pippa said. "Where'd you learn that?"

"Previous yacht," he said with a wink.

Lunch lasted forever. The ladies devoured every ounce of sashimi.

They nibbled their salads one grain at a time. Zombies disappeared as fast as two bartenders could make them. Pippa finally figured out why: no one was about to leave the ballroom while Phelps was visiting tables in his Speedo bikini. After he left to catch a plane, Pippa coaxed everyone into the tent. The mock Westminster dog show began. It was a huge success, marred only by the poor sportsmanship of Dusi Damon, furious that Kappa lost Best in Show to a pug named Studs. Dusi regained a partial will to live after being awarded one of the fiberglass fire hydrants from the Luxor as consolation prize.

Out came coffee, sorbet, and chocolate cookies. Shocked at how quickly the afternoon had gone, Leigh's guests made a final pass around the gift exhibit, the Poussin, Rudi, and the rococo harpsichord. Pippa knocked on the door of Moss's study. "Sir?"

"What can I do for you, Cosmo?" he called with chilling insincerity.

Pippa peered around the heavy door. Moss was seated at his Louis Quatorze *scriban* studying an ancient encyclopedia of birds. "Your guests are leaving. Would you care to see them out? It would be a very gracious gesture from the man of the house." He didn't move. "I'm sure Signora Bowes would appreciate it."

"I'm sure she would." He carefully turned a yellowed page. "Come here, Cosmo. I need your advice."

Pippa brightened. "Of course, signor."

"Which bird do you like better?" Moss flipped between two pages. "The red or the blue?"

"The blue one has a beautiful beak."

"I'm not talking about the beak, you dope. I mean the feathers."

Realizing Moss would exterminate fifty thousand of whichever bird she picked, Pippa said, "I really couldn't say. They're both so adorable."

"They're quite rare." He chuckled. "About to get rarer."

Pippa was aghast. "May I ask, have you considered synthetic feathers?"

"No, I haven't." He returned to the book. "Go away. You're useless."

Pippa stopped at the library door. "I thought you were interested in joining the country club, signor."

"That I am. It's just that I'm not terribly interested in standing anywhere near my wife at the moment." He stared at Pippa's uniform for an uncomfortable length of time. Pippa was sure he was studying her flattened boobs and was about to ask her to remove her jacket. To her relief, when Moss opened his mouth, it was merely to say, "That silk captures pigeon green perfectly."

"Thank you." Pippa waited a moment. "Please, Signor Bowes. Without you we're doomed. All your good money would be wasted." Thayne always used those lines to great effect.

They worked on Moss, too. He stood with Leigh as three hundred exiting guests raved about her stupendous, fabulous, delightful, truly magnificent party. Best of all, they *meant* it. Only Dusi Damon, first to arrive, last to depart, seemed less impressed. "Well! That was quite a show."

"Did you enjoy it?" Leigh asked, instantly anxious. Pippa could have kicked her.

"Certain elements were well done. Other elements could have been finessed."

"You're not suggesting we bribe judges from the Westminster Kennel Club," Pippa cut in. "That's a valuable fire hydrant, by the way. I'm told Frank Sinatra urinated on it."

Dusi opened her mouth, thought about what to say, and went with, "Congratulations on the Poussin, Moss. It goes perfectly with the gold drapes."

"Yes. I always try to match my paintings to the drapes."

As usual, Dusi couldn't tell if he was serious or not. For someone who desperately wanted to get into the Las Vegas Country Club, Moss displayed shockingly little respect for her power to make or break his dreams. He was the only man in Las Vegas who hadn't noticed her new DDD breasts; even now he preferred to ogle the tassels on Cosmo's jacket rather than Dusi's stunning décolletage. He would have to be disciplined immediately.

Dusi extended a gloved hand to Leigh. "Come to my home for lunch tomorrow, both of you."

"Are you free, Moss?" Leigh asked.

"Forgive me, I meant you and Cosmo. Twelve sharp." Dusi couldn't help but shake her head one last time at Leigh's rosewood doors. Noses high in the air, she and Kappa left.

Pippa immediately slammed the doors. "We don't need to wave goodbye."

Leigh looked agitated. "What did she mean, 'certain elements could have been finessed'?"

"Absolutely nothing. Thank you for making an appearance, Signor Bowes. I'm sure it's tedious pretending three hundred strangers are your friends." Pippa's father always had the good sense to drink half a bottle of sherry before stumbling downstairs. "Especially that woman."

"Cosmo!" Leigh gasped. "We owe Dusi everything."

"Or so she'd like you to think. When are they going to decide on your membership?"

"Within the next two weeks."

"About time." Moss trained his hard blue eyes on Pippa. "I want every invoice from this pooch fest on my desk tomorrow. Get the pool drained and disinfected. Whose idea was the dog bath?"

"Mine," Pippa admitted. "It was a swim meet, not a bath."

"We'll deduct the cleaning from your fee."

"You ass!" Moss's wife cried. "You should be on your knees thanking Cosmo for such a brilliant idea. People will be talking about it for years."

Pippa thought Moss would punch both of them. Her suspicion was confirmed when he asked, "Where's Samson?"

"I fired him. Cosmo's my bodyguard now."

"At no extra cost," Pippa bowed.

"Such a deal." Moss got a walkie-talkie from his belt. "I'll be in the car." He left.

Pippa closed the front doors. "Does he understand that getting into a country club is only slightly less expensive than running for president?"

"He understands. I'm not sure he wants me as his running mate, though." Leigh was on the verge of tears. "Excuse me. I need a drink."

Pippa was left alone in the foyer with Titian chewing her shoelaces. Cole appeared, wearing his driver's cap. "Great show, Cosmo. You got everyone here but the guys from E!"

Pippa shuddered: she'd had enough of E! for the rest of her life. "Thanks for slicing the fish."

"At your service." The way he said it made her blush.

In two hours all traces of Titian's party were expunged from Casa Bowes. Pippa found Kerry in the bowling alley, sleeping off the river of beer she had consumed with the bodyguards. They set to work dismantling the gift table. Moss maintained an enormous wine cellar, Pippa discovered as she carted case after case downstairs. Kerry kept note of all incoming stock in her BlackBerry. "Are you the sommelier?" Pippa asked.

"The what, Mo?"

"Wine steward. My name's Cosmo. Two syllables. What are you writing there?"

"I just like to keep records. For my own protection."

"Let me guess. That's your diary. You're working on an exposé."

Kerry nearly dropped a case of Viognier. "Are you spying on me? I'll break your faggot jaw."

"Get a life. There's one of you in every house. In case you're screwing Signor Bowes, be aware that the market's already flooded with kiss-and-tell memoirs. Written by nannies who majored in English." Encouraged by Kerry's dismay, Pippa took a long shot. "Signora Bowes already knows about you and Samson. I'd worry about my own jaw if I were you."

"Holy Mother of God! Does she know about Rudi, too?"

"Can I give you a piece of advice? If you're going to hit on everything that moves, get a job with Howard Stern."

Pippa went to the kitchen. She hadn't eaten all day and had a thrashing headache. Rudi was tautening Saran Wrap over every container in the refrigerator, muttering about escaping odors. Seeing Pippa slumped at the table, he brought over a crock of shrimp salad. "You did a great job today, Rudi."

"Zose ladies zink I am zat *Schweinehund* Wolfgang Puck!"

"They loved you." Pippa watched Rudi stack leftover cookies in a tin. His devotion to his art reminded her of Slava Slootski, the greatest clown on earth. How was that poor man doing? And Pushkin? Suddenly she missed them terribly.

"My shrimp salad iss bad?"

"It's wonderful." Pippa stood up. "I'm just really tired. Good night."

She went to her room, kicked off her leaden nubucks, and unpeeled her mustache. She hung up her uniform and moved on to the high point of her day, unzipping the jogging bra. Pippa checked in the mirror to see that neither breast had gangrened. She flopped on her bed and dialed Olivia. "The party was a huge success."

"Yes, yes, I heard. Leigh was on the phone with me for an hour." Dead drunk but coherent enough. "She adores you."

"She's a nice person. May I have my diploma now?"

"Now?" Olivia repeated with exaggerated surprise. "I don't understand."

"That was the deal, wasn't it? Get Leigh through the party?"

"I believe the arrangement was that you would get her through the *week,* Lotus. Perhaps more." Olivia had just wheedled an extra twenty grand out of Leigh if Cosmo stayed on until Labor Day. "Have some pity. You know I desperately need the money."

The answer would have been no were it not for the beguiling presence of Cole. Pippa had had another naked dream about him last night. "Okay. One more week."

"You're a dear girl. If I had a daughter like you, I'd be the happiest woman alive."

Olivia's comment nudged her into melancholy. Pippa fell blankly asleep, only to be wakened by another altercation in the Jacuzzi. She couldn't believe that Leigh and Moss could hurl such crippling words at each other and still live under the same roof. Even her parents in their vilest moments had the good sense to keep their mouths shut, get into separate cars, and hit the golf course or Neiman Marcus. It always blew over because silence expressed both everything and nothing and, at the end of the day, most arguments were about nothing. Nothing that could be fixed, anyhow. Pippa winced as the fight escalated to four-letter words containing *u*'s.

A soft knock on her door around midnight: Cole. "Cosmo? May I use the bathroom?"

"Of course," Pippa called from the bed.

"Did I wake you?"

"Hardly."

"Have you had dinner?"

Pippa crept to the door. "You haven't eaten?"

"We just got back from a meeting with a snakeskin exporter."

"That sounds gross."

"It was. Come on, let's raid the kitchen. I'm starving."

Now that he mentioned it, so was she. "Why don't you bring some food back here? I don't want to run into Leigh or Moss in their present state."

Pippa made her bed. She squished back into the sports bra and glued her mustache on. She had just finished buttoning her jacket when Cole returned with two of Rudi's salads, a bottle of wine, and a huge crock of pickles. "Gee, Cosmo, you didn't have to get all dressed up for me."

"All I brought were uniforms. I hadn't planned on staying longer than the birthday party. Now it seems I'm stuck here another whole week."

That news made his day. Cole handed her the bowl of shrimp salad. She looked cuter than ever with the mustache on upside down. Beneath the mousy-brown dye job, he suspected she was a blonde. "Are we that bad?"

"It's a long story." Pippa realized she was sweating profusely: she hadn't sat on a bed with a heterosexual male since Prague. Cole hadn't exactly placed himself in the far-off corner, either. "How long have you been here?"

"Six months."

"You worked on a yacht before then?"

"That's right." *Thanks for reminding me.*

Pippa waited for further details: none forthcoming. "How'd you end up here?"

"I answered an ad. It went something like 'International businessman seeks valet. Must be discreet and fond of birds.' I thought 'birds' meant 'girls' so I sent my résumé."

"There must have been a million applicants," Pippa frowned.

"I actually do know something about birds. My mother belongs to the Audubon Society."

"I'm sure she'd be delighted to know what Moss is doing to the worldwide avian population."

Cole didn't answer. She wore a Patek Philippe watch: that was a lot of buttered toast. Settling on the pillow, he dug into a bowl of chicken salad. "Tell me about yourself, Cosmo."

"What would you like to know?"

Why are you pretending to be a guy, for one. What were you doing at the Phoenix Ritz-Carlton, two. Do you have a boyfriend, three, four, and five. "Where'd you get the Maserati?"

"Oh, that," Pippa laughed, cursing the day its paint dried. "It's a gift from my—" Oh, boy. "Previous employer."

"For services rendered?"

Pippa blushed fiercely enough to ripple the wallpaper. "I got him over a little hump. Actually a big hump." That sounded worse. "It's not the sort of hump you're thinking of."

"Sounds illegal."

"No, just impulsive and stupid."

As Cole poured her a glass of cabernet, he caught her looking at his watch. "A gift from my previous employer. No humps involved. Cheers."

She tried not to stare too blatantly at Cole's throat as he sipped his wine. "Is this from the cellar? It's excellent."

"Moss told me to help myself. He doesn't drink and Leigh prefers Gallo in gallons."

"Is he a nicer guy when he's not around her?"

Cole tore his eyes away from her mouth. He was already fantasizing about peeling the mustache off. "You've got to understand where Moss is coming from, Cosmo. He grew up in a tenement in Buffalo. He doesn't like to see his money evaporate."

"Then he should join the Masons, not the country club." One of Thayne's favorite lines. "So what do you do all day? Sit in the car and wait for Signor Bowes to need a ride?"

"Something like that."

"That sounds pretty boring."

"It beats organizing birthday parties for dogs." Winking, Cole refilled her glass. "Where'd you get the idea to call the Westminster Kennel Club?"

"My previous employer was a party girl. She thought big and just picked up the phone. You'd be amazed at the insane things people would do for her."

Odd that Cosmo never mentioned who these previous employers might be. Majordomos were normally the crassest name-droppers. "So she had private dog shows and swim meets?"

"No, those were my idea." Pippa sighed. "Signor Bowes is going to hit the roof when he gets the bills tomorrow."

"Maybe he'll just hit Leigh instead."

"You think those fights are funny? I couldn't imagine treating my husband like that." Aghast, Pippa realized her mistake. Damn wine! "I mean my wife."

Cole couldn't resist teasing her a bit. "Which is it, Cosmo?"

Pippa tried to think. If she said "husband," Cole would think Cosmo was gay. If she said "wife," he'd think Cosmo was a guy. "Whatever," she mumbled. How lame! Pippa crashed the bowl of shrimp salad onto her night table. "Now if you'll excuse me, I'll say good night before I make a complete fool of myself."

"No pickles?" Cole chomped the tip off the largest of them. "They're delicious."

"I hate pickles." Pippa sprang off the mattress, caught her foot in the bed skirt, and fell flat on her face. Yves Saint Laurent's eyeglasses shot under the chair. "Whoa!" Cole picked her up. "I'm sorry. I shouldn't have pried like that. Are you all right?"

"I'm fine." Actually Pippa felt much worse after he let go of her.

Cole swished his hand under the chair, trawling for her eyeglasses. To Pippa's horror he found not only the glasses but her jewelry roll. "What's this?" As she stood petrified, he untied the ribbon and emptied the contents into his hand.

They both stared at Pippa's magnificent diamond necklace from her grandfather, her diamond earrings from Lance, and her diamond barrette from Rosimund. Pippa knew that he knew the rocks were real. "A going-away gift from my previous employer," she explained. Sadly, that was very close to the truth. "When I get a chance I'll sell them on eBay."

Cole quietly replaced everything in the jewelry roll. "That must have been one hell of a hump, Cosmo." He gathered the empty bowls from the night table. "Would you like to keep the wine?"

"I've drunk enough for one evening, thank you."

At the door he paused. She looked so pale and deflated that he felt like reading her a bedtime story. "I'm glad you're here. Hope you stay awhile."

She didn't move for quite a while after the door shut behind him. Cole was no ordinary chauffeur.

Eighteen

Following Titian's birthday party, Dusi Damon had to admit that Leigh, Casa Bowes, and Cosmo were the talk of the town. That house! Those games! Door prizes! The tuna! Millions of cell phone minutes were expended regarding Leigh's baseball cap, sequined belt, and hand-sewn Italian shirt. Was she making a fashion statement or was she just a clueless tramp? Consensus was finally reached: perhaps jeans, and not a prim designer suit, *had* been the correct attire for a dog's birthday fête. Cosmo had obviously dressed his mistress and, as anyone could see, Cosmo was in a sartorial class of his own. Only a pioneer would wear a purple sombrero and matching silk pantaloons in public. Gray socks and nubucks: revolutionary. Half the Las Vegas fashionistas swore his jacket and eyeglasses were Saint Laurent. The other half swore they were Versace. Try as she might, Dusi could not refocus the spotlight on herself. It was an ugly, helpless feeling.

Following Leigh's lead, she fired her bodyguard Giorgio. Instead of a haute couture suit, Dusi dressed in tennis clothes and a baseball cap for her luncheon the next day. She was chagrined to see Leigh show up in an apple-green Dolce & Gabbana suit, Prada shoes, and not one sequin. Cosmo wore his customary uniform, which already felt classic, like Tom Wolfe's white suits. "Welcome to Castilio Damonia," Dusi effused, feeling ridiculous in her ruffly panties. "I hope you don't mind that I will be going straight from lunch to a croquet lesson."

"Obviously," Cosmo answered dryly.

Ignoring Leigh, Dusi took Cosmo's arm and proceeded down a long, dark foyer lined with thirty-six full coats of armor. "Castilio Damonia is modeled on Blusterwell, the seat of the Marquess of Ashberry in County Durham. It has four ballrooms, thirty guest rooms, and fifty large fireplaces."

"Winters must be brutal in Las Vegas."

"I'll tell you a little secret, Cosmo: we turn the air-conditioning to fifty-five, then light the fires." Dusi paused to admire a stuffed horse, in full armor, at the end of the hallway. "My husband Caleb's armor collection is one of the finest in the northern hemisphere. In fact, he's in Normandy as we speak, negotiating for a suit worn by Ethelred the Unready. I just don't know where we're going to put it!"

"How about the kitchen? You can hang pasta over the spear."

"What a splendid idea. I will consider that."

Leigh had never been invited to Dusi's forty-thousand-square-foot castle before. Her head was spinning. "Wow! This so reminds me of Harry Potter."

Dusi glanced backward with disdain. "I presume that was a compliment, Leigh."

"Signora Bowes is comparing your home with the Bodleian Library and Lacock Abbey." Pippa was a big Harry Potter fan. "I would consider it a huge compliment."

"In that case, thank you." Dusi detested suits of armor. However, since they were flashy, unique, and appallingly expensive, she allowed Caleb to gallivant all over the planet augmenting his collection. "Let me show you a modest hobby of my own."

They entered an enormous room crammed with dolls in glass cases. The place looked like a cross between a preemie ward and a midget mortuary. Dusi meandered from case to case, reciting how much she had paid for each doll and where she had bought it.

"Do you ever play with them?" Leigh asked.

"My dear girl! Would you 'play' with the Shroud of Turin?" Dusi stopped at a large glass case. "This doll belonged to Tsarevna Anastasia.

I bought it in Istanbul for four hundred thousand dollars. It is now worth three times that."

The doll bore an unpleasant resemblance to Chucky. As she stared at its harsh green eyes, Pippa recalled that several years ago Thayne had gone with Dusi on a trip to Istanbul in search of a doll that had purportedly belonged to Tsarevna Anastasia. Thayne had raved for months about the doll's green garnet eyes. After a worldwide search, she had finally managed to find herself an outstanding specimen of the gemstone and had it mounted in a brooch. Fortunately, the name was easy to remember.

Pippa leaned over the case. "Is that demantoid?"

"My God, Cosmo! How did you know?"

"Mined in the Urals. Very rare horsetail inclusions. A favorite of Fabergé." *Thank you, Mama.* "My previous employer had a dozen in the knob of his walking stick."

Rattled by the condescension in Cosmo's voice, Dusi said, "Well! Who's ready for a drink?"

Horatio, her ancient butler, brought three room-temperature martinis to the library. "The bar is so far away and he's so slow," she apologized. Dusi didn't apologize for the cheap gin. "Light me please, Horatio."

"That's a stunning holder," Leigh said as the poor man hobbled across the room to hold a flame to his mistress's cigarette.

"Thank you. It belonged to Lola Montez." Dusi had spent years and another fortune collecting the cigarette holders of immortal *femmes fatales.* She wasn't about to let a little lung cancer prevent her from showing them off. "It was a gift from her lover, Ludwig the First of Bavaria."

As Leigh listened in awe to a disquisition on mad King Ludwig, Horatio brought another round of warm martinis containing both olives and twists of lemon. "He's been with us forever," Dusi sighed by way of a second apology. "Would you consider trading Cosmo for Horatio, Leigh?"

Pippa immediately cut in. "I'm sorry. I have an exclusive contract with Casa Bowes." She glared at Leigh to discourage any waffling. "And I'm very happy there."

"Too bad! May I be the first to know if the situation changes?"

"Absolutely," Leigh smiled.

Pippa leaned meaningfully forward. "How are you progressing with Signora Bowes's membership to the country club?"

Dusi needed a moment to recover. She had thought Cosmo was about to inspect the emerald pendant lost in her cleavage. "It is progressing more slowly than I had hoped."

"And why is that?"

Dusi exhaled a long plume of smoke. "Leigh, may I be frank? Your background is not aristocratic. Nor is that of your husband. Despite your admirable qualities, you are still first-generation plutocrats."

"So are you, if I'm not mistaken," Pippa said.

"Who told you such a thing?" Dusi gasped. For years she had been repeating the canard that she was a descendant of Jay Gould.

"It is common knowledge." Pippa removed the olive from her martini and placed it in a lapis lazuli ashtray. "Please continue."

"There is incredible competition for the two open memberships. The least blunder could be fatal. Floridia Ventura was a shoo-in until someone wrote to the committee that she was seen wearing the same Badgley Mischka dress two years in a row. Tori Batterson was a sure thing until her chef reported that he had been instructed to purchase store-brand groceries."

"You've got to be kidding," Pippa muttered in disgust.

"It's the truth." Dusi looked toward the doorway. "Yes, Horatio?"

Dusi's butler entered with an ornately framed diploma. "Madam, you requested to see this the moment it arrived."

"Oh, that thing. Yes, yes, show it to the guests."

"You've been inducted into the Frequent Bentley Society." Leigh excitedly read the fine print. "Ten Bentleys in eight years! That's fantastic."

Dusi was in the habit of having a few martinis and driving into the moat surrounding their castle. "Please hang that in the hallway outside your room, Horatio," she said, waving him off. "As I was saying, Leigh, one tiny misstep and you're finished. I will protect you as far as humanly possible but remember, you are nothing but a tap dancer." Dusi was gratified to see Leigh's lips tremble. "From Buffalo!"

"May I ask how *you* gained entrance into the Las Vegas Country

Club?" Pippa interrupted. Via Thayne she already knew that Dusi, after hiring six private detectives, had finally found enough dirt to blackmail two philanderers on the membership committee.

"My qualifications spoke for themselves," Dusi replied with a straight face. "I must congratulate you on that party yesterday, Leigh. It generated a lot of positive feedback from people who were—how do I say this?—previously unenthusiastic about your pedigree."

Horatio reentered. With white-gloved hands he presented Dusi with a little silver tray. On the tray was a little card. Dusi took the card. "Lunch is served," she read aloud.

They repaired to the dining hall, a masterpiece of English Gothic architecture. One hundred heraldic flags hung from the rafters. In the dark corners Caleb had managed to stash another stuffed horse and a quartet of fully armored knights, their lances all pointing at the long refectory table. Horatio had lit the two candelabra closest to the end where the ladies were seated. Sixteen candles didn't go far toward dispelling the gloom; however, Dusi considered the effect sensationally dramatic. She noticed Cosmo staring at her candlesticks.

"Are you admiring my regency silver, Cosmo?"

"No, I'm wondering whether I should allow Signora Bowes to lunch at a table lit by candles in daytime. I would never allow such a lapse at Casa Bowes."

Mortified, Dusi could only twitter, "Bravo, Cosmo! I was testing you." Nevertheless, she kept the candles lit rather than risk Cosmo noticing her filthy chandeliers.

Discussion of the Bowes's chances of joining the Las Vegas Country Club continued over congealing beef Wellington. In Dusi's opinion, dinosaurs had a better chance of roaming the earth than had Leigh of getting six yes votes from the membership committee. One abstention, one tiny anonymous letter of objection, and Leigh was out. The last forty candidates had not passed muster, and they were all people of stellar merit. Ten were billionaires. "Wealth was not enough," Dusi warned. She could not go into further detail because she had taken an oath of secrecy. "Unfortunately, Leigh, some people think Cosmo is the classiest item of furniture in your house."

"You know how important this membership is for Moss and me," Leigh whispered, again on the verge of tears.

"Furthermore, the club frowns on unstable couples. You two are definitely unstable."

"My employers are sublimely happy, Madam Damon. Who gave you such poor information?"

"I have my sources. And I have eyes in my head. Moss was definitely *not* staring at my neckline yesterday afternoon as I left Casa Bowes."

Pippa needed a moment to process how not ogling Dusi's boobs made Moss's marriage unstable. "Must everyone stare at those two bazookas you acquired in Rangoon?"

"My God, Cosmo!" Dusi nearly choked on her Yorkshire pudding. "Who told you such an outrageous lie?"

"Again, common knowledge." Pippa folded her napkin. "Thank you for lunch, Madam Damon. I believe Signora Bowes and I have heard, and eaten, enough." She headed for the door.

"Wait! I did say the situation was difficult, but it's far from hopeless. Yesterday's party was a good start. Leigh needs to follow up with a knockout punch."

Pippa turned. To her irritation Leigh was still seated at the table, fork in hand, paralyzed. "What do you suggest? We have no more pets with upcoming birthdays."

Leigh sprang to life. "We could celebrate Dusi's induction into the Frequent Bentley Society."

"An excellent idea!" Dusi agreed at once. "Leigh, you have more imagination than I thought. I'll send a guest list tomorrow. This could clinch it for you if you do it right." She beamed as Horatio entered with a dark, gummy mound on a silver platter. "Ah, the figgy pudding."

Pippa's digestive tract was spared by the entrance of a thirtysomething man in white pants and polo sweater. He had the tanned, even looks of an Abercrombie model now given over to full-time freeloading. "Pardon me," he cried in surprise. "I didn't know you were having company, Dusi." He looked quizzically at Pippa, whose gender was open to question. "I'm Harlan Scott."

"Cosmo du Piche," she replied, limply offering her hand.

Harlan instantly concluded that Cosmo was not his type. Leigh was another story. "Good afternoon to you," he leered.

Dusi took immediate preemptive action. "Harlan is croquet instructor at the club," she said, rising. "And my chaperone when Caleb is out of town." Translation: hands off. "Now if you'll excuse us, I believe we're late for my lesson." Fusing herself to his forearm, Dusi marched Harlan toward the door. "Think about my offer of a trade, Leigh."

"What was that all about?" Leigh whispered after the front door had slammed.

"That means Harlan is more than her croquet teacher."

"What trade is she talking about?"

"Me for Horatio. Don't even think about it. Are you interested in that figgy pudding?" No way. "Then let's get out of here. This place gives me the creeps." Pippa cupped her hands over her mouth. "Thank you, Horatio," she called to the butler standing discreetly at a side table. "Everything was exquisite."

"My pleasure, sir." He showed them to the front door. "Good day."

Leigh's apricot Duesenberg was parked in the stable beside Caleb's collection of royal horse-drawn carriages. Pippa slowly drove over the moat bridge separating Dusi's castle from the real world. "She's got some nerve calling Casa Bowes gaudy."

"I think Dusi's home is magnificent."

"Will you stop defending her? Anyone who lives with two stuffed horses is not sane."

"I think she has a crush on you, Cosmo."

"That just proves my point. Please don't encourage her."

"I can't believe Floridia Ventura was rejected! She's a descendant of the first governor of Rhode Island." Leigh's mood deteriorated with each mile Pippa put between them and Castilio Damonia. "Maybe Dusi's right. There's no hope. I'm just a social-climbing ex-Rockette with an unstable marriage."

"She's playing mind games with you. She needs to keep you in a state of perpetual insecurity. It's the way she is."

"Why would someone be that mean?"

"It's easier than being nice." Pippa tried to buoy Leigh's spirits by taking her to Picasso at the Bellagio for an edible lunch. "Why don't you personally collect checks from all those ladies who got their pictures taken with Michael Phelps yesterday? It's the perfect opportunity to meet some club members one on one. Just be yourself. Charm them."

"But what should I wear?" Leigh moaned.

"We'll go shopping. Leave everything to me."

Presuming that anyone who wore a purple sombrero and those outlandish glasses was a very important player in Las Vegas, the maître d' at Picasso led Pippa to a prominent table. As she followed him through a sea of curious stares, Pippa realized that she rather enjoyed playing the role of Cosmo du Piche. For once her alias did not feel alien. Cosmo exuded a confidence that had hitherto appeared to her only in fragments. His bizarre charisma actually bent others to his will. Pippa smiled: so this was what it felt like to be Thayne.

"Did Dusi really get her boobs in Rangoon?" Leigh asked after they had ordered.

"Last June."

"How do you know all this, Cosmo?"

"It is my business to know. The better to serve and protect you."

Leigh put her hand over Pippa's. "I think you're terrific. Don't ever change a thing. Not even that mustache."

They were discussing how to inform Moss of yet another blowout party when a comely but drunk woman, minus a shoe, sloshed to their table. Each hand was wrapped around a martini glass. Pippa vaguely remembered her from Titian's birthday party. "Wyolene!" Leigh gasped. "How nice to see you. Please join us."

"I jus rezeived a note," Wyolene revealed, weaving like a reed in the breeze. "Hand delivvrd while I wz playn brij."

Pippa and Leigh eventually pieced together the disjointed segments of Wyolene's story. After spending three hundred thousand dollars on parties, gifts, and abject brownnosing, Wyolene had just learned that her application for membership in the Las Vegas Country Club had been denied. All Dusi could tell her was that someone had written a letter to the committee, alerting them to the fact that Wyolene owned a Shih Tzu named Mambo. Naming a dog after a corrupt dance raised concerns about Wyolene's character.

"I wz blackBALLd!" Wyolene shouted, draining both martinis.

The maître d' hurried over. "Is this woman bothering you, sir?" he asked Pippa.

"She's had a bad shock. She'll be all right."

"No aright!" Wyolene staggered into the next table. One of her martini glasses fell into someone's cream of celeriac soup. "I goin' back to Palm Bich! Screwwww Vegaz!"

A waiter led Wyolene away. "She didn't get in because of *Mambo*?" Leigh asked, barely eking out the words.

"Your dog is named Titian," Pippa reminded her, signing the check. "Let's get out of here before we run into any more rejects."

Unfortunately they ran into Esmeralda at Armani, Karla at Fendi, and Bibi at Simayof, all of whom had just received hand-delivered notes similar to Wyolene's. All three women were crushed. Not one had a clue as to why her petition to join the country club had been blackballed. Pippa couldn't figure it out, either: these were wealthy, elegant, socially responsible ladies. Their dogs were named Rembrandt, Dwight, and Eiffel. Esmeralda had taken Dusi to Madrid to see a bullfight. Karla had given Dusi a triple-strand necklace of nine-millimeter Mikimoto pearls. Bibi had not only given Dusi a Warhol to hang in her mudroom but she had bought a stuffed pony for Caleb. Evidently none of these gestures had been enough to turn the tide. "Did anyone actually get into the club?" Pippa asked.

"Wallace and Peggy Stoutmeyer," Bibi sobbed, handing a credit card to the cashier. She was purchasing a little pick-me-up cocktail ring for eighty thousand dollars. "He's a damn chicken farmer. She looks like a tractor."

"That means there's only one space left," Leigh said.

"Don't get your hopes up," Bibi snapped, stalking out.

The mood in the Duesenberg was funereal as Pippa and Leigh headed home. "Under the circumstances, should we even go ahead with this Bentley ball?" Pippa asked. "Dusi's got a great little scam going."

Leigh was nearly beside herself. "I have to give this my best shot, Cosmo. Moss is counting on in it."

Pippa pulled into the driveway of Casa Bowes behind the Zappo Pool Sanitizers truck. The apricot Mercedes was parked under the portico. Pippa smiled: Cole was home. Unfortunately, so was Moss. "What the hell's he doing here at this hour?" Leigh demanded.

Pippa groaned: in her rush to dress Leigh for lunch, she had neglected to put the bills for Titian's party on Moss's desk. "Leave everything in the car, signora. If we're going to talk him into another party, the last thing he needs to see is ten Armani bags."

They parked in the garage, where Cole was polishing a black Porsche. "Hello, ladies," he called. "Excuse me. Lady and gentleman."

"What are you two doing home?" Leigh repeated.

"I believe you and Mr. Bowes are meeting your biggest Lurex supplier for five o'clock cocktails."

Leigh had forgotten all about that. "Yoo-hoo," she twittered as she and Cosmo crossed the threshold. "Titian! Where are you, darling?"

Nowhere. They found Moss in his library inspecting a mound of black feathers under a halogen light. "Have you seen Titian?"

"I just sent him to obedience school. Caught him chewing on my best *Turdus merula.*"

"You sent my dog away without telling me? Damn you!"

"He'll be back in a week." With a few bruised ribs. "Where have you been?"

"At a long, productive lunch with Dusi," Pippa said. "She lives in a spectacular castle filled with coats of armor. She showed us her doll collection and her—"

"Where are the bills from the pooch fest?" Moss cut in.

"I'll get them for you, signor."

When Pippa returned with her folder, Moss had commandeered Leigh's wallet and was calmly totaling all the credit card receipts from that afternoon's shopping excursion. "Eighteen thousand six hundred ninety-eight dollars," he remarked. "Was that before or after Dusi showed you her doll collection?"

"We only bought absolute necessities," Pippa reported as bravely as possible. "Signora Bowes seriously needs a new look."

"Shut up, Cosmo. Give me that folder." Moss again went to work with his calculator. He added everything twice then strolled to the window. "Forty-eight thousand bucks and change," he mused, staring pleasantly outside as if Botticelli's Venus had just stepped out of a clam shell onto his patio. Without warning Moss grabbed a globe and hurled it at Leigh. "For a dog's birthday party!" he screamed. "Are you out of your mind?"

Pippa, an experienced soccer player, made a diving catch, sparing both the globe and Leigh's costly nose. "Really, Signor Bowes," she said, brushing herself off. "That was beneath your dignity." She replaced the globe in its stand. "Now *you* sit down and shut up. I have something to say to you."

Moss was so surprised that he obeyed. Pippa proceeded exactly as Thayne had over the last twenty years whenever her spouse got tetchy over operating expenses. "You are a very successful man, blessed by marriage to a beautiful and loyal woman who chose *you* out of all the eligible, handsome, and extremely generous men in Dallas."

"Buffalo," Leigh whispered.

"Wherever. Your wife must reflect your success or she is not fulfilling her sacred duty to your name. In exchange you must provide her with the means of maintaining a superior social position."

"Says who?" Moss shot back.

"Please don't interrupt!" Pippa regretted that last warm martini at Dusi's; it was causing her to forget the most persuasive paragraph of Thayne's speech. "A few thousand dollars here and there are peanuts to a man of your good fortune. Furthermore, this isn't a matter of money. It's a matter of respect for the woman who has given you every ounce of her life and blood. This is your opportunity to be truly gallant." That was all Pippa remembered of Thayne's "Burn Me at the Stake" monologue. If Moss was anything like her father, he'd be slamming doors any second now, so she plunged ahead. "You wish to become a member of the Las Vegas Country Club. You have put your wife in charge of that Mission Impossible. You must now back her up."

"What's impossible about it?"

Pippa sighed as if she were explaining "two plus two equals four." "This afternoon we ran into four women who were also trying to become members of the club. Each had spent between three and six hundred thousand dollars to that end. Each woman received a handwritten letter of rejection this morning."

Moss sat very still. "What went wrong?"

"They were blackballed."

"What does that mean? Something like bushwhacked?"

"Someone wrote an anonymous letter to the committee raising objections."

"Anonymous, my ass. Who?"

"It's a secret meeting. The vote must be unanimous."

"The Stoutmeyers got in," Leigh blurted. "Can you believe that?"

"Shhh!" Pippa turned to Moss. "To date you have spent a measly eighteen thousand on clothing plus forty-eight grand on one party plus a few thousand for entertainment."

"Don't forget the sixty-five grand for yourself."

"Fine," Pippa snapped, her brain crunching the numbers. "That still only totals one hundred and thirty thousand dollars, which to be blunt, is barely enough to buy you two votes out of six. You can't afford to look cheap now, Signor Bowes. How badly do you want this membership?"

He mulled that over. "You've got something up your sleeve, you little runt."

"Moss! I'll not have you speak to Cosmo that way."

Pippa shrugged. "Call me what you will. I propose a masquerade ball. Two hundred thousand dollars."

"I'll give you thirty."

"One hundred forty."

"Ninety."

"Done."

"Now you tell *me* something, Cosmo," Moss growled. "Where does the membership committee meet?"

"At the club, I would presume."

"When's the next meeting?"

"Why do you need to know? You can't attend. You can't even pretend to care when they meet."

"You do it your way. I'll do it mine."

Pippa's upper lip tickled. Running her tongue over the offending itch, she was chagrined to feel bristle. Her mustache was sliding off: it had been a long, sweaty day. "Excuse me," she said. "I'll begin organizing the ball at once."

"Wait! What will I wear tonight for the Lurex people?" Leigh cried as Pippa headed for the door.

"The yellow Herrera with the raspberry pumps. Pearls and a hairband if you've got one." Pippa dashed to her room, there to verify that her mustache was barely hanging on by a few cross weaves. Worse, this morning she had left her tube of glue uncapped and most of it had oozed onto her dressing table. She ran into the bathroom to get a Q-tip and rescue some of it.

Cole stood naked at his sink, shaving. "Omigod!" Pippa shrieked. "I thought we agreed to knock, Cosmo," he said, not particularly concerned.

"I thought you were out washing cars!" Pippa stumbled back into her bedroom and slammed the door. She had never been so mortified in her life. For a moment Cosmo vaporized and the old, traumatized Pippa resurfaced, ready to bawl. She was about to fling herself on her bed and soak the pillowcases when she heard Cole whistling "What a Wonderful World." She held her breath, listening. He sounded happy. Really happy.

The whistling eventually stopped. "I'm done, Cosmo," he called through the door. "Bathroom's all yours."

Snapping out of her trance, Pippa phoned Olivia Villarubia-Thistleberry to vent. She got Cornelius informing her that Olivia and her lawyers had gone to Colombia to buy off a judge. Next Pippa called Dallas. "I'm so happy to hear you're back in the office, Sheldon."

"Most of me is back," he corrected her. "I'm seeing a hair regeneration specialist about the part that isn't."

"You'll be happy to know I'm still in school."

"That chambermaid camp?"

"I'm interning now. I'll be graduating in a week if a big party goes well."

"I'll believe that diploma when I see it."

"I need you to do me a tiny favor."

"I just sent you a Maserati, a phone, ten thousand dollars, and the lighter that singed off my eyebrows. You have about eighty thousand in your discretionary account. Don't tell me you've spent that on starch for your aprons."

"I need you to send four mustaches," Pippa said. "Overnight. Morning delivery. Nice ones. You know Inspector Clouseau? Like his, but light brown. Plus extra glue formulated for the desert. Hypoallergenic if you can find it."

"Desert? I thought you were in Aspen."

"Were you listening? I'm interning in Las Vegas. Toupees and mustaches are part of my routine here."

"What sort of employer would want his chambermaid to glue a mustache on him? Sounds like sexual harassment." Sheldon's voice lifted. "Maybe you should sue."

"The mustache is for me. I'm now a majordomo named Cosmo du Piche."

Sheldon didn't speak for a long moment. "Why don't you just quit shaving your legs and call it a day? Or move to Lesbos?"

"I like being Cosmo." Pippa had to spell the name three times. She gave Sheldon the address of Casa Bowes. "How's my mother doing?"

"She's in London. The BBC is thinking of doing a documentary about her. I advised her not to go but she didn't listen, as usual."

"At least she hasn't been in any fistfights for the last couple weeks."

"Nothing major," Sheldon replied vaguely. "You concentrate on that diploma now."

Another shouting match erupted in the library. Pippa went to her window just in time to see a soapstone owl smash through a window and land on the patio. She saw Cole walk to the garage and back the limousine out to the driveway. Moss hustled Leigh, attired head to toe in gold sequins, into the rear seat. As the Mercedes pulled away, Pippa's phone rang.

"Could you call Painless Panes, Cosmo?" Cole's voice was barely audible over the shouting. "Five on the house speed dial."

"No problem."

"Would you like to raid the kitchen with me later?"

That depended on how much mustache adhesive she could scrape off her dresser. "Maybe."

"Hey, Mo!" Kerry was pounding on her door. "The Zappo guys are leaving."

"Gotta go." Pippa rescued enough glue to hold her mustache in place for a few more hours. She signed the pool cleaners' receipt and waited for the same glass crew who had been there yesterday to come back and fix the broken window in the library. Kerry and Rudi left to play the slots, leaving Pippa alone at Casa Bowes. She toted the booty from that afternoon's shopping spree upstairs. On the fifth trip to the garage, obeying an impulse, Pippa went to the black Porsche parked next to her Maserati. She opened the door and sat in the driver's seat, inhaling Cole's vapors. She was sure this was his car, not Moss's. The keys were in the ignition. Pippa started the engine and cruised once around the block. Her secret ride felt as exhilarating as a stolen kiss. Cole had given the Maserati a thorough washing and waxing, she noticed. For the first time in weeks she wondered how Lance was doing. Training season would start any day now. Pippa laughed, shocked: she really didn't care.

She washed her jogging bra and, on another impulse, shaved her legs with Cole's gold razor. At midnight, hearing the front door slam, she felt her whole body quiver alive. She heard Leigh and Moss go upstairs, drunk but mostly yelled out for the evening. Their bedroom light went on, then off. Her phone rang. "Sorry, Cosmo," Cole said. "Something's come up. I won't be able to make it."

"No problem," Pippa lied.

After she heard his Porsche roll down the driveway, she consoled herself with leftover flank steak and some grand cru burgundy. Halfway through, Rudi and Kerry entered the kitchen, twenty bucks ahead of Flamingo for the first time in history. They finished off the bottle and a tray of Rudi's eggplant lasagna. Eventually Kerry burped in porcine satiety. "Hey Mo, where's Cinderfella?"

"Excuse me?"

"Cole. His Porsche is gone."

"I believe he's running an errand for Signor Bowes."

"Don't wait up for him," Kerry laughed.

Pippa did anyway. He never came back.

Nineteen

Chippa had been a fixture of Cole's imagination ever since she'd whapped him in the face at the Phoenix Ritz-Carlton. Next morning he had blown her a kiss across the lobby; if anything, that speeded her escape to a limousine waiting outside. Hoping to reconnect with her, Cole had gone to lunch with an inebriated psycho named Marla, who would only reveal that Chippa loved pickles and garlic and had a Polish lover who couldn't play poker to save his ass. Marla had then tried to grope him under the table. Cole left Phoenix that afternoon; he had been there picking up an Airstream doghouse for Titian. He never thought he'd see Chippa again.

He found her reincarnation as Cosmo both amusing and unsettling. Normal women didn't hop around the country using aliases. What was she really doing here? It was a serious issue because, in addition to valeting Moss and keeping all motor vehicles in pristine working order, Cole was in charge of security at Casa Bowes. After a rash of letter bombs in the neighborhood, Moss had ordered him to inspect any incoming packages that did not come from known sources. Cole happened to be parking his Porsche in the garage when a FedEx van pulled into the driveway at eight the next morning. "You got a Cosmo du Piche here?" the driver asked.

"Yes." Cole signed for the small, light package from a law firm in Dallas. Then he opened it. Cosmo had received four mustaches in a velvet case, six tubes of hypoallergenic adhesive, a pair of silver mustache-trimming scissors, a tiny comb, mustache wax, a brochure for villas in Lesbos, and twenty thousand dollars cash.

Frowning, Cole resealed the box. He was quite sure she had taken his Porsche out last night while he was squiring Moss, Leigh, and the Lurex people around Las Vegas. The car hadn't been parked anywhere near straight in its slot in the garage. Was she spying on him? If so, she was colossally inept. Maybe that was part of a larger deception. "Incoming package, Cosmo," he called, knocking on her door. "Would you like me to open it for you?"

"Absolutely not!" Her door cracked an inch. "Please push it into my room."

"What's inside, tassels for your cap?"

"None of your business." The lock clicked.

She sounded peeved. Cole found that a poor way to start the day. "Are you okay?"

Of course not! Pippa felt like screaming. The past eight hours had been hell. In Phoenix, when she had asked Cole how his love life was, he had immediately replied, "Fine." The rational side of her argued that *of course* a guy like Cole would have a girlfriend with whom he would have fantastic sex seven nights a week. *Of course* the woman would be madly in love with him, and vice versa. *Of course* Pippa's jealousy was childish and petty, if not downright stupid, considering he didn't even know she was female. The irrational side of Pippa just wanted to find this woman and kill her. Mostly she was furious at herself for dreaming impossible dreams.

Kerry had not helped Pippa's insomnia by groaning through several bouts of sexual congress, either with Rudi, Moss, or herself. Maybe all three.

On the plus side, Pippa's new mustache glue worked like a champ. Shortly before nine, after she saw Cole and Moss leave, she dragged herself to the kitchen. Rudi was there making johnnycakes. Dressed in a peignoir with lots of feathers, Leigh sat at the window nursing a cup of coffee and calling every dog obedience school in Las Vegas. She had yet to locate Titian.

"Good morning, signora. Did you have a nice time with the Lurex people?"

"I don't remember. Thanks for fixing the window." Leigh's blood-shot eyes settled on Pippa's upper lip. "You did your mustache. It's lighter. I like it."

"Thank you. I devoted several hours to personal grooming last night."

"Poor thing, you've been working too hard. You look exhausted."

The doorbell rang. Pippa went to the foyer. Dusi's Bentley stood in the driveway. Her butler, Horatio, sweating buckets in tuxedo, white gloves, and wool cap, presented her with an envelope. "Good morning, sir. I bring word from Castilio Damonia regarding the Bentley Ball."

"Come in," Pippa said. "Have some pancakes. Rudi's on a roll."

Horatio hesitated; his normal breakfast at Dusi's was a day-old baguette. "I would be grateful for a glass of water," he answered care-fully.

Pippa dragged him to the kitchen. "You boys relax while Signora Bowes and I read our marching orders." She and Leigh adjourned to the formal dining room. Pippa opened an envelope with *Castilio damonia* embossed in such huge gold letters across the top that there was no room for stamps, which was the whole point: Horatio was Dusi's postal service.

Pippa cleared her throat. " 'Dear Leigh, I think that a masquerade ball in honor of my induction into the Frequent Bentley Society is a marvelous idea, considering all that I have done for you. A masquer-ade is a festive and fanciful event, therefore I would like the men to come dressed as chauffeurs circa 1930, driving vintage Bentleys (they can be rented anywhere for a song), and I would like the women to come dressed as cars such as Pintos, Mustangs, Jaguars, and the like. You must have Rudi prepare a supper similar to that served to King Edward the Seventh, another member of the Frequent Bentley Society. The menu will include pressed beef, snipe, lobster, partridge, oysters, ptarmigan, truffles, quail, grouse, jellied eel, and lamb tongue; eight varieties of Persian melons; nectarines in French Sauternes; a selection of fruit jams and cream biscuits; four varieties of gently steamed veg-etables, with their blossoms; and toasted almonds. For dessert you must offer persimmon flan, steamed quince pudding, and fruitcake (without walnuts, please! I'm allergic) soused in heirloom rum; and of course, have a generous quantity of alcoholic beverages on hand. Décor: I do love gondolas and harlequins! If you can get hold of a few tigers (on leashes, of course) to roam the grounds, that would be so exotic and stunning. I leave the music to you, but please hire at least a seventy-piece orchestra so that we can hear it. Have tons of gardenias, my very favorite flower. You may dispense with the relay races in the swimming pool, but please make the bowling alley available again for valets and personal attendants. Do not serve pepperoni pizza to them this time. Barbecue flown in from Dr. Hogly Wogly's in Los Angeles would be ever so much better, with Pilsner Urquell in kegs. Please have the Delta Force snipers back in the trees for our protection, as there will be major jewelry in attendance. Following is a guest list. I have been up all night winnowing this down to four hundred. You should have no problem hand-delivering the invitations, as everyone on it resides within two hundred miles of Las Vegas. I advise you to construct a raised dais with soft lighting so that we may have an appropriate ceremony at the stroke of midnight. As you know, I will be joining Caleb in Normandy tomorrow as he purchases Ethelred the Unready's suit of armor. I will be back in Las Vegas only briefly before leaving for a long-overdue vacation to Algeria. Therefore my only available date for Masqueradia Dusiana will be seven days from now, at eight in the evening. I so look forward to seeing how you fare with this large-scale effort, Leigh, and hope that with Cosmo's help, you will be not only the toast of the town, but also the newest member of the Las Vegas Country Club. With affection, Dusi. P.S. Very important: this must be a surprise party!' "

Pippa let the pages flutter to the floor. "Sure, no problem."

Leigh went whiter than the feathers in her peignoir. "That's a million-buck bash. You only got ninety grand out of Moss." She headed for the decanter on a side table. "We're toast."

If they were, then so was Pippa's diploma. "Nonsense!" She removed the decanter from Leigh's quaking fingers. "Stay sober, signora. You're about to make a few hundred house calls."

"You really think we can pull this off?"

"It is nothing. Get dressed and meet me in your office as soon as possible."

Pippa went to the kitchen, where Horatio was consuming pancakes as fast as Rudi could flip them. "Please tell Madam Damon we love her proposal."

She sat at Leigh's desk with a legal pad. What the heck was a snipe? If she managed to feed four hundred mouths for a hundred bucks apiece, that would leave fifty grand to play with. Booze would cost at least ten, the orchestra twenty. Flowers she could get for five. That left a measly fourteen thousand bucks for wild animals, harlequins, and gondolas. Pippa massaged the numbers this way and that. Each time she got the bottom line to work, she realized she had left something out, like the barbecue in the bowling alley.

Leigh came in wearing one of her new Armani pantsuits. Pippa handed her fifteen pages of guest list. *Delegate as much as possible to useful idiots.* "Start planning your route. You'll be visiting one hundred people each day."

Leigh stared at the printout. " 'Page and Zelda Turnbull of Las Vegas' "?

"Obviously Dusi thinks she lives in Edwardian London. You'll have to look up everyone's street address online."

"That is a major pain in the butt."

"I believe that is the whole point." Pippa removed her eyeglasses. Today they seemed to weigh ten pounds.

While Leigh was researching addresses, whimpering about her missing bichon frise, Pippa ordered stationery from Neiman Marcus. She designed the invitation and even found a Bentley icon online. Pippa tried not to guffaw as she typed "Masqueradia Dusiana: A Surprise Party" across the top line in Olde English font. At the stroke of ten she rousted Kerry from bed. "Be in Signora's office in five minutes."

There Kerry was handed a map of Las Vegas and instructed to mark every one of Leigh's addresses with a dot. "What for?"

"You're going to be driving to each of those dots in the next few days."

"I ain't driving anywhere. I'm the linen and silver person, period."

"Would two thousand bucks change your attitude?"

"Yeah, I guess so."

Pippa paid her immediately from her own slush fund. Downstairs,

Rudi was just seeing Horatio out with a picnic basket. "Rudi, we're having a party next week," Pippa said, accompanying him to the kitchen. "It's going to make you famous." She presented him with the menu Dusi had proposed.

His eyebrows nearly shot off his forehead. "Who makes diss? Too many dishes."

Never accept no. "It's a historical menu prepared for English kings when they came back from hunting. Could you do it for a hundred bucks a head?"

He took another look. "For twelf people?"

"For four hundred."

"*Nein!* Impossibell!"

Pippa immediately threw herself to the floor. "Please, Rudi," she wailed, clutching his ankles. "If you don't, I'll lose my job. I'll have to go back to New Orleans." That didn't get much traction. "My house is washed away. People beat me up down there." No dice. "The alligators ate half my mother." She looked up. "The top half."

"Okay," he finally snapped. "One hundred fifty per person. Othervise *schlecht* qvality, I cannot allow. Plus you must get me five sous chefs from Flamingo."

Pippa kissed his clogs. "Thankyouthankyou, Rudi! You're the greatest."

"And you giff me five tousand bonus."

"Absolutely! I have it right here." Rudi was paid on the spot.

Pippa staggered upstairs to help Leigh and Kerry, who had narrowed their focus to the fifty-odd names on Dusi's list with out-of-town addresses. When the blank cards arrived from Neiman's, Pippa printed four hundred invitations. In flowery script she wrote names on envelopes and tucked those envelopes into larger envelopes. She shuddered: this was almost like getting married again. By two o'clock the delivery route was complete.

"Don't spend more than three minutes at each place or you won't get back for a week," Pippa advised Leigh. "And remember to tell everyone it's a surprise party."

"But it's not."

"Just do it," Pippa snapped. "You do know how to drive a Duesenberg, Kerry?"

"A car's a car."

After that expedition to Erewhon shoved off, Pippa worked with Rudi on the menu. The price of snipe, partridge, quail, eel, and lamb tongue was ruinous. Rudi insisted on renting a refrigerated truck for eight thousand bucks and began pawing through ancient gastronomic encyclopedias in search of recipes. He was showing Pippa a recipe for pressed beef in horseradish aspic when the phone rang: Dusi calling from her jet over the North Pole.

"I forgot whelks and periwinkles," she said. "Please add them to the menu."

"Thank you, Madam Damon. It will be done."

"Cosmo, you sound exhausted. You must be overwhelmed trying to put on this little party all by yourself. Were you at Castilio Damonia, I'd hire a staff of twenty for you. You'd barely have to lift a finger." When that got no response, she added, "Whatever Leigh's paying you, I'll double it."

"We're doing fine, Madam Damon. Bon voyage." Pippa slammed down the phone. "Add whelks and periwinkles to your shopping list, Rudi."

"Velk? Vatt iss dat?"

"Just get them," Pippa shouted. The phone rang: this time it was Leigh, thirty miles away. Miscalculating a turn, Kerry had knocked over a park bench. The Duesenberg's rear fender was history.

"Moss is going to kill me," Leigh wailed. "You can't fix these cars for less than twenty thousand bucks. It's part of the mystique."

"Where's Kerry?"

"Trying to revive the old lady who was sitting on the bench. You've got to come get us, Cosmo. I can't be seen in a car with a dented fender. That would be an immediate blackball."

"Stay calm. I'll send reinforcements." Pippa called Cole. "Are you busy?"

She sounded quite sarcastic. However, the sound of her voice sent him over the moon. "I'm waiting for Moss to finish a meeting. Sorry about last night. Something came up."

I'll bet it did, you horny bastard. "Kerry and signora just trashed the Duesenberg." Pippa provided a few terse details. "Can you fetch them?"

"I'd love to, but Moss is my primary responsibility."

"I understand." Furious, Pippa hung up. "I'll be back in a bit, Rudi. Do not answer the phone."

Like Pippa, Cole had gotten very little sleep the previous evening. First he had to chauffeur Moss, Leigh, and four Lurex salesmen to a number of revues on the Strip. At midnight, after shoving Leigh upstairs, Moss had asked to be driven to the Las Vegas Country Club, where he was meeting some guy named Harlan to discuss croquet lessons. They stayed there until the bar closed. After dropping Moss back at Casa Bowes, Cole proceeded to an all-night cybercafé because Moss wanted an immediate background check on Cosmo. Leigh had hired him in a rush and something about the guy just didn't add up.

Cole's investigation began with an old school chum, now a police chief in Texas. He learned that Cosmo's blue Maserati with LOTOPO plates was registered to a Vernon Pierce care of Sheldon Adelstein, the Dallas lawyer who had sent the mustache kit. That sounded a bit convoluted so Cole had his friend run the serial number through a number of insurance databases. He discovered that the car replaced a Maserati previously owned by Lance Henderson. The Cowboys quarterback? Was he the "previous employer" Chippa had gotten over a hump in exchange for that dazzling diamond necklace? Seething, Cole Googled "Lance Henderson."

Eighty million links appeared. Few of them related to football. Cole was shocked to see a picture of Lance and . . . that woman . . . the bride . . . he zoomed in . . . Chippa? She was ravishing! Blond. No glasses. Those diamonds circled her delicious neck. What a dress! Her name was Pippa Walker. Big oil family. Wedding of the century. Mesmerized, Cole read until four in the morning. He learned that Pippa had disappeared after jilting Lance at the altar. Grandfather shocked stiff . . . mother berserk . . . father AWOL . . . mother-in-law rabid . . . media circus . . . who could blame her for evaporating? Apparently she had dumped the quarterback for someone else: that was weird, considering how hard she had hit on Cole in Phoenix. Granted, it had been a brief, bizarre conversation at the Ritz-Carlton but he would swear that the ditzy blonde drinking rusty nails was unattached. On the other hand she had offered him ten grand to have it off with Marla. Were they some kind of gender-bending psychopaths? That was an unpleasant concept.

At breakfast Cole reported back to Moss. First and foremost, he said, Cosmo was totally on the level. The employment agency, the references, everything checked out. The boy looked bizarre but he got the job done. Moss should quit worrying about him.

Moss looked up from his soft-boiled egg. "I still say there's something off about the guy."

"I'll stay on his tail, sir."

Cole had been parked outside Fine Feather, Inc., when Pippa phoned with the Duesenberg problem. To his regret Cole couldn't assist: he'd be fired on the spot, and Moss was his priority. When Pippa hung up on him, he felt impaled. The ice in her voice wasn't just about the car. Sighing, he returned his attention to the conversation transmitting through his earbuds. Reception inside Fine Feather headquarters was loud and clear.

"Account 8020347–2," he heard Moss say into the tiny microphone hidden in his lapel. "Bangkok General. You'll have it tonight."

Cole entered the numbers in his BlackBerry. "Gotcha."

When Cole and Moss finally returned to Casa Bowes, the Duesenberg was parked with its smashed fender facing the wall of the garage. The Maserati was gone along with Cosmo, Leigh, and Kerry. Rudi was in the kitchen whipping through piles of old cookbooks. He looked like a smallpox boil about to explode. "Rudi says the ladies went for a joyride," Cole reported to Moss.

"May it be a long one."

While Moss settled into the Jacuzzi, Cole inspected the damage to the Duesenberg's fender. He drove the car to the body shop, then called Cosmo's cell. "Where are you?"

"Delivering invitations to the masquerade ball."

That was the first Cole had heard of it. "Here?"

"A week from now. Four hundred guests."

No wonder she sounded frazzled. "How can I help?"

"Fix the car."

"Way ahead of you, Cosmo. I'm calling from the body shop. Tell me about the ball."

"Not now. We have six more invitations to deliver. Under no circumstances ask Rudi to make dinner." She hung up.

Cole got Thai food on his way back to Casa Bowes in a courtesy vehicle. He was serving Moss on the patio when the ladies finally returned. "Do you two have something against postage stamps?" Moss asked.

Leigh dug into a carton of pad Thai. "You obviously know nothing about style."

"Nor do you, or you would have taken the Duesenberg instead of that wopmobile."

"My Maserati gets excellent mileage," Pippa objected. "We're on a strict budget, if you recall." Mere mention of the word "budget" tied her stomach in knots: extra sous chefs, the refrigerated truck, bonuses for Kerry and Rudi, not to mention whelks and periwinkles, had already shot everything *thirty-four grand* overboard, and that was just day one. "Have a pleasant evening," she said, leaving. "Be careful of the new windows, signora."

Cole caught up with Pippa as she was knocking, to no effect, on Kerry's door. "Where'd she go? She was supposed to start polishing silver after driving the car back this afternoon."

"Maybe she ran away. It's not an insignificant repair."

He stood only inches away. Overcoming a violent urge to close the gap, Pippa took a step backward. "When will it be fixed?"

"I'll pick it up at six tomorrow morning. Moss won't see a thing. Don't worry about the bill. I'm in charge of a small discretionary fund."

She went into her room and shut the door. Cole put his nose to the wood. "Cosmo? Did I say something wrong?"

"I'm just tired," came her weary voice. "Please leave me alone."

Cole went to the kitchen. Nearly beside himself, Rudi was still ripping pages out of cookbooks. He didn't even notice Cole putting together a supper tray. Outside on the patio, Leigh and Moss were mired in another fracas. She hadn't located Titian at any obedience school and Moss wasn't about to reveal the dog's location until his ribs healed. "You hired a hit man, you bastard!" she cried. "You never liked him!"

"Why pay someone to wipe out a dog when I could just drown it?" Not the best reply.

Cole smiled: Casa Bowes was paradise. He knocked on Pippa's door. "I brought supper, Cosmo." He waited. "Come on, be a sport." He had to chew on his fists not to break down the door. "Are you sure you're not mad at me?"

"No. I mean yes." Nevertheless she opened the door. "Come in."

"Sorry I couldn't help this afternoon," he said, sitting on the corner of her bed. "Moss has been running me ragged lately. I was up until five doing a security check for him."

Pippa slowly blinked: so he hadn't been with a woman. Ten tons of mud lifted from her psyche. "I'm sorry I was so short with you."

"You have a lot on your mind. Here. Eat." He handed her a plate of roasted peppers. "Smell that garlic. Yum yum." When she only wrinkled her nose, he offered her a crock of pickles. "My favorite food group."

"So I notice." She took the Waldorf salad instead. "May I ask you a personal question?"

"Shoot."

"What are you doing here?"

"In your room?" That was obvious, wasn't it?

"No, here at Casa Bowes. You seem overqualified to be a chauffeur."

He didn't answer at once. "The pay's good and the work's easy. Plus I like Vegas."

"You seem the sort of man who prefers a more challenging job."

"Believe me, this one's a challenge." Especially now that you've arrived. "Why are *you* here? You're obviously not a run-of-the-mill majordomo."

Pippa blushed. Her fingers flew to her lip, checking that the mustache was still on. "I know my uniform is strange."

"I love the uniform. I was referring to you. Personally."

After a brief internal debate, she decided not to add more lies to the pile between them. "Can you keep a secret? I'm interning. In a week, if all goes well, I'll get a diploma from the Mountbatten-Savoy School of Household Management."

"Congratulations. Then what?"

I can start repairing the damage I've done. "I can raise my rates." That seemed to amuse him. "You think I'm kidding?"

"Sorry, Cosmo, I didn't realize you were that hard up."

"What about you? Do you plan to stay here?"

"Maybe."

The silences were becoming long and dangerous. *Get the damn diploma, Cosmo.* Pippa slid off the bed. "Do you mind if I take a bath? It's been a long day."

"Go right ahead." As he lay in bed listening to the water swishing on the other side of the wall, imagining her without clothes and especially without a mustache, Cole composed the huge thank-you note he was going to send Lance Henderson someday.

The next day, as Leigh fretted about her missing dog, Pippa engaged forty waiters with harlequin costumes. She got a deal on flowers from the very people Thayne had used for her nonnuptials. However, every gondola and festive tent in Nevada was spoken for. In the middle of another erotic dream involving Cole and a bearskin rug, Pippa had a brainstorm. First thing in the morning she called a number she had sworn never to call again.

"Henderson residence," a familiar voice answered on the first ring. "This is Harry."

Pippa affected a French accent. "Allo. I am Cosmo du Piche, majordomo at Casa Bowes in Las Vegas. In ze near future we will bee having a party for four hundred guests. It has come to my attention zat you have recently purchased four tents representing ze four seasons plus bandstands, two gondolas, clouds, bocce equipment, fountains, and cages of birds. I would like to rent zem from you."

Harry was too stunned to reply. Following the wedding debacle, he had stashed all that junk at a remote ranch, where it would stay until Lance's little sister got married off.

"Five zouzand dollars." Pippa waited a moment. "I do not see zat you need to inform anyone about zis private matter between majordomos. I am happy to send cash vizzin ze hour."

"Could you make it seven, Monsieur du Piche? I'd like to retire soon."

Pippa was tempted to pay the long-suffering man ten. As they settled the details, she heard Cole singing in the shower. He was sweet to
have brought supper last night. And he was sweet to be picking up the
Duesenberg this morning. He was trying very hard to be kind to her.
Him. Whatever. Pippa shut her eyes as the water stopped gushing. She
imagined Cole walking to the sink. Picking up his gold razor. Those
long legs . . . that butt . . .

Get the damn diploma, Cosmo.

Pippa was surprised to see Kerry stumble into the office at nine
o'clock. "Where were you yesterday afternoon?"

"Off. It's in my contract."

"I paid you two thousand bucks to stick around 24/7."

"Well, here I am."

Fresh from her soft shoe lesson, Leigh came in. No sparkly eye-
shadow. Another new Armani pantsuit. "You look beautiful, Signora
Bowes."

"I'm learning, Cosmo."

The doorbell rang. A case of Pol Roger arrived with a note for
Leigh: "Thinking of you. Love, Bekka." "Word's gotten out," Pippa
said. "Every social X-ray in Vegas is going to be chewing her fingernails hoping you'll drop by today." The bell rang again. "Maybe I
should just leave the front door open."

Leigh's cell phone rang. "Hello, dear!" She listened at length. "Absolutely no problem, Dusi. Right away." She handed the phone to
Pippa.

"What now, Madam Damon?" Pippa asked, barely masking her irritation.

"I just wanted to say hello from Normandy," Dusi burbled.

"Hello. Now goodbye." Pippa hung up. "What did she want?"

"She forgot to pack her false eyelashes. I said I'd pick them up at
Castilio Damonia and bring them to the airport. Her jet will take them
to France in time for a photo session with the new suit of armor."

"Come on! Why can't Horatio bring them to the airport?" Kerry
demanded.

"He's with Dusi."

"They don't sell false eyelashes in France?"

"Kerry, once you get a pair that fits, you stick with them."

"You're far too understanding, Signora Bowes. This little favor is going to put you hours behind schedule." Dusi knew that, of course. "Please be more careful with the car today, Kerry."

"Would you like to drive, Mo?"

Pippa signed for a delivery of four dozen roses. "Leigh—just celebrating YOU. Love, Nicoline." "I'll be here if you need me."

For the remaining daylight hours Pippa attended to an avalanche of details. The doorbell never stopped ringing. Rudi kept savaging cookbooks. Dusi called twice, to request that jugged hare be added to the menu, then to dictate the opening lines of her Frequent Bentley Society ceremony. Cole called once, asking if Pippa needed anything. Leigh and Kerry returned from their postal deliveries after midnight and went directly to bed. Despite her exhaustion, Pippa dozed but couldn't sleep: Cole hadn't brought a midnight-snack tray to her room. Around two o'clock she went to the kitchen to put together a tray of milk and cookies. Maybe he was waiting for her to bring food to *his* room for a change.

Rudi looked up from a mountain of whelk recipes. "Vere you go vit all ziss food?"

"Cole and I are hungry."

"He iss not home. He visits a voman."

"Cole has a girlfriend?" Pippa choked. "Are you sure?"

"*Ja,* I ask him vere he goes tonight. 'My boss lady,' he tells me. Big secret."

"Thanks for keeping your mouth shut," Pippa muttered. She went to his room and knocked. "Cole?" Silence.

Once all the invitations were hand-delivered, Leigh began seeing Dr. Zeppelin, a therapist specializing in pet bereavement. She told Moss she would continue doing so, at two hundred dollars an hour, until Titian returned. For once, he said nothing.

Day by manic day, plans for Masqueradia Dusiana fell into place. Unfortunately, each day Pippa went another ten grand over budget. She now understood what Thayne was up against throwing her legendary parties year after year. *Cut one corner and another will bite you in the arse:* right on, Mama. Pippa slaved from dawn until midnight. If nothing else, she could thank Dusi for keeping her mind off Cole, who had been quietly driving his Porsche out the driveway after everyone had gone to bed and creeping it back around four in the morning. No matter how soundly she slept, Pippa always heard him return. When she couldn't take it anymore, she contrived to run into him in the hallway as he was tiptoeing back to his room.

"Cosmo!" He was stunned to see her. "What are you doing up at this hour?"

"Planning a party." She glared at his stubble. "I certainly hope Signor Bowes is paying you overtime."

He caught up with her in five steps. "It's not what it looks like."

"Sir, your personal life is not my concern." Wow! Of all the lies she had told since the wedding, that was by far the grandest. "The bathroom is all yours."

One morning as Pippa stood at the Bolivian rosewood doors signing for a crate of Persian melons, a moving van pulled under the portico. Texas plates. Her stomach rolled over: Rosimund's tents. Pippa held steady as the movers hauled miles of canvas, two bandstands, fleecy clouds, bocce gear, fountains, and bird cages to the backyard. Sight of the two gondolas, however, put her over the edge. She was suddenly back in Texas Stadium with Rosimund's maudlin Tunnel of Love. The orchestra was playing waltzes. She was dancing with her grandfather. Lance got up to speak and everything went into a death spiral.

Get the damn diploma, Cosmo!

"The boats go in the pool," Pippa ordered. When all of Rosimund's props were unloaded, she gave everyone a tip and hit the bar for a stiff drink.

Leigh bounced in, aglow from her morning ballet class. "Cosmo! What's the matter?"

"A spot of indigestion, signora. Thanks for asking."

"It must be stress. But everything's going well, isn't it?"

"Yes, if two hundred thousand over budget means nothing."

"Don't worry. Moss is just hot air. He fully expects this party to cost half a million."

"I would not want him to fire me, signora. That would be catastrophic."

"That will only happen over my dead body." Leigh evidently didn't consider that a possibility. She glanced at her watch. "Where's Dusi today? She usually calls by ten."

The doorbell rang. Finishing her bourbon, Pippa chuckled, "Speak of the devil."

Sure enough, Horatio stood outside. He looked embarrassed. "Good morning, sir. Madam Damon was in the neighborhood and thought you might enjoy a brief visit."

"Absolutely not," Pippa retorted. "She's supposed to be in Europe."

"Couldn't stay away, dears," Dusi waved from the rear seat. "May we come in?"

"We don't have time for this, signora," Pippa fumed as Horatio helped Dusi and a few friends out of her new Bentley.

"I can't say no to her." Leigh suddenly panicked. "God! I'm not wearing any jewelry!"

Pippa unbuttoned the collar of her jacket and removed her diamond necklace. Lately she had been wearing it under her uniform for moral support. "Put this on." Seeing Leigh's eyes pop, she added, "It was a gift from my last mistress."

"Cosmo, darling!" Bursting into the foyer, Dusi clasped Pippa in a lingering embrace. Today she wore a purple sheath that a streetwalker might consider immodest plus the usual ton of gold. "I just had to introduce you to my friends. They've heard *soooo* much about you, they almost think you're a member of my staff. You remember Harlan, of course."

The croquet gigolo. "Sir," Pippa nodded.

Harlan was much more interested in Leigh. "Don't you look sweet in that leotard."

"Thank you. I've just finished my ballet lesson."

"So we see," Dusi sniffed. "This is Peggy Stoutmeyer, the newest member of the Las Vegas Country Club. We are all so proud of her."

"Madam." Pippa nodded to a pudgy, vulgar woman in a jumpsuit.

"Love the pantaloons, Cosmo," Peggy laughed. "Weeeeehaw!"

Leigh shook her hand. "Congratulations, Mrs. Stoutmeyer."

"Call me Peggy, hon."

"And this is my dear friend Thayne Walker from Dallas. I ran into her at Harrods and just had to bring her back with me. I'm sure you can squeeze one more person into Masqueradia Dusiana, can't you, sweetheart?"

Twenty

As the last member of Dusi's party stepped forward, Pippa felt her heart go still. Thayne looked frail and shell-shocked. The diamonds that she had always worn so proudly now seemed too brilliant for her. She did, however, manage a creditable glare at Pippa's uniform: in Thayne's book, a majordomo wore a tux. Period.

"Madam." Pippa bowed, lowering her voice an octave.

Thayne never conversed with other people's servants. She pointedly took Leigh's hand. "This is quite a mansion, Mrs. Bowes."

"Call me Leigh. It's a replica of Versailles, as you may have noticed."

Hard to miss. "My home is a replica of Fleur-de-Lis, palace of the Comte de Mirabeille outside Toulouse. He was beheaded in the French Revolution."

"That's fascinating! Would you like a tour? We can compare notes."

"I'd love that."

Nausea knifed through Pippa: the remains of the Henderson Ball littered Leigh's backyard. "A quick word before you begin, signora." She took Leigh far down the hallway. "Under no circumstances let anyone near the rear windows. I'm going to shut all the drapes on that side of the house. There are some things floating in the pool."

"Good Lord!"

"Stall them at the front door until I get back." Pippa tore through Casa Bowes, ripping the drapes shut. Leigh was still expatiating upon the Bolivian rosewood bas relief, and Dusi was still complaining about the wood stain, when Pippa returned to the foyer with a tray of martinis.

"Thank you, Cosmo." Dusi swallowed thirstily. "I needed this."

The group entered the first ballroom. "Why are those drapes drawn, Leigh?" Dusi noticed immediately. "You're not trying to save on air-conditioning, I hope?"

"Far from it, Madam Damon. We wish at least one element of your masquerade ball to be a surprise. Please stay away from the window."

Thayne gasped. "How dare he speak to you like that, Dusi."

"Thayne, you are such a stiff," she laughed. "Cosmo and I have our own private language. You wouldn't understand."

Thayne merely stood there. Pippa couldn't believe it.

Leigh took Thayne's arm. "Everyone's in love with Cosmo. I can't thank Olivia Villarubia-Thistleberry enough for sending him to me."

"Really! She sent my new majordomo also. We have something else in common." Thayne smiled, having just bestowed the ultimate compliment on another human being.

"Cosmo, come here with those martinis." Dusi extended her glass as she fluttered her globe-trotting false eyelashes. "Are you trying to get me drunk, naughty boy?"

"Perish the thought. That's a very nice cigarette holder, Madam Damon."

"It belonged to Greta Garbo."

Pippa tossed it into the fireplace. "No smoking in Casa Bowes. I believe we've been through this once already."

As Thayne emitted an operatic gasp, Dusi cooed, "You're such a tyrant, Cosmo."

Leigh conducted a magnificent tour of Casa Bowes. Thayne was very taken with the six dressing rooms and ballrooms, the gargantuan silver chest, and the Louis Quatorze *scriban* in Moss's library. An hour later they ended up in the kitchen. "Last but not least, this is Rudi, my Austrian chef."

Rudi barely nodded to the intruders. He was contemplating three hundred plucked baby ptarmigan lying on the counter. They were much smaller than he had imagined, ergo stuffing each tiny cavity with a filbert, a date, and a crab apple would take eons.

"My God! What are those awful little carcasses?"

"Ptarmigan," Pippa replied. "Butchered at your behest."

Dusi had thought a ptarmigan was a fish. "Perhaps we could serve Dover sole instead."

"In addition to lobster, oysters, periwinkles, and whelks?"

"I suppose that would be a bit much," she admitted. "Rudi, would you mind whipping up a few mushroom omelets for us? It's nearly lunchtime."

Rudi responded with a blitz of Teutonic profanity. "Really, Dusi! Can't you see the man's busy?" Thayne scolded.

Moss and his briefcase now made a surprise entrance. "Sweetheart!" Leigh showered him with kisses to show that her marriage was stable. "Dusi was kind enough to drop by with a few friends. Can you join us for lunch?"

"Not today." Sarcasm soured his voice. "Sweetheart." Noticing a sparkle, he unzipped Leigh's sweatshirt to expose the diamond necklace beneath it. "I hope that's fake."

Dusi leaned forward to inspect. "Moss, you devil! You had me worried there for a moment. I haven't seen this piece, Leigh."

"I purchased it at Cartier this morning," Pippa cut in, casting Moss dire looks. "Signor Bowes instructed me to find a bauble for his wife to wear with her leotard."

Thayne now stepped in for a closer look. She immediately recognized the mine-cut diamonds as those from the Walker treasury. For the first time in her life, she directly addressed someone else's servant. "You got this at Cartier, Cosmo?"

Fibs have no reverse gear. "In estate jewelry, madam."

Thayne's eyes closed. "She pawned the family diamonds," she whispered, and fainted.

"Thayne!" Leigh shrieked. "Moss! Help!"

Moss and Harlan carried the victim to a sofa. As Leigh tried to revive her with pepper vodka, Dusi announced, "It's that daughter from hell again. I've told Thayne a hundred times to put out a contract on her and end the agony."

"She's already disinherited," Pippa retorted. "That's the same thing, isn't it?"

"Cosmo! Where do you get this information?" Dusi was tremendously impressed. She lowered her voice. "How much did you pay for that necklace?"

"MYOB, Madam Damon. Excuse me." Pippa dragged Leigh into the hallway. "Give Thayne the necklace."

"*Give* it to her? It's worth a fortune. How do we know she's not making this up?"

"Do as I say. Tell her you would never wish to own another family's heirloom." When Leigh still looked doubtful, Pippa added, "If such a grand gesture doesn't get you into the country club, nothing will."

Done. As Leigh removed the offending jewelry, Thayne moaned, "Pippa, is that you?"

"Wake up, Twinkie." Dusi roughly shook her shoulders. "You've had a shock."

Moss followed Pippa to the kitchen. "What was that all about, you weasel?"

"All you need to know, Signor Bowes, is that you did not buy that necklace. Thank you for playing along with our little charade." After he left, Pippa slumped against the refrigerator. She felt as if she had just gone over Niagara Falls in a gondola.

"Cosmo." Cole stood inches away. "Are you okay?"

Pippa's eyes briefly locked on his. "Can you make omelets? I don't dare ask Rudi."

"My specialty."

He wasn't kidding. As an impromptu three-course lunch was served in Leigh's formal dining room, Peggy Stoutmeyer regaled everyone with the latest blackball stories from the club. Apparently there had been a membership meeting last night. "Did you hear that Dayton and Belva Hutchins were turned down? They were seen flying economy on the New York–Washington shuttle."

"But there is no first class on the shuttle," Harlan the gigolo pointed out.

"In that case they should have flown their own plane. Or hired one. And you'll never believe what Lurette Bock did. She served lobster bisque in consommé cups!" Peggy's raucous laughter made the chandelier quiver.

"We haven't gotten around to your application, Leigh," Dusi mentioned. "There were so many incredible people ahead of you."

Thayne squeezed Leigh's hand. She was still overwhelmed that Leigh had simply given her Pippa's necklace, no questions asked. " 'Were' is the operative word, dear."

"Don't give the woman false hope, Twinkie," Dusi said irritably. "Masqueradia Dusiana will decide everything."

Silence fell over the table as Pippa served red grapes and Debauve et Gallais truffles. "I'm so looking forward to the ball," Peggy Stoutmeyer raved, attacking the chocolates. "I'm coming as a falcon. What's your costume, Leigh?"

"That is a secret, madam." Pippa's retort earned another searing glare from her mother.

"Pooh! What's your costume, hon?" Peggy asked Thayne.

Thayne, recovering a bit of her old mojo, waited a few seconds for the suspense to build. "I will be Marie Antoinette."

Harlan looked nonplussed. "I never heard of a car called Marie Antoinette."

Dusi launched her grape scissors at him. "If she wants to come as Marie Antoinette, let her."

"Sorry, gorgeous," Harlan lied twice.

"I will be Aphrodite, goddess of spring," Dusi announced. "Please, everyone, that information must not leave the table. It is a very elaborate costume. My seamstress has been working on it all week."

"I never heard of a car called Aphrodite, either," Harlan said.

"Why should I come dressed as a car? Every other woman will be dressed as a car." Dusi glared across the table. "Except for Marie Antoinette. Whatever possessed you to disregard my request, Twinkie?"

Thayne's fingers played over her beloved necklace. "I am not an automobile."

Touché, Mama!

Dusi could only sit fuming as Thayne described every stitch of her vintage Parisian gown. Her wig and shoes had been previously worn by Princess Belgioioso, a rumored amour of Liszt's. "Only one element in my outfit is missing," Thayne said finally. "The perfect antique brooch for the bodice."

"Brooch?" Dusi complained. "Your fainting fit just got you a diamond necklace."

"You must try Kuriakin at the Trump Tower," Leigh said. "I go in once a week. They have the most gorgeous estate pieces."

"Why don't you girls go on a little expedition tomorrow? I have a membership meeting that will last all day." Dusi discoursed for the next twenty minutes about her trip to Normandy. Throughout Harlan tried to play footsies with Leigh; Peggy Stoutmeyer finished all the chocolates. Luncheon ended with liqueurs and coffee. "I can't have one little peek into the backyard before we leave, Cosmo?" Dusi asked.

"No." Pippa yanked her chair away from the table. "You've already overstayed your welcome."

"The gall of him!" Thayne gasped again.

Dusi merely laughed. "Twinkie, get a life." She took Pippa's arm and led her procession to the foyer. "Thayne has been impossible," she whispered. "Thank God I unloaded her on Leigh for a day."

"Madam Walker looks perfectly normal to me."

"My dear fellow, she beaned her husband with a candelabra. She put a Korean masseuse in the hospital. She strangled her wedding planner with her bare hands. It's all that wretched daughter's fault. I never liked the girl. She was a conniving slut from the get-go."

"I don't think she liked you much, either."

Dusi clasped her bosom. "You're sure of that?"

"I am. Good day, Madam Damon." Pippa watched impassively as Dusi's party piled into her Bentley and drove away.

The moment the door was shut Leigh asked, "Did we survive?"

"Yes. Plus you made a new friend."

"Yes. But you behaved terribly, Cosmo."

"On purpose, signora. According to legend Madam Walker loves to be offended by the poor manners of others. I did my best to accommodate her."

"She and you are the only people I know who aren't terrified of Dusi."

"Thank you. I'm quite proud of that." As Leigh went upstairs to prepare for Dr. Zeppelin's house call, Pippa reopened all the drapes in

Casa Bowes. She was surprised to find Cole in the kitchen washing lunch dishes. He looked severely fetching in an apron.

"Another triumph, Cosmo?"

She took a towel. "I wouldn't call it that. No." She became lost in thought.

"Come here." He gave her a nondenominational hug. For days they had been treating each other with utmost professional courtesy, a feat on a par with fasting. "You were great. Who was that ice goddess with the spun-sugar hair?"

"Her name is Thayne Walker."

He nearly dropped a platter. Her mother! No wonder Pippa was out of it. "Is she just passing through?"

"She's coming to the ball."

Moss stalked in. Whatever business he had just finished in the library had not lightened his mood. "What are those boats doing in my pool, Cosmo?"

"They're gondolas, signor. For the guests."

"No way. I don't have the liability insurance." Moss glared at Cole. "Ditch the apron. You're my valet, not the dishwasher."

He dragged Cole away before Pippa could properly thank him for making lunch. Fatigued, she went to her room. She was relieved that Thayne had not recognized her, mortified that Thayne hadn't immediately seen through the mustache, brown pageboy, and eyeglasses. Her mother had aged. Thayne's face and the figure were still perfect but a light had gone out of her eyes. Without that light she looked bitter and homeless. She was still swift enough to identify Pippa's diamond necklace; on the other hand, she was equally swift to believe that Pippa had pawned it.

Kerry pounded on her door. "Mo, come see the tents."

Instead Pippa took the Maserati for a ride in the desert. She practiced J-turns just for the hell of it. She thought about Cole in an apron, flipping omelets. When that got too warm, she thought of him with his girlfriend. If it wasn't what it looked like, why hadn't he explained? *Because he thinks you're a man, you idiot.* Oh. Right. Pippa envisioned Thayne in her Marie Antoinette costume. Despite her mother's weakened condition, one thing was certain: all hell would break loose when she recognized Rosimund's tents.

———

Leigh had arranged to pick up Thayne at one o'clock for their shopping excursion. As the Duesenberg approached Castilio Damonia she asked one last time, "Are you sure you can't come with us, Cosmo?"

"Madam Walker is a legendary shopper. I will wait in the car."

Leigh stared glumly ahead. Last night she had discovered a streak of lipstick on Moss's jockey shorts. He had attempted to explain it away as some sort of Magic Marker but eventually gave up. Another Tiffany lamp had been defenestrated, inflicting substantial damage on one of Rosimund's gondolas. "I'm leaving him," Leigh said. "This marriage is a joke."

"We're all under stress right now," Pippa said, patting her knee. "Maybe Dr. Zeppelin can provide some further insight."

"We've already determined that I prefer my dog to my husband. That's enough insight for me."

Pippa drove over the drawbridge to Castilio Damonia. She had barely opened the rear door when Thayne skipped outside, ready to burn a little plastic. "Good afternoon, Madam Walker."

Casting her a brief but foul glare, Thayne ducked into the rear seat. "Don't you look smashing, Leigh."

"So do you, sweetheart." Air kisses.

"I feel as if I'm escaping the Tower of London. Dusi has been a tribulation ever since she bought those breasts."

Having bought only slightly less imposing breasts of her own, Leigh could not attack Dusi directly. However, she could in good conscience say, "Harlan is far beneath her dignity."

"Honey, you haven't seen Caleb. He hasn't been home in thirteen years. He just keeps sending armor back to Las Vegas."

"And I thought *my* marriage was in bad shape."

"Dusi's infatuation with your—" Thayne raised her voice so that Pippa could hear everything. "Your eunuch is simply beyond belief."

"I'm not so sure about that." Leigh leaned over to whisper, "If Cosmo's gifts from his mistresses are any indication, he's a world-class stud."

"What a revolting thought!"

Conversation turned to Thayne's brooch. Thayne was looking for a mabe pearl surrounded by rubies set in gold filigree. The pearl had to be at least the size of an egg yolk, set with proportionately large rubies. Matching earrings would not be frowned upon. "I will of course be wearing the diamond necklace you returned to me yesterday," Thayne said. "To break up the monotony."

Pippa dropped the ladies off at Kuriakin, a sumptuous boutique in the Trump hotel, and proceeded to valet parking. She cut quite a figure in Duesenberg, purple sombrero, and Saint Laurent glasses. Tourists, even other chauffeurs, kept asking for her autograph. She created such a traffic jam that the bellman finally came over. "I'm sorry, sir. You'll have to park over there."

"Do you know who I am?" Pippa thundered.

"No, sir."

"Neither do I." Pippa pulled to a remote lot, where she kept an eye on the Trump entrance while phoning greengrocers, linen services, Porta Potti professionals, ice companies, and liability insurers. She was negotiating with Dr. Hogly Wogly's barbecue in Los Angeles when she saw an apricot Mercedes limousine pull up to the hotel. For a horrible moment Pippa thought that, fearing for his wallet, Moss was going to pull Leigh by the hair out of Kuriakin. Then she saw Moss step out with a beautiful Asian woman in a red dress and five-inch heels. She clung to him like peanuts on a PayDay bar. They went into the hotel together.

Pippa's mouth was still wide open when a severely curvy redhead in black leather approached the Mercedes and, without even knocking on the window, slipped into the front seat with Cole. They were not unfamiliar with each other, Pippa saw at a glance as he drove into the hotel garage. Speechless, her thoughts a whirlwind, Pippa waited for thirty minutes. Cole, alone, returned to the curb moments before Moss emerged, alone, from the hotel. He got into the back seat. They drove away.

Two-timing bastards!

Pippa slowly realized that the windmills across the street were Leigh and Thayne waving their arms at her. "Sorry, signora. I was tied up with the Persimmon Association."

"Speak when you're spoken to," Thayne snapped, diving in. "Take us to Fred Leighton's at the Bellagio." Her voice softened as she turned to her new best friend. "I don't know. Should I get the cabochon ruby parure for two hundred fifty or the emeralds for two seventy-five? I hate to comparison shop but my circumstances have been reduced and I have to count pennies from now until the day they bury me in Crockett."

"What happened to the mabe pearl brooch?" Pippa called over her shoulder. "That wouldn't have cost more than a hundred twenty tops."

"My God, that is one cheeky servant you've got, Leigh."

"I know." Leigh caught Pippa's wink in the rearview mirror. "Don't you go falling in love with him now."

Pippa waited for them outside the Bellagio. Then outside Kuriakin. Then the Bellagio. Thayne finally decided to go with the cabochon ruby parure at Kuriakin for two hundred and fifty grand. "Once upon a time I never would have batted an eyelash at twenty-five thousand dollars," she repeated. "Now I have to worry about who will support me in my old age."

"Your daughter will." Leigh patted Thayne's hand. "Girls never leave their mothers."

"Even when their mothers have disowned them?"

"You cut off your own flesh and blood? My God, Thayne! What did she do?"

"You don't read the newspapers?"

"I'm sorry. Redecorating Casa Bowes has taken every ounce of my energy for eight months. Well? Tell me what she did. I hope it was at least a triple murder."

Thayne dabbed a handkerchief at her tears. "I spent months organizing a beautiful wedding for her. Two minutes before tying the knot she backed out." Thayne was shocked at how innocuous that sounded.

"You mean she was a runaway bride, like Julia Roberts?"

"You could say that. But she also announced there was someone else."

Leigh burst out laughing. "You disowned her for being honest?"

"You had to be there, Leigh. I was very angry and hurt. Very betrayed."

"I'd say she did everyone a favor by coming clean. That must have taken a lot of guts, although I suppose the timing could have been better."

"Why does everyone sympathize with the criminal instead of the victim?" Thayne cried in exasperation. "I am so tired of being treated like Lady Macbeth. My sole concern was for the family honor." Having provoked no further sympathy, she continued, "In any event, that mess is over. I must move on. Lately I've been thinking of having another child. Cedric, my majordomo, is giving me a run for my money."

Both ladies screamed as the Duesenberg nearly drove off the road. "Cosmo! What's going on up there?"

"A bee in the front seat, signora," Pippa wheezed. "I have killed it."

Leigh didn't need Dr. Zeppelin to deduce that Thayne's self-inflicted wound was at the root of her depression. "Dear, why don't you repair bridges with the daughter you already have before you go about making another?"

Thayne hit her with an obelisk stare. "How many children do you have, may I ask?"

"Zero. I just have a dog named Titian. Moss took him away from me. That dog was the light of my life. I can barely face the day without his little black eyes shining at me in the morning."

In the rearview mirror Pippa saw a tear creep down her mother's cheek. "I'll be honest with you, Leigh. I miss my girl. Every day I think about her and worry about her. I spend eons crying over old scrapbooks. She was the best daughter in the world. She idolized me, God knows why." Thayne looked morosely out the window. "Her betrayal was a death blow."

"What betrayal? Death blow to what?"

"I've been trying to figure that out," Thayne admitted. "How did we get on this dismal subject? I need a drink."

Pippa passed a flask of scotch from the glove compartment to the back seat. "Madam."

Thayne took a belt, shocked at the intimate conversation she had just had with a woman she barely knew, in the presence of an eavesdropping servant. She was even more shocked that she hadn't scratched Leigh's eyes out for suggesting she was a less than perfect mother. "I must be going soft in my old age," she half laughed.

"It suits you, madam," Pippa said.

"You must get rid of that fellow, Leigh. Do yourself a favor and unload him on Dusi."

Leigh shook her head. "Not a chance."

The shopping excursion ended when the Duesenberg's trunk could hold no more. Pippa was a wreck when she finally dropped Thayne back at Castilio Damonia. She had learned more about her mother in the last few hours than she had in the previous twenty-two years. Thayne had studied to become a criminal lawyer, maybe even a judge, but had put those aspirations aside after becoming a Walker. She had married Robert on the rebound; her previous suitor, a flamboyant rancher and the love of her life, had crashed his Cessna into the prairie on a clear summer day one month before their wedding. Robert Walker was a gentle man. Their marriage was serene. Yet Thayne had not felt vibrantly alive again until the moment Pippa was born. "I did not marry an alpha male," she confessed to Leigh. "Perhaps if I had, I would not have focused every atom of my being on my daughter." Thayne had had two miscarriages prior to Pippa and two following. She described how proud she had been at her daughter's debutante ball, at her sorority initiation, her first ride on a horse . . . it was all Pippa could do not to rip off her glasses, mustache, and sombrero and dive into the back seat shouting, "Here I am, Mama!"

Get the damn diploma, Cosmo.

"That poor woman," Leigh said after dropping her off. "Talk about blowing it."

"You're her only friend in the universe, signora. If I were you, I'd urge her to swallow her pride and get her daughter back. I could certainly find the girl for you. Rumor has it she'd give anything to be reunited with her mother."

Leigh, of course, had other priorities. "Let's get through the party first."

Neither spoke for the rest of the journey home. As they approached Casa Bowes, a red Mustang shot out of the driveway, nearly hitting them. "Idiot!" Leigh shouted out her window. She saw her linens specialist standing in the doorway. "Who was that maniac, Kerry?"

"He delivered a case of Champagne. I've been answering the door all day." One would think she had been asked to walk on hot coals.

Dr. Zeppelin was waiting in one of the ballrooms. Leigh had a brief consult with him before going upstairs with her seamstress. Meanwhile Pippa checked in on the kitchen. Rudi had acquired a megaphone, through which he was barking commands at his five sous chefs from Flamingo in order to be heard over the mariachi music blazing from their radios. Since they barely spoke English and his accent was thick as mashed potatoes, the kitchen was, literally, a madhouse. Pippa walked to the backyard.

The gondola damaged by the Tiffany lamp had been repaired. A bill for two thousand dollars was taped to its hull. Stuffing that in her pocket, Pippa strolled through Rosimund's four tents, which had been arranged in four spokes around a central platform for the seventy-piece orchestra. Electricians on ladders were hanging lanterns and fleecy clouds. Fountains gurgled. Mechanical birds trilled from brass cages. Pippa was beginning to think that maybe, just maybe, Masqueradia Dusiana would fly when the doorbell rang.

There stood the Asian woman she had seen with Moss that afternoon. Red vinyl raincoat and black vinyl boots caused her to sweat profluently. "I want Moss Bowes," she demanded, waving a pistol.

Pippa snapped into Walker survival mode. "Is this a robbery, madam?" she asked, stepping aside. "The silver's in the second room to your right. Help yourself."

"No silver! I want Moss Bowes."

"He isn't home. Look." Pippa pointed to the open garage. "No car. May I get you a glass of soy milk while you wait?"

"You make fun of me, mister?"

"Not at all! You look thirsty. Please. Come in and make yourself at home."

"You a big idiot." The woman took aim at a French Empire porcelain vase and, with one shot, blew it to smithereens. "Next bullet for Moss."

Pippa watched her black Miata rocket out of the driveway. It had all happened so fast that she hadn't been able to get properly terrified. To add to the surreality, Dusi's Bentley now rolled up to the portico.

"Yoo-hoo! Cosmo! I was just passing by on my way back from the membership meeting."

"We're still here, as you can see. Feel free to continue passing by."

"Actually, I was looking for Harlan. Has anyone seen him?"

"I don't believe anyone at Casa Bowes is taking croquet lessons."

"Don't toy with me, Cosmo." Dusi sidled inside then, two steps at a time, charged upstairs, splitting the back seam of her pants. "I know he's with Leigh."

"That's impossible," Pippa shouted, running after her. "We just got back from shopping."

"I saw him leering at her yesterday." Bashing open the door to the master bedroom, Dusi found Leigh standing in front of a mirror as her seamstress zipped up the back of a sheath plaited with thousands of yellow, black, and white feathers.

"Dusi! What brings you here?" Leigh managed to gasp.

"Where'd you hide him?" Dusi tore the duvet, ten pillows, and half the sham off Leigh's bed: nothing. She ripped apart Leigh's six closets, Titian's nursery, six upstairs bedrooms, and the master bath. Still nothing, but that didn't deter Dusi from stomping back to the bedroom. "You've been screwing Harlan!"

"The croquet instructor, signora," Pippa reminded her.

To her credit Leigh didn't burst out laughing. "I'm afraid there's been a misunderstanding. The last time I saw Harlan was at lunch here."

"He said you were pretty in pink!"

"I'm sure he was just trying to be sociable." Leigh put an arm around Dusi's quaking shoulders. "It never crossed my mind he would find me *that* attractive. Particularly in comparison to you. That's simply unimaginable."

"I suppose you're right," Dusi sniffled after studying her reflection in a floor-to-ceiling mirror. Her curves looked spectacular in bottle-green Christian Lacroix. "You don't even come close."

"Would you care to have the seamstress repair your pants while you're here, Madam Damon?" Pippa asked.

"Thank you, but I'll have my jet take them back to Paris." Dusi stepped gingerly over the heap of pillows and shams she had just made. "What is that costume all about, Leigh?"

"I'm a lark. Remember the classic Studebakers from the sixties?"

"I'm not familiar with the Studebaker. It sounds very middle class."

"From the Pierce-Arrow line," Pippa informed her. "Surely you're familiar with that."

"I thought a lark was brown. Small and inconspicuous."

"The horned lark is brown. The meadow lark is yellow." Pippa escorted Dusi downstairs. "How did the membership meeting go, Madam Damon?"

"We still didn't get to Leigh, if that's what you mean." Dusi leaned out the front door. "Horatio!" She impatiently tapped her foot as her majordomo doddered up the steps. "The seam in my pants has given way. Give me yours to wear until we get home."

"But then I will have none, madam."

"I didn't ask for editorial comment, I asked for your pants." Adding insult to injury, Dusi said, "I do hope they're clean."

"Let me get you a pair of Rudi's," Pippa told Horatio.

"Don't give the man ideas! We have no time." Dusi nearly stripped Horatio's pants past his knobby knees. She slipped into them and hustled him back to the Bentley. They drove off.

Leigh leaned over the banister. "Did Dusi really think I was having it off with that smarmy gigolo?"

"You handled the situation very well, signora. Brava."

Leigh noticed the mess in the foyer. "What happened down here? You must replace that vase before Moss gets home. Go to Antiquités de Napoléon right away. They had two in the window last time I looked."

"Do we have a line of credit there?"

Leigh dropped a wallet over the banister. "Keep going until you find a card that works." She returned to her fitting.

Kerry, her face streaked with silver polish, wandered into the foyer. "What was that noise I heard? Sounded like a gun."

"You mean ten minutes ago? Thanks for rushing to help." Pippa thought of something. "Did Harlan drop by today?"

"Har who?"

"Dusi's boyfriend. The greaseball with the bedroom eyes."

"Never heard of him." Kerry noticed the smashed vase. "Uh-oh."

"Sweep it up, would you? I have to replace it before Moss gets home. And straighten the upstairs. Madam Damon went on a small scavenger hunt."

Pippa took the Duesenberg to Antiquités de Napoléon. By maxing out six of Leigh's credit cards, she scrounged together fourteen thousand bucks for a French Empire vase with robins. Leaving, she noticed a tiny stuffed bird lying in a bowl. Its red feathers matched the ruby parure Thayne had bought that afternoon. "How much?" she asked, blowing dust off its wings.

"One thousand dollars."

Pippa counted the cash from her purse and arranged for the bird to be delivered to Castilio Damonia. "The note is to say 'If I were a bird, I'd fly to you.'"

If I were a bird? The guy already looked like a barn owl. "Very romantic, sir."

By the time Pippa returned to Casa Bowes, the workmen had departed for the day. A white Lexus was the only vehicle in the driveway. As Pippa put the new vase in place, her shoes crunched over many bits of porcelain still embedded in the carpet: typical Kerry cleaning job.

The doorbell rang. "Where's Leigh?" mewled a woman one might describe as gorgeous were it not for viscous liquids streaming from eyes, nostrils, and mouth. Her toy terrier barked in sympathetic morosity. "I must see her."

Pippa led the woman to the bar, only to find Leigh already there with another hysterical reject from the Las Vegas Country Club. "Vivianne!"

"Kristel! You, too? *Waaaaaa!*"

Pippa made several quarts of martinis as, over the next hour, the number swelled to eight, not including dogs. Dusi's membership meeting had barely adjourned, yet letters of rejection had been dispatched with such speed that one might suspect they had been typed before the meeting began. Dusi had signed them all with her fountain pen formerly owned by Gloria Swanson. Each note ended with a handwritten "P.S. I'm so sorry, dear!" in garnet ink. Each woman had immediately phoned Dusi, who had taken thirty or so seconds to explain that an anonymous letter of protest had arrived, squelching further consideration. The points of protest? Kristel had a son whose boutique Napa vineyard just won a blue ribbon (possible alcoholism in family). Vivianne had sold her Matisse to an Egyptian (unpatriotic, possible terrorist). Gina, a Ph.D. in astrophysics, had sent away for home-schooling materials in lieu of brochures from Choate (dangerous fundamentalist). Jocelaine possessed only thirty pairs of shoes (automatic expulsion). No one could figure out how Peggy Stoutmeyer had made the cut. She walked, talked, and dressed like Roseanne Barr. She wasn't even that rich.

"If it makes you feel any better, I'm probably next to get the axe," Leigh told everyone after the fourth round of martinis. "My application is on top of the pile now."

"But Dusi adores you, honey!"

"She adores Cosmo. I'm just the chum."

"What are you going to do if you don't get in, Leigh?"

"Rejoin the Rockettes." Leigh unsteadily placed her martini glass on a side table. "Let me take you to dinner, girls. We can cry on each others' shoulders."

"I'll get the car, signora."

Pippa ran into Moss and Cole in the foyer. She hadn't even heard them come in over the keening in the bar. As Moss was inspecting the new French Empire porcelain vase, Cole knelt on the carpet, picking up the larger pieces of porcelain Kerry had failed to vacuum. "Another hen party, Cosmo?" Moss asked.

"Eight more ladies didn't make the cut at the country club. They'll be leaving in a moment."

"I preferred the vase with orioles," Moss mentioned, his voice flat. "These are robins."

"Then take it up with the chick who thought she was shooting skeet," Pippa snapped. "Maybe you know her. Mole on her right cheek, red vinyl coat, black vinyl boots, wears too much Shalimar." He got the picture. "I believe she carried a Smith and Wesson thirty-eight. The bullet's still in the wall. There."

Moss's face went white as his new vase. "She came *here*?"

"Oh—she left a message—the next bullet's for you."

Moss grabbed Pippa's sleeve as she walked past him. "Does Leigh know?"

"I didn't see any point in informing her, signor."

"Good boy." Moss and Cole took off like a pair of elk. They didn't return until well after Pippa had tucked Leigh, inebriated and despairing, into bed.

Pippa was expecting the knock on her door. "Come in."

Cole wasn't surprised to see her up and fully dressed: that last look she had shot him in the foyer was a definite "See me in my office, sonny." He sat on the chair rather than on her bed. She remained standing, arms crossed. "I owe you an explanation," he began. Pippa said nothing. "It's not what you think. That woman controls the biggest feather syndicate in Asia. Moss needs to keep her happy."

"How happy?"

"Very." Cole didn't have to elaborate.

"Then I'd say he was doing a lousy job." Pippa tossed back some scotch from a glass on her dresser. "I saw her with Moss at Trump Tower yesterday. While we were shopping."

She took her liquor neat, he noted with admiration. "Her name's Bing Bing."

"Thank you for that heartwarming detail."

"How did you know what sort of gun she was carrying?"

"My mother owns one similar to it."

"Tell me what happened."

"The doorbell rang. Bing Bing stood there demanding to see Moss. I told her he wasn't home and invited her to wait inside."

"Obviously you didn't know she had a gun."

"Of course I knew. She was waving it in the air. She probably rang the doorbell with it."

"And you invited her in?" He almost choked.

Pippa gave him a withering glare. "What was I supposed to do, slam the door in her face and call the police?"

Well, yes. If you were a normal person. "Why didn't you?"

"Bing Bing wasn't interested in anything but putting a few holes in Moss." Pippa almost added, *You'd have to be a woman to understand that.* "When she realized he wasn't home, she vented on the vase and left. It was all over in fifteen seconds."

Cole sat staring at his hands. "You've got balls, Cosmo," he said finally. "It could have ended very differently."

"You could say that for a lot of things."

What did that mean? And she was still mad at him, damn it. "For the record, I don't approve of what Moss is doing. But I'm in no position to tell him off."

"Of course. You're just the innocent chauffeur."

Cole realized that she had seen him with the redhead. There was nothing he could do about that right now. "I try to do my job. Good night."

Twenty-One

Leigh did not remember much about her evening with the girls except that Cosmo had tucked her into bed and the bill for dinner was two thousand bucks. When she finally opened her eyes around ten in the morning, she was surprised to see a large bouquet of roses on the bed table. "Tonight's our ball. Let's dance. Moss."

Moss hated to dance. *Our* ball?

Hungover, Leigh dragged herself downstairs in an aqua peignoir. Dozens of people buzzed hither and yon with napery, bottles, and floral arrangements. Cosmo stood in the middle of traffic with a clipboard and policeman's whistle. "Good morning, signora. Ready for your big day?"

Leigh rubbed her throbbing cranium. "Whatever."

"I put a Thermos of coffee in your office. You'd best stay out of the kitchen."

Beside the Thermos was a bottle of aspirin. Leigh swallowed eight as she leafed through the invoices on the blotter. To date Masqueradia Dusiana was running slightly over two hundred thousand dollars. That was peanuts, Leigh thought as bits of last night's party floated back to her. Kristel had spent nearly four hundred grand on two bridge parties with Omar Sharif. Beverli had blown six hundred reserving Dusi a nonrefundable seat on a future shuttle mission. Jocelaine had donated an enormous Hadzi sculpture to the club to plant behind the eighteenth hole.

No one's husband had been enthusiastic about the huge gambling expense. Vivianne had silenced her spouse by procuring an online credit report proving they had nothing to worry about. An excellent strategy, Leigh thought, turning on her computer. She went for the fifty-buck superspecial report and was waiting for results when Pippa walked in with a small, ornately wrapped package.

"For you. From Kuriakin." Pippa watched as Leigh unwrapped a diamond choker. "Fantastic, signora!"

"I told you all this bellyaching was just hot air." Leigh opened the little envelope. Her smile faded. " 'To my adorable Bing Bing. Love forever, Moss.' " She looked oddly at Pippa. "Bing Bing? He's never called me that."

"Let him call you anything he wants. It's a stunning necklace." Heart pounding, Pippa slipped the offending card into her pocket. "We'll leave for the Ritz in thirty minutes. I've booked you for the full-day treatment at Vita di Lago." That would get Leigh out of the house. "Are you listening, signora?"

Leigh was way more interested in the credit report that had just come onscreen. She had no idea she had that many credit cards, each about twenty grand in the red. Moss still owed forty on the Duesenberg. The mortgage on Casa Bowes remained four million, signed by Leigh and Moss Bowes. The mortgage on his condo at Trump Tower was two million, signed by Moss Bowes and Bing Bing Kao.

Pippa stood paralyzed as Leigh connected the dots, or rather, the Bing Bings. "He got himself a little *pied-affaire*," Leigh whispered after an eternity. She ran to the kitchen, dropped the necklace down the garbage disposal, and flipped the switch before anyone could stop her. "That's what I think of Bing Bing," she shrieked over the terrible metallic gnashing.

Rudi emitted a howl. He couldn't care less about adultery. He was now without a functioning garbage disposal for the biggest party of his life. "Leaf my kitchen!" he cried, brandishing a carving knife. "Or I chop your head off!"

Leigh got a heavy ladle from her silver chest and proceeded to smash the new French Empire vase as well as Moss's rococo harpsichord to pieces. She heaved his soapstone owl through the library window again and was about to start tearing his bird books apart when Pippa shouted, "Enough, signora! You've made your point!"

"I haven't *begun* to make my point!" Before Pippa could stop her, Leigh rampaged through Casa Bowes, laying waste to Lladró figurines and antique grandfather clocks, throwing anything she could out the nearest window. She beat the Bolivian rosewood doors until the silver ladle looked like a Giacometti sculpture. Finally exhausted, she crumpled to the floor. "How could he do this to me, Cosmo?"

"Get back to work," Pippa snapped at the half-dozen guest workers gathered around them. Murmuring, they scattered. "You must pull yourself together," Pippa whispered.

"What for? First my dog, then Bing Bing! My life is over!"

Pippa helped Leigh to her feet and up the grand staircase. "You're going to spend the day at Vita di Lago. Tonight you'll be belle of the grandest ball Las Vegas has seen in years. By Monday you'll be the newest member of the country club." *By Tuesday my diploma and I will be out of here.* "I'm sure this is all a misunderstanding. You only have one side of the story."

"A diamond choker, 'my love forever,' and a *pied-affaire*? How many sides do I need?"

"Believe me, I know how you feel. I had a similar episode in Prague a few years ago."

"Did you kill her?"

"I simply left. Within four weeks I was reengaged." Pippa walked into Leigh's middle closet. All of the clothing Dusi had torn off the racks yesterday was still lying on the floor. She found a beige knit ensemble. "Put this on."

"Those nights away. Those months working late. How could I have been so blind?"

"Stop torturing yourself, signora! Get dressed now. Quickly."

Leaning over the banister, Pippa screamed a few orders to the people scurrying about downstairs. How the hell had that mix-up happened? If Bing Bing got the jewelry intended for Leigh, she might return to Casa Bowes with a missile launcher this time. Pippa speed-dialed Painless

Panes and told them to get over immediately, with one of everything. She called Cole's cell. "Leigh received a diamond necklace this morning. The card was for Bing Bing."

"Oh, shit."

"Half the downstairs is smashed to pieces. I'm missing eight windows. Signora found out about the condo at the Trump Tower."

"I'll be right over."

"Leave Moss behind, if you don't mind. Unless he's really good at vacuuming glass." Pippa made one final call, to Dr. Zeppelin. "Signora Bowes just learned her husband is having an affair. Go to Vita di Lago and hold her hand."

"Will you throw in a deep-tissue massage?"

"You can do the whole-day treatment together."

Leigh exited her bedroom looking like a wraith, thanks to the sedatives she had just swallowed. "Why am I going to the spa, Cosmo?" she asked in a childlike voice.

"Because Dr. Zeppelin will be there waiting for you." Pippa guided her downstairs. "Watch the glass," she shouted over her shoulder, keeping a firm grip on Leigh's arm as she opened the front door. "I'll be right back."

Who should be standing on the stoop but Dusi, dressed in a vintage shirtwaist. Her Bakelite necklace and bracelets gleamed in the sunlight. Her face looked tight and rodentlike beneath a plaid hairband. "Good morning! May I come in?"

"Can't you see we're just leaving, Madam Damon?"

"My lord, Leigh, you look as if you've been through the wringer."

"Signora Bowes has just had a ballet lesson with Mikhail Baryshnikov," Pippa replied. "She will be spending the rest of the day at Vita di Lago." Dusi didn't budge. "Is there anything we can get for you? Several tons of caviar, perhaps?"

"Actually, I brought something for *you*." Dusi unearthed a large silver ladle from the depths of her Prada handbag. "It is from King Edward the Seventh's court. I'll need it back, of course."

"I believe we have plenty of ladles."

"Really?" Dusi smiled triumphantly. "That's not what I hear."

Pippa swore she felt Leigh's body temperature drop ten degrees.

"Signora, could you please see yourself to Vita di Lago? I will be detained here and I don't want you to be late."

"Of course." Leigh sleepwalked to the garage.

"Disgraceful," Dusi huffed. "That woman is unfit to join Alcoholics Anonymous, let alone the Las Vegas Country Club."

"I congratulate you, Madam Damon. And your informant." The house was crawling with people: could have been anyone. "You wasted no time getting over here."

"I had to know if that rampage rumor was true. I have an obligation to the membership committee." Her voice turned sly and wheedling. "May I come in?"

"No. Go home and play with your stuffed horses."

Dusi sighed. "Then I must presume the worst. I will be morally obligated to write a letter objecting to Leigh's membership in the club."

"In that case, the party's off."

"How dare you blackmail me, Cosmo!"

"I'm simply playing your game. The score is tied at zero." Pippa turned to go inside.

"Wait. I can make this a win-win situation." Dusi clutched Pippa's sleeve. "I can guarantee that Leigh and Moss will succeed in their membership."

Pippa knew what was coming. Nonetheless she asked, "And in exchange?"

"You will come to work at Castilio Damonia for one year. I will give you a staff of twenty."

"I'd rather sweep mines in Afghanistan."

"Six months and a staff of thirty."

"One month and a staff of fifty," Pippa countered.

"Three months and a staff of forty."

"Two weeks and a staff of sixty. That is my final offer. You will announce Signora's membership tonight," Pippa said. "At the ball."

"That's impossible. The committee doesn't meet until Monday."

"I'm sure you know how to make a conference call. Do we have a deal?"

"Well—I—Cosmo, you are ruthless." A staff of sixty! Dusi was speechless with admiration. "Yes, it's a deal."

They shook hands. "How is Madam Walker today?" Pippa asked.

"In seventh heaven. She received a little stuffed bird with a mash note. It must be a practical joke of some sort. Who in their right mind would fly to *her*?"

"I sent her the bird. And the note. I find her gloriously attractive."

Dusi looked as if she had just been whacked in the face with a dust-mop. "You!"

"Please don't tell her." Pippa knew perfectly well that hell would freeze over before Dusi did that. "I prefer to worship her from a distance."

"Well! Aren't you full of surprises." Shaken to the core, Dusi retreated. "I'll see you tonight, Cosmo. Remember that I will be Aphrodite, goddess of spring."

"I thought Persephone was goddess of spring."

Pippa slammed the Bolivian rosewood doors. She took a deep breath then turned apprehensively to face the foyer. Unfortunately Leigh's wilding had not been a dream: Casa Bowes looked as if Mitzi and Bobo the elephants had just trampled through. The damage easily ran into the millions. As Pippa was considering a remedial dose of arson, Kerry roared in. "Mo, get to the kitchen. It's really bad."

One of the sous chefs, covered with blood, was chasing another sous chef, also covered with blood, around the island. Everyone had knives and everyone seemed to be bandaged and screaming except Rudi, who was focused on stuffing three hundred ptarmigan with a date and a filbert. "What happened?" Pippa cried.

"He was trying to dig something out of the disposal and the other guy threw the switch." Kerry winced as a rack of stuffed courgette blossoms crashed to the floor. "This is not good."

"Let's tackle the first guy."

"Are you nuts? He'll decapitate us. They're like wild dogs."

Dogs! Hey! "I have something for that."

Pippa dashed to her room for the MatchMace. She tested the white button: an arc of flame shot over her bed. Obviously the black button was the Mace. She dashed back to the kitchen and blasted each of the combatants in the face: chase over.

Outside, Cole screeched the Mercedes to a halt inches behind the Painless Panes truck. He bolted up the steps. The rubble in the foyer took his breath away. He followed the screams to the kitchen, where a couple of sous chefs were rolling around the floor, hands to their faces. Two other sous chefs were wrestling over something in the sink. Rudi was sweeping up a pile of stuffed squash blossoms, talking to himself. Pippa stood immobile as the Statue of Liberty in their midst.

Cole hustled her to the patio. "You weren't kidding, Cosmo. This place is out of control." He rolled up his sleeves. "Let's get to work."

Pippa would remember only one thing about the next hours: Cole was there. He not only got Casa Bowes swept up, a miracle in itself, but managed to get Antiquités de Napoléon to *lend* him nearly everything in their showroom. He replaced all five sous chefs and rescued about half the diamond necklace from the disposal. He took all deliveries. When Leigh and Dr. Zeppelin returned from Vita di Lago, he stashed them in an upstairs closet and told them to emerge at eight o'clock, ready to party. All smashed windowpanes were repaired. Rudi began cranking food out of the kitchen. The orchestra, the tigers on leashes, and the barbecue from Dr. Hogly Wogly arrived. The sun went down. Candles were lit.

At ten before eight, Cole sagged onto a sofa. He smiled at Pippa, who had collapsed there moments before. "Want to flip a coin for the bathroom, Cosmo?"

"You can go first," she said.

"I don't know. You look like you need a serious bath."

"I need a serious drink."

"Later. We're not out of the woods yet."

No kidding. Thayne had yet to see the tents. "Where's Moss?"

"He'll show up at the stroke of eight." This was not the time to reveal that, having received an emerald necklace with a love note for Moss's wife, Bing Bing had driven to Fine Feather and caused a lot of faux fur to fly. "Tell you what. You stay here and rest. I'll change."

Pippa shut her eyes. As long as Cole was in the house, she felt safe. She had never felt that with Lance or André. Maybe she should ask for his help in keeping Thayne out of the tents. Short of tying her mother up, Pippa had no idea how to keep her from wandering into the backyard.

Some time later, warm breath grazed her ear. "Your turn," a voice whispered.

Cole was leaning over her. Freshly shaven. He wore a handmade tux. He looked stupendous. "I must have dozed off," she said.

"That was the point, Cosmo."

Pippa showered and changed into a fresh uniform. She added a few extra drops of glue to the tips of her mustache. She cleaned her eyeglasses and opened a small red box that had materialized on her dresser. From Cartier with a note: "Have a ball tonight." Presuming she had been the third beneficiary of Moss's guilt complex, Pippa removed the diamond pin that spelled COSMO from its velvety perch. It fit perfectly on her collar. Feeling a little reckless, she daubed her neck with Thayne perfume. Before returning to the ballrooms she slipped MatchMace into her pocket in case that Asian assassin returned.

"Nice," Cole said. That was the understatement of the year. "New cologne?"

"I just have a few drops left. It's for special occasions."

"We're going to have a great party, Cosmo. If this doesn't earn you a diploma, nothing will." For some reason that made her shudder. "Let's do one last cross-check before the deluge."

Pippa almost took his arm as they promenaded through Casa Bowes. "How do you know so much about parties?"

"I observed my mother in action, same as everyone else."

Vintage Bentleys, Rolls-Royces, Hudsons, Packards, and Morgans began arriving at the stroke of eight. Casa Bowes filled with women dressed as cougars, pintos, falcons, impalas, and jaguars. Their men had almost all dressed as chauffeurs, albeit with heavy doses of sequins and paisley. A few wore goggles. Bonhomie bobbed on rivers of Champagne. Pippa found Leigh circulating in the tent with her therapist. She would remain there all evening; Moss would remain inside the house. Under no circumstances were they to get within two hundred feet of each other.

"Signora, you look spectacular," Pippa said. She really did. Leigh's headdress of ostrich plumes towered three feet above the horde. Thousands of yellow, white, and black feathers shingled her outstanding curves. Only on close inspection did one notice her eyes were red.

"Another bauble from your mistress?" Leigh asked, noticing the pin. "You must be one hell of a stud, Cosmo."

Pippa squeezed her hand. "This will be a triumphant night."

Leigh floated away with Zeppelin and a glass of Champagne. Whatever sedative he had given her was working perfectly, so Pippa went to Leigh's bedroom and slipped four pills into her pocket. She slogged through the Lurex to the Bolivian rosewood doors, where Moss was glaring at people as they invaded his house. He looked like an undertaker in black livery with solid gold buttons. Pippa noticed two parallel scratches on his cheek and teeth marks on his earlobe. "How are you managing, Signor Bowes?"

"No comment."

"Thank you very much for the pin."

"I can do without your sarcasm." He shook a woman's hand so tightly that she winced. "Delighted to see you." Ditto the husband, who also received a shove inside. "Look at these doors," Moss snarled once they had passed. "They look like they were in a bullfight."

Pippa had to admit that Leigh had done significant damage with her ladle. "Signora was very upset."

"Hello," Moss said, crunching another woman's hand. He shoved the husband inside. "All these chauffeurs are giving me the creeps."

"Pay attention, signor. You have to give one of them a prize for best costume."

"Oh, God. Look who's here. The bride of Frankenstein."

Dusi's face and upper body were covered in green/gold paint. Her breasts, crammed into a golden bustier, looked like a pair of tarnished Lombardi Trophies. She wore gold harem pants. A green organza robe hovered over everything like smog over Mexico City. Her jewelry, a flock of hand-hammered gold butterflies, was more plague than adornment. In her waist-length wig were silk flowers and a tiara that redefined the term "fender."

Moss took Dusi's green-gloved hand. "What a vision."

"Ouch!"

Moss crushed Harlan's hand next. "Where do you chauffeur? *Star Trek*?"

"Harlan is wearing the uniform of the Swiss Guard," Dusi divulged. "Pope John Paul the Second personally blessed this entire outfit."

"I don't care who blessed it. He looks like a wind sock."

"Your costume is divine, Madam Damon," Pippa bowed.

"Thank you, Cosmo. *Your* opinion means something to me."

"Signor Bowes," Pippa whispered after they had swept inside. "Please restrain yourself. I have made a deal with Madam Damon but she could still change her mind."

Moss's eyes were riveted on a cumulus of white silk, lace, crinoline, and satin inching up the steps of Casa Bowes. Marie Antoinette couldn't have proceeded to her own coronation with more hauteur than did Thayne Walker, whose three-foot-high wig, white-powdered face, diamonds, brooch, and earrings were already causing jaws to drop. Pippa's stuffed bird perched in her wig like a cherry in a yard-high mound of whipped cream.

"Good evening, madam," Pippa said, bursting with pride. "You look radiant."

Ignoring her, Thayne sniffed the air. Someone's perfume smelled awfully familiar. No females in the area: perhaps her own hair spray was inducing an olfactory hallucination. Thayne offered the host her hand. "Good evening, Moss."

For once he didn't squeeze any fingers to a pulp. He simply gazed, awestruck, at the bird in Thayne's wig. "That's a Venezuelan black-hooded red siskin. *Carduelis cucullata.* I never thought I'd live to see one." He kissed Thayne's hand. "May I touch it?"

Thayne rolled her eyes. "I wear rocks worth two million and all he notices is the bird in my hair," she sighed in mock despair to the couple standing behind her.

"That 'bird' is worth twice your rocks, my dear. Less than five have been sighted in the last half century."

Color rushed to Thayne's floured cheeks as the crowd forming around her murmured in excitement. She had almost tossed Pippa's gift into the trash this morning. At the last moment she had decided to stick it in her wig so as not to look too pale next to Dusi. "I am well aware of its rarity, sir."

"Where'd you get it?"

"You ask such a question before even offering me a glass of Champagne? Ruffian."

Pippa took a flute of Roederer from a serving tray and slipped four tiny pills into the bubbly. She didn't know where this siskin business was going but she wanted to make sure Thayne didn't focus too squarely on Rosimund's tents and gondolas: those fragile high spirits might come crashing down for good. "Champagne, Madam Walker?" *Forgive me, Mama.*

"Black-hooded red siskin," Thayne repeated, swallowing everything. "Is there such a thing as a red-hooded black siskin, Moss?"

"No. There isn't."

Frowning, disappointed in God Almighty's lack of creativity, Thayne lifted a second glass of Champagne off a passing tray. "I do hate singletons."

"Come to my library. I'll show you the definitive canary encyclopedia. Take over the welcome wagon, Cosmo." Folding Thayne's arm over his, Moss led his prize away.

"What car is that woman's costume?" the next woman inside asked.

"A Grand Marquis, I believe." Relieved that Thayne and Moss would be out of circulation for a while, Pippa remained at the door greeting flocks of incoming guests. Cole cruised by every fifteen minutes. Pippa invariably asked him if he had seen Moss and Madam Walker emerge from the library. The answer was always no.

"Things are heating up in the tent," he eventually reported. "Dusi's dancing."

"Where's Signora Bowes?"

"Sitting in the fountain. Thinks she's Donald Duck."

Pippa was aghast. "What's her therapist doing about it?"

"Sitting next to her. Quacking. Love your pin. From the old hump again?"

"None of your business. Could you please find Kerry? She can greet for a while."

Kerry was never located, not even in the bowling alley with the bodyguards. At quarter to twelve, desperate, Pippa planted a harlequin at the front door. "Don't let in any Asian women with guns, okay?"

Leigh was indeed sitting in about four inches of water, playing pattycake with Dr. Zeppelin. "Signora," Pippa whispered, wading over. "Get up. We're about to make the Frequent Bentley presentation."

"I think Leigh should stay where she's happy," her therapist said.

Fine. Pippa went into the tent. Guests were fressing pressed beef, oysters, lobsters, jugged hare, puddings, melons, and steamed vegetables as if their jaws had been wired shut for months. Dusi, drunk, trailing chiffon, was prancing about the dance floor, foisting herself on any male she could pick off from the herd. Her green makeup had rubbed off in spots, rendering her a scrofulous pastiche of Salome and Norma Desmond. Harlan, not surprisingly, had abandoned ship.

"I'm Parsippany, goddess of spring," she cried, unlacing her bodice another inch, dragging another chauffeur onto the parquet. "Dance with me!"

To pass the time onlookers had placed bets regarding when Dusi would have a wardrobe malfunction, with which breast. Pippa knocked on the library door. "Signor Bowes, it's time for the presentation."

Cole appeared. "Should I start moving everyone to the grandstand?"

"It's very quiet in there. I'm worried."

Her perfume was driving him crazy. He fought another roaring urge to peel Pippa's mustache off with his teeth. "They're probably making out on the couch," he suggested.

"That's ridiculous! I'm going in."

Pippa flung open the doors. Moss lay on the floor, groaning. He looked as if he had been attacked by a dozen vultures and a baseball bat. Thayne lay on the leather couch, asleep.

Cole spoke into his collar. "He's down. In the library."

Dusi bustled in. Her rigorous dancing had not done wonders for her complexion. "Cosmo, it's five of twelve. I want my presentation to be at the stroke of midn—" She stared at Moss, then unleashed a shriek audible in three time zones.

Moving fast as a cat, Cole clamped a hand over her mouth. Dusi elbowed him in the stomach until, out of patience, he karate-chopped her neck. She went down like a mud slide. "That's better." He dragged her to an empty chair.

Meanwhile Pippa tried to roust Thayne, without success. She detected a weak pulse beneath many layers of silk and lace. "She's been drugged." When Cole just stood there looking dubious, she added, "I did it."

He put two fingers on her neck. "She'll be fine."

"Call the damn ambulance," Pippa screeched.

Leigh and Dr. Zeppelin, dripping wet, made their entrance. Leigh vaguely recognized the cabochon ruby parure but Thayne's wig befuddled her. "Is that Bing Bing?" She took a few menacing steps forward.

"Stay away! It's Madam Walker!"

Presuming that anyone with such a chalky complexion must be dead, Leigh swooned. Dr. Zeppelin, a hand covering his mouth, ran out.

As Cole was propping Leigh in the last available chair, a harlequin strode in. She whipped off her mask and knelt over Moss. Pippa recoiled, recognizing the redhead she had seen hopping into Cole's limo the other day. "Who are you?" she demanded.

"Special Agent Ballard," Cole replied for her. "FBI."

The woman removed a tiny memory card taped to Moss's foot. "Who did this?"

"Don't know."

"Is he going to make it?" Pippa cried.

"He'd better."

The library became very quiet after the woman left. "What's going on?" Pippa said in a dull voice.

Cole took a deep breath. "I work undercover for the FBI. We've been investigating Moss for months. Trafficking in endangered species. Money laundering. I'm just the valet, okay?"

Two cops came in with an emergency medical unit: Pippa had learned from Thayne to always have an ambulance handy for parties over fifty. "They're all okay," Cole said, referring to the trio of inert females. "He's not."

Moss left on a stretcher. "What happened?" a cop asked.

"We don't know yet." Cole introduced himself as the valet. "His name is Moss Bowes."

"He's the chauffeur here?"

"No, he owns the place. All the male guests are dressed as chauffeurs tonight," Pippa said.

"Who are these three . . ." Call girls? Two of them were way over the hill.

"That is Signora Bowes, Moss's wife. That is Dusi Damon. That is Thayne Walker. Friends of the family. They are unhurt."

"And you would be?" Girl, guy, what?

"Cosmo du Piche, majordomo at Casa Bowes."

"Any drugs involved here?"

"Only alcohol," Cole quickly said. "Cosmo and I found Bowes lying on the floor. Madam Walker was asleep on the couch. The other two came in and fainted."

"That's a lot of fainting."

Leigh revived and saw two men in uniform. Thinking they were bodyguards, she said, "Beer's in the bowling alley, guys."

"Thanks, but we're on duty. Your husband's had a serious accident."

"Hip hip hooray."

"Signora!"

"What makes you say that, Mrs. Bowes?"

"Ask his fucking girlfriend." Leigh wavered toward the door.

"You! Du Piche!" the policeman barked. "Stay right there. You, too, Mrs. Bowes."

As Leigh returned to her seat, Dusi shuddered to life. "What happened?"

"We're trying to establish that. Tell us what you've been doing tonight."

"I've been dancing with a legion of admirers. This party is in my honor. I've recently been inducted into the Frequent Bentley Society." She gasped. "Cosmo! We're late with the ceremony! We must get back to the tent."

"Who do you think is going to present your plaque, madam? Signor Bowes is in an ambulance. His wife is in shock."

Dusi tapped her fuchsia-shod foot. "I should have known something like this would happen. Leigh is disgracefully unreliable. Moss would go out of his way to embarrass me."

"Including hit himself in the head with a blunt object?"

Dusi's hand flew to her mouth. Her lips quivered as tears inched down her green cheeks. "I had no idea he was that spiteful."

Thayne's eyelids fluttered. She was coming out of a bizarre dream involving her signature perfume and a ten-acre white gown. "Pippa?"

"That damn daughter again," Dusi muttered. "Wake up, Twinkie! You're safe."

Pippa assisted her mother to a sitting position. Miraculously, Thayne's wig stayed on. She stared around the library, trying to piece the bits together. Nothing fit, especially the cops. "Did I do something?"

"No," Pippa assured her. "Signor Bowes was showing you a book about the black-hooded red siskin. Do you remember?"

"Vaguely."

"You'll have to do a little better than that," Dusi frowned.

"What's a siskin, Mrs. Walker?" a cop asked.

"A rare Venezuelan canary. Only five have been sighted in the last half century. Mine is worth over four million dollars."

"I hope you're not talking about that ratty little bird in your hair," Dusi said.

Thayne reached high up on her wig. "It's gone! Someone stole it!"

"Did Bowes try to take it from you? Is that why you bopped him?"

Thayne glared at the policeman. " 'Bopped'? I'm not familiar with the term."

The cop noticed a half-open drawer in Moss's Louis Quatorze *scriban*. Its contents looked pilfered. Sliding his hand into a latex glove, the cop removed a bunch of Montblanc pens, an inch of Casa Bowes stationery, six pairs of Buccellati cuff links, and three gold ingots. "Mrs. Bowes," he called to Leigh, who was sitting in a stupor playing with her ostrich feathers. "Are these what I think they are?"

Leigh looked over. "Yes, that is gold bullion."

"Why are they in the desk drawer?"

"Moss kept them handy so he could bribe his way to the front of the gas line. In case of an oil crisis."

"What else was in this drawer? Besides these junky old gold bricks?"

"How would I know? Ask his valet."

The cop was getting frustrated with all the strange terms these people used. "What is a valet, exactly?"

"A valet is a man's personal dresser," Thayne informed him. "He chooses ties and socks, irons shirts perfectly, and sees that every shred of his master's clothing is in perfect condition. He also functions as a personal secretary, scheduling important social engagements as well as appointments with manicurists, hairdressers, doctors, and tennis pros. A top-notch valet will also walk the dog, drive the limousine, run to the ATM, and serve breakfast in bed."

"Gee, I've got one of those at home," the cop said. "She's called my wife."

Only the other cop laughed. "Okay, Cole. What have *you* been doing all night?"

"Attending to four hundred guests."

Thayne frowned at Pippa. "You allowed a valet to circulate with the guests, Cosmo?"

"Cole is not a mere valet, Madam Walker."

One of the cops pricked up his ears. "Are you two more than valet and majorhomo?"

"Domo," Pippa corrected, her face burning. "Our relationship is strictly professional."

"Whatever. Did you happen to pop your head into the library any time tonight, Cole?"

"I don't generally pop my head in when my employer is having a tryst. Nor does Cosmo."

Unfortunately that put the heat back on Thayne. The policeman took a closer look at her mountainous white curls: she could easily stash a shillelagh in there. "Would you mind removing that hat?"

"I certainly would." As he stepped forward, Thayne grabbed Moss's Waterford letter opener off a side table. "Don't you dare touch me."

Pippa leaped over the couch and planted herself between the policeman and the razor-sharp glass. "Officer! Please! Asking a lady to remove her wig is like asking her to strip naked. You simply can't do that."

"Then you're coming to the station," the policeman said. "You can remove it in the privacy of a jail cell."

"Jail? Again?" As Thayne reeled into the bookcase behind the desk, the hoops of her skirt knocked over two globes. "Will I be frisked?"

An electric shock ran from Pippa's head to her toes as she realized that Thayne was carrying her tiny pistol, as always, in a garter above her knee. "Put those handcuffs away!" she shouted in the cop's face. "Madam Walker has done nothing wrong."

"She's threatening me with a dangerous weapon. Plus she was the only one in the room when Bowes was attacked."

Before things got any worse, Pippa grabbed Thayne's wrist. "Give me the letter opener, Madam Walker," she said softly but firmly. "Now."

After a long pause, Thayne obeyed. "Please sit down. Let me take off those tight old shoes. Are you a size eight?"

"How did you know?"

"Cosmo knows everything, Twinkie," Dusi sighed.

"We're the same size," Pippa told her mother. "Come. Allow me to trade shoes with you." Pippa glanced at the cop standing behind her. "Would you mind not staring, sir? Only a husband should see a lady's ankles."

Shaking his head, the cop looked away. Pippa slid her hands under Thayne's gown and located the revolver in a garter above her mother's knee.

"Damn it, Cosmo! Your hands are freezing!"

"What's going on back there?"

"Nothing, Officer." Pippa slipped the offending hardware into her pocket. "These old pumps are murder to remove without a shoehorn."

That voice: that perfume: Thayne passed a hand over her face as Pippa traded shoes with her. "Cosmo?" she asked weakly, looking about the room. "Pippa?"

"Get a grip on yourself, Twinkie," Dusi clucked. "Pippa is disowned. She no longer exists and you must forget about her. Cosmo is Leigh's majordomo. For the moment," she added before turning to the policemen. "Thayne has recently suffered a family trauma. She's got lawsuits coming at her right and left. Her mind is unhinged. She has been assaulting people from coast to coast without provocation. She has driven a Maserati into the swimming pool of a Dallas motel frequented by prostitutes. Last week I found her in Harrods wearing a fringed tweed suit that went out of fashion four years ago. If that isn't a sign of dementia, I don't know what is." Dusi sighed heavily. "It's all that damn kid's fault."

"One more word about my daughter and you're eating that tiara."

Pippa stalked over to Dusi's chair. "Say no more. You're not helping in the least."

"Forgive me, I forgot," she laughed. "You have a crush on the glorious Madam Walker. You sent her the dead bird."

"I knew there was something weird about that guy," one cop whispered to his partner.

"A stuffed bird is not a dead bird," Thayne snapped. "Dusi, you should be the last person to criticize a bit of taxidermy, considering your boobs looked like two dead slugs before you went to Rangoon."

"Why, you bitch! At least I didn't force a slut to marry a quarterback!"

Thayne got both hands around Dusi's green throat before a policeman wrangled her out of the library. "That woman is a walking A-bomb," Dusi gasped, clutching her neck.

"You're even worse," the cop replied. "Get out before I lock you up with her."

Cole put a restraining hand on Pippa's arm. "Stay calm," he said under his breath. "We need you here."

Having seen Moss into the ambulance, Agent Ballard returned to the library. "Where did you get that costume, Mrs. Bowes?"

"It was made for me by a Fine Feather designer."

Ballard plucked a dark plume from the bodice. "This is from the Tasmanian double-variegated cockatoo. An endangered species."

"That schmuck! He dresses me in illegal feathers?"

"We'll have to impound it as evidence."

"Fine, but I'm not wearing any underwear."

"I'll take you upstairs."

After Leigh and Agent Ballard left, Pippa asked, "When may I fetch Madam Walker from the police station? She was asleep when the attack occurred."

"Why do you say that, Sherlock?"

Pippa looked imploringly at Cole, who kept his mouth shut. She felt like kneecapping him with her mother's pistol. "The Walkers don't clip their enemies in the back of the head. They shoot them in the chest, like respectable people."

"Thank you for that insight. Go fluff your mustache now."

Pippa slammed the library door with all her might. It hardly made a dent in the ambience at Casa Bowes, which had become a riot of sequins, booze, music, and dance. The tigers on leashes were performing tricks in exchange for stuffed ptarmigan. Pippa found her sentry still on duty at the front door. There seemed to be twice as many harlequins circulating as before, but she couldn't be sure. "Everything under control?"

"Some fairy godmother just left in a police car," he said. "Swearing like a trooper."

Pippa found Rudi in the kitchen, apoplectic that no one was eating his whelks, tongues, jugged hare, or eels. She was halfway to the backyard when her cell phone rang: Sheldon. Presuming Thayne had called him en route to jail, Pippa said, "I'll make bail, whatever it is."

"Bail?" Sheldon didn't want to know what that meant. "I've located Officer Pierce. He's selling used cars in Milwaukee."

"Send him a ticket to Vegas. He can pick up his new Maserati tomorrow."

"At the same address I sent the mustaches?"

"Yes. Have you heard from Mama tonight?"

"Far as I know she's in London on a shopping trip." Sheldon heard raucous music in the background. "Are you at another wild party?"

"I'm working. What's the penalty for carrying a concealed weapon in Nevada?"

"First offense has got to be a gross misdemeanor."

"What if you smack someone's head so hard he goes to the hospital?"

"My God! What have you done this time?"

Pippa hung up and proceeded to the patio, where Dusi had decided to go ahead with her Frequent Bentley presentation. She had climbed into the gondola in the swimming pool, where her plaque was resting on an easel covered with a dropcloth. As the gondola drifted over the water, Dusi waited for the crowd on the patio to calm into reverential silence. When that didn't happen, she threw two floral displays into the pool. That didn't work, either.

She noticed a wireless microphone on a cushion. "Welcome to Masqueradia Dusiana. What a wonderful evening! First I have a bit of news to report. Moss Bowes has been mugged in his own library. If anyone here did it, please let Leigh know so she can thank you personally."

The laughter became a little uncertain. "Get to the point," someone shouted.

"The point is this." Dusi tore the dropcloth off the easel. " 'To Dusilla Damon, in recognition of the purchase of her tenth Bentley.' Is this not gorgeous?"

Five Persian melons, launched from various sites around the pool, flew into the air. Each struck either the plaque or Dusi herself. "How dare you!" she spluttered.

"Go screw yourself," a heckler shouted as a second volley of melons found their target.

Peggy Stoutmeyer, the only person at Casa Bowes whose dreams Dusi had not destroyed, rushed to the diving board. Never a good judge of distance, she could see even less wearing a falcon mask. She grabbed the bow of the gondola, lost her balance, and splashed into the water, taking the boat down sideways. Cheers broke out as Dusi plummeted into the drink.

"Madam Damon!" Pippa cried, diving in. Heroics weren't necessary, Dusi having fallen into the shallow end, but Pippa was taking no chances. Peggy Stoutmeyer was paddling to a ladder in the deep end, apparently comfortable as a walrus in the water.

Pippa went to the cabaña for a terry robe. To her disgust it had just been used as a fornicatorium. A cheesy pair of red nylon panties and a man's orange thong had been left behind. Tucking both into her pocket, intending to dispose of them the moment she passed a trash can, Pippa grabbed a fresh robe and returned to the pool.

"Why are they throwing things at me?" the sodden goddess of spring whimpered. She espied Harlan, her lover. "Give me your jacket! I'm not walking out of here in a terry robe."

He divested himself of half his Swiss Guard uniform, unaware that fresh love scratches crisscrossed his upper body. Fortunately Dusi only had eyes for her plaque floating under the diving board. "Get that, Harlan!"

Pippa saw the three of them to the door. "I will never forget the horror of this night, Cosmo," Dusi announced, boarding her Bentley. "Home, Horatio."

Pippa watched the Bentley float away, sure that her diploma floated away with it. She stood in a trance, dripping water onto the portico, until one of the harlequins came up beside her. "Check the mustache, honey," he whispered.

The right edge was slipping off again. "Thank you."

Pippa went to her room. She changed into a dry uniform and refreshed the glue on her whiskers. As she was reaffixing her Cosmo pin, Cole knocked. He looked weary but still agonizingly handsome in his tux. "Thanks for leaving me high and dry," Pippa said, furious. "You really let me down."

He stood at the door. "I've been working undercover for six months. I still am."

"You know Madam Walker didn't hurt Moss."

Cole looked her in the eye. "Actually, Cosmo, I don't know."

"*If* she did, she would have been on the phone with her lawyer in one minute flat. The defense team would already be here eating Rudi's snipe."

"You seem to know a lot about Thayne Walker," Cole retorted, annoyed. He had told Pippa he was an undercover FBI agent. She had offered no reciprocal confession.

"I should. She's my mother."

To her surprise, he quietly said, "Thank you for telling me."

"Bing Bing could have come over disguised as a harlequin."

"Unlikely, as she's under round the clock surveillance."

"Maybe Moss fell off the ladder." That didn't have much gravity. "What did your girlfriend take out of his sock?"

"A memory card that will put him away for a long time. What did *you* remove from beneath your mother's skirt?"

He saw that? Good eyes. "Her gun."

"That was risky, Cosmo." Insanely so. "Where is it?"

"In my pocket."

Cole confiscated it. "Your mother's a consummate actress. She had me convinced she had never seen you before."

Pippa's face felt hot as lava. "She really doesn't know I'm me. I look a lot different than the last time we met."

"What's this about a disowned daughter? Your sister? She sounds awful."

"She's had a streak of bad luck," was all Pippa would say. "Now if you'll excuse me, I've got to bail Thayne out of jail."

"You can't leave now. We've got a party to wrap. Nothing's going to happen to your mother for the next few hours." Something might happen to Cosmo, though; those gray socks paired with her mother's pointy satin shoes were driving him mad with lust.

They went back to the ballrooms, where Masqueradia Dusiana was raging at force five. Leigh, her therapist, and her missing bichon frise Titian blew in around three in the morning. All things considered, she looked radiant. "There you are, Cosmo! Dr. Zeppelin and I just got back from Bing Bing's. He thought we should meet face-to-face and he was absolutely right. Can you believe that bastard gave my dog to his *mistress?*"

"Just for the week," Dr. Zeppelin said. "Still inexcusable."

Leigh nuzzled her pet's neck. "We had a cathartic session. The FBI just arrested her. Serves her right for trying to dress me in double-variegated cockatoo feathers."

Pippa frowned at Dr. Zeppelin, who seemed proud of his day's work. "Shouldn't you be with your husband in the emergency room, signora?"

"Surely you jest. Where's Dusi? I want to throw a persimmon at her. Dr. Z and I are getting rid of all my oppressors tonight."

"She's gone home for the evening. All that dancing exhausted her."

Cole's phone rang as Leigh and her emancipator wandered off. "That was Agent Ballard," he said, hanging up. "She just arrested Moss when he woke up."

"Is she your partner?"

"She's my boss. We've been on the case for six months." Was that a gleam of jealousy in her eye? Hallelujah! "If you mean romantic partner, no. No one is." *Put that in your pipe and smoke it, Cosmo.*

A tsunamic blush rolled from Pippa's head to her feet. Not the girlfriend not not not: her heart had just been let out of a cage and soared far above Casa Bowes. In a daze, Pippa bid departing guests adieu. Few asked and no one seemed the least perturbed not to see Moss and/or Leigh on the way out. Cole visited the Bolivian rosewood doors every hour or so to check that Pippa's feet were still on the ground. By sunup only a few vintage cars remained in the driveway. Loath to leave while Rudi was still cranking out food, the Stoutmeyers had started a bridge tournament in the first ballroom. A few drunks slumbered in the gondolas. An accordion octet sat in their underwear in the Jacuzzi.

Leigh found Pippa at the front door. "That was a great party, Cosmo. You are the best."

Pippa accepted a loving hug. "I'm sure Madam Damon will call with a wonderful announcement any moment now."

"She can take her country club and stuff it. I'm divorcing Moss and going back to the chorus line. That's where I was always happiest."

As they were waving goodbye to a few bedraggled guests, Kerry appeared on the porch with Dusi's ladle. "What do we do with this ugly thing?"

"Give that to me."

Cole caught up with Pippa as she was backing the Maserati out of the garage. "Going somewhere?"

"I'm returning Dusi's ladle. Then I'm getting my mother out of jail."

"Mind if I come along? We just discovered that Moss wired sixty thousand bucks to Harlan's account. I've got a few questions for him."

They drove a while in silence. Cole found himself staring at Pippa's jacket. Two healthy breasts lurked under that gray serge, yearning to be freed. And her thighs . . . each time she depressed the clutch, her long, smooth muscles rippled beneath her silk shorts. Tossing those eyeglasses out the window would be the crowning achievement of his life. She would look fantastic with mascara and gray eye shadow. Lipstick! He nearly groaned.

Pippa looked sweetly over. "I couldn't have done it without you, Cole."

"Loved every minute." He noticed the huge ladle on the floor. "Dusi's?"

"Yes. It's Edwardian silver. Weighs a ton."

A zillion-volt current crackled across the bucket seats as they both had the same thought: had Dusi's ladle dented Moss's skull? "I don't believe it," Pippa said. "Why?"

"Let's find out." *Fast. I wouldn't want to lose Harlan.* To his delight, Pippa read his mind. She was also a natural fast driver: Cole thought he had just died and gone to heaven.

A red Mustang shot past them on Dusi's moat. Their rearview mirrors kissed on the narrow drawbridge. "That car nearly hit us the other day," Pippa said. "Horatio!" Dusi's majordomo, his old eyes crusted with sleep, was still standing on the stoop. "Who was that?"

"Harlan, sir. He and Madam are going to the airport. They will be visiting Algeria for a few months."

"Which airport?" There were three possibilities.

"The one where her plane is, naturally."

"Thank you." Pippa shut her window. "What's the closest airport?"

"North Vegas."

She blasted north. "Call Leigh for me." Cole held the phone to her ear. "To which airport did you deliver Madam Damon's eyelashes a while back? Thank you."

Pippa yanked on the emergency brake and executed a textbook J-turn. "Driving school," she offered by way of explanation. The Maserati's speedometer climbed to ninety. "We guessed wrong. They're leaving from Henderson." She chuckled at the name. "Should have known."

Fortunately, traffic was light; unfortunately, Harlan hadn't observed any speed limits, either: Pippa and Cole arrived at the small executive airport well after his red Mustang. "FBI," Cole shouted, flashing his badge as he and Pippa tore to the runway. "Nothing takes off. Tell the pilot to stay in the cockpit."

They bolted up the stairway into Dusi's Learjet seconds before the steward closed the door. He was summarily evicted. Inside the cabin, Dusi sat at a table smoking one of her long *femme fatale* cigarettes, sipping a martini as she held her lighter beneath a sheet of paper that wouldn't ignite. Thayne's black-hooded red siskin perched in her safari hat. Beer in hand, Harlan was studying a coat of armor wired to the back wall. Both of them had changed from Masqueradia Dusiana duds into Patagonia khakis.

Dusi dropped her lighter in surprise. "Perfect timing, Cosmo!" She ogled Cole head to foot. "And I get Moss's valet in the bargain? That's very generous of you."

"We're not reporting for work," Pippa said. "We need to ask Harlan a few questions."

"Tell us about the sixty grand Moss Bowes deposited to your account," Cole said.

In reply Harlan yanked the spear away from the coat of armor, taking down half the rear wall. "Harlan!" Dusi screamed as a codpiece skittered across her table. "You've just destroyed the armor Sir Gilbert Umfraville wore to Agincourt!"

"Leave me alone," he growled, brandishing the spear. "I didn't do nothing."

"Then put the spear down." Cole removed Thayne's pistol from his vest. "Or I might have to shoot you."

"Stop! I will not have my servants behaving like the IRA! Put that

spear down, you meathead. You, drop that gun in here." Dusi removed
the lid from her martini shaker. "Now." Cole dropped the pistol into
the gin. Dusi glared at Harlan until he reluctantly set down his spear.
"Sixty thousand! I don't pay you enough for services rendered?"

"Moss needed personal information."

Dusi clapped her hands over her face. "He paid you *sixty thousand
dollars* to learn what I like in bed?"

"Actually, he wanted to know what was going on at the membership meetings."

The cigarette holder dropped from Dusi's mouth into her cleavage.
"*You* gave him those photocopies?"

"Sixty grand is a lot of dough."

"How dare you! We all took a blood oath of confidentiality."

"What could possibly be so bad, Madam Damon?" Pippa said. "If
I understand correctly, you did nothing at those meetings but read
blackball letters."

Dusi slowly regained her color. "I suppose you're right, Cosmo. As
always." She took a belt of her martini. "Moss was looking for dirt in
the wrong place."

Seeing Dusi's eyes flit to the papers on the table, Pippa managed to
grab a wad of them a split second before Dusi could. They were all
damp and smelled of chlorine. Pippa read the first page. " 'I object to
the membership of Gina Crane. She intends to homeschool her children
instead of sending them to a reputable institution such as Choate.' "
She read the second page. " 'I object to the membership of Vivianne
Cross. She has just sold her Matisse to a citizen of Egypt. Her patriot-
ism is highly questionable.' " All of the pages contained similar messages. "Why were you trying to burn these, Madam Damon?"

"That's part of my job." Without skipping a beat, Dusi reached
into her pocketbook and scribbled out a check. "Cosmo, here's a little
something for your trouble. Thank you for bringing Harlan's repre-
hensible behavior to my attention."

Pippa stared at the check for five hundred thousand dollars. Those
odd squished *m*'s . . . those crooked *t*'s and oversized *d*'s . . . suddenly
she was back in matchmaking school listening to Marla Marble ana-
lyze her students' handwriting. Pippa took another look at the letters
to the membership committee.

"What's the matter?" Dusi snapped. "Not enough money?"

"I believe you wrote all these letters." Why were they so wet? *Aha!* "They got soaked when you fell into signora's pool."

"After you took them from Moss's *scriban*," Cole chimed in.

Another zillion-watt lightbulb went off in Pippa's head. "And you tried to silence Signor Bowes when he confronted you."

"Cosmo, you're hallucinating. I was with Harlan every minute last night."

"Every minute," Meathead confirmed, slightly too enthusiastically.

Pippa took a wild stab in the dark: *Hang on, Mama.* She reached in her pocket and dropped a man's orange thong on the table. "Then I suppose that would be yours, Harlan." Pippa dropped the tacky red nylon panties on top of them. "And these would be yours, Madam Damon. Size nine."

Dusi nearly gagged. Size nine! *Nylon!* Words escaped her as she tried to figure out what Harlan's monogrammed thong was doing with that red abomination. She soon reached the only conclusion possible. "After all I've done for you," she spat. Dusi removed the gun she kept under the table in case a terrorist tried to fly her Learjet into the Empire State Building.

She aimed for Harlan's heart but only clipped him in the shoulder. Dusi's second bullet was more successful, ricocheting off Sir Gilbert Humfraville's helmet into Harlan's gluteus maximus. "Get off my plane!" she screamed.

Howling, Harlan staggered out, leaving an impressive trail of blood.

"You." Dusi pointed the gun at Cole. "Leave."

He didn't budge. "Do as she says," Pippa said.

"I'm not leaving you here, Cosmo."

"Madam Damon and I have business to discuss. I'll be fine." Cole left, with a door slam that shook a couple more pieces of armor off the wall. Pippa settled into the leather seat opposite Dusi's. Her fingertips tingled as she ratcheted into Walker survival mode. "There's one thing I don't understand. Why did you let Peggy Stoutmeyer into the club?"

Dusi realized that denying her guilt, at least to Cosmo, was futile. "I wasn't about to let a rich, attractive woman into the club to take croquet lessons with Harlan. As you can see, he's a bit of a tomcat."

She emptied her glass. "God! I'm so glad you're working for me now, Cosmo. If I drink one more warm martini, I'll lose my mind."

Pippa eyed the bird in Dusi's hat. "You treated Madam Walker very badly."

"She'll live! A top-notch defense should get her off with a few thousand hours of community service."

"But you were the one who smacked Signor Bowes with the ladle. Madam Walker didn't do anything but fall asleep."

"Bad luck." Dusi clicked her gold lighter a half-dozen times, to no effect. "Damn! I used up all the lighter fluid trying to burn those papers."

"Allow me," Pippa said, drawing the MatchMace from her pocket. "You must really quit smoking, Madam Damon."

Twenty-Two

Thayne awoke from a fitful dream with a cramp in her leg and a stitch in her neck. Her wig weighed a ton and her corsets were squeezing her blood blue. She sat in a jail cell with a pair of transvestites who had arrived minutes after she had last night. The two of them were still debating whether Thayne was a fellow transvestite, a well-preserved English actress from the sixties, or the mistress of a Russian Mafioso. Her gown and jewels were beyond magnificent but the nubucks confused them. Thayne hadn't helped matters by refusing to utter a word.

She was lost in thought, her mind full of surreal images: Moss on the floor, masked harlequins serving Champagne, a Kafkaesque legion of chauffeurs, green Dusi. Thayne could not fathom how she had ended up in jail. She remembered feeling sleepy. She remembered a little red bird. Mostly she remembered Cosmo.

As dawn tinted her skirt gold, Thayne thought about the young man who had literally read her mind. Had he not removed her pistol before she was dragged to the police station, God knows where she would have opened her eyes this morning. Dusi had said Cosmo was extraordinarily well informed, but knowing about a pistol in her garter? Then slipping it into his own pocket? Incredible.

Thayne thought back to the moment she first saw him. He had

bowed to her. She had been less than courteous in return. Was it his uniform? Now that she was used to it, Thayne thought Cosmo's ensemble was uniquely beautiful. She couldn't imagine him in the black livery of an ordinary majordomo. She was even becoming fond of his eyeglasses and that anemic wisp of a mustache.

She cringed, remembering how she had ignored him, thinking he was merely a servant while she was Thayne the Magnificent from Dallas. Any other domestic would have responded to that treatment by spitting in her caviar. Cosmo had responded by defending her honor again and again while her supposed friends remained silent. Devotion of that magnitude reminded her of . . . she felt an ache in her heart . . . Pippa.

Cosmo did bear distinct similarities to her daughter. His voice. His slender body. When he blushed, he could be mistaken for Pippa's fraternal twin. Whenever he walked into a room, Thayne felt an elevation of pulse, of life force, that she had only ever felt with Pippa. Maybe the two of them had been born on the same day, at the same minute. Cosmic twins. Cosmic Cosmo: Thayne smiled with great melancholy. She was in love with him. It wasn't sexual. She just felt a massive longing to hear his voice every day, to have him in her house, fill that gouge in her chest . . . look, she was crying.

Cosmo was a very private fellow. Dusi hadn't been able to get one word out of Olivia Villarubia-Thistleberry concerning his origins. Thayne wondered where Cosmo was born. Europe? Northern Africa? Turkey? Where had he acquired his superb sense of style? What was his mother like? Thayne envied the woman, whoever she was: she had everything that Thayne did not, and she would have it forever. That was because Cosmo's mother would not peevishly disinherit her child for calling off a wedding. She would not go on a tirade across the continental United States because her child had taken a different path than the one she had imposed on him. Cosmo's mother was no doubt a wise woman; Thayne didn't deserve the title mother.

Had he really sent her that black-hooded red siskin? With the note about flying to her if he were a bird? Thayne smiled ruefully. Cosmo must have felt very sorry for her indeed.

Keys jangled in the iron door. Thayne was too depressed to even look up until she heard the voice that made her life worth living. "Good morning, Madam Walker."

She bolted off the cot, then passed a hand over her face. "I must look a wreck."

"We all look slightly below par, I'm afraid." Cosmo wasn't kidding. The sleeve of his gray jacket was torn. Two buttons were missing. The valet Cole was equally disarranged. "I'm sorry we couldn't get here sooner."

"I will pay back every cent of bail. At once."

"There is no bail. You're free to go home."

"My God!" Thayne clasped her beloved in a long embrace. "You've single-handedly saved my life."

Pippa smiled at Cole. "Not entirely."

They brought Thayne up to date on events at Casa Bowes. When the saga ended with Dusi being led away from her Learjet in handcuffs, Thayne could only shake her head. "I'm not surprised. That woman always considered herself above the law. I used to be that way myself."

After an awkward silence Pippa asked, "Will you return to Dallas now, madam?"

Maybe it was her lack of sleep, maybe it was the early sun on Cosmo's cheek: Thayne was stunned to hear a woman dressed as Marie Antoinette blurt, "You will think this very odd, Cosmo, but I'd like to visit your mother and personally thank her for bringing you into the world." Such a deep silence ensued that Thayne feared the worst. "I'm sorry. Is she living?"

Cosmo blushed violently. "Yes, madam, she is."

"Too bad," Thayne sighed. "I had hoped to adopt you."

Pippa looked imploringly at Cole. "Trust me, Cosmo," he whispered. "Close your eyes."

She slowly lowered her lids. She felt her eyeglasses being lifted off. Then she felt Cole kissing her cheek. His mouth proceeded south, stopping at the end of her mustache. She felt him grab one end of it *in his teeth* and tug. Then Pippa felt a breeze on her upper lip. Cole kissed her. She really kissed him back.

"You can open your eyes now," he said, stepping away.

Thayne gasped. Of all events over the last two days, this was by far the most surreal. "Pippa?"

Her daughter smiled and bowed. "At your service, madam."

They hugged and cried and laughed like two paupers who had just won the lottery. Eventually Thayne became aware of the handsome valet who had rather seriously kissed her daughter. "I'm sorry. You said your name was Cole?"

"Madisson. From Pittsburgh."

"My God! You used to work for the Pittsburgh Madissons?"

"I *am* one of the Pittsburgh Madissons."

Thayne thought she might faint: the Madison steel fortune was ten times larger than Rosimund Henderson's paltry petrodollars. "And all this time you've been pretending to be a valet?"

He winked at Pippa. "Great minds think alike."

Pippa tried to look displeased. "How long have you known?"

"From the moment I saw you." He took her hand. "Forgive me?" Another kiss.

"Let's leave this awful place," Thayne said. "Take good care of this," she called, tossing her wig to the transvestites. "It belonged to Princess Belgioioso."

Twenty-Three

Reader, this is your intrepid Dallas Morning News *society reporter Zarina breaking a white-hot scoop from Fleur-de-Lis. Pippa Walker, wedding dodger par excellence, has just married Cole Madisson (that's Madisson with two s's, as in all the steel in Pennsylvania) one year to the day after they met. Unlike Pippa's last attempt at matrimony, this was a very modest affair. The guest list was small and, shall we say, special. Besides Elmo and Geneva Madisson, the groom's parents, those who witnessed the event were Wyeth McCoy, the wedding planner (didn't do this one, though—way too small!); Lance Henderson, who shocked the world last January by coming out of the closet one day after winning the Super Bowl for the Cowboys (hmmm! think that had anything to do with Pippa's dodging the bullet last time around?); Lance's partner, Woody Woodrow, a "physical" therapist; Ginny Ortlip, just back from the source of the Nile; Officer Vernon Pierce and his bride, former socialite Leigh Bowes, who is expecting a bambino (they met over a Maserati then began ballroom dancing); Mike Strebyzwynkiwicz (where's my aspirin?), inventor from Phoenix whose company, MatchMace, just went public; Olivia Villarubia-Thistleberry of Aspen, who goes nowhere without her six teacup poodles but managed to attach herself within ten seconds to aforementioned inventor; Horatio Jones, someone's antique butler; two dashing Cub Scout leaders from Philadelphia; and a pair of Russian clowns and their trained bear, Pushkin, who danced with Pippa all night long as her indulgent husband looked on.*

The ceremony was performed in the gorgeous "backyard" of Fleur-de-Lis under a canopy that (I can't believe this!) previously served as Pippa's bridal train in her nonwedding to Lance. Sheldon Adelstein, the family lawyer, officiated. Pippa made a decent speech at the altar this time around, mostly thanking her mother for forgiving her. She closed by saying the only thing that would have made the day happier would have been the presence of her grandfather Anson. (We know the old boy was there in spirit!)

The bride wore a simple white dress, the better to show off an heirloom diamond necklace and a sparkly pin spelling "Cosmo." No one at the wedding would reveal what this meant. Pippa also wore cowboy boots with a HUGE pair of platinum spurs, a wedding gift from her mother. Go figure! The weather cooperated perfectly. A stunning meal was provided by a chef named Rudi, who specializes in stuffed ptarmigan. For some reason there were lots of Polish pickles on the menu.

Oh! Forgot to mention the bride's parents! Robert Walker, delayed at the nineteenth hole, almost missed escorting his daughter up the grassy aisle. I am thrilled to report that Thayne Walker, the mouth that sank a thousand ships, has turned over a new leaf. She was quiet as a mouse throughout the afternoon. A happy mouse, stunning in a gray Saint Laurent jacket and flowing pants of the most exquisite purplish-greenish silk. A little red bird perched on her shoulder—very well behaved—maybe it was stuffed! She did nothing but smile and dab her eyes with a handkerchief as the couple exchanged vows. Perhaps she was thinking about the army of carpenters who will soon be constructing a fifty-thousand-square-foot addition to Fleur-de-Lis for the grandchildren "if and when."

As for the bridal couple, what can I say? They're in love. They're beautiful. After a nice cozy honeymoon on the Madisson yacht, they'll return to Washington, D.C., where Cole has a top-tier FBI job no one can talk about. Shh-hh-h. Pippa will be taking the reins of the Anson Walker Foundation, which she created last month with a small donation of a billion bucks. The foundation is devoted to family counseling, with particular emphasis on "premarital compatibility education" (whatever that is).

Oh! How could I forget! Proudly on display was a huge diploma from the Mountbatten-Savoy School of Household Management in Aspen. "What did you learn there?" I asked the radiant bride.

"How to fly," she answered. Then Pushkin the dancing bear swept her away.

Acknowledgments

A special thank-you to Marcelle and Robert Frey.

*Our gratitude to Nick and Elizabeth for introductions
and the first dance.*